"*Songs from the Stars* i[...] [...] tion set free from its good old-fashioned puritan taboos. Clear Blue Lou is a judge of the tribes in post-atomic Aquaria, an isolated national fragment in a broken world. . . . We find ourselves following Lou on a traditional Quest for the secret of the Dark Power, led of course by his soulguide anima. . . . Clear Blue Lou and Sunshine Sue are destined for each other . . . bound together by the dark power, as a god hero and his consort should be."

—Walter M. Miller, Jr.,
author of *A Canticle for Liebowitz*

"Bravo! . . . The most intelligent, loving, precisely hopeful, sophisticated, practically-survival important book . . . so far!"

—Timothy Leary

"Dense and meaty, multi-leveled . . . as if Norman considers it a sin, as I do, to bore the reader or waste his time. . . . Spinrad leads the reader gently toward wider and more awesome vistas, expanding his mind as he goes."

—Larry Niven

"Remarkable. . . . Beautiful. This is one of the truly uplifting works I've read. . . . Not a false word uttered."

—Philip José Farmer

Other books by Norman Spinrad

SONGS
FROM
THE STARS

Norman Spinrad

BANTAM BOOKS

TORONTO • NEW YORK • LONDON • SYDNEY • AUCKLAND

SONGS FROM THE STARS

A Bantam Book / published by arrangement with
the Author

Bantam edition / July 1985

ISBN 0-553-24879-0

Published simultaneously in the United States and Canada

Bantam Books are published by Bantam Books, Inc. Its
trademark, consisting of the words "Bantam Books" and the
portrayal of a rooster, is Registered in U.S. Patent and Trademark Office and in other countries. Marca Registrada. Bantam Books, Inc., 666 Fifth Avenue, New York, New York
10103.

PRINTED IN THE UNITED STATES OF AMERICA

H   0 9 8 7 6 5 4 3 2 1

For
David Hartwell,
gentleman and scholar

Clear
Blue Lou

Cruising southeast on a golden afternoon for eagles, Clear Blue Lou had left the world behind him. Below, the Sierra foothills were a chiaroscuro tapestry of crumpled green velvet, and the cloudless sky filled his soul with clear blue glory. His spirit was absorbed into a birdlike awareness of the dips and slips of the mountain airstreams. He was Clear Blue Lou, perfect master of the Clear Blue Way. In the towns and communes and farmsteads of Aquaria below, that meant cleansing *other* people's karma, but up here all alone in the Clear Blue, he himself found his own Way. Every master must dance his own song.

Lou hung suspended in time and space beneath the clear blue helium-filled eagle; from the ground, he appeared to be riding beneath an almost invisible wing of air. From where he sat in his saddle slung beneath the eagle, the glider wing was a sunshade lens attuning the blue of the sky to a deeper and more tranquil vision. Nowhere else was he more totally in the Way.

So blissfully was Clear Blue Lou riding the Clear Blue

Way that before he knew it, sunset was creeping up behind him.

Oh shit! he suddenly realized. I've done it again!

Long streaks of purple and carmine were playing over the eagle wing, and the ribwork of the lower surface had become a cathedral archwork of lengthening shadows. Below, inky pseudopods were oozing east through the rugged canyon bottoms of south-central Aquaria, and the tops of the scattered clouds were turning mauve and pale orange.

Clear Blue Lou might be in sync with the law of muscle, sun, wind and water, but of this white tetrad of sanctioned powers, the one that made him grunt and sweat was the one he liked the least. And now, to pay back this golden afternoon of sweet karma, he was going to have to pedal.

The solar eagle is a helium balloon in the form of a subtly flexible glider wing. Hanging below it in a saddle, the eagle rider flexes and warps it with the control lines like an aerial puppeteer riding beneath an avian marionette. Given the right wind, an ace like Clear Blue Lou could follow a general vector with no power at all. Unfortunately, such optimum karma occurred maybe a dozen times a year.

And today was not one of those days. A light headwind was blowing up from the east, there was less than an hour's sun left, and the last eagle's nest between here and La Mirage was at least eight miles away. He was going to have to pedal.

The upper surface of the eagle wing is covered with solar cells that produce enough electricity to power two pusher props halfway out toward the tips. In still air, the sun can move the eagle at about ten miles per hour. When it is up.

When it is not up or when the wind blows the wrong way, there is a central pusher prop run by the pedals. No true eagle freak enjoys pedaling. If he did, he'd be a cycle sailor, who enjoyed that dubious pleasure every time he lost his wind.

Nevertheless, muscle *was* part of the Way, and there *were* perfect masters of certain ways who taught that sweat was good for the soul and sprinted about their rounds on bicycles. There were even those who thought that solar eagles were tinted a suspicious tone of gray.

As Clear Blue Lou hit the pedals, as his legs established a rhythmic pump and he let his muscles drive his lungs, flesh warped consciousness closer to immediate reality, and Lou was forced to remember that the Eagle Tribe who had built his sky chariot were deeply involved in this mess in La Mirage. They were under a cloud whose belly was black with the shadow of sorcery.

The sky was deepening to darkness behind him, and the land below had cloaked itself in shadows that made it seem more craggy and forbidding as Clear Blue Lou pedaled laboriously east through the sweet sunset musk given off by the forested foothills. On the eastern horizon, the jagged peaks of the Sierras themselves blazed redly in the setting sun. Beyond them . . . the Great Waste, from whose depths black science oozed its subtle way into Aquaria, grayed by the time it reached La Mirage, and ostensibly pure as the driven snow by the time it cleared the Exchange.

Somewhere between here and the other side of the Sierras, someone's hand was quicker than the eye. Or, anyway, eyes that chose to look away. No taint could be pointed to on the whiteness of solar eagles, no molecule made by the hand of man, no power other than that of sun and wind and muscle. Well within the letter of the law.

Of course, the solar cells had to come from somewhere, and the fabric of the glider balloon was a rather outré derivative of cellulose, and the Eagle Tribe's train of supply drifted back ambiguously into the hermetic mountain william canyons way up in the eastern slopes of the central range where the righteously white did not care to risk sticking their noses.

Clear Blue Lou did not make a habit of questioning the karma of that which sweetened his own, and he believed in doing likewise for the good karma of others. If it tastes good to the spirit, you can eat it.

But now, with the landscape gone sinister and his own misattention trapping him in the penitive task of pedaling, Lou was reminded that not even a perfect master could count on a perpetual free lunch. Perhaps having to keep in the Way by force of will over protest of flesh *was* good for the soul, a cautionary cosmic zinger.

Right now it reminded him that this was no joyride after all, that he had been summoned to give his justice in a dispute that touched on the karma of this selfsame eagle that had transformed him from a high-flying rider of the wind to the beast of his own burden with the setting of the sun.

Good for the soul, like peyote, he told himself sourly,

leaning into the pedals. But that didn't mean he had to like the way it tasted going down.

Within the hour, the land below had sunk into a black abyss, the moonless sky blazed with pinpoint lights like the landscape of some eldritch pre-Smash city, and Clear Blue Lou had had more than enough of the yoga of pedaling.

So it was with a certain sense of relief that he finally spotted the eagle's nest beacon, a powerful 200-watt reflector beam winking at him like a grounded star from the next ridgeline. He shifted gears, and a portion of his footpower was shunted into the pump that recompressed wing helium to kill the eagle's lift for a glide-in. This did not make pedaling any easier, and by the time he established his descent curve, he was groaning and wheezing, and it was pure ecstasy to stop pedaling for good and float down like a moth toward the light.

Down he came into a high mountain meadow shining ghostly pale under the stars. Only one other eagle was tethered to the hitching rail. Millions of insects circled in the beam of the spotlight on the roof of the single-story rambling lodge cabin.

The main room of the cabin had walls of undressed timber, smooth-hewn tables and chairs, and a big wood stove where Matty the cook presided over two big iron kettles and a pot of cider, which blasted out food odors that went straight to Lou's empty stomach.

"Food and flop, Matty," Lou called out. "I've been pedaling for hours."

"In such a hurry to get to La Mirage?" The only other customer was a tall willowy woman in a yellow Sunshine messenger jumpsuit who sat alone over the remains of her meal, beckoning him to her table. She was neat, she looked a little mean in all the right places, and she seemed just a little hostile.

"As a matter of fact, I've got all the time in the world," Lou said, beaming invitingly at her as he sat down across from her.

The Sunshine Girl ran her tongue over her lower lip and smiled back ironically. "Are you soliciting a bribe, oh giver of Clear Blue justice?"

"Are you offering one?" he asked.

The Sunshine Girl shrugged. "It might enliven an otherwise dull night," she said.

Matty set a bowl of rice fried with vegetables under a sauce of soybean chili before him, and Lou considered the karma as he savored the first welcome mouthful.

Sunshine Sue's whole operation could be on the line when he gave his justice, and from what he had heard, it had been the Eagle Tribe who had first suggested him, not the Sunshines. And here he was, flying in on their product. It could be argued by a good enough sophist that he owed the Sunshine Tribe some counterbalancing equivalent, which might be most pleasantly provided at sport with this member who was both willing and a turn-on.

On the other hand, the hoary maxim that a stiff prick knows no conscience was not the bottom line for Clear Blue Lou.

"Is it against your rules to discuss our case?" the Sunshine Girl asked.

"What's your name?"

"Little Mary Sunshine," she answered dryly.

"Well Mary," Lou said, "that depends on whether I'm talking to Little Mary or to Sunshine Sue's Word of Mouth."

"Off the record. Cross my heart."

Lou eyed her narrowly. Sunshine Sue's Word of Mouth earned its way by carrying other people's messages, but it also carried public news up and down the length of Aquaria. News that it collected however it could. If he didn't want to trust Little Mary Sunshine, he wouldn't be Clear Blue Lou, but if he trusted her implicitly, he wouldn't be Clear Blue Lou either.

"And hope to lie?"

Little Mary laughed. "No, really," she said. "I just want to tell you something. The Sunshine Tribe isn't into black science; we're no grayer than anyone else who does business in La Mirage."

"That's not exactly a certificate of karmic purity," Lou said dryly.

"I'm leveling with you, Lou. Sure, you could say that some of our electronic components might not be ultrabright, but our radios are as white as your eagle."

"I can't think of a blacker science than atomics," Lou said. "Can you?"

5

"That's what I'm telling you!" Little Mary said in a tone of some exasperation. "We wouldn't mess with sorcery like that! What do you think we are, monsters?"

"But you were caught with radioactive power cores in twenty-five radios. Or do you dispute the facts as charged by the Eagles?"

"*The Eagles?* Where do they come off so whitely righteous? How did they know about the power cores in the first place? We didn't."

"You didn't?"

Little Mary reached out and touched his hand. She looked into his eyes. "Really we didn't," she said quietly. "We bought them on the open market from the Lightning Commune, and we've never had trouble like this with them before; they've always been a reasonably white outfit. And now suddenly they set us up for a sorcery judgment. . . ."

"How come the Eagles knew about the atomic cores if you didn't?"

"Now you're catching on," Little Mary Sunshine said.

I am? Clear Blue Lou thought. But to what? This side of the story didn't add up. And it wouldn't until he got an explanation from the Eagles. And he had an uneasy feeling that they'd have a hard time giving him a straight answer too. And he didn't at all feature whom this was all beginning to point to. He also realized that this discussion had gone a little too far. He had already asked some questions that could be turned into items by Word of Mouth with a little embellishment.

"This *is* all off the record?" he said. "It's not going to be all over Aquaria that I discussed this with you in the course of coming on?"

"Whose karma would that sweeten?" Little Mary said. She smiled. "So you admit you'd like to while away the night together?"

Oooh, this was getting tasty. But it was also getting dicey. The mind game that was going on would make for fiery sport. But that would tie another Gordian knot in the skein of karma he was being called upon to unravel, with something more intimate than his finger tied up in it.

At times like these, he could do with being a little less Clear Blue.

"I admit I'd like to," he said.

Now she was touching both of his hands. "So would I."

Lou's flesh surged toward her, but his head held him back. "Some good things," he said dryly, "were not meant to be."

She sighed and relaxed back against her chair. "Can't blame a girl for trying," she said easily.

"Were you really trying?" Lou asked.

"Was I really trying *what?*" Little Mary Sunshine drawled ingenuously.

"To suborn a giver of justice with your sweet charms," Lou said half seriously.

"Was the giver of justice maybe using the situation to see if he could get it down?" she asked slyly.

"Would I contemplate a thing like that?"

"Are you sure you don't want to talk that over in my room?"

"Much as I'd like to, the karma isn't clear," Lou said regretfully. "If we sported, either you'd incline me favorably toward your tribe, or I'd bend over backward the other way to be fair. Unjust either way."

He laughed. "Besides, right now, neither of us could figure out what was fucking whom anyway."

"It might be fun trying."

"I'm sure it would, but I'd hate myself in the morning," Lou said, getting up from the table. He kissed her hand. "Maybe when this is over, we can wake up one morning in bed together and remember this with a smile."

"I sure hope we all come out of this smiling," Little Mary Sunshine said dubiously. "Nobody's smiling now."

"That's what I'm here for," Clear Blue Lou said. It was as good an exit line as any. But with his glands sulking in frustration and his mind already whirling through the numbers, he went to bed already warped into the karmic maelstrom. And he was still a good morning's flight from the scene that awaited him at La Mirage, where the winds that were blowing had more of a whiff of the east about them than usual.

Next morning after a solitary breakfast of wheatola and hot cider, Clear Blue Lou took off through the damp mist that fogged the high mountain meadows, his spirit soggy with last night's missed pleasures and the sorcery-tainted karma that had trapped him in its evil spell of chastity.

But soon he was above the fog, soaring rapidly east on a

favorable wind and a high mountain sun that warmed his body to wakefulness and clarified his soul.

The karma that he was being called upon to judge had already prevented two innocent people from sporting together, and *he* was one of them. As far as Lou was concerned, that was proof enough that somewhere at the bottom of this lay a mindfuck pattern, a violation of free will, an outrage to both himself and the Great Way. The seeking of justice had already begun.

For the giving of justice was no neutral intellectual process. In order to clear karma, a perfect master must enter its realities. Otherwise, he would be writing law, not fulfilling destiny; he would be acting like a government. What was left of the world could do without people who thought they could be unmoved movers.

Atomic power cores aside, karmic imperialism was at work here; it had already quite literally grabbed him by the balls. And justice would require that this karmic debt not go unpaid.

The fair following wind was taking him rapidly toward the beginning of the central range of the Sierras. No rolling foothills below him now, but apprentice mountains rising up toward him.

This was the beginning of where the world ended. Or at least the world that the whitely righteous knew. No eagle could cross the High Sierras powered only by sun and wind and muscle. Beyond that immense wall of mountains was the greatest of all Wastes, Aquaria's knowledge of its extent petering out into the infinity of legend. Great was the megatonnage that had fallen upon the eastern slopes of the Great Divide during the Smash. Still deadly was the vast radioactive wound which the hand of man had gouged in the body of the Earth.

But the world did not end in a bleak abyss or with an unseemly suddenness. Now Lou's eagle was flying abreast of the peaks of the higher foothills, and he was ascending into a great aerial river system of canyon passes leading on into ever higher and more forbidding mountains, awesome in their beauty.

Here was truly a land untouched by the unclean hand of man, a world unto itself that had existed in its impenetrable vastness for transhuman aeons. The Smash had not touched it. Even the awful black science of the pre-Smash Americans had not been able to seriously mar these mothers of mountains. All they had left behind was a sparse network of roads where tall trees burst from the shattered concrete. Lou soared past fir-covered slopes where hawks and eagles circled, high verdant meadows where sheep and deer grazed. The world ended in a wilderness Eden whose far boundary was impenetrable to man. What irony that beyond the highest peaks of this primeval majesty lay a radioactive hell and the lairs of sorcerers!

In all of this mountain fastness, the only significant human settlement was La Mirage, one of Aquaria's major towns, a long day's flight from anything of significance and two days from Palm by wagon on the torturous back-door road.

What this bustling town was doing way out here in the middle of nowhere was generally considered best left unsaid. La Mirage was near nothing but the fuzzy mountain boundary between Aquaria and what lay beyond.

And now the sorcerers beyond the mountains had showed their hand at work with uncool clumsiness. More than the fate of the Eagle Tribe, the Lightning Commune, and Sunshine Sue's Word of Mouth was at stake. La Mirage itself was now under a heavy cloud of black science of the most blatant sort.

And the fact was that Aquaria needed La Mirage for the very reason that made it content to leave the doings in the shadow of the High Sierras out of sight and out of mind.

An arcane chemistry took place here upon which the civilization of Aquaria depended. The children of Aquarius had built a civilization based on the white sciences, under the law of muscle, sun, wind and water. Now they could fly like eagles, and generate electricity, and pass messages along by solar radio. White science advanced year after year, and its mages and merchants did their business together in the La Mirage Exchange. New technology was manufactured most often in the workshops and factories of the town and from there diffused slowly outward.

It was conveniently said that the scattered mountain william tribes in the eastern back country had preserved certain manufacturing techniques from pre-Smash days, and it was certainly true that these simple people zealously guarded their so-called trade secrets.

It was also true, however, that somewhere up in the Sierras, mountain william country ended and the haunts of the

Spacers began. It was hard to believe that there was no interpenetration. It was hard to believe, but most people tried.

Expeditions too high up into the mountains had a way of not coming back. Besides, bounty flowed across the land from La Mirage, and none could prove that the law of muscle, sun, wind and water was violated by eagles or solar radios or sophisticated batteries and wind generators.

Such was the delicate balance that allowed La Mirage to flourish. By such a nonexistent pact with the unnameable did Aquaria ultimately thrive in its righteous whiteness. Some perfect masters saw this as a fatal flaw, but Clear Blue Lou didn't believe in being bad for business. Which was why he was the favorite perfect master of La Mirage.

Which was also why the nature of this klutzy confrontation pointed to machinations by the Spacers. Sunshine Sue might very well be capable of knowingly purchasing atomic-powered radios—her reputation was well grayed to say the least. But the Eagle Tribe had no percentage in wanting to expose her. Shining unwanted light into someone else's dark corner was against the rules of the game, if only because you yourself might be next.

Around the next bend, the canyon that Lou was following widened out into a steep green meadow that swept upward before him. He valved more helium into his eagle and nosed it upward, slowly inching up above the steep slope, making his final climb to La Mirage in a long climbing arc.

On the high mountain plateau above him was a town that had summoned his justice, a town that trusted him and which he had perhaps come to love. Perhaps that might prove to be a stain on his karma. Certainly the missed night of sport with Little Mary Sunshine had already made things personal.

As he soared upward through the most beautiful country in his world, the Eden below seemed to mock him with its purity and innocence. For the shadow of black science lay heavily across this mountain greenery where the domain of sorcery touched the lives and fortunes of men.

Sunshine
Sue

As always, Sunshine Sue was in a hurry, and as always, her world moved too slowly. There was a great bleeding freight wagon clogging the road up ahead of her, just as the wind was finally getting some speed out of this stupid contraption!

Her current mode of transport was a sail cycle. She had made it down the coast from Mendocino by boat in under three days, but from Barbo, her way to La Mirage had become a crawling nightmare. Endless hours on a dumb smelly horse to Javelina and then two bloody more days to Palm by coach, where she missed her connection to La Mirage because of a busted axle and was told she'd have to lay over for eighteen hours.

Fortunately the Sunshine Tribe maintained a messenger station in Palm and had its own transport. Of a kind.

Now her sweet ass was riding a few inches above a rock-strewn dirt roadway in the saddle of a speeding sail cycle. With a good wind, this thing could really move—right now she must be doing nearly thirty miles an hour. But the trouble was you lost your following wind around every other bend in the road, and most of the time, you had to lean against the torque of the angled sail to keep on the ground. And when the wind died, kiddo, it was hit the pedals.

The sail cycle had two small wheels up front for steerage; behind was a big pusher wheel that rode free under sail and was driven by the pedals when the wind died. Sue reclined low against the road in her saddle behind a deerhide fairing to minimize drag. The triangular sail rode on a boom behind the rear wheel and was controlled by a crank through a system of ratchets.

She had been told in Palm that the record time to La Mirage in one of these things was under thirteen hours, whereas the coach would take nearly two days—and that after a layover.

She had also been told that she was crazy, that you had to be in shape for pedaling, that you needed to know what you were doing, but Sunshine Sue was burning with adrenaline and impatience, and she would've hitched a ride on a passing mountain lion to get to La Mirage a few hours sooner.

In the Word of Mouth business, she was fond of telling apprentice messengers, the fastest transport between any two points was the one you took. The fastest transport was always too damned slow anyway.

She had been up in Mendocino, setting up a net node station for the new fifty-mile radio transmitter whose arrival should have been imminent. Instead, word had crawled up the coast that the entire shipment had been interdicted by Levan the Wise. For sorcery.

A black science interdiction in *La Mirage?* By *Levan?* Atomic power cores in the transmitter circuits? What the fuck was going on down there?

Sue sent a blizzard of questions into the Word of Mouth net, but she didn't sit around waiting for answers. She knew that her presence was required on the spot the day before yesterday.

She grabbed the first ship south and couldn't make radio contact till she got to Barbo. There she had learned that the Eagle Tribe had supposedly discovered an atomic power core in one of the new radios which the Lightning Commune had tried to sell them. When the Eagles righteously blew the whistle, even cool old Levan had been forced to interdict the twenty-five examples of this black science that the Sunshine Tribe had taken delivery of in La Mirage.

That did not exactly clarify the logic, but it did transmit

the brimstone smell of the shadowy Spacers. The Lightnings might just have the collective intelligence to assemble the devices, but no one who did business with them seriously believed that they were really reproducing pre-Smash designs. And anyone who believed that even more brain-burned mountain williams farther back in the woods supplied their components from pre-Smash stashes might as well have believed that solar cells and microcircuits grew on trees. Someone somewhere out of sight was making this stuff and using the williams as a thin camouflage which fooled only those who wanted to be fooled, namely, any reasonable person.

The Eagles might buy solar cells and electric motors from the Lightning Commune, but they didn't buy radios. They didn't know squat about radios. So how come they found the atomic power cores hidden in the circuitry when our own aces didn't? And why would they want to blacken the reputation of their supplier of solar cells and motors?

Sunshine Sue had pondered these questions during the endless horseback trip to Javelina without coming up with answers that satisfied the test of self-interest. And this was too complex a mess to be the result of mere random fuck-ups; uncool things like that just did not happen in La Mirage. Therefore, someone with a *hidden* self-interest was pulling strings from out of sight, and that meant the damn Spacers.

Who else could hide atomic power sources so thoroughly in the transmitter circuits that they could get past the radio mechanics of the Sunshine Tribe? The Eagles could not have discovered the atomic cores unless they were meant to.

But why? Why would even the Spacers pollute Aquaria with atomic power sources and then somehow arrange to have their own dupes exposed for the blackest of sciences?

Before she left Javelina, Word of Mouth came from La Mirage that Levan had decided that this situation required justice from a perfect master. The Eagles had suggested Clear Blue Lou and the Lightnings had accepted. Would she agree? Of course, she had to decide immediately because otherwise they would have to await her arrival to negotiate another choice of perfect master, and it could take a week for one to arrive whereas Clear Blue Lou was two days away, and in the meantime, the Sunshine Tribe might find itself under sorcery boycott until the situation was resolved. . . .

Some "freely agreed-upon choice of judges!" It was Clear Blue Lou, or this mess would fester for weeks. And of course it was common folklore that Clear Blue Lou was in love with his solar eagle; no doubt the pea-brained Eagles thought that would shield them from any repercussions.

But Word of Mouth on Lou was that he really *was* Clear Blue; few people lost when he gave justice. And he was practically the patron saint of La Mirage. He and Levan saw eye to eye on keeping things cool. Furthermore, the solar cells in Lou's eagle came from the same source as the Sunshine radios. A perfect master like Clear Blue Lou would be wise to the wider implications, and he himself already owned a piece of this karma.

Finally, Clear Blue Lou was a perfect master who boogied. Better him than some whitely righteous celibate or vibrating lady!

So she sent her agreement down the net and hauled ass for La Mirage, hoping to get there before anyone else had a chance at working on Clear Blue Lou's head.

That is, if you could call *this* hauling ass!

Sue sounded her klaxon, and up ahead the wagon began to inch to the right side of the so-called road. But not fast enough. She would have to lose some momentum by using the brakes, or she'd hit the damn thing going by.

She slowed down to under twenty, centered the boom, and slipped by. Then she found the road going into a rising bend, lost the wind, and had to pedal, puffing and cursing, to gain the crest.

And that was what this whole bleeding trip had been like! Finding out about things days after they happened and not being able to make your reaction felt until more days later. It was a source of wonder to Sunshine Sue that anything ever managed to get done in Aquaria at all.

She but dimly remembered how much worse it had been before she took leadership of the Sunshine Tribe and established the Word of Mouth net. In those days, it could take a week to get a hand-carried message from Mendocino to La Mirage, and there was no such thing as public news. Now at least the Sunshine Tribe had enough solar radios to relay messages all up and down Aquaria while the sun was up. Well, almost. The damn things had only a five-mile range— less in hilly country—and you still had to shift them around to set up Word of Mouth chains. And if too many radios had been shifted to the wrong places, it could take days to set up the right chains.

Last year she had purchased a solar-and-battery-powered computer, which had magically appeared on the Exchange, and now at least the radios she had could be moved around to reform new chains with maximized efficiency. But it was still nothing like the old networks.

Sue crested the ridgeline just as her lungs were starting to give out. Before her, the road circled down a few bends, then debouched upon a long straight dry lake bed without a bend or a dip until it reached the famously awful switchback road that climbed torturously up to La Mirage.

Those new radios should have been the beginnings of a real Sunshine Radio Network. With their fifty-mile range, they would form an unbroken chain of relay stations covering all Aquaria. *Voices* could be transmitted up and down the land instead of secondhand messages. And the Lightning Commune had promised her cheap and plentiful solar receivers for next year. With the beginnings of a Sunshine Radio Network already broadcasting, she could have marketed them to every town and commune and farmstead in the land. It would have been the beginning of the new electronic village.

Sue had to ride the brakes as the sail cycle nosed over and began to speed down around the curves toward the dry lake bed. Now all that was down the willy hole because of the atomic power cores that had been found in the key piece of hardware. And if this situation came out badly, who knew how much of the Sunshine Tribe's equipment might end up proscribed!

Sunshine Sue had never met an admitted Spacer, nor had she met anyone who admitted to dealing with Spacers. Who, after all, would *admit* a connection with black science, even in La Mirage? But she had always felt that the unseen sorcerers somehow favored her enterprise.

When she needed a large supply of the old radios, the Lightnings had magically managed to triple their production. When she was ready to make good use of a computer, up popped that piece of legendary arcana, white as the clouds in the sky, or maybe almost. And the new fifty-mile radios had seemed like the latest gift from the trolls who apparently were her silent partners twice removed.

Hell, everything up until then had checked out ultrabright,

hadn't it? If these pure white devices had been dropped in her lap, who was she to find out more about their ultimate source than was good for her to know?

Sunshine Sue accepted the law of muscle, sun, wind and water as the distilled wisdom of human history. The black science of atomics had poisoned the vast continent beyond the Sierras and who knew how much of the rest of the world, and filled the air of the planet with carcinogens. Unnatural chemistry had killed the fish of the sea. And the burning of black coal and black petroleum rotted the lungs and made the air unfit to breathe. Every human on Earth was still paying for the sins of black science with a reduced life span, and the species itself might eventually pay for its folly with extinction. Black science *was* evil, and the Spacers *were* sorcerers.

Or were they? After all, none of the technology that seeped across the mountains was demonstrably other than white. None of the equipment she had bought did anything but sweeten the karma of Aquaria.

Until now, that is.

Was this karmic punishment for her flirtation with black science? Now her whole enterprise was threatened by the very distantly removed black science that had allowed her to build it to this point in the first place. Could this bad karma be *just?*

The sail cycle rounded the last descending bend and whooshed out onto the long straight road up the dry lake bed. She ratcheted the sail around to catch the following wind blowing north toward La Mirage, and the sail cycle began to pick up even more speed. Twenty, twenty-five, thirty, nearly forty miles an hour, fairly skimming along this well-maintained high-speed section of the road. Faster than a horse, faster than an eagle, faster than any yacht, faster than anything else in the world save Word of Mouth. Almost fast enough.

Justly earned bad karma, my ass! Sue thought. The karma that took me this far has been sweet, for me, and for mine, and for Aquaria too. I've been true to my destiny, I've walked my own Way.

Admittedly, it had been a Way that no other feet had trod in centuries, a Way that narrow minds might find streaked with black had she revealed the true path now, before its time. More Rememberers' hoards than not were burned for sorcery when discovered, and the dim remnants of this mysterious ancient tribe were shunned by the whitely righteous.

Even *her* first reaction had been a certain dread when she stumbled upon the abandoned Rememberers' hut on that long-ago late fall afternoon in the redwood country northeast of Mendocino. She had been plain Susan Sunshine then, a teenaged messenger carrying a packet through the mountains from Mendocino to Shasta. She had stopped along the road to relieve herself and improperly tethered her horse. By the time she had gotten her breeches back on, the animal had wandered off into the forest.

The waning sun sent intermittent shafts of ruby light through the dark aisles of giant trees. Bird sounds seemed abnormally far away, and the still forest air was redolent of resin and loam and cool with impending night. The atmosphere seemed pregnant with mysterious import.

And then she caught up to her mount, sipping placidly from a little brook. On the bank of the stream, half-hidden by the saplings and brush that had grown up around it, was the crumbling log hut.

She tethered her horse to a tree—very carefully this time —and gingerly entered the abandoned hut through the open portal where the door had fallen from its rotted leather hinges.

Inside, moldering rough-hewn furniture, semi-darkness, and the earthy rank odor of the pallid mushrooms that grew all over the dirt floor. Bits and flakes of paper scattered about like dirty snow. When she fingered one of the larger fragments, one surface felt slick as glass. Holding it up to a thin shaft of sunlight filtering through a crack in the log wall, she saw the right upper quarter of a woman's face impressed upon the parchment. Her heart skipped a beat.

A "photograph!" The perfect likeness of a human face printed on the magically smooth paper by lost pre-Smash black science. Now she knew what this place was and what it was doing here hidden in the depths of the woods. This was a cabin of Rememberers, abandoned for many years by the look of it.

Dread not unmixed with a certain morbid curiosity chilled her spirit as she poked about. The Rememberers were a dying breed, and their reputation was well streaked with black. A century ago, there had been thousands of them scuttling about the land in small groups, zealously guarding their hoards of pre-Smash books, photographs, and publications. Aquaria had never entirely made its mind up about the Rememberers. It was clear that they venerated these pathetic remnants of pre-Smash black science, but it was also clear that these bits and pieces of the lost and evil world were entirely beyond their dim comprehension. Periods of uneasy tolerance alternated with pogroms. Hoards relating to the obviously black sciences were righteously burned, but some hoards relating to less clearly black arts were sometimes allowed to remain with their guardians or just as often seized for study. The Rememberers themselves were frequently slain and universally abominated.

Now, Rememberers were few and the discovery of a new hoard a major event. By the look of this ruin, nothing remained here but debris and fragments. Still, something made Sue search through the abandoned hut, kicking over fungi, rifling through piles of rotting wood, peering into decayed wooden boxes.

The light was fading fast when she found the metal box under a heap of amorphous filth. It was about the size of a saddlebag, silvery, but too light to be silver. She almost dropped the unholy thing when she realized what it was. The strange light metal had to be aluminum, a pre-Smash metal whose manufacture involved obscenely vast amounts of electrical energy. How many carcinogens had been pumped into the atmosphere to make this thing, how many lives had it cost down through the ages?

But of course she had to know what was inside. The lid opened easily, and within were a few moldering ancient magazines, a handful of photographs, and a single decaying book.

The cabin interior was nearly totally dark now. She removed the hoard from the aluminum box and tossed the black thing away into a corner. The forest outside was a cavern of black shapes and shadows, and the creatures of night had already begun their eerie symphony. Of necessity, Sue made camp for the night, got a fire going, gulped down some bread and dried fruit, and by the flickering firelight, began to examine the hoard she had discovered.

The photographs seemed a random lot—faces of the long-dead, a silvery bird flying through the clouds, a strange device like a glass aquarium but with tiny manikins inside it, playing an unknown game on a grassy field. The magazines were called *Time* and *Radio Digest* and *Listener's Log* and *TV Guide*. The lone crumbling book was called *Understanding Media* by Marshall McLuhan.

Far into the night, Sue studied the Rememberers' hoard, alone by the firelight in the dark forest, trying to make sense of the arcane lore, trying to decide whether this science called "media" was white or black or something in between.

She took the hoard with her in the morning and down through the years studied it still. Much of it remained beyond her grasp. "Television," some strange form of radio which transmitted pictures that moved. "Ratings," which seemed to be a pre-Smash form of numerology. "Prime time," which did not seem to be a unit of duration.

But buried in the mass of incomprehensibility and the nearly impenetrable dialect of the book and the magazines was the concept that came to rule her destiny.

The pre-Smash world had been blanketed by things called "networks," immaterial electronic webs of radio and television messages. If this lore were to be believed, there were millions of radio receivers and "TV sets," and almost everyone had access to one. Huge transmitters, powered by black science, broadcast "programs," messages in the form of plays and stories. These transmitters or "stations" were organized into "networks" so that everyone in the world could receive the same messages at the same time.

The networks also broadcast something called "news," messages about events happening all over the world, aimed at all the "viewers" or "listeners" as a whole.

Thus the people of pre-Smash times had been united by plays and stories and news which they all received at the same time. Anything that happened anywhere was immediately known to all. McLuhan believed that these message networks changed the consciousness of the people by knitting them together into something he called "the electronic global village." These "artificial senses" changed the very nature of human thought and magnified intelligence even as the invention of printing had aeons before.

Thus the "electronic villagers" had not merely possessed black sciences lost to modern man, *their minds themselves* were more cogent.

True, these selfsame electronic villagers had destroyed their world and poisoned Sue's own by their fatal affair with black science. But it was the devices of black science, the "hardware," that had brought man to ruin, not the "software," which was concept and spirit alone, a path of the Way, independent of science, white or black.

Now the world lay poisoned perhaps unto death; a person's world was the area in which he lived and what sparse news moved up and down the creaky Word of Mouth net, and before Sue had built Word of Mouth with her secret software lore, not even that.

How limited we are if only we knew, Sunshine Sue thought as she sped up the dry lake bed toward La Mirage with the speed of the wind. How fast I seem to be moving and yet how slowly our thoughts crawl from town to town and mind to mind! Now, as so often since that day in the Rememberers' hut, she felt like a poor lorn creature trapped outside her proper time. The secrets she alone knew tormented her soul with impatience for the distant rebirth of the electronic global village that might one day reunite the scattered remnants of the species in a web of consciousness beyond her poor imagining, a worldwide community of spirit that might yet heal what was left of the shattered Earth.

Up ahead, she could see wagons inching up the switchback road that ascended the mountain to La Mirage, and beyond, the great central peaks of the Sierras that rimmed the known world. East of the horizon lay the terra incognita of black science—out of sight, but hardly out of mind.

Yes, the law of muscle, sun, wind and water was the Way. But could the present world of crawling, limiting isolation truly be called good?

It was destiny that had taken her to that Rememberers' hut, destiny too that had made her a member of the Sunshine Tribe where her secret knowledge could be put to use. And if destiny required that she risk graying her soul in the service of her dream, then so be it. For surely that dream was in the end whiter than the rigid narrowness of the asshole righteous.

And if her silent patrons now sought to destroy what she had built for their own unknown reasons, those Spacer bastards were going to have one hell of a fight on their hands.

"Move, damn you, move!" she shouted into the wind, pushing against the steering gear as if she could squeeze more speed out of the sail cycle by sheer force of will. Why couldn't this bloody thing go faster?

* * *

The mountains began abruptly at the northern end of the dry lake bed; from this angle, the Sierras were a vast ziggurat staircase reaching upward and eastward. La Mirage was built atop one of the lower flattened steps of the cordillera stairway, and the lake-bed road ended abruptly at the foot of a severe three-thousand-foot slope.

Here the road became a torturous zigzag, climbing the mountain in an endless series of steep switchbacks, forty miles of crawling agony to ascend three thousand feet. A procession of horse-drawn wagons inched up this nightmare back door approach, dwindling away to insectlike dots toward the heights.

Barreling along the valley road at top speed to the last minute, Sunshine Sue slammed on the sail cycle's brakes and came to a screeching stop in a cloud of dust right outside the cabin that the Sunshine Tribe had built many years ago at the foot of the mountain road. Half a dozen sail cycles with furled yellow sails and four Sunshine yellow solar eagles were tethered to the hitching rail. No sail cycle could ascend the mountain road, and the geography precluded radio contact with the town, so from here to La Mirage, Word of Mouth—and Sunshine Sue herself—would travel the last three thousand feet straight up by eagle.

Teddy Sunshine, the station honcho, emerged from the cabin even as Sue was shakily unwinding her cramped legs from the long drive. Sue pointed to the line of solar eagles, not wanting to waste even a minute, and they met under the golden shadow of the nearest eagle wing.

"What's the word from La Mirage?" she asked breathlessly, stowing her gear behind the eagle saddle. "Lou arrived yet?"

"Not yet," Teddy said, as Sue climbed into the saddle and began strapping in. It seemed to Sue that he was not exactly eager to meet her eyes.

"What's wrong, Teddy? What's the bad news *now?*"

"Worst possible," Teddy grunted. "The Lightnings are now claiming we knew about the atomic power cores when we bought the radios."

"WHAT?" Sue screamed. "Those lying brain-burned sons of bitches!" Bloody fucking hell! If Clear Blue Lou ended up believing *that*, he might very well decide to disband the tribe! And *I* could end up in karmic rebirth!

She studied Teddy, who seemed to be studying *her* most peculiarly.

"You don't believe that shit, do you!" she demanded. "Do you think for a moment that I'd—"

"Of course not!" Teddy interrupted none too convincingly. "But . . . uh, maybe Gloria might have, uh, gotten a little carried away. . . ."

"No way! I made that deal myself, remember?"

"Then why—"

"It's a set-up, it's got to be!"

"But who—why—?"

"Who do you think made the power cores?" Sue asked sharply. "As for why . . ." She nodded toward the east, shrugging. "That's what I'm going to find out," she said. "Now please untether this thing."

Teddy slipped the hitching rail bolt. "I'd never fool with atomic power," Sue told him earnestly. "*That* black, I'm not. You *do* believe me?"

But the eagle shot skyward before she could hear his response, and Sue found herself contemplating what the electronic villagers would have called her "image" with a new sense of unease. If my reputation is so gray that even my own people can half believe I'd knowingly fool with atomic power, how am I going to convince Clear Blue Lou that the Lightnings are lying? And why would they tell a lie that convicts *them* of black science out of their own stupid mouths?

The eagle bobbed upward along the mountain face where the string of wagons groaned laboriously toward La Mirage. Rapid though her rise was relative to these groundlings climbing in the dust, it seemed achingly slow to Sunshine Sue. She valved the last of her helium into the wing and nosed the eagle skyward. The eagle began to climb even more rapidly but still not fast enough.

"What's going *on* up there?" Sunshine Sue demanded aloud, craning her neck upward.

Muttering imprecations, she began to pedal.

La Mirage

Clear Blue Lou's eagle soared along the ascending meadow, and then was buffeted upward and backward for a moment as it crested the lip of the plateau and hit a sudden swirl of freer air. After this dramatic fanfare, it regained its forward momentum, and in a few minutes, Lou was floating high above La Mirage.

From this perspective, the name of the town seemed a poetic image of innocent purity. La Mirage was the lone handiwork of man in a vast vision of primeval grandeur. The colorful buildings and groved avenues seemed to spring like magic mushrooms from the center of an oval meadow rimmed on three sides by a sheer drop into immensity. The ascending cordillera east of the town formed a dwarfing backdrop that reversed Lou's aerial perspective, an amphitheater of the gods looking down from on high on man and all his tiny works. Here the upland meadow unraveled into a seemingly infinite complexity of canyons that began as fingers of brown raking the green plain below, and then climbed and branched and grew in scale as they became the texture of the mountains towering away high above his eagle.

Lou circled over the center of La Mirage and began to recompress helium with his pedals, descending in a lazy spiral that was also a dance of arrival for the benefit of the town below.

How serene it looked from this deceptive viewpoint, how in harmony with the wilderness to which it served as a humble human grace note. And what a *mirage* that vision of bucolic tranquillity really was!

The town streamed eastward from Market Circle like the thinning corona of a comet about its head. West of the Circle toward the abyss, it quickly petered out into residential groves and isolated farmsteads. To the east, the main avenues fanned out into a sweep of manufactories, workshops, residential neighborhoods and manse grounds, attenuating back into the canyons that climbed up into the higher Sierras, as if the town had chosen to turn its back on the western landscape that sent the soul soaring out over vast natural vistas to bask in the craggy ambiguity pulling the mind toward the looming mountain strongholds of the unknown to the east.

The tradehouses and inns and civic buildings of Market Circle were built along the rim of the circular park in the center. Trees dappled most of the park, but its center was a clear circular bullseye where scores of varicolored eagles were tethered like carnival balloons. As Lou descended toward them, he saw that scores of people were drifting through the park toward his landing point; his Clear Blue Lou blue eagle was an easily recognizable ensign and by now, most of the town would be aware of his arrival.

A small crowd was already milling around as he landed, waving and shouting his name in greeting. By the time he set foot on the grass, someone had tethered his eagle, someone else had unfastened his pack for him, and he was surrounded by a babble of greetings, invitations, and the inconsequential, as if this were simply another casual visit by La Mirage's favorite perfect master. Dinner invitations, pleas for personal council, sexual come-ons—both subtle and overt —a wineskin tossed into his hands, a pipe of reef stuck in his mouth—welcome to La Mirage!

Puffing on the reef between courtesy swallows of wine, Lou made his way out of the park amidst the ebb and swirl of his casual reception committee. None of the major mavens had turned out to greet him, nor had any Lightnings or Eagles—though of course there was a Sunshine messenger hanging back at the periphery. Apparently, the movers and shapers were trying to be as cool as was possible under the circumstances.

People began to melt away into the general traffic as he circled around the thoroughfare toward the Exchange. Market Circle was crowded as usual, but the vibes were all wrong for this time of day. The taverns and smokehouses were buzzing with nighttime-sized crowds, and the general tune of the conversation was not exactly a holiday air. Many of the tradehouses he passed did not seem open for business. The establishments of the astrologers and soothsayers, on the other hand, were bursting at the seams with worried customers. La Mirage had the ozone reek of a storm waiting to break, and you could hardly say the town had no reason to be nervous.

The big redwood-and-glass geodesic dome of the Exchange dominated the northern quadrant of Market Circle, and ordinarily merchants and mages would be pouring in and out of the main entrance and a dozen wagons would be lined up outside the freight dock. The Exchange was the commercial and karmic heart of La Mirage. Here the mountain william tribes came to sell their components to the manufacturers and craftsmen of the town and Aquaria beyond. Here La Mirage displayed its products for out-of-town buyers. Here white scientists came to acquire somewhat gray knowledge by osmosis, though of course they wouldn't admit it. Here presided Levan the Wise, Arbiter of the Exchange, passing on the whiteness of questionable goods, adjudicating commercial disputes, renting out space, and in general maintaining the dynamic harmony.

But today the Exchange seemed neither dynamic nor harmonious. The place was more than half-empty. The outer ring of the Exchange floor under the dome was divided up into display areas rented out by purveyors of La Mirage's products. Ordinarily, this would be a continuous sweep of marvelous goods on sale for fancy prices, awash in buyers and hype. Now half the stalls were vacant. The central area was usually a raucous camp of mountain williams, selling the components that made all of it possible, getting stoned, making music, dancing, and doing everything but setting up cookfires to make it like their upper canyon camps. Now there were no williams at all. The central aisle around the william encampment was usually filled with hawkers selling food and drink and smoke, as well as astrologers and sooth-sayers. Now there were fewer refreshment stalls and more soothsayers, who seemed to be garnering most of what customers there were.

The lair of Levan was a roofless cubicle on the outer north rim of the floor. Inside, the old man held court reclining on a green divan, beside a large table heavily laden with wines and medicines and smokes and an endless untidy smorgasbord of unappetizing snacks. Vases of cut flowers were everywhere. It seemed more like a sickroom than a place of business, and the frail bedrobe-draped body, the mess of thinning white hair, the liverish wrinkled face, completed the illusion of a dying doddard. Only Levan's bird-brilliant eyes and the product of his twisting mobile mouth gave the lie to this impression of decayed senility.

But that was more than enough. The old man was railing away at a constipated-looking fellow dressed in the severe Castrotown mode, all blacks and whites. "Local interdiction be damned, I'll take no further action until justice is given! Look at what's happened to business already! Everyone's afraid they're going to get stuck with interdicted goods and hardheads like you have apparently convinced the mountain williams that La Mirage is under some kind of curse!"

The old man's face lit up when he saw Clear Blue Lou, but he quickly rearranged it into a simulacrum of petulance. "Lou! It's about time you got here! The town's going crazy! Don't you have any compassion for a sick old man?"

"So you're Clear Blue Lou," the Castrotowner said. "I hope you'll be willing to take more righteous action to protect the whiteness of Aquaria, unlike friend Levan. We must make sure that the rest of the questionable science that is purveyed in this evil place is freer from sorcery than—"

"When I see, I'll speak," Lou said frostily, "and when I speak, I'll speak justice." Whatever the facts, this kind of strident white righteousness always rubbed him the wrong way.

"Lou and I have some serious matters to discuss, if you don't mind," Levan said, vibing Lou his thanks.

"Of course," the Castrotowner said obsequiously. "And of course, everyone has faith in the justice of Clear Blue

Lou." He shot a parting glance of distaste toward Levan. "Especially the gray folk of La Mirage."

"Thanks Lou," Levan said when he had gone. "The righteously white have been crawling all over me to go further ever since the latest. Suspending trade in Lightning components and making it impossible for anyone to buy eagles or radios or electrical equipment isn't good enough for them! Now they want me to interdict everything the Sunshine Tribe uses and shut down the Word of Mouth operation. Next, they'll want me to ban Lightning-type components generically and shut down what's left of business in this town, as if I'm not unpopular enough already!"

"But that can't be decided until I give justice," Lou said, taking a seat at the foot of the divan.

"Oh, that's not good enough for them now, not since the Lightning Commune started saying that the Sunshine Tribe *knew* that the radios they bought had atomic power cores."

"WHAT?"

Levan peered at Lou owlishly. "You didn't know? Oh yes, now it's all over town that those brain-burned williams claim that Sunshine Sue knowingly bought loathsome black science from them, and now everyone's looking at everyone else as if they were the black plague and searching for Spacers in the woodwork."

"But that's an open admission that they're practicing black science themselves. . . ."

"You think I don't know that?" Levan said. "What's more, my instincts tell me that they're lying. Sunshine Sue isn't *that* black, she's certainly not that stupid, and she's always played by the rules of the game. She's been set up; you can't tell me she hasn't."

"But how and why and by whom?"

"How?" Levan snorted. "The Lightnings sold her the radios and then tipped off the Eagles, who for some reason got a sudden attack of righteous whiteness and denounced her. Why? The answer to that one is who, and we both know who really made the piece of black technology that's at the heart of this situation, now don't we?"

"The Spacers deliberately set up Sunshine Sue?" Lou said. It didn't make sense. "But why would they want to ruin the Sunshine Tribe?"

Levan lit a pipe of reef, puffed, shook his head, and spoke more slowly. "It could be part of something *really* sinister,

Lou. Everything's at a standstill already. What if the karma of this situation forces us to disband Word of Mouth and ban Lightning-type components generically? Imagine Aquaria without solar cells or eagles or Word of Mouth and with everything else that comes out of La Mirage smeared black with the scandal. . . ."

Lou took Levan's proffered pipe, toked deeply, and tried to make sense out of it. Without the La Mirage free market, Aquaria's supply of electronic components would dwindle away to a trickle of inferior imitations. It might even be worse, since only the mountain williams "knew" how to produce these goods at all. In short, without what was permitted to sleaze through La Mirage, Aquaria's white civilization would be crippled. Without the venial gray sins that were committed here, virtue would be unworkable.

"It doesn't add up," Lou said. "Why would the Spacers help us build a white technology on the sly and then create a situation that cripples it?"

Levan shrugged. "My soul may be well flecked with gray, but I'm no Spacer," he said. "Could this be preparation for some kind of invasion? Cripple our technology and then—"

"It could never happen," Lou blurted instinctively. "We'd never let—" He stopped in mid-sentence, for the flow had brought him to a clearly flashed vision of the likely truth in all its subtle awfulness.

"I smell a satori," Levan said, eyeing him narrowly.

"Could be," Lou said slowly. "I mean, if we're forced to dismantle half our technology to prove our righteous whiteness to ourselves, we just won't do it. Instead, we'd have to admit self-consciously that our vaunted white science has a black lining, that without a certain amount of black science, the law of muscle, sun, wind and water is unworkable. They may have caught us in a nasty karmic paradox."

Even Levan the Wise, Levan the Cool, blanched at this prospect. After all, his whole life had been spent in the maintenance of the very necessary ambiguity that these Spacer machinations seemed designed to resolve into disaster, the vital illusion that was the spirit of La Mirage. And from the look of the town, that wire-walking act was getting pretty shaky already.

"Is this karma punishment for our sins, Lou?" Levan sighed half seriously.

Lou laughed ruefully. "Somehow," he said, "I can't see

the Spacers as the avenging angels of righteousness. Perhaps they seek to make the temptations of black science more open and watch as we're forced to blacken our souls to survive. They make much more sense playing the snake.''

Levan sat up, leaned forward, and tried to assume a grandfatherly pose. ''Whatever you do, you must also restore the harmony of La Mirage, my young master,'' he said. ''You know how this town feels about you, Lou. You won't let your people down, will you, my son?''

''Would I do that?'' Lou said, and he meant it. But he also knew that he would be beyond the bounds of such affection and loyalty when the voice of justice spoke through him.

After a dose of what awaited her at the Sunshine Tribe's transport depot and tribal hostelry in the eastern suburbs of La Mirage, Sunshine Sue decided to avoid the Market Circle headquarters of the tribe for the moment. Everyone she wanted to avoid was clamoring to see her, and everyone else was asking her politely to keep her distance.

After a quick meal, she had grilled Gloria Sunshine and the craftsmen who had examined the sorcery-tainted radios in the office she had commandeered while casually tending to a vast assortment of business with other people. While she let them convince her that only a true black scientist could have discovered the hidden atomic cores in the merchandise, she hoped that this public performance would convince her own people that the Lightnings were lying, that she hadn't knowingly betrayed her tribe to black science.

Then she went through the blizzard of messages awaiting her. Levan wanted to see her at once, half a dozen scribes wanted interviews, and most of the astrologers and soothsayers in town were eager to improve her destiny for a stiff fee. There were dozens of notes from old friends and lovers telling her they were with her in spirit, but asking her to accept their regrets for wanting to make discretion the better part of valor.

To hell with it all! she decided. I'm just going to take a bath and see no one for the rest of the day.

She was just toweling herself down in her quarters and beginning to cool out a little when some bozo knocked on the door, despite the message she had left not to be disturbed.

''Go away!'' she shouted. ''I don't want to be bothered.''

"Not even by a representative of Space Systems Incorporated?" said a basso voice on the other side of the door.

"What?" Sue shouted. *"What did you say?"*

"I'm a representative of Space Systems Incorporated. I must speak with you privately on a matter of vital mutual interest."

Sure you are! Sue thought sourly. And I'm the wicked witch of the west! Still, anyone who was crazy enough to claim he was a Spacer deserved some craziness back. So she went to the door with the towel wrapped low under her armpits, exposing a goodly amount of breast. Maybe I'll just tease this maniac and see what happens, she decided.

A creepy-looking young man stood in the doorway, heavy with pudge, bald on top, doughy like a baby around the jowls, and weird looking around his intense watery blue eyes. He seemed to stare right through her half-draped body without reacting. This is a sinister black scientist? He was a total turn-off, his seeming indifference to her fair flesh infuriated her, and she felt like an asshole. But she was damned if she was going to show it.

"So you're a Spacer?" she purred sardonically. "Well come on in and let's get acquainted."

The pudgy man took a seat by the dressing table while Sue reclined provocatively on the bed, letting the towel ride high up her bare thighs, determined to get a sexual rise out of this creature so she could torment him with rejection. "So?" she said in a sultry voice. "What do you really want?"

"I'm John Swensen, and I represent Arnold Harker, Project Manager for the implementation of this scenario," the so-called Spacer said. "He wants to meet with you at once; the scenario calls for it." He did seem a little sweaty now, staring carefully at a fixed point slightly above her head as Sue let the towel drop a little, exposing the aureole of one nipple. "A great opportunity will be yours if you follow the scenario nominally."

"Scenario? Nominally? Great opportunity? What the hell are you talking about?"

"The scenario that brought you to La Mirage. It has been followed nominally thus far. You bought the radios, our operative in the Eagle Tribe arranged for the so-called black science to be revealed, and here you are to be judged by Clear Blue Lou. Phase two requires—"

"Shit, this is serious, isn't it?" Sue said, sitting upright and drawing the towel more protectively around her. Suddenly she felt all too naked. This confirmed her worst conjecture—the damn Spacers *had* set her up, and this creature had just established his credibility by telling her how. Unlikely as he seemed in the role of a sorcerer, he was the real thing.

"Of course it's serious!" the Spacer said in his first display of excitement. "It's a moment of great destiny for you and for the world. Phase two of the scenario will reveal the true reasons for what we've done and present you with a gift that will make you forever grateful for your compliance."

"Grateful!" Sue snapped. "My compliance! You try to destroy everything I've built and you expect my compliance! You tell your Project Manager that he can stick his bleeding scenario up his—"

"Phase two will undo all the damage caused by phase one, I assure you," the Spacer said fretfully. "You'll regain all you've lost and reap far more if you follow it." His fat face seemed to harden suddenly as he reached the down-and-dirty bottom line.

"Besides," he continued in a much more threatening tone, "if you don't follow the scenario, you'll be judged guilty of black science, your tribe will be disbanded, and you'll lose your current persona through karmic rebirth. Phase one guarantees all that. You cannot rationally refuse to follow phase two. To deviate from nominality is to assure your own destruction."

Sunshine Sue studied the Spacer with disgust, anger, loathing, and no little fearful respect for the powers his unprepossessing person represented. The bastards had her. They had set this up with hideous precision, and her only hope was that they were telling the truth about extricating her from their own trap. Certainly no one else was about to. Their ironclad logic did indeed compel her compliance with this "scenario" of theirs, but if they thought they'd ever get any gratitude from her for trapping her in their dirty mindfuck, they had another think coming.

"Okay, so you've got me for the moment," she admitted belligerently. "Now what, sorcerer?"

"My directive is to take you to the Project Manager at once," the Spacer said, rising from his chair. "He's waiting up in the mountain william country away from watching eyes. I'll be waiting over Canyon Boulevard in a silver eagle to lead you. We have to leave at once to get there before we lose the sun; it's a long flight up."

"And how do I know you'll let me return?" Sue asked skeptically.

"You have to take our word for it," the Spacer said almost pleadingly. "Besides," he said more coldly, "you really have no choice, do you?"

And with that, he departed, taking any vestigial illusion of Sunshine Sue's free will with him.

Just how far up into the mountains is this person taking me? Sunshine Sue wondered as she soared up a jagged rocky cleft that seemed to climb up forever into the mountain fastness that now towered all around her. Long shadows already obscured the rugged land below, and only the tops of the peaks still gleamed in full sunlight.

She had been following the silver eagle for hours, and now the sun was starting to sink. Up here even the mountain william encampments were few and far between; in fact she didn't remember seeing one below for the better part of an hour.

Where the hell am I? she wondered. What am I doing here? I must be crazy.

She didn't know how far east they had come, but it was certainly far enough to become frightening. Outsiders didn't penetrate too far up into mountain william country if they knew what was good for them, and now it appeared that she was flying through country that the williams themselves were none too eager to brave. This was terra incognita already. No one ever dared fly this far east. Soon the sun would be down, which meant that this was farther toward Spacer country than she could return from without spending the night where no whitely righteous foot ever trod. Where did Spacer country begin? And was she already in it?

She shuddered in the sunset breeze that blew up the gorge through which she was flying. The canyon walls around her were deeply shadowed, forbidding and ominous in the pregnant aura of oncoming twilight. What might be slithering about the unseen landscape below?

This *is* insane, she decided. I'm not following my way up here, I've been forced into this. Without being able to stop myself, I'm following their bloody scenario. I've got about as much free will as a gear in some Spacer machine.

Up ahead the Spacer eagle veered off down a side canyon which opened out into what seemed like the last highland meadow before the central peaks of the Sierras rose up as an impassable barrier. A tongue of deep shadow extended east up most of the meadow, but the upper quarter was still a bright green where the day yet held back the creeping onset of night.

~~Something round and bright~~ gleamed high atop a peak of rock that loomed over the upper terminus of the meadow. Squinting against the brilliant contrast of light and dark, Sue made out a cluster of buildings at the top of the meadow and a cluster of eagles tethered beside them.

An eagle's nest? All the way up here? It made no sense; there was no eagle traffic at all this far up into the mountains.

But there it was, for all the world like any rest stop on the way from Mendocino to Lina, up here in the mysterious shadowy territory where the whiteness of Aquaria ended.

After leaving the Exchange and checking into his usual free room at the La Mirage Grande several blocks away from Market Circle, Clear Blue Lou spent the afternoon making the rounds of the taverns and smokehouses, trying to pick up an inspiration for his choice of place of justice—and perhaps some sport for the night.

Within reason, a giver of justice could ordinarily choose any place he fancied for the scene of his big party, and within a few days, it would be gladly turned over to him and rearranged to his liking. The present circumstances, however, seemed to demand that the Court of Justice be convened quickly, by tomorrow night if possible. This limited Lou's choices. On one level, he couldn't expect to have the town clear out the Exchange or a major public house overnight. On another, he knew damn well that La Mirage would be only too happy to let him run such a power trip under the current paranoid circumstances. But if he took advantage of this psychic injustice, the Court of Justice would open to bummer vibes. So he needed a place that would be immediately available without gross imposition.

In the Sorcerers' Saloon, he ran into Kelly the Munificent, an old bedfriend who owned the Palace of Dawn. She let it be known that both her music hall and her bedchamber would be happily available to him on instant notice. The Palace of Dawn was the largest music hall in La Mirage and eminently suitable. Kelly was big and blond and a noble sportswoman of fucking. However, she was literally the intimate of most of the key figures in town, and involvement with her karma at this point promised too many additional complications.

"The trouble with you, Lou, is that you really *are* Clear Blue," Kelly told him good-naturedly when he explained his polite regrets. Perhaps they could sport after the giving of justice was over, he told her, and in any case, of course, she would be invited to the Court of Justice.

His next stop was the Smokehouse, where the reef was the best in town, and the soothsayers and mages gathered to engage in dialectic, and where, if legend were to be believed, black scientists got stoned with the locals incognito. Today, however, Spacer machinations were the sole topic of conversation, and any black scientist in attendance would have gotten his ears scorched.

An intense lady astrologer assured Lou that while Sunshine Sue's stars were bad, the heavens were about to look on La Mirage with favor. She also assured him that the stars would smile on their union if he cared to come to her place. It was the opinion of the La Mirage mages that Sunshine Sue was too cool to have dealt knowingly with black science, though opinions on the true color of her soul varied. The Lightning Commune was held in the general contempt reserved for mountain williams.

But aside from the enigmatic Spacers, the true ire of the denizens of the Smokehouse seemed reserved for the Eagle Tribe, and there seemed to be a general conspiracy to paint them as the villains in Lou's eyes. Whether or not Sunshine Sue was guilty of black science, it was pointed out to him forcefully, the Eagles were flagrantly guilty of assholery.

"Where's there percentage in this?" Mithra the Biomaster demanded indignantly. "Now their own manufactory is shut down too."

No one seriously considered that the Eagles had acted out of a sense of selfless virtue, and it would have been jejune of Lou to suggest this possibility in this company, especially since he found the idea hard to swallow himself.

"Business is terrible," Dusty Windman complained. "You can't even sell some farmer a simple wind generator without his insisting that it be examined by a neutral expert for sorcery. You've got to reharmonize the vibes, Lou, and if that means sanctions against the Eagles, well, they're the ones who really violated the rules of the game."

"Lou understands that. He's been around."

"On his *eagle!*" someone blurted, and at that point, Clear Blue Lou decided it was time to leave. The lady astrologer was sidling up to him again with unwelcome stars in her eyes, and the mind games being run on him were starting to get personal. He could see what was coming. Use his well-known love of his eagle to put him on the defensive, and he might bend over backward when the time came to prove the purity of his justice by punishing the Eagles. And for what? For doing their civic duty?

He cut off the conversation by inviting most of the patrons to the Court of Justice, including, softheartedly, the lady astrologer, and continued his round of Market Circle until the sun started to set and his stomach began to rumble from the afternoon's overload of come-ons, mind games, and aperitifs.

Clear Blue Lou was used to being offered a constant choice of bed companions, and especially in La Mirage. But the problem with being a perfect master was that it was hard for most women to treat him as a mere lover or sporting partner. Even a single night with a master was filtered through the vision of transcendent expectations. Many perfect masters found this no problem at all since expectation usually led to at least the illusion of fulfillment, and not too many men, perfect master or no, failed to get off behind a mirror image of their own wonderfulness in a lover's eyes.

Lou, however, got off behind being a pure sexual organism in bed, whose consciousness was totally involved in the act of making love itself, not in the mind games that drove it. As far as he was concerned, the ideal fuck was like a flash of satori, where verbal thought dissolved into a oneness with the timeless ecstatic moment.

This, aside from a suitable place of justice, was what Lou was looking for—and this was what was looking hard to find in La Mirage at the moment. Usually this town abounded with ladies cool enough to sport with Lou as if he were just another natural man. But now he couldn't get away from being Clear Blue Lou, the giver of justice in a case in which no one in La Mirage could feel entirely uninvolved, and it would not be the Way to fuck anyone who was out to fuck *the giver of justice*.

Lou brooded over this during a solitary dinner of stuffed artichokes and wheat noodles with curried mixed vegetables in the small dining room of the La Mirage Grande. Somehow it synced with his difficulty in finding a suitable place of justice. Neutral vibes were hard to find.

After dinner he bathed, chose new clothes from his pack, and lazed around so that he would hit the night after the action had fairly started.

Under a brilliant canopy of high mountain stars, La Mirage boogied. Music halls rocked with dance bands, and smokehouses offered your choice of esoteric talk or comic entertainment. Deals were proposed and concluded at parties in the suburban manses of magnates. Orgies were not unknown, and if you hadn't been invited to any, there was usually the mountain williams' open-air insanity in the park. The taverns buzzed with gossip, shop talk and assignations.

And tonight the town was seething with nervous tension and in a mood to blow it all out. And of course wherever Clear Blue Lou went, the determination to boogie away the bad news blues was heightened by the frantic desire to show him what a good time La Mirage was, how sweet his karma was here, how much everybody loved him, and how essential it was to all that he give justice that would let the good times roll on.

Well if Clear Blue Lou didn't like to boogie, he wouldn't be Clear Blue Lou, and if his favorite place to boogie wasn't La Mirage, he wouldn't be the town's favorite perfect master. Besides, the giving of justice required a personal openness to the total karma out of which justice must come. You had to dance to the music before you could give it words. So if the music got down and dirty, why, you did a down-and-dirty dance if it seemed like fun.

So as he hopped from tavern to smokehouse, Lou refused not the reef and wine that were thrust upon him, not a sip or a toke, enjoying it all for the good-natured bribe it was. And as the night rolled on, his sexual fastidiousness began to transform itself into inspired compromise; since mindfuck games were the life of tonight's party, he would allow himself to succumb to some honest dishonesty if such could be found. As long as everyone knows what they're doing and knows that everyone else knows, there is no blame along the Clear Blue Way, or so he told himself.

Nevertheless he had hardly expected to end the night in a

ménage à trois with a Sunshine and an Eagle. He had met the two star-crossed lovers in a tiny food shop where he chanced to stop for a beer and a spinach pie in the wee hours after midnight. The place was empty save for the two women who sat together nursing the remains of a large flagon of wine and apparently saying tearful goodbyes. Laurie Eagle was tiny and blond, with narrow intense eyes and an appropriately aquiline nose. Carrie Sunshine was larger, darker, and rounder, her sadness vulnerable, whereas the smaller woman seemed to rage against the dying of their light.

When they saw him enter, it was Laurie Eagle who asked him over to their table with a request for his counsel too insistent for him to deny, even had he known what he was about to get involved in. When they told him their story, he knew that the Way had taken him to the karmic heart of the night.

Laurie was now an Eagle and Carrie was a Sunshine, but they had grown up together back in mountain william country where everyone got it off with everyone else of any sex, and the two of them were, in effect, sister-lovers. Carrie, the elder, had ambitions beyond the life of a simple william and had managed to join the Sunshine Tribe. Through the influence of her new tribe, she had gotten Laurie into the Eagles so that they could be together in La Mirage.

Now, however, their relationship was under double pressure from their respective tribes. Since the Eagles had denounced the Sunshines for sorcery, the blood between the two tribes had become bad indeed. Both of them would have lain on the edge of expulsion for continuing to consort with each other, even if they hadn't grown up as mountain williams together.

But since everyone felt that black science country began just east of their own karma, the williams had a black reputation even among the gray worthies of La Mirage. And here were two girls from the upper canyons united by a bond that went back further than their tribal loyalties, back east in space and time to their mountain william origins.

And since the Lightnings had openly admitted to sorcery, williams were in particular disfavor now.

Their respective tribes had made it quite clear that each must give the other up in order to prove their whiteness and loyalty.

"So where is the Way?" Carrie asked plaintively. "Do we

part and lose the best part of our lives or stay together and be banished to the canyons which are no longer our home?''

"And prove to the whitely righteous of this town that once a william, your soul is always tinged with black," Laurie said bitterly.

"But we'd have each other," Carrie said softly, clutching at Laurie's hand.

Lou was saddened by this story, but more than saddened, he was outraged by the unfairness of it all. His heart was touched and his sense of justice was angrily aroused.

"You stay together," he said firmly. "And you stay with your tribes."

"But that's the one thing they won't let us do!"

"Justice demands it," Lou said. "I won't stand for this shit."

"But this is a tribal matter," Carrie said. "You can't give justice unless our tribes both request it."

"Which they won't. . . ."

"There is justice that speaks when spoken to and there is justice that speaks up for itself," Lou declared. And as the words passed his lips, the Way opened up to him, clear and blue.

All night, he had been searching for a lady he might sport with without involving himself in the mind games that swirled around him. Now he was confronted by two loving women torn asunder by the very karma his justice was called upon to unravel. Now the giver of justice would make love and the natural man would get off on justice. He might not find sport, but love he would make.

Then again, these ladies might just still be into their old mountain william ways. . . .

"How about I make you ladies a loving down-and-dirty proposition?" he said. "What say the three of us go to the Garden of Love and rent a cloud chamber? There, for the world to see, Laurie of the Eagles, Carrie of the Sunshines, and the giver of justice to both their tribes will sport together openly. My karma will be your karma. I magnanimously offer you my body to sanctify your union before the assholes of this town. What I join together, let no tribe split asunder!"

He winked at each of them in turn. "Which they sure as shit won't after tonight, seeing as neither of them is exactly anxious to arouse my displeasure."

"You'd do that for us?" Laurie eyed him somewhat suspiciously, whereas Carrie's eyes shone with gratitude.

"Uh—of course, I'm not suggesting we actually get it on," Lou said deliberately unconvincingly. "All we have to do is rent a cloud chamber and go to sleep. . . ."

Laurie's suspicion evaporated. "You really are what they say you are, aren't you?" she said.

In more ways than one, Lou thought, his lips creased in a fey little smile. Carrie looked at Laurie. Laurie looked at Carrie. They both beamed at Lou. Ah yes!

"Is there something wrong with us?" Carrie said archly.

"Wrong with you? What could be wrong with you?"

"You're risking your reputation for us," Laurie said, "and we're two healthy william girls who grew up believing in sharing their joy. And you suggest the three of us rent a cloud chamber and *just go to sleep?*"

"Pretty insulting."

Lou laughed. "Well I didn't mean to be all that insistent about it . . ." he owned.

"Thought you didn't," Laurie said, licking her lips. The three of them laughed together and then the two of them kissed Lou on either cheek together like a sly little fox and the three of them rambled around Market Circle to the Garden of Love, arm in arm in arm, nuzzling and feeling each other, to the somewhat scandalized delectation of passersby.

They spent a conspicuous ten minutes in the big tavern downstairs, drinking brandies at the bar until even the groups of public lovers enjoying their own pleasures in the open cloud chambers around the tavern floor were constrained to notice the politically improbable trio signaling their outrageous intentions with eyes and hands and frank caresses. Clear Blue Lou, called upon to judge the tribes of these star-crossed lovers, was going to sport openly with them in a public cloud house. Outrageous!

It was an act of bravery, an act of charity, and a demonstration of loving justice, La Mirage style, that could not fail to charm the town's convoluted gray heart. Even La Mirage liked its love stories to have happy endings, and now the town could not help but embrace the love of Laurie Eagle and Carrie Sunshine in its own. Blessed be the loving justice of the Clear Blue Way.

Upstairs, in the curtained cloud chamber, with its pink-tinted aphrodisiacal incense and its soft featherbed floor, sweet love likewise embraced justice far into the small hours of the morning. Not until joy had thoroughly exhausted flesh did love and sated languor merge into a common downward drift into black velvet sleep.

Clear Blue Lou awoke briefly at the sun's first dawning with two lovely sleeping heads tucked into his shoulders, with the two lovers' hands clasped together in sleep across his chest. He sighed contentedly. He laughed sardonically.

Justice had been well served tonight, and so had he, both in more ways than one. He had saved a love and been lovingly treated himself. And without quite realizing it at the time, he had told the town that he cared.

And as he drifted back into sweet sleep, hugging his bedmates to him, he realized that he had found a place with the right vibes for the Court of Justice.

What better place of justice than the Garden of Love, now that he had made it forever an emblem of the path between, the Clear Blue Way!

Eagle's Nest
Syndrome

Down came Sunshine Sue, following the Spacer eagle into the tethering rail of a most peculiar eagle's nest. In addition to the main cabin, there were four barnlike sheds, a corral full of burros, and four eagles at the rail with camouflage wings of sky blue wisped with white. Strangely, there seemed to be no beacon light. Stranger still was the big round antenna high atop the overhanging crag, pointedly facing east toward the unknown lands of black science.

You didn't need to be the Queen of Word of Mouth to figure out the color of the birds that nested here!

Swensen led her past the sheds and corral toward the main cabin. A bearded mountain william, hunched over against the psychic shadows that seemed to hover over the place, led a string of burros toward the first of the sheds. The door was ajar on the second, and inside Sue saw a whole team of williams loading panniers onto burros, regarding the intense-looking man who supervised the operation with no little unease.

Inside the cabin, down a long hallway past a series of closed doors, and into a big bare room at the other end, which looked out across a backyard where a dozen or so male mountain williams sat on the ground in front of a fire, eating potatoes and passing the hose of a hookah. The room itself was furnished with odd chairs and couches—angular frames of burnished steel slung with a material that did not quite look like black leather. A single huge painting hung on a wall, done with a realism that would've convinced Sue that it was a photograph except for the impossible subject depicted—great Saturn, with its banded rings. Faint and eerie music seemed to waft into the room as if some invisible orchestra were playing in the yard outside—strings and horns and reeds, both exalting and yet somehow blandly soporific, phantom musicians playing an ethereal and ghostly symphony, soothing to the ear but chilling to the spirit.

Two more williams squatted together on the floor fitfully toking pipes, apparently knowing how out of place they seemed in this strange lair.

"Wait here," Swensen said. "I'll inform the PM." The mountain williams exchanged uneasy glances as he left, and then their stoned-out eyes fixed uneasily on Sue.

"Never seen ya before, and ya don't look like one of *them*," one of the williams said. "Who your mates? What the demons giving ya?"

"Live Oak Commune," Sue said off the top of her head. Demons? Giving me? What's going on here?

"Never heard of no Live Oaks. . . ."

"Uh—we like to keep to ourselves. Don't know what the demons are giving us yet. What they giving you?"

"Computer chips, they say. Sell 'em to the Lightnings."

"Aw, you guys ain't gonna sell no more chips to the Lightnings. Not since they got caught selling demon stuff. Clear Blue Lou gonna bust 'em up."

"So we find someone else to buy 'em."

"Ah, I dunno. All the lowlanders are scared of demon stuff now."

"Lightnings ain't exactly lowlanders."

"Yeah, but all the tribes that buy demon stuff from us gotta sell the stuff they make to lowlanders, and the lowlanders are scared of demon stuff now."

"Assholes are scared of it, but they gotta have it."

"Ah, I dunno. What you think, Live Oak?"

Oh shit! Sunshine Sue thought. What have I gotten myself into?

Now she knew what this place really was, and it terrified her that they were letting her see it. This was where the Spacers passed the components they made on the other side of the mountains to the outlying mountain william tribes. This was the place no one wanted to know about, the bottom-line point of entry of black science into Aquaria, where the williams were dealing directly with sorcerers and knew it. This was far deeper into black science than Sunshine Sue cared to get—especially since she didn't see how the Spacers could afford to let her out. And now these williams were looking at her very peculiarly. Gods forbid that these brain-burn cases should ever cop to who she really was!

"Uh, I think the lowlanders'll be scared off for a while, but when Clear Blue Lou takes care of things, they'll be buying again," she said. "The whitely righteous ain't all that white and they ain't all that righteous. They ain't gonna do without the demon stuff for long."

The mountain williams laughed. "Yeah, they end up serving the demon god same as us, 'cept they ain't got the balls to own up to their karma."

Sunshine Sue blanched. This stoned-out bullshit was starting to cut a little close to the bone.

"Mike, your burros are loaded now. Thor, your people will receive four burroloads of solar cells; these are not to be sold to the Eagles."

A tall spare man loped briskly into the room. His black hair was cropped close to his skull with a hard line between hair and skin at the neck and around his ears—the weirdest male hairstyle Sue had ever seen. He had a similarly cropped black beard that dramatically framed his angular face and set off his piercing blue eyes. *This* one really looked like a sorcerer, he spoke with precise tones of absolute authority, and the two williams shambled to their feet as he made his entrance.

"I'm the Project Manager," he said, turning to Sue with the same arrogant assurance. "Follow me please."

He turned on his heels and loped down the hallway, forcing Sue to trot after him like a good little girl. It was hate at first sight.

The Spacer led her into a medium-sized room decked out with more of the steel-framed sling furniture; the black material definitely didn't feel like leather when Sue gingerly lowered herself into a hammocklike contraption. A fortune

43

in energy units blazed from an electrical light in the ceiling and another on the burnished steel desk. There was a thing in a corner that looked like a much more advanced version of the computer she had bought from the Lightnings last year. One wall was an amazingly huge and perfect mirror, something she would have thought impossible to craft. Each of the other three walls displayed utterly realistic pictures of utterly unreal subjects—an image of planet Earth floating in space, something like a steel eagle flying over a nightmare landscape that might have been hell, and another picture of ringed Saturn.

There was no attempt to disguise this lair as other than it was. It crowed of black science in all its evil glory; it reeked of unnatural craft, of petroleum fumes, and coal dust, and smashing atoms—of all that the world shunned. And unguessably more.

What did anyone really know about the Spacers anyway? That they favored La Mirage with laundered sorcery? That they manufactured electronic components beyond the Sierras using black power sources? That their black science had been handed down in a direct line of evil perfect masters extending back beyond the Smash?

But how much was legend and how much was fact? Truth was, no one really *wanted* to know, and Sue already had the feeling that she knew more than was good for her as the "Project Manager" settled himself in a chair behind the desk and fixed her with those eyes of fiery ice.

"Arnold Harker, Project Manager of Operation Enterprise," the Spacer said coldly. "First I will tell you something that will cause you to loathe me; then I will tell you a wonderful thing that will change your mind and your life."

Sue stared back woodenly at this strange creature. It was hard for even the Queen of Word of Mouth to think of a comeback to a statement like that!

"You have been brought here as part of the scenario for Operation Enterprise," the sorcerer continued brusquely. "You were selected as the optimum female operative by a program factoring in all known parameters, so rest assured, we know what we're doing. The nominality with which the scenario has been actualized thus far is further proof of that —you *are* here and Clear Blue Lou *is* in La Mirage to give justice in your case, and this *was* the sole goal of phase one of the scenario. You will go operational in the next phase. Your assignment is to bring Clear Blue Lou to us."

"You're right so far, you fucker, I loathe you!" Sue snarled, choking on this rotten morsel. "You admit you set me up, and now you expect me to help you abduct a perfect master? Take it and stick it, you dirty sorcerer!"

But Harker acknowledged this outburst with nothing more than a thin smug smile. "Now I will tell you a wonderful thing that will change your mind and your life," he said. "I will tell you one of the Company's most highly classified secrets."

He rose dramatically from his chair and struck a pose in front of the picture of planet Earth floating in space. "Once men flew through the air faster than the speed of sound," he said. "Once great cities blazed at night. Once man mastered the secrets of the atom. Once men left their own planet and dreamed of building cities in space, of traveling to other worlds circling far-off stars, of boldly going where no man has gone before."

He touched a palm to the picture behind him. "*Not* a painting," he said. "A copy of a *photograph* taken by an employee of Space Systems Incorporated when the Company was involved in many of the greatest projects of the lost Age of Space. We've kept the dream alive through all these centuries, and now at last the Age of Space will soon be reborn!"

The sorcerer beamed weirdly at Sue, as if he were already assuming that they were willing fellow conspirators. "This is the wonderful thing I promised to tell you," he said. "Just before the Smash, the Company was involved in the most advanced project of the Age of Space—a great space station and a network of satellites to service it."

He moved over to the computer and leaned against it, mesmerizing Sue with his unholy fervor, a fervor that for some reason he apparently expected her to share.

"For hundreds of years we've known what was waiting for us up there. The space station and the satellite network were designed to operate indefinitely on solar power. There's no reason why they shouldn't still be operational."

He loped over to Sue's seat and stood over her, babbling in a frenzy, or so it seemed to her. "For centuries, the remnants of the Company kept what knowledge they could alive, keeping to the wastelands where the fools who thought us demons dared not go. For centuries, we rebuilt our infrastructure, developed our technology, and labored over plans. For fifty years, we have been laboriously crafting a man-rated space shuttle capable of reaching the Company's space station. Soon it will be ready. And you and I have the honor of being the midwives, as it were, to the birth of the New Age of Space!''

He smiled at her. He positively glowed. ''Have I not told you a wonderful thing? Have I not changed your mind?''

Sue goggled up at him. ''You're crazy,'' she said matter-of-factly. ''You do realize that? A New Space Age? One Smash wasn't enough for you? You want to make the same mistakes all over again and kill what's left of the world? And you expect me to help you? Just how black do you think I really am?''

And *these* are the sorcerers whose aid I've pretended didn't exist? she thought, not like the answer she found bubbling up from the pits to her last question.

''Black enough, Sunshine Sue,'' Harker said. He sat back down behind the desk and spoke at her through steepled fingers. ''You may lack the vision to share the dream of a New Age of Space, but you won't be able to resist the spin-off.''

He leered at her with infuriating smugness. ''Those are *broadcast* satellites up there in orbit,'' he said. ''A radio network that can cover the world, in place and legally powered by the sun, if your scruples are *really* so punctilious. That's *your* payoff for following the scenario nominally. For *that*, wouldn't you be willing to overlook a little of what you choose to call black science? Might not you be willing to taint your soul a bit to fulfill *your* dream?''

''You're . . . you're serious . . . ?'' Sue stammered. ''These broadcast satellites really *are* up there . . . ?'' McLuhan *had* mentioned such satellite broadcast systems; they really *had* existed. She studied the sorcerer more closely. An evil maniac? Or a man following his own great dream, black though it might be? And if I told anyone *my* secret dream, wouldn't they call *me* a sorcerer? ''Solar powered . . . ?'' she said slowly. ''They don't poison the Earth or use atomic power . . . ?''

Harker grinned fatuously. ''White as the driven snow.''

Sue sighed. She looked across the desk at him with hard

46

bargaining eyes. "All right," she said coldly. "Let's hear your price."

He had told her a wonderful thing which had changed her mind.

"When our spaceship reaches the station, we'll reactivate the satellite system and give you a ground station that can command it. By relaying your broadcasts through the satellites, you'll be able to reach every operating radio in the world. And all we ask in return is that you help us get the spaceship launched."

"This ground station you're going to give me, it's atomic powered, isn't it?" Sue guessed. "And this spaceship of yours, I'll bet it's not exactly ultrabright either, right? And you're going to reactivate something actually built by pre-Smash sorcerers. . . . This isn't just gray, it really *is* black science!"

"It's *science*," Harker said, shrugging. "These distinctions of white and black are superstitious drivel. Surely you're intelligent enough to realize that by now."

A spiritual vertigo came over Sue. Everything she knew of her world told her that she was contemplating a pact with evil. But she didn't feel evil. To her, *Harker* was evil, but she was convinced he wasn't evil to himself. The world would call her evil if they knew what she planned, just as they would react in a murderous frenzy, a holy war, to the launching of a spaceship by sorcerers. So how to judge black and white, good and evil? How can I consider myself one and this sorcerer the other? And how can either of us hope to realize our wicked dreams?

"Science or sorcery, it won't work," she said, surprising herself by the tone of disappointment in her voice. "Launch a spaceship, and there'll be a holy war, a jihad, a pogrom. You've survived so far because people fear your power more than anything you've yet done. But if you go *this* far, they'll fear what you've already done more than what you still might do, and a horde of the whitely righteous will swarm over these mountains and . . ."

She grimaced, realizing the ironic truth as it passed her lips. "And in that atmosphere, I wouldn't be able to use the broadcast system I sold my soul for anyway. . . ."

But Harker just nodded as if all this had been anticipated in that scenario of his. And from what she had seen so far, she wouldn't bet against it. "That's why we need Clear Blue

Lou," he said. "If Clear Blue Lou judges our cause just publicly, Aquaria will listen."

"Clear Blue Lou is going to tell Aquaria that the Spacers are whitely righteous? After you kidnap him?"

"But we're not going to kidnap him," Harker said. "You're going to seduce him."

"I'm going to *what?*" Sue shouted self-righteously. But it was mostly for show. What else could her part in this "scenario" be? They hardly needed her for muscle, now did they?

"You don't think you can do it?" Harker said slyly. "Rest assured, computer comparison of your personality profiles predicts a high probability of success. And you'll have the advantage of studying his profile, as well as the advice of Company motivators."

"If I want to seduce someone, I can do it by myself!" Sue snorted in outraged feminine pride.

"Your self-confidence is heartening," Harker said dryly.

"So I seduce Lou and then what?" Sue sighed, realizing after the fact that the sorcerer had trapped her again. "You must really think I'm something if you believe I can simply lead a perfect master to you by his crotch." She laughed. "Well, just maybe I can," she owned. "But you don't *really* believe that even I can make a perfect master think with his cock. Not when it comes to something like this!"

"The scenario doesn't require that," Harker said. "Inevitable logic has convinced *you* to follow the scenario, and the logic of the truth will cause Clear Blue Lou to reach the same conclusion when you go through karmic rebirth with him and input what you have learned with the force of shared truth."

"WHAT!" Sue roared. "Karmic rebirth! You double-crossing bastard, you promised you'd get me out of this mess you put me into!"

"I said nothing of the kind."

"You certainly didn't say that this scenario of yours had set me up to be found guilty!"

"Why fear a mere Aquarian ceremony when in fact the real karmic rebirth has already taken place?" Harker said knowingly. "Hasn't your destiny *already* been transformed? Doesn't a new persona as creator of the new global electronic village already await you? Haven't you *already* transcended your previous karma? No, Sue, it is *Lou* who will be reborn. He'll taste your truth—the truth we have given you—and he will choose to follow the scenario too."

"And I'm supposed to trust all that?"

Harker shrugged. "The scenario is behavioristic," he said. "Your trust is not required. Your motivation does not enter the equation. You'll follow the scenario because you must. You *will* undergo karmic rebirth with Clear Blue Lou. That sequence is already locked in."

"You really *are* an evil son of a bitch, aren't you?" Sue said softly, not without a certain painful admiration for his strange unprecedented style of low cunning. The Spacers really *were* sorcerers. No one had ever been able to . . . to control her very karma like this!

"But I can still choose not to get it on with Lou," she said wanly, trying to salvage some remaining illusion of free will.

Harker shook his head. "Locked in too," he said. "The programmed confrontation has too much libido behind it. Out of thousands of possibilities, the computer picked *you* as the woman most likely to fascinate Clear Blue Lou."

He grinned a sly grin at her, and for the first time, Sue detected a human vibe, nasty though that vibe was. "And of course Clear Blue Lou was chosen as the perfect master most likely to fascinate *you*," he said.

"You shit. . . ." Sue whispered. This . . . this cold demon has programmed a love affair between me and Clear Blue Lou, and he's told me up front there's nothing I can do about it. And gods help me, I believe him!

But Clear Blue Lou *was*, after all, a perfect master. Might not *he* have the power to free both of them from this mindfuck scenario? She suddenly realized that in Clear Blue Lou, the Spacers were flinging her together with the strongest possible ally she could have against their power. If she could make him one.

Or was *that* thought part of the scenario, too?

"You think of everything, don't you?" she said.

Harker laughed. "You're beginning to look forward to it, aren't you?" he said.

"What kind of man are you? Don't you have any feelings? How can you treat people like this?"

"Like what?" Harker asked ingenuously. He really didn't seem to know what she was talking about.

"Like things! Like pawns in your game. Don't you Spacers have any respect for freedom of the spirit?"

"Aren't we all pawns in the game of our choosing?" Harker said with a slight whine. "Haven't you chosen your own destiny for yourself?"

"I'm beginning to wonder," Sue told him. All the more reason to open my spirit to Clear Blue Lou, she thought. Great gods, how many levels did this game *have?*

It seemed to her that Harker was able to use even his own blindness to the feelings of his pawns as one more weapon. He knew they existed; he knew how feelings determined action, and how action altered feelings. He knew all too well that he was committing the sin of bending human spirits to his will by brute psychic force.

The terrifying, and yes, sickeningly fascinating, thing about it was that he just didn't seem to care. Was that, in the end, what truly made him a sorcerer?

After her meeting with Harker, Sunshine Sue was shown to a spartan bedchamber where she was served an unsettling supper built around a huge slab of some unidentifiable meat. Like most Aquarians, she would dare a bit of upper-food-chain fare now and again; the poisons and carcinogens concentrated in the flesh of birds and mammals were cumulative, and it would take a steady diet of the stuff to significantly cut the lifespan. A tainted treat now and then did little harm and the danger added a gourmandizing spice. But this badly cooked Spacer meal had the plainness of commissary food cooked and eaten the same way every night. She guessed that the Spacers ate meat daily. Did that mean they just didn't give a damn about their health, or *what?*

She found her door unlocked, and far too wired to sleep, she wandered about the empty cabin at will. The mountain williams had gone, every door was closed, and the windows of the common room looked out across a dark expanse of lawn on the invisible rock wall behind the eagle's nest. She might as well have been alone in their bleeding space station, floating in the middle of nothing. Cosmic loneliness overcame her. Here she was, warped against her will into the reality of black science, with no kindred soul in all the world to tell her troubles to.

She was almost glad when she ran into Arnold Harker as she drifted back to her room. Almost? Hell, she *was* glad. Maybe she could suss this dude out better if she caught him in a personal moment before they released her to do their bidding in the morning.

Harker, on the other hand, did not seem pleased to find her wandering around in the night. "Why aren't you in your room?" was his cold greeting. From a natural man, it might have been the opening line of a come-on, but from this Spacer, it was simply an expression of distaste. I get no sexual vibe out of this man at all, she realized. Though she was far from burning with passion for the sorcerer, it irked her that he seemed immune to what experience had taught her were her obvious charms, that her femininity availed her nothing with this cold son of a bitch.

"I might ask you the same question . . . Arnold," she cooed. I'll get a rise out of you yet, she decided. I'll make you come on so I can have the pleasure of turning you down.

"I was looking at the stars," Harker said.

"How romantic."

"I was searching for unplotted satellites," the Spacer explained drearily. "Hundreds of them were orbited before the Smash. No immediate scientific value, but . . ."

"So at least you have a hobby. How human of you."

Arnold Harker frowned. His icy eyes suddenly seemed a tiny bit vulnerable. "Why are you so sure I have no feelings?" he said petulantly.

"Because you don't care about anyone else's feelings, Arnold."

"I'm a cold passionless manipulator, is that it?"

"Well aren't you?"

"You think me cold because I don't share the piddling feelings of your limited little world," Harker snapped angrily, "and yet to the greatest passion of all, you're cold as ice yourself!"

Well, well, well! Sue thought. He does have some strings after all and I must just have pulled them. "Try me, Arnold," she said.

"I already have and you didn't even know it," he said. He looked at her speculatively. "But I'm willing to try again. Let me show you."

Oh really? Sue thought. Well what have I got to lose? "I'm all yours," she said. "For the moment."

But strangely, Harker didn't lead her to his bedchamber. Instead, he took her outside the cabin to a little porch on the roof of the building where a thick black tube pointed up at the starry sky. He sat her down on an upholstered bench by the tube, from which vantage she saw that it terminated in an optical eyepiece at her eye level. "Look through the telescope," Harker said, squeezing in beside her.

Sue squinted upward into the eyepiece. A circle of stars, millions of them all crammed together, flickered skittishly in the focus of her vision. "What do you see?" Harker asked softly.

"Stars," she said, trying to make it sound ingenuous rather than snide. "What am I supposed to see?"

"The destined home of man," Harker told her fervently. "Not the remnants of a once-proud species scrabbling for survival on a ruined planet around an insignificant sun, but worlds without end, ours for the taking. Once they seemed finally within our reach. Then came the Smash and we threw away our chance. You talk of passion? Can you imagine the passion of keeping that dream alive all these centuries, of dedicating your life to redeeming your species no matter what the cost?"

Sue looked away from the meaningless dancing image in the telescope and stared at Arnold Harker, sorcerer, his face blazing with energy now, wistful yet angry.

"But you can't understand, can you?" he said bitterly. "That's the final tragedy of it all, a species that can no longer even comprehend what it's lost. We're evil black sorcerers, and that's the end of it."

"I know what it is to dream of things that were and might yet be again," Sue said somewhat defensively. "And I admit I may have bent my virtue a bit in the process too."

She leaned forward into his body space and watched him flinch. "But what's really black about your karma is what it's made of you, Arnold," she said. "Maybe this destiny of yours is really worth it to you, but if you ask me, you've paid too high a price to follow it. You tune out other people's feelings, and you end up turning off your own."

She could see old Arnold blush under his beard. "You have no right to say a thing like that to me!" he whined.

"Oh don't I?" Sue said, moving even closer, speaking her words into the air he was breathing. "What if I were to offer to sport with you right now, under these stars of yours? Could you untangle yourself from your scenarios long enough to be a natural man?"

Harker started. He gaped. He flinched back again. He eyed her narrowly. "Practicing your technique for Clear Blue Lou?" he said snidely. "More proof that we've chosen well."

"That's just what I mean. You're not man enough to take me seriously."

"As seriously as you intended?" Harker said, leaning forward into her body space. "So you could then salve your wounded ego by making a fool of me in your own eyes?"

"But I've done that already, haven't I, Arnold?" Sue said lamely, trying to cover up the shock she felt at having this creature, turned off or not, see right through her completely.

"Really?" Harker said. "Well, then I might as well return the favor." He moved even closer, daring their lips to touch. "I'll take you up on your offer, unless of course you're not really the natural woman you pretend to be."

And with that, he kissed her full on the lips, pressing his mouth to hers lightly, challenging her to pull away and show her true cock-teasing colors. Sue could not tell for all the world whether he was messing with her mind again, or whether this down-and-dirty game was starting to turn him on, too.

"Of course, you know that this means war," she said, undoing the front of her blouse.

"What a peculiar thing to say," Harker said woodenly as he ran his hands mechanically over her cool bare flesh. Sue found herself shrinking from his unwholesome touch—and yet that very queasiness filled her with an equally unwholesome lust.

"Let's see what you've got, sorcerer," she said, thrusting a hand into his crotch as she slid down onto the bench and drew him down on top of her.

Harker removed the remainder of her clothes with unsensuous speed and clumsiness, and Sue gritted her teeth in anticipation of a clumsy and fetid grudge fuck.

But old Arnold turned out to be not quite what she had expected or indeed like anything she *could* have expected. He was reasonably dexterous and quite thorough but cold as ice. No false kisses of feeling lip to lip, no feigned sounds of passion. He knew exactly what he was doing, and he knew exactly what this was.

He was maddeningly patient and in tireless control of his mechanically proficient performance. So much so that Sue tried to prolong the necessity of his effort as long as possible, partly to make a point and partly because this was a unique sexual experience, to say the least, and one which she knew she would not have the stomach to try again.

He stayed with her like a hero—or like a well-lubricated machine—and made sure she was both satisfied and exhausted before he allowed himself a loathsomely controlled release in utter silence.

"Well," he said when it was over, "have I proven to you that I'm a natural man?" He seemed to be studying her face for a reaction as if it really seemed to matter to him.

You really think you're good, don't you? Sue thought. And she had to admit that by his own criteria of competence and control, the wretch had a right to think of himself as an accomplished technologist of sex. I could never tell you how awful you are in terms you could understand, she realized.

"Let's just say you've made your point and I've made mine, Arnold," she said, disengaging herself from him and retrieving her clothes.

He looked at her peculiarly, and for a moment, Sue thought she could see hurt and confusion flicker across his face. But then the sorcerer's mask reformed itself in its facade of arrogance and control.

"Maybe they were the same after all," he said sardonically. "Maybe what just happened was as inevitable as what will happen when you meet Clear Blue Lou."

Sue measured him in somewhat fearful amazement. Is he laughing at me inside? she wondered. Have I just been had? Did this son of a bitch just run another of his scenarios on me? Who had just mindfucked whom? She quivered in disgust and confusion.

She had fallen into the realm of dark sorcery indeed.

The Court
of Justice

Clear Blue Lou hated to be early to any party, even his own. The giving of justice was a social event, but the meaning of "social" went deep. The giver of justice chose the place of justice, decreed the refreshment and entertainment, and summoned whom he would to the Court of Justice. All parties to the dispute and all parties whose karma had been touched by it. Anyone he thought might contribute to the richness and complexity of the vibes. Anyone anyone else wanted to have there, within reason. Gate-crashers who were in no wise discouraged.

Thus began an open-ended party that truly represented the totality of the karmic moment, a party that threw everyone even remotely involved together in a high-proof distillation of their common reality itself and let them boogie together until it all hung out.

No reason why justice shouldn't be fun, and every reason why it should be a social event. Hopefully, good vibes in, good vibes out. And as a social event, a Court of Justice could at least be counted upon to be royally catered, since the perfect master ordered up the fare and the parties to the dispute paid the bill. Any hint of mingyness would be bad karma indeed, and disputants usually vied with each other in the addition of their own extras. Everybody was trying to prove that the vibes they contributed to the whole were noble and beneficent, and of course, no more so than to the master of the Court of Justice himself.

"Punishing the guilty" and "exonerating the innocent" were merely enforcing the law. One who would give sweet justice must make it a boon to all. Ideally, no one should leave the party feeling bad.

Needless to say, this was not always possible. The giving of justice was an art, not a science, and the degree of perfection was determined by the material at hand as well as the skill of the artist.

And as he waited upstairs at the Garden of Love in his private cloud chamber for things to really get underway before he made his grand entrance, Clear Blue Lou wondered whether it was going to be possible to come up with happy endings for all this time around.

Sunshine Sue was guilty of sorcery in point of fact, the meaningful question being only the color of her honest intent. The Lightning Commune had openly proclaimed their own blackness. The technically righteous Eagles should have been the heroes of the hour, but in reality, justice that did not chastise the "innocent" Eagles would leave La Mirage seething with paranoia and resentment. If he went far enough to clear the karma of La Mirage in the eyes of the whitely righteous, he might destroy what he was trying to preserve and play right into the unseen hands of the Spacers. But if he didn't go far enough, black science would win a public victory, and the sorcerers would also reap the reward.

Lou could see no way around it: when justice was given, he was going to have to kick ass. And that was the part of giving justice that he liked the least. Sorcery cases were rare; most often disharmonies arose from the equal evil of mindfucking. There could be no greater crime against the Way than the theft of free will, and it was Lou's conviction that the villain himself was also the victim of programming that had seized his karma and bent it into disharmony.

Thus the sweetest justice was obtained not by edict but through satori for all concerned, as he had achieved last night in saving the love of Carrie Sunshine and Laurie Eagle.

He had cleared the tribal control programs through shame, not diktat.

But when a perfect master could not achieve justice in this ideal manner, he had to be willing to take the moral responsibility for telling people what to do—in effect, committing a kind of mindfuck himself. Lou always felt like something of a hypocrite inside this paradox, and the only thing that let him accept such karma was the knowledge that a giver of justice who *didn't* feel like a hypocrite in such circumstances would not be truly walking the Great Way.

And here, where the Way had been poisoned not by disharmonies among those who tried to walk it but by sorcery from outside, there seemed no way through to justice that would not involve the kicking of unwilling asses.

I don't like the headspace I'm getting into, Lou thought, as he left the cloud chamber and descended into the Court of Justice he had convened below. But of course, the headspace he was getting into was the headspace that needed him to be there. Getting into it was what the Court of Justice was all about.

The cloud chambers around the outside of the tavern floor had been converted to private booths with tables, curtained off from each other but open to the rest of the scene. Sex was not the obsession of this party, nor would it be the entertainment. What liaisons of the bedchamber that might arise in *this* atmosphere would likely be intense and private, for intrigue, not casual sport, was definitely the vibe.

Lou had timed his entrance well. The place was already fairly crowded, and many people of import had already arrived. Levan the Wise, hovered over by two liveried ladies in his employ, reclined in one of the booths, surrounded by traders from the Exchange and a dense cloud of smoke. In another booth, North Eagle, one of the four leaders of the tribe, sat alone nursing a flagon of wine, the glum object of many passing dirty looks. There were plenty of people in Sunshine Yellow in evidence, mingling freely and spreading their own Word of Mouth. Sunshine Sue had apparently not yet arrived, and the mountain william Lightnings would have stood out at once even in this mob scene.

The long bar along one wall was laden with pastries, curries, pillaws, bowls of fruit, platters of vegetables, tureens of soups and chilis, and even a single large platter of roasted deer meat. Bottles of wine and distilled spirits lined the bar behind the food like a picket fence. At the Court of Justice, everyone served themselves, and there was a solid press of people attacking the buffet. Mages, merchants, Sunshines, Eagles, astrologers, magnates, soothsayers, and the unknown children of the night passing food and drink to each other, unified for the moment by the ceremony of culinary chaos.

In the center of the room was a round table piled high with reef, peyote, arcane mushrooms, powerful herbs, dried unnameables, and vials of magic extracts—the full Aquarian pharmacopeia of natural foods for the head. This smorgasbord of the psyche was not as crowded as the buffet spread as yet—the vibes were still too tight for all but the most daring or desperate.

The rest of the tavern floor was a seethe of bodies and psyches, dancing from table to table, sliding sparking against each other in the process.

And people were still pouring in. Here comes Kelly the Munificent and . . . uh-oh, isn't that the overeager lady astrologer from the Smokehouse?

"Lou!"

"Lou!"

Kelly and the astrologer both spotted him at the same time. Then they spotted each other spotting him and started snake-dancing through the crowd toward him, shooting poisonous glances at each other. Flattered though the natural man might be, the perfect master had other things to think about tonight.

The astrologer got to Lou first. "You chose your place of justice well," she said, sidling up to him. "The stars say—"

"There you are Lou—uh, excuse me—I've got to talk to you before these people start bending your brain about the Eagles!" Kelly had arrived, fairly bumping the lady astrologer out of the way with a swipe of her ass, grabbing Lou by the elbow, and was already talking as she dragged him away. Neat move, Lou thought, glancing back over his shoulder with a gentlemanly shrug of regret at the lady astrologer.

"Look Lou, North Eagle and I are bedfriends from way back if you know what I mean, and he feels just *awful* about the way people are treating the Eagles. . . ."

"Without making a judgment myself, I'd say the town feels pretty awful about the way the Eagles treated *it*."

"Well North Eagle feels bad about that too, it wasn't really their fault, if you'll just talk to him, look how sad he looks!"

Without even knowing it was happening, Lou had been steered over to the booth where North Eagle brooded alone, perhaps already slightly in his cups. Well, this was going to have to be confronted sooner or later. . . .

"Hello Lou," North Eagle grunted unhappily as Lou sat down, with Kelly shoving in beside him, neatly trapping him in this reality. Lou knew North Eagle slightly himself, and he had always been a good-time boy. But now he seemed morosely loaded.

"Hello, North Eagle, how's your karma?"

"Very funny. But then you probably think we smell like shit, too."

"Hey, don't put the man on your bummer!" Kelly said, punching North Eagle affectionately on the shoulder. "He's here to sweeten your karma, isn't that right, Lou, so give him a chance!"

"Gonna have to deal with some bad shit if he's gonna do that," North Eagle grunted with defensive belligerence. "Some really bad people . . ."

"Like who?" Lou asked, pouring himself his first drink of the night.

"Who do you think? Double-crossing Spacers, that's who! You think we *wanted* to create this mess? Tell me what we're getting out of it, man!"

Over his shoulder, Lou saw that people were indeed eyeing this meeting with suspicion and distaste. Sunshines were drifting together to talk strategy. Levan dispatched one of his female minions into the crowd to drift casually in their direction. North Eagle, too, picked up on what Lou was seeing.

"Yeah, we sure gained a lot of friends being good citizens, didn't we?"

"And that's all you were doing, being whitely righteous?" Lou said archly. "You called the present unpleasantness down on your own heads because of your righteous wrath against black science?"

North Eagle sipped at his wine, shrugged, grew calculatingly more intimate. "Aw, you know how it is, Lou," he said. "To make eagles, we need solar cells, which come from mountain williams like the Lightnings, who get them from . . ." He deliberately let the unsaid hang in the air. "Dealing with the williams isn't easy; you never know what may spook them. So we had this Eagle, Joe, who came from near their country, who the Lightnings insisted on dealing with. Had a whiff of gray about him, but what can you do? So the Lightnings try to sell this Joe this radio, and the assholes *tell him* about the atomic power core. So Joe goes to the tribal council and convinces us the Sierras are trying to trap us—he got the story out of the Lightnings by getting them loaded, or so he says. See, the Sierras paid the Lightnings to run this number. If we play it cool, which they're counting on, then we get denounced for not denouncing the radio, all the williams get spooked out of doing business with us, and the Sierras can take over the eagle business."

"That's the biggest load of shit I've heard in quite a while," Clear Blue Lou said unsympathetically. "You're trying to tell me you couldn't smell it?"

"No . . . yes . . . Aw. . . ." North Eagle sighed. "Okay, okay, so we weren't exactly surprised when Joe disappeared, and maybe he *was* . . . kind of . . . our Spacer connection, and maybe we sort of knew that someone east of here wanted us to do what we did. . . . But what difference did that make? I mean, it was pretty clear that if we didn't denounce the atomic radios, we'd have a hard time getting solar cells, one way or the other. . . ."

"So you played a little *quid pro quo* with black science?"

"Ah come off it, Lou!" North Eagle snapped. "Look around this place! Who isn't playing a little *quid pro quo* with sorcery! Without it, there's no La Mirage." He looked Lou straight in the eyes for the first time. "And you flew here in your *eagle*, didn't you?" he said more quietly. "If we're so black for doing what we had to do to make it, how whitely righteous does that make all you happy eagle freaks?"

Kelly winced, clearly of the opinion that this zinger was not exactly calculated to win the pleasure of the giver of justice. But zinger it had been, and not without justice. The Eagles *had* only been playing the same old game, and not too many people here, including perhaps Lou himself, were in a position to be too whitely righteous about it. Black science was not their karmic stain. Nor was naive klutziness.

However, what they *had* knowingly done was allow sorcery to blackmail them into creating this bummer to save their own commercial asses. And that, Clear Blue Lou decided, was karma that would have to be paid back.

"Levan would like to see you when you have a moment." A young lady in Levan's livery spoke up from the swirl of people in front of the booth. How long had she been standing there? How much had she heard? Did it matter?

"Okay," Lou said, shooing Kelly out of her blocking seat and sliding away from the table.

"Tell Levan I'll be there in a bit," he told the Arbiter's emissary after she had covered his retreat into the crowd. He didn't want Levan's opinion on what to do with the Eagles at the moment. Instead, he made his way to the head-food table, which was much more crowded now. The party was rolling and people were no longer trying to hold back the changes. Couples and threesomes and foursomes were beginning to ease upstairs to the cloud chambers. Seers and mages were holding forth in a stoned-out manner. Someone was playing a guitar and a few fancy dancers were going into a clothes-throwing frenzy.

Lou loaded a pipe with reef and turned away from the table, taking his first smoke of the night. "May I?" said a tall blond lady as she plucked the pipe from his mouth. It was Little Mary Sunshine.

"Saw you talking with North Eagle over there," she said, taking a puff. "And I heard about your wonderful little threesome last night. So . . . ." She leaned an elbow on his shoulder, propped her head in her hand, and blew breath-scented smoke at him.

"So I thought you might be in a less righteous mood tonight," she said. "I mean, you've already gotten it on with a Sunshine and an Eagle, and you've already had your little talk with North, so don't you think maybe it's my turn?"

"What did you have in mind?"

She glanced around the room conspiratorily. "Is there someplace we can be alone?" she said nervously. "I want to show you something."

Huh? Lou thought. Just when I'm ready to ride with the wind that's blowing, I find out I'm reading the signals wrong?

"Uh, upstairs," he said, and he led her through the crowd and up the staircase, acutely aware as it was happening that people were making up their own minds about what they were seeing. Have I been had?

Inside the cloud chamber, Lou put his hands on his hips, and cocked his head at Little Mary Sunshine suspiciously. "Now what was it you wanted to show me?" he said.

Little Mary Sunshine seemed to be choking back a giggle as she stared soulfully into Lou's eyes. "This," she said, flipping off her blouse proudly to display a superb pair of naked breasts with purposefully erect nipples.

Lou broke up. He couldn't help himself. "Oh ya got me!" he cried, collapsing into giggles. He bent over and addressed Mary's nipples as if they were the eyes of her face. He pointed an admonishing finger between them. "But I don't want to hear a word about Eagles or Sunshines or sorcery!" he said. "Keep your mouth shut and attend to business!"

Little Mary laughed. "That's not going to be easy," she said, tumbling him backward onto the softly padded floor of the cloud chamber.

It took quite a while for Little Mary Sunshine to attend to business, and she didn't keep her mouth shut most of the time either, but true to the spirit of bedfriendship, she refrained from attempting to use their fleshly intimacy to influence him on behalf of her tribe afterward.

Paradoxically, Lou was feeling warmer toward Little Mary as they came down the stairs together, and perhaps through her, toward the Sunshine Tribe itself. Maybe she had achieved what she set out to do by running no number at all. And if *that* had been her number in the first place, well, who could deny the sweetness of that . . . ?

Apparently everyone who might have a stake in whatever it was Clear Blue Lou might be feeling.

A sea of eyes tracked them down the stairway, and the fact that the measuring glances were doing their poor best to be covert only made the seething vibes that much more obvious. Clear Blue Lou has gotten it on with the Sunshine Tribe—that was where it was at as far as all these nondetached observers were concerned. North Eagle muttered imprecations to three of his fellow tribesmen at the headfood table and then pointedly turned his back. Sunshines flashed vibes of tribal appreciation in the direction of Little Mary. Levan smiled knowingly in his booth, apparently pleased by his interpretation of the implications. Eagles measured the reactions of Sunshines and Sunshines measured the Eagles reacting to them.

Though on an obvious level, Lou had indeed been had by the Sunshine Tribe—and quite royally too, thank you—on a higher level, the cause of justice had been well served by the pleasures of the flesh. The vibes had been intensified, and Lou's vision of justice was beginning to come together.

The karma of the Sunshines tasted sweet in his mouth, whereas the karma of the Eagles tasted sourer every moment. Such had been the general perception of La Mirage all along, but now Lou was synced into that vibe, the aesthetic conviction that seemed to contradict the legalistic facts of the situation. The Eagles had stained their tribal karma knowingly, whereas the karma of the Sunshine Tribe gave off no foul odor of self-knowledge of evil. If the Sunshine Tribe had knowingly dealt with sorcery, the sin had been Sunshine Sue's alone; her people believed in their own innocence.

There was no reason why an erection could not dowse out justice and every reason why a giver of justice should allow himself to be a natural man.

Lou kissed Little Mary a chaste public good-bye, pulled a vibrational cloak of privacy around himself, secured more reef and wine, and commandeered a solitary booth from which vantage he could observe the configurations of the ripening party.

The common room was jammed now, and he suspected there was little going on in the cloud chambers above. The buffet was beginning to look ravaged, spirits were flowing like there was no day after, and a fogbank of reef had rolled in. Eagles and Sunshines gathered by themselves in little groups; the vibes were now too intense for them to mingle. Indeed, most of the partyers were divided up into groups and factions, tables, booths, and clots of them; soothsayers and mages, mavens and magnates, craftsmen and astrologers, locked in private paranoid realities. The vibes were keening toward longed-for karmic release, and the energy level was building.

Thus there was an audible mass intake of breath and then a babble of frenzy when the Lightnings entered the Court of Justice.

Two mountain william men and four women, all naked to the waist, their chests draped with long necklaces of beads and medallions and animal bones. The men wore fringed pants of crudely tanned buckskin and the women short skirts of the same material. All six of them had long manes of untidy hair, and their eyes were reddened, their pupils enormous. They floated through the mob scene as if they were in their own reality, and the people of La Mirage gave them plenty of body space.

As well they might. Not only were they mountain williams, not only were they fried to the eyeballs, they were the people who had created this foul karma, and they were self-admitted servants of sorcery. Waves of sullen anger not untempered with a certain paranoid dread swept the Garden of Love. The villains of the hour had arrived.

But the Lightnings seemed unaware of the protective aura of danger they gave off; they slithered around like nervous serpents anticipating the booted heel. Lou stood up and commanded their presence with an imperious crook of his finger. By the time they reached his booth, everyone in the room had focused in on this confrontation. A tide of bodies surged forward. The blond male Lightning whirled around to glare at the hostile circle of eyes. His black-haired mate cringed and spun him around. The Lightning women were totally elsewhere, swaying to unheard music.

"Everybody cool it," Lou ordered. "I want to have a little talk with these people."

A murmur of approval swept the room at his harsh inflection of the last, and a bubble of psychic space formed around them as the Lightnings sat down—the males across the table from Lou with a woman on either side, and the other two women sandwiching Lou between them.

"Thanks man," the black-haired man said, "that was getting a little heavy and we're flying high. I'm Nate and this is my mate Buckeye, and we're as good as any of these lowlander shits."

"That's right, who they kidding, they serve the demon god just like us," Buckeye said with belligerent vehemence.

Lou studied the two williams narrowly. *Demon god?* It appeared they were already too stoned to know what they were saying.

"You mean the Spacers?" he said.

"Spacers, demons, sorcerers, all the same thing," Nate said. "Serve 'em, and you get gifted; cross 'em, and you get cursed."

"Theirs is the power," Buckeye said nervously. "You serve 'em like they tell you, or you end up doing what they want anyway; they don't give a shit."

Lou had the feeling these williams weren't connecting up with reality at all. They didn't seem to know what they were saying, and they certainly didn't seem to realize whom they were saying it to.

"Hey, I'm Clear Blue Lou, remember?" he said, snapping his fingers in their faces. "The giver of justice in your case? And you're sitting here totally whacked out telling me that you're servants of black science?"

Nate seemed to come down from somewhere and realize to some extent where he was and what was happening. But Buckeye, his eyes wild and his body vibrating, continued to rave on. "We all serve the demons!" he roared. "Theirs is the power! Nobody thwarts their will!"

The whole room was listening now, and Buckeye finally grew aware of it. "Lowlander assholes!" he shouted. "You're as black as we are! You just don't have the balls to admit it!"

A knot of male Eagles came surging through the crowd from one direction and a mob of Sunshines from another, and scores of hands were balled into fists. *Ug*-ly! Lou bolted to his feet and held up his arms.

"We don't have to listen to this shit!"

"Not from mountain william assholes!"

"Break 'em up, Lou!"

"Let's have some justice *now!*"

"I'll speak justice when and how I see it!" Lou roared. The tumult guttered into silence. "And I don't like what I'm seeing right now," he said more quietly. "As for *you*," he said to the Lightnings for the benefit of the sullen onlookers, "get your asses upstairs, all of you!"

Talk about bearers of bad karma, these Lightnings seemed to *enjoy* being walking bummers! How black did this sorcery get?

Sunshine Sue entered the Garden of Love as the recipient of the best vibes the Court of Justice had to offer at the moment, or so it seemed to her. Salutes and high signs and greetings from all and sundry, for some strange reason. The only bad vibes came from the Eagles and, unsettlingly enough, from a few of her own people who apparently still weren't convinced she hadn't gotten the tribe in over its head.

If only they knew, she thought wanly. If only all of them knew.

Across the crowded room, Levan was motioning her to his booth; since Clear Blue Lou was nowhere in sight and Levan could be counted upon to have all the strands of the web in his hands, she made her way through the crowd in his direction.

"Hi Sue!"

"We're with you!"

"Damn Eagles!"

Something really weird was going on. *Why* was everyone save the Eagles openly showing her their support? It was as if they *expected* her to come out clean. Even if the town's sympathies were really with her, the movers and shapers of La Mirage did not make a practice of standing too close to someone in danger of being painted black.

And of course, she was now guiltier by far than anyone but she herself knew. She was in fact here as an agent of sorcery, whether she liked it or not. She was deeper into black science than she had thought it possible to get.

Arnold Harker had gotten to her on levels where she didn't even know she *had* levels. The prize of a Sunshine World Broadcast Network would probably have tempted her into this plot even if she had real free will. But it terrified her to know that the Spacer scenario was so cogent that her will didn't enter into it at all. "The scenario is behavioristic," Harker had said. She still didn't know quite what that meant, but the vibe at least was all too clear. An utter ruthlessness that chilled the soul.

Yet Arnold had also shown her that this ruthlessness was far from cold-blooded. The Spacers followed their dream with a burning passion, sterile and pointless though it might seem to her, a passion that seemed to have leached Harker of all other feeling. What could be blacker than that?

Yet, on another level, how different was it from her own obsession? Like the Spacers, was she not selling the clarity of her soul for a dream that went beyond the ultimate question of black or white?

As she made her way to Levan's booth, she felt an unsettling psychic distance from the sophisticates of La Mirage, whose peer she had always felt herself to be. There was an insubstantiality to them, a diminishment. They were children who dared not look behind the programs that ran their lives, who risked not their souls in the service of dreams which seemed to transcend accepted definitions of good and evil.

And wasn't that very attitude the essence of sorcery?

"So you finally find the time to pay your respects to a poor old man," Levan said by way of greeting. "Where have you been? Didn't you get my messages?" The old man slumped back in his chair, puffing a reef pipe, while one of his young cuties hovered in attendance.

Even Levan seemed less cogent now, less alive and real. His only dream was to preserve an illusion that was breaking apart before her eyes and against her will, whatever *that* was now. Who the hell am I? Sue wondered. What's *happening* to me?

"I was out selling my soul to the Spacers, and the fine print in the contract took a lot of negotiating," she said dryly as she sat down. "What's going on, Levan? Where's Clear Blue Lou? How are things looking for me?"

Levan shooed his girl away in search of more goodies, leaned forward, and smiled crookedly at Sue. "Your cause is looking up," he said. "Lou is upstairs with the Lightnings, singeing their dirty hides, I hope. And after he talked to North Eagle, he repaired to his cloud chamber with one of your tribeswomen, a gesture lost on no one. You can get good odds now if you want to risk a wager on the survival of the Sunshine Tribe."

"*What?*" Sue exclaimed. He's already gotten it off with one of my tribeswomen? Politically advantageous to her cause though it obviously was, she found herself consumed by a flash of anger. Who the hell was it? That's *my* business! But of course she couldn't let any of this on to Levan. And she did not at all like the irrational jealousy she felt at the thought of someone else getting it off with the horny son of a bitch.

"Surprised?" Levan said. "But then you don't know Lou. Last night he had a tryst with two star-crossed lady lovers whose tribes were tearing them asunder. A public statement of support, as it were."

"How romantic," Sue snorted.

"The town seems to think so," Levan replied with a smirk.

"And you, I gather, have a somewhat more cynical assessment?"

"Oh no, no, no," Levan oozed. "Lou really is as warm-hearted as he is hot-blooded. But he's also a man who knows how to deliver a message subtly enough so that its political intent is accomplished without calling attention to itself. Bedding an Eagle and a Sunshine together was his way of showing La Mirage his intent to deliver a justice the town can live with."

"And getting it off with one of my tribeswomen . . . ?"

"Why, a gesture of intent to deliver justice that the Sunshine Tribe can live with, of course!" Levan told her.

"You make him sound like quite a man," Sue said dubiously.

"Oh he is, he is," Levan replied. He cocked an ironic eyebrow at her. "I'm sure you'll enjoy meeting him." He laughed around a cloud of reef smoke, slumped back, and regarded her shrewdly. "In fact, I'll wager you're thinking about it already."

Does this old man see right through me? Sunshine Sue flashed through a moment of panic.

But Levan seemed to be regarding her less with suspicion than with grandfatherly amusement. He seemed to think that it was Clear Blue Lou who was moving toward *her* as lover and savior, having already signaled his intent in cryptic fashion. Perhaps Levan even thought he had had a hand in crafting this politically desirable liaison. No, even Levan the Cool, Levan the Wise, was an innocent when it came to this level of sorcery. It was *she* who saw through *him*.

Nate and Buckeye Lightning hunkered down on the soft floor of the cloud chamber as if they were facing Clear Blue Lou across some tribal council fire. Lou himself was barely aware of the incongruity of the setting—the soft candlelight, the pink incense fumes, the memory of the lovemaking that had taken place here not so long ago. Only the four Lightning women seemed to sync into the sensual vibes of the chamber, reclining together in a stoned-out heap, brain-burned into a simpler and sweeter world.

"All right, now let's get to the bottom of this," Lou said firmly. "You've openly admitted that you're servants of black science. You want a chance to deny that now? Because otherwise, you know what I'm going to have to do. . . ."

"Aw, we're all really ripped, is all," Nate whined. "Buckeye didn't mean—"

"Don't tell me what I mean!" Buckeye shouted angrily. "I know what the fuck I mean! And I also know that this dude can't touch us—"

"Shut up, Buckeye!" Nate hissed, elbowing him in the ribs.

"Let him speak!" Lou commanded.

"That's right, you tell him!" Buckeye growled, bleering at Lou. "You fly an eagle, don't you, perfect master, and the solar cells for it came from us, and you know where *we* got 'em from. The demons gifted you too. You're as black as we are. The demons have you too."

"I'll be the judge of that," Lou said. But he didn't like the ring of justice in the ugly truth he was hearing. These Lightnings were self-admittedly evil, and they had open contempt for anyone less honest about his tainted morality than themselves. And who could say there was no truth in that?

"That's not what the demons tell us," Buckeye said smugly.

"*What?* What's not what the demons tell you?"

"The demons have protected us with a curse," the mountain william told him. "We're under their protection. You disband the Lightnings, and *nobody* gets gifted with solar cells or nothing anymore. You got the balls to do that, lowlander?"

Great was Lou's ire. Nobody was crazy enough to threaten a giver of justice in the middle of the process. Not even the Spacers would likely dare that. Surely they didn't suppose they could save these assholes from disbandment with such a crude threat. More to the point, would they take such a risk just to save a tribe of mountain williams that they had set up in the first place? No way! Those blackhearted bastards!

"You really believe that?" he said. "You really believe the Spacers can save your tribe from disbandment after you've openly admitted to peddling atomic power?"

"You can't afford not to let us get away with it," Buckeye insisted belligerently.

"Come on," Lou said, "you're not really that stupid.

"You think the Spacers care enough about your dirty hides to risk playing a game like that just to save them?"

"But they said . . ."

"The demons . . . *the demons lied to us?*" Nate said softly. Finally the message was getting through.

"What do *you* think? That the Spacers are so righteous that they wouldn't lie to you to get you to do their bidding? That they'd throw away everything they're doing just to avenge your disbandment? Are you really *that* stoned?"

"Oh shit," Nate said woodenly. "They just used us. They told us they'd protect us, and now they'll just throw us away."

"And you were so stupid you didn't see it coming?"

"Y' don't understand," Nate said shakily. "Y' don't know what the demons are like. They told us what we had to do. If we didn't do it, we'd never be gifted again."

"And you'd be forced to make a righteously white living," Lou said unsympathetically.

"You don't understand," Nate insisted. "We didn't know the Eagles would find the atomic cores in the radios. But when they did and when the Spacers told us we had to admit we knew about it, what could we do? We were caught anyway, and who else was going to protect us? You? Lowlanders? Man, you can't fight the demons, they don't just tell you what to do, they make you do it."

"And you had no choice in the matter?" Lou said harshly.

"We had to serve them!" Buckeye said shrilly, apparently finally realizing the deep shit his tribe was in. "We couldn't help ourselves."

"And I suppose the Spacers forced you to accept their gifts too?" Lou snapped. "They forced you to start trafficking in black science, is that what you expect me to believe?"

"Aw . . ."

"Everybody does it. . . ."

"But not everybody gets caught, is that it?"

Both of the mountain william men hung their heads and stared at the floor. It seemed to Lou that they were finally coming to realize that they had brought their current bad karma upon themselves. They had played with sorcery and they had lost. They might have been mindfucked into it by the Spacers, but it was their own greed that had allowed it to happen. The Lightning Commune had proven its own karmic unworthiness. It would be better if they could admit it to themselves.

"What—what are you going to do with us?" Nate asked, looking up at Lou with pleading eyes.

Lou pondered his answer long and hard. Obviously, the Lightnings had to be disbanded. But the purpose was to cleanse, not to punish, and he would do well to remember that. If these williams were now ready to serve justice, perhaps justice might be able to serve them.

"That depends on you," he finally said. "Your tribe must be disbanded. The Lightning Commune's collective karma has become so thoroughly blackened that no one will ever dare do business with you again, even if I were to permit it. *That* much justice you've given yourselves already."

He paused, hardened his eyes, and spoke more slowly, chewing over each word as he said it for effect. "However, *personal* justice for each of you is something I must decide. You could each be exiled from the towns of men forever. . . . you could each be karmically reborn. . . . you could be required to work off restitution debt for the rest of your lives. . . . Or you could give me a reason to be merciful. . . ."

Nate and Buckeye's ears pricked up at this. Poor bastards! Lou found himself thinking. True justice was going to be hard to find in any of this. The Lightnings. Sunshine Sue. The Eagles. All of them had been led to blacken their karma, but the real villains were the Spacers, and those fuckers were beyond his grasp. Absolute justice demanded that he judge *them*, and that was impossible. The whole process, therefore, was beginning to seem a little hollow.

"You must choose to stop serving the Spacers and serve justice," he told them. "Justice not for yourselves but for those whose karma you have blackened. You must tell me the truth: did Sunshine Sue or any of her tribe know that the radios you sold them were black, or was that a lie that the Spacers ordered you to tell?"

Nate and Buckeye exchanged fearful glances, which alone was enough to tell Lou what he wanted to know. Levan's instincts had been right—Sunshine Sue *had* been set up. By the Lightnings, and the Eagles, and the sorcerers whose pawns they were.

"And if we tell you . . . ?" Buckeye said in a bargaining tone of voice.

You've already told me, asshole! Lou thought. But I won't rob you of the chance to choose your own fate. "I'm not bargaining with you," he said. "I'm asking you to serve justice of your own free will."

"Aw . . . shit, all right," Nate said. "Truth is, we don't know. Yeah, the demons told us to say we told Sue about the atomic power cores. No, we didn't really tell her—"

"But that don't mean she didn't know!" Buckeye said belligerently. "Them Sunshines know as much about radio circuitry as we do by now; they *coulda* known! That Sunshine Sue's so black she'd sure as shit not care if she *did* know!"

"But you do admit you told the Spacers' lie for them?"

"Theirs is the power," Nate said, hanging his head.

"Over your tribe," Lou said, "not over each of you, not anymore. Your tribe existed only to serve the demons. Now I disband it, and you will all be scattered, each to follow his own personal Way and make of it what you will. Do try to walk a little more carefully from here on in."

The mountain williams regarded this with sullen acceptance, an inevitable bitter morsel which must be swallowed. Justice did not yet taste sweet to them. Lou hoped that some day it would. He hated justice forced upon the unwilling; if it tasted sour to those who received it, it could not taste sweet to him.

And how much more bitter food for the soul would he have to hand out before this skein of evil could be unraveled? What will *my* karma taste like after justice is finally given for all? he wondered.

"Here he is now," Levan said, and Sunshine Sue followed his line of vision to the stairs leading to the upper floor.

Six glum and unsavory Lightnings were slinking down the stairs trying to look invisible. Behind them was a spare man of medium height in a blue flying suit. Long brown hair fell in well-groomed waves to his shoulders, his mobile mouth was twisted in an ironic smile, and his big green eyes radiated a deceptively tranquil power, hooded, held back. Every eye in the room tracked him as he descended, but he didn't seem to acknowledge this tense and rapt attention. Or perhaps more accurately, he refused to let anyone see him acknowledging it.

So that's Clear Blue Lou! Sue thought as she watched him

make his way toward their booth in a bubble of private body space. He didn't use this aura to brush off the people who crowded around him, but he didn't let his way become impeded either. Formidable without being arrogant. The cock of the walk so sure of himself that he could play against it. Sue could not help pondering how this would manifest itself in the bedchamber, and she was forced to admit that the fucking scenario still seemed to be working "nominally." The *fucking* scenario indeed!

"I have a feeling you've made up your mind about the Lightning Commune," Levan said when Clear Blue Lou reached the booth.

"I'll speak my justice on the Lightnings when I give justice for all," Clear Blue Lou said loftily, sliding into a chair opposite Sue.

And just when Sue had begun to discount her first impression and decide he was a pompous ass, he turned those big green eyes on her, beamed her a look complexed with promise and danger, and said, "And how can I speak justice for all until I get to the bottom of *you*, Sunshine Sue?"

Did he mean that the way I *think* he means it? Sue thought. The way he looked her up and down seemed to leave little doubt. "And you're a man used to delving the depths of whomever you want to, Clear Blue Lou?" she said dryly.

"I don't usually have any problems."

Sue slowly and deliberately stripped *him* with *her* eyes. "I'll bet you don't," she said somewhat snidely. But he had her playing his game already, or at least so he thought. A few double entendres, a zap with those eyes, the karma of the moment, and the bastard assumes I'm going to get it on with him already. That they both knew she was going to make him fight for it only added to the instant sexual tension and made the outcome that much more inevitable. And perhaps that much more tasty.

Levan grinned knowingly. "I knew you two would get along," he said smugly. The old shrewdie had them in the bedchamber together already. Indeed, he probably thought he had set it up himself, so thoroughly did it suit his own purposes.

"What do you mean by that?" Clear Blue Lou said archly. "The lady and I don't even know each other."

"But I know both of you quite well," Levan said with a leer.

"What is this, a public flesh market?" Sue snapped. "What am I, a fancy dancer auditioning for hire?"

Lou wagged a finger of mock admonishment at Levan. "You're a dirty old man," he said. "Do you dare to suggest I could be persuaded to get it on with someone I'm supposed to judge?"

Levan just snorted.

"And are you suggesting I'm so corrupt as to offer my admittedly irresistible favors to a giver of justice?" Sue said, joining in the game of mock outrage.

Clear Blue Lou smiled ruefully at her. With her. He shrugged, cocking his head toward Levan. "A dirty old man," he said. "He assumes I'm as horny as he is."

"For sure," Sue said. "Imagine him thinking I'd get it on with someone like you."

Zingo! Lou's eyes widened. *Oh really?* they seemed to say. Skies above, what a game this is turning out to be! Sue thought.

"I mean, a perfect master and a giver of justice," she drawled, running her tongue over her lips. "An unattainable paragon of detachment and righteousness. Why I'll bet you're under a vow of celibacy for the duration."

Levan coughed on his reef. Lou, too, came close to breaking up. "At last a woman who understands me," he said dryly. Their eyes met and held. Perfect or not, he was surely a master of *something*.

"As I hope you'll come to understand me," Sue said, cutting through the play with an unwavering stare that in itself raised the game to yet a higher level.

Lou's voice hardened, his mouth tightened, and his eyes seemed to suddenly stare right through her. "I think we're beginning to understand each other already," he said. "Shall we mingle a little and discuss it?"

And damn it, her body began to tingle with anticipation as he took her hand, bowed ironically to Levan, and led her away from the booth. So this is what a perfect master is like as a man! It hadn't taken Clear Blue Lou long to get to her on levels where she didn't even know she had levels. The bastard knew all too well what a tasty morsel he was. He knew what the game was before she could even start playing, and he had let her know he was accepting her invitation to duel.

You think you're so good do you? she swore to herself.

THE COURT OF JUSTICE

I'll show you! I'll show you a game that will leave you gasping for air and wondering what happened.

But she had a feeling that was exactly what he had in mind.

And where is the Clear Blue Way *here?* Clear Blue Lou wondered as he handed Sunshine Sue a glass of wine, clinked it with his own, and watched her eyes watching him watching her over the lips of their glasses.

Small but generously fleshed, almost muscular, she pulsed with sexuality, at least on his wavelength, and he knew that his mind could not hope to judge her clearly until they had cleared these sexual vibes in the only way possible. Which was to say that both wisdom and foolishness told him that he absolutely had to bed her. And he could tell she felt the same way about him; a woman after his own heart, she had made that clear up front.

But there was something more, something darker. True, there was good pragmatic reason for her to want to make political love to him, and there was too much measuring in those deep brown eyes for him to believe she was hot for the natural man alone.

Yet Sunshine Sue burned. That sweet little face under those deceptively angelic blond curls flamed with an intensity that was almost unwholesome. There was certainly nothing pure and simple in her vibes. She burned with some inner passion, breathtaking in its intensity, that cloaked her in tantalizing danger. Lou wasn't so far gone that he supposed this was mere mad lust for him, but he was certainly far gone enough for it to inflame his desire with an illusive energy he had never quite experienced before.

"Well, are you or are you not a sorceress?" he said. "That's the essential question, and I don't know how I'm going to decide."

"Oh don't you?" she said evenly.

"You have a suggestion?" Lou said. What he wanted to say was let's get it on and get it over with. Why were they locked into this crotch-teasing game? And why was this game turning him on?

"Don't you?" she said, turning the screw a little tighter. If this went on much longer, he was liable to grab her right here.

"Should I?"

"Well, since you've already shared your cloud chamber with an Eagle, two Sunshines, four mountain william girls, and who knows what else, I assumed you had a healthy lust for naked justice," Sunshine Sue said, deliberately projecting her voice and creating an instant audience.

"So you think my justice can be bought in the bedchamber?" Lou shot back.

"Oh no, I just think you're a natural man. A fair man who believes in tasting fully of all points of view."

What's she doing? Lou wondered. What am *I* doing? What's going on? They were crowded up against the buffet bar, and about three dozen people were doing a bad job of pretending they weren't listening to this.

"And you want an opportunity to get yours in more fully?"

"Don't *you*?" she said.

Lou could hear choked-back laughter over his shoulder and see two astrologers sputtering in their drinks. What was she doing? Challenging his manhood publicly? Daring him to make a public display of bedding her?

As he had with Carrie and Laurie? And Little Mary Sunshine? Ooh, so that's it! he realized. She's letting the world know this is a karmic fuck. She's betting her destiny on it, right out in the open.

What a woman! he thought lustfully. And what a subtle game she's playing, he realized more clearly. You're a perfect master yourself, Sunshine Sue!

He leaned closer and touched her lightly under the chin. "This is getting a little too personal," he whispered. "Or not personal enough."

"Shall we go upstairs and get personal in private?" she suggested, touching her upper teeth with the tip of her tongue.

Not quite yet, lady, Lou decided. You're not gonna get me just the way you want me. "What I had in mind," he said for the benefit of the eavesdroppers, "is you and me just go outside and have a little talk."

Sue sniffed up her nose at him, another exaggerated public gesture. "And here I thought you were such a natural man," she said to all and sundry. "And all you want to do is *talk*."

At this, the onlookers could not keep from breaking into audible moans, and everyone turned pointedly away, some of them shaking their heads in rueful appreciation of the knot she had tied him into. If they didn't get it on, he would not only have publicly refused to pick up her gauntlet, he could stand accused of shallow justice. And now, when they *did* get it on, as they both knew bloody well they were going to, there was no way that what went on between them in private could be kept out of the public giving of justice.

Just like that, she had him—by the Way and by his balls. If she *was* an evil sorceress, she sure was good at it!

But perversely, Lou found himself enjoying every minute of it. It had been a long time since anyone had been able to play with him on *this* level. Whatever her true color turned out to be, no one could say she was innocent.

Outside the Court of Justice, alone in the quiet darkness of Market Circle Park with him, Sunshine Sue began to get a little wary of Clear Blue Lou. No audience to play to now, she thought as they walked down a deserted path under a thick canopy of night-dark trees, just the two of us, one-on-one. And this was no mere teasing little sex game to end in laughing sport. Everything was at stake here. They would not sport together, and what they would make would certainly not be pure enough to be called love.

She had to bear in mind that this was not merely a quick-witted and attractive man, but a perfect master; even the Queen of Word of Mouth could not assume she was his match. Might he not penetrate her inner being and see the true color of what lay within?

And isn't that black? she thought. Aren't I an agent of black science at this very moment? Won't I be following a sorcerer's scenario even as we fuck? And am I really doing all this so unwillingly? Haven't I already decided that a World Broadcast Network is worth selling my soul for without even being aware of when it happened?

And if he finds that out . . .

Lou came to a halt beside a big tree, leaned one hand up against the rough bark, struck an insouciant pose, and challenged her with his eyes. "Now that we're alone . . ." he said.

Sue leaned her face close to his, their lips not quite touching. Slowly, she opened her mouth, rolled her tongue, closed her eyes, and made him come to her.

Their lips came together in a sudden release of tension, and Sue poured her tongue into the depths of him, throbbing in the groin and quaking in the knees but determined to make *him* respond to *her*. After a moment of this, he returned measure for measure, and the kiss became a delectable and at the same time rankling contest of wills, each trying to arouse the other, and each succeeding royally.

Sue pressed her body against him, and they moved together liquidly, thigh on thigh, until they both moaned. She pushed him back up against the tree and pressed her mouth to his ear.

"Right here, right now," she whispered. "I'm game if you are."

Slowly he pried her away and held her under the armpits at arm's length, his thumbs resting on the sides of her breasts. "What about our little talk?" he said.

"At a time like this?"

"Especially at a time like this. I think you think you have me thinking with my cock."

"Don't I?" she teased, slowly running a finger up the vee of his flying suit.

He laughed. "Don't get me wrong, I'm yours to command," he sighed ironically. "*Except* when it comes to the giving of justice. Just so we understand each other. I *do* know what you're doing."

"Oh you do, do you?" Sue shot back. But it was false bravado, for he had sent a sudden tremor of fear through her. How deep did that go? Could he taste the sorcery that tainted her soul? Could she keep that back from him when their bodies were one? So much of her being was involved, and her body was already not exactly under her control.

"I think so," he said. "And I think we're both enjoying it. No reason why justice can't be down and dirty. Just don't think he can be bought."

"I don't," Sue said, realizing that now she meant it truthfully. "But I'm hoping he likes what I'm giving away."

Lou kissed her teasingly on the lips. "I wouldn't like it half so much if I really believed you were giving it away," he said dryly.

"Back to your famous cloud chamber at the Garden of Love?" Sue said, touching a finger to his nose. "Or would you rather keep it a secret and have me right here on the ground?"

He laughed and pressed a mocking kiss into her palm. "I'm not much for outdoor sport," he said. "Let's go back to my quarters in the La Mirage Grande, where nobody will know for sure. Or do you insist on a public fanfare?''

"What's between you and me is between you and me," Sue said, taking his arm. Besides, she thought, I've already had the public fanfare. Still, she was certain that whatever happened between the two of them would not be something entirely encompassable by Arnold Harker's personality profiles and scenarios.

Everything really was coming down to one-on-one between herself and Clear Blue Lou. Therein lay both hope and danger.

The Giving
of Justice

Unfortunately, the walk back to the La Mirage Grande gave Clear Blue Lou time to think. The night was wearing on into the fringes of morning, and he could almost taste the tension in the empty streets. No one would rest easy until justice was given, and what was the perfect master of the Clear Blue Way doing? He was following his throbbing dowsing rod into danger and confusion, that's what he was doing!

No reason why justice couldn't give you an erection, but no reason why an erection guaranteed justice, either. And when they finally found themselves alone behind the closed door of his room, he knew all too well that it was hardly justice that he lusted for right now. This fiery creature was going to quite literally fuck him for all he was worth and all she was worth as well. And she had let him know it, daring him to refuse the challenge.

It was mad, it was brave, it was down and dirty, it was the most deliciously nasty game he had ever played, and oh, how it turned him on! It was also a little frightening, for when the truth was revealed in all its naked splendor, he just might find himself in bed with sorcery and liking it.

And he didn't understand why *that* possibility was just making the moment that much tastier.

"Well, here we are," Sue said, glancing around the room, her eyes lingering for a moment on the bed. "And here I am."

And she fell forward into his arms, her mouth reaching up for his. Lou moaned, and quivered at the knees, and his mind shut off, and he found himself eagerly flowing around her, surrendering to the overwhelming energy that she seemed to be pouring into him by near-desperate act of will.

They staggered to the bed and toppled back onto it, Sue uppermost, still locked in the long charged kiss. She ran her hands up his thighs in a purposeful seeking that sent a bolt of lightning up his spine and made him break his lips away in a moan when they found their mark.

She smiled smugly down at him, catching him in the opaque hidden depths of her eyes as she undressed him with teasing fingers. "And now for a taste of justice," she said, gobbling him up in her masterful mouth.

For masterful was the word for how she seized the mainline that went right to the core of him and caught his being in the iron grip of ecstasy. Slowly and teasingly, feeling out his responses, then fully and openly, until he felt his soul would pour out into her, did she catch him in her spell, a protoplasmic pleasure that reached down into his very cells, to which he could not but surrender.

Almost.

No woman who could do this could have cold void at her heart. But no woman who could do this with those knowing eyes wide open could be doing it without purpose either.

Not quite, lady, not quite yet, Lou thought, taking her by the cheeks and pulling her head away. Before he would surrender what was left of his will to the natural man, he had to see those eyes in the truth of uncontrolled ecstasy, and he was damned if he'd take his own pleasure until he did.

He pulled her to him, kissed her with mocking chasteness on the mouth, rolled her under him around the kiss, then propped himself up on his elbows looking down at her.

"And now for a taste of truth," he said.

He slowly stripped off her clothes, staring steadily into her eyes with an expression of ironic appraisal. She arched her back up toward him as he slid her garments out from under her, looking back at him with prideful self-knowledge as her breasts bobbed up into his face.

Ah, she was lovely, and oh, did she know it, and ooh, how Lou loved that!

"Well?" she demanded. "Am I worth it? Are you glad you're compromising yourself?"

"There'll be no compromises here," Lou said throatily, and he fell on one of those small perfect breasts, nibbling and licking the sweet hard nipple until he heard her whimpering in pleasure. Then he slowly trailed his mouth down over her body, savoring every inch of it—the swelling curve of her breast, the hollow of her stomach, the silly grace note of her navel, the taut skin of her inner thighs, the heat and smell and taste of her. She curled her hands into his hair and pretended to resist, but he sensed that the game was purely sensual now, and when he began to slide toward the quick of her against the teasing tension, she sighed and melted backward into the luxurious taking of pleasure, the natural woman surrendering the last veil.

Oh Lou, I think I'm afraid of you! Sunshine Sue thought as she danced on the tip of his tongue. For with that tiny point of connection, he was letting her know just who he was and how deep into her being he could reach. He had pierced the games and scenarios to the essence and left her hanging helpless on a lance of pleasure.

Oh, he was a perfect master all right, and his mastery went deep. He was dissolving her fears in pleasure, and what a loving thing to do! Her heart could not help but respond to the sweetness of that any more than her body could help respond to his mastery of her flesh.

Yet she knew all too well that this pleasure had a higher purpose than its own. He was opening her up to him, he was letting her know he could do it, he had accepted her challenge and turned it back upon her. The game was still on, but now the levels reached higher than she would have ever believed possible. Ah Lou, Lou, you're as subtle a creature as I am, what a wonderful thing to find! We both play the same games. How fortunate that we both enjoy it. And how nice that we're evenly matched.

She reached down with both hands, pulled his mouth up to hers, and then they were kissing, mouth to mouth, a dance of acknowledged equals, tongue on tongue, ego on ego, a kiss that took and acknowledged pleasure in every level of this ultimately earnest game.

"Nice to know you," Sue said, as she welcomed him deep inside her with a rolling twist of her hips.

Sunshine Sue regarded him with open and sapient eyes even as Lou felt her dancing a challenging counterpoint to his rhythm, rubbing the edge of her pleasure against his own, letting him feel her feeling him, then sending him off on a trip of his own where the master became the ecstatically willing student. Her mouth twisted and flowed in abandoned taking of pleasure even as her eyes read his with a certain knowing amusement.

It was a place he had never quite been before, a place whose elusive truth he sought with the focus of his being. He could feel the sweetness of her; he felt that in a certain sense he was looking down into her honest heart; he felt the pleasure she took in the pleasure she was giving, and the pleasure she gave in the pleasure of taking. The intimacy was real. He tasted her spirit and found it good.

Yet he knew that he neither possessed her fully nor comprehended the whole. There was something burning deep inside her that had nothing to do with him or this moment, an inner secret she both guarded and longed to have released.

Fuck me! her body seemed to tell him. Fuck me out of my mind! If you dare. If you can. It was a new level of the game, perhaps the final level; the feat of cocksmanship to which he had been challenged and the truth he sought were both somehow aspects of the path to justice.

Trust me, he tried to say with his body, with the rhythm of his hips and the depth of his stroke. Open up to me, let me all the way in. Ride me to wherever it is that you want us to go.

Up and over the top into new country went Sunshine Sue, with her legs wrapped around Lou's body, and her spirit wrapped around the taking of pleasure that she now allowed herself to the full, open to the goodness of his power to lovingly overwhelm.

For overwhelmed her he had, matching her karmic challenge measure for measure, playing every level of the game she was calling like the master he was, and now fucking her into truly letting her be fucked by him.

At the peak of this orgasm of the body and spirit, Sue felt herself floating up weightlessly toward the bright sun of ecstasy, felt Lou releasing himself into the arms of her soul, surrendering himself to the sweetness he saw there, and thereby holding up to her the mirror of her own essential goodness as she tasted him drinking deep of what he found there.

I'm all right, she thought as she lapsed into sweet repose. For *he* was all right, and he found her good. He was indeed a perfect master and a giver of justice, and the truth of this had been proven to her by the natural man.

She snuggled into the crook of his shoulder and just relaxed for a long moment listening to the synced rhythm of their heavy breathing. Finally he spoke softly against her ear.

"Okay, you win, lady. You're going to get what you came for."

Whatever it was, he had done it to her again. She sat up beside him and studied those big green eyes. There was amusement there that seemed of a loverly kind, but there was also the cool clear unfathomableness of the perfect master. It seemed that the game wasn't over after all.

"Are you playing another game with me after all we've meant to each other?" she said archly.

"Same game we've been playing all along," he said. "It's called the seeking of justice. And now I see how it can be found. I'm going to give you your heart's desire. I'm going to let you choose justice for yourself."

"What?"

"Isn't that what you were after all along?" Lou said slyly. "Isn't that why you seduced me?"

"*I* seduced *you?*"

He laughed boyishly. "Well, you tried," he said. "And you certainly succeeded in wrapping the giver of justice up in your karma. I can't kid myself into believing I'm a detached observer. So you've won the right to speak justice on yourself."

"Hey, this isn't funny," Sue said. "I'm beginning to think you mean it."

"I do."

"But after the scene I made at the Court of Justice, everyone will think you're a fraud if I come out too clean."

Lou nodded. He smiled at her sardonically. "That's part of your karma now too," he said. "You can't say you didn't ask for it."

Oh no! Sue thought. I can't make you look like a fraud now. And you know it. Because you're *not* a fraud. And you know that too, you son of a bitch!

"You really *are* a perfect master, aren't you?" she said.

"I try," he said dryly. "But now it's your turn. Tell me what to do with you."

"You *know* what to do with me," Sue said archly, throwing herself into his arms. But it didn't work. He gently pried her loose. "This is real," he said with deadly seriousness. "Justice must speak through you. Don't blame me, lady, that's the way you set it up yourself."

And damn it, he was right, righter than he even knew. All her life she had taken her own destiny in her hands. She had been karmically arrogant enough to act on the conviction that the dream she followed was a higher good than any of which her fellow beings were aware. Indeed, she had been willing to take the evolution of the human spirit into her own hands, and she had been pretty ruthless about it. This was her Way, and it had brought her to this moment.

And here she was, having willingly sold her soul to black science, being told to judge herself, and being unable to avoid agreeing with the justice of that sentence. Harsh would have been the justice she gave on herself in her heart of hearts were it not for one thing—her destiny still tasted sweet to her in the face of all logic and Lou had shown her that he thought so, too.

"Ah, you don't know how deep that cuts," she sighed.

"Don't I?"

No you don't! she thought. You may be a master, but you're not perfect. She longed to tell him everything, especially that which she didn't understand herself. But there was more at stake here than her own feelings.

"Lou, do you think my soul is black?" she asked tentatively.

"I think your soul is many colors."

Ah, what a perfect Clear Blue answer! But he was also

deliberately evading the heart of the matter, or rather not allowing her to put off any of what she was feeling on him. All right, she decided, you asked for it.

"Hear my justice on the Sunshine Tribe!" she declared with mock pomposity. "Neither I nor any of my tribe knew we were buying black radios. The Sunshine Tribe has done nothing to stain its karma beyond the usual standards of La Mirage. As giver of justice, I therefore declare the Sunshine Tribe white as the driven snow and hold it blameless of all wrongdoing."

"And you?" Lou asked solemnly.

"Me?" Sue sighed. "You have no idea what I've done. What I'm doing right now. What I believe must be done."

"But *you* do," Lou said. "That's why you must speak justice for yourself."

"I can't, Lou. I honestly don't know how."

Lou studied her narrowly. "Are you *asking* me to do it, then?" he said. "You want to tell me about it and accept my justice with an open heart?"

Sue studied him back. Great gods, was this a trap all along? She sighed. If so, it was a *perfect* one. Is there anything else I can do? Once I'm forced to admit that I can't judge myself, is there anyone else I can turn to?

She sighed again. She gritted her teeth. "Everyone knows that the Spacers set me up," she said fatalistically. "What no one knows is *why*."

"And you do?"

Sue nodded. "The only thing the Spacers want out of this is *you*," she said.

"*Me?*" Lou exclaimed, and Sue knew that she had reached territory where even his Clear Blue vision would probably be clouded.

"You, love," she said softly. "I've met the sorcerer behind all this. The whole situation was set up so you'd be my giver of justice and we'd make love and I'd convince you to meet with sorcerers, and I think I'm going to do just that."

"WHAT?"

"Things don't look so Clear Blue anymore, do they?" she said sadly. "And it's even worse than that. They want you to aid them in a kind of sorcery. And I want you to do it too."

Lou managed an ironic intake of breath. "Uh, I'd be interested in knowing what the hell you're talking about," he said.

"The Spacers are weirder than anyone knows," Sue told him. "I got off with one, and I don't even know if I had any choice in the matter. I probably didn't even have any choice not to do what I'm doing right now. I don't like them, and I'm doing what they want me to do, but I've got to convince you to do what they want anyway."

"And what might that be?"

Sue took a deep breath. She looked into his eyes. Incredible as it was, he seemed to be withholding judgment even in the face of this. He had spoken truly when he said she would give justice for herself. What clarity it took for him not to hate her now! But how far could he really walk with her? How sure was her own step?

"Black science is building a spaceship," she said. "They want you to help them let it fly. And so do I."

Lou just goggled at her, speechless. Oh Lou, how can I make you understand?

"They're building a spaceship," she repeated. "I don't understand why *they* think they're doing it, but I know why *I* want it to fly. Badly enough to risk doing what I've done to help them. Badly enough to try to persuade you to help us, even though it convinces you I'm the blackest person you've ever met."

"Do you realize what you're talking about?" Lou said incredulously.

"I know exactly what I'm talking about," Sue said testily.

"A *spaceship?* Like the rockets that destroyed the pre-Smash world? Burning thousands of tons of carcinogenic filth? Black science polluting the very heavens with their evil? Stirring up a holy war against themselves for the twisted pleasure of slaughtering a children's crusade? *Do you realize what you're saying?*"

"I'm afraid I do," Sue said. "And I'm afraid I still believe it's worth it."

"What could be worth that . . . ?" Lou said. But there was as much fascinated curiosity in his voice as anger or dubious disbelief. Oh Lou, she thought, maybe you *will* understand.

And if you don't? she thought. If *you* find my dream black at its heart, might not I stand convicted of sorcery in my own eyes? But either way, she would at least be released from the paradox in her own heart as she shared it with the only person she could trust. The person she had no choice but to trust.

"I'm going to try to tell you," she said. "For better or worse, I'm going to tell you who Sunshine Sue really is, and what I believe, and just how far I'm willing to go. Then you tell me whether I'm white or black, Lou, because I'm not sure I even care anymore."

The longer he listened, the more Lou understood about Sunshine Sue, but the more he understood, the more complex the problem of justice became. Truth be told, he had been close to the final vision even before he met her—the Lightnings to be disbanded, the Eagle Tribe slapped on the wrist, the Sunshine Tribe to be allowed to continue to function after all its equipment had been recertified righteously white. Only the question of justice for Sunshine Sue herself had hung in abeyance pending the tasting of her soul.

And now that he had tasted her and found her sweet, it seemed that on the ultimate level, her spirit had to be the same shade as his. If we taste good to each other, we must be the same flavor.

But what flavor was that?

It was certain that the dream that burned inside her would be called sorcery by anyone outside the ambiguous reality of La Mirage. Hidden lore from a Rememberers' hut. An "electronic village." Linking human consciousness electronically to recreate the higher unity of pre-Smash man. It all stank of sorcery. After all, the "mass consciousness" she was trying to recreate had slaughtered billions and poisoned the Earth.

Yet you could point to nothing about it that seemed to violate the law of muscle, sun, wind and water. This "software science" of "media" seemed neither white nor black. An art purely of the spirit, "independent of the hardware," or so she claimed.

On the other hand, Lou could see that such a "radio network" as Sunshine Sue dreamed of creating could become an instrument of mindfucking on a scale beyond anything the blackest heart lusted after if put to the wrong use.

But what Sue seemed to sincerely find in this dark art was exactly the opposite, a new Way, a path to greater clarity that all the peoples of the Earth might walk together hand in hand. "Extended electronic senses" to bring anything that happened anywhere into the consciousness of everyone all at once. Surely that could only bring the vision of all closer to the Way and form a commonwealth of consciousness and a brotherhood of man.

He loved her for this vision and through that love tasted the whiteness of her soul and the sweet karma that seemed to be the pot of gold at the end of her rainbow. The perfect master, the giver of justice, and the natural man all longed to take her hand and be her companion along this Way.

But it could not be denied that those who had walked this Way before had been monsters of evil, black scientists who had destroyed their world. And the Spacers had proven that they were worthy karmic successors to these evil sorcerers of old. They had threatened the stability of Aquaria, halted commerce, and had been readily willing to wreck lives just to bring the two of them together in this configuration of destiny.

And yet . . .

And yet they found each other sweet. And yet Lou believed that Sunshine Sue's heart was good even though she believed in this dream with a burning intensity. More, he found *that* sweet too; logic could not deny the reality which he felt.

If she's tainted black, then so must be I, in my heart of hearts, he thought perplexedly.

"And so that's why I'm willing to deal with the Spacers," Sue said, openly pleading for understanding. "Once they get to their space station, their karma is no longer mine. The World Satellite Broadcasting Network will be as white as the sun that powers it. Where's the black science in using it to bring the scattered tribes of our ruined world back together again? You can see that, can't you, Lou? You'll help me do it, won't you?"

And he could. And he wanted to. But what would be the cost? How much evil had to be done before her electronic village could be built? Would not the bad karma of the means poison the result? Was this not how black science had once before seduced a world to its doom?

"I want to believe you, really I do," he said. "But this ship they're building must burn millions of gallons of petroleum to get into space. And what about the energy units to build it? I don't see how you can send a spaceship into outer space without black science, and lots of it."

Sue looked downward at her breasts. "I didn't say they weren't sorcerers," she said softly.

"And you didn't say you wouldn't be willing to overlook sorcery to get your world radio network either," Lou said, wincing as the force of truth pulled the words from his lips.

Sue hesitated, then looked up at him, her eyes suddenly burning with defiance. "No I didn't!" she said. "Maybe we *do* have to taint our souls with a little sorcery to lift what's left of the human race out of the dust! Fuck it! So be it! Tell me, Lou, what's really more important, the pristine purity of your own soul or the destiny of the world? Neither of us are karmic virgins! If sorcery is what it takes to get a world radio network, then you can paint me black—and proud of the guts it takes to admit it, oh perfect master!"

A surge of lust poured up Lou's spine as she shamed him with her bravery. Willing to commit her own spirit to a cause that seemed beyond good and evil and willing, too, to accept what karma that would bring her. In her, he saw something that must have gone out of the world long ago, to be rekindled by chance or destiny in a young girl in a Rememberers' hut deep in a darkening forest.

That in itself smelled of sorcery, and the pride of her courage to brave regions beyond the law wrapped the cloak of dark arts around her like a banner. He knew this, he felt this too, and yet it made him throb with dark desire.

He touched her on the shoulder and felt electricity shoot through him. Her posture was defiant, her nipples pointed upward in pride. Oh gods, Lou thought, if this creature is evil, then I am lost!

"But the results of this . . . this necessary sorcery . . ." he half stammered. "The poisoning of air and life . . . ? Would you kill what's left of the world to save it?"

"Will one spaceship trip do more harm than what we let pass through La Mirage just to ease our comfort and pleasure ourselves?" Sue demanded. She peered at him narrowly. "Is out of sight out of mind the true measure of purity, oh favorite perfect master of La Mirage?"

Now she really *had* shamed him. For what she was saying was undeniable truth. All Aquaria was tainted with gray if you dared to look with open eyes. People knew it and chose not to know it and tried to walk the path between. And was not that path the Clear Blue Way? Did Sunshine Sue not simply have the courage to admit openly what he hid from himself in the guise of creative ambiguity?

Yet once this was openly admitted, was not clarity lost? Was the whiteness of Aquaria a lie and the sweetness of its karma hollow? Or could a little necessary evil somehow promote the cause of good?

"You're making me think strange thoughts, lady," he said, meeting her eyes again. "I've got to admit you make temptation look pretty good. You've got me half believing black is white."

"Black, white, gray, is that really all that matters?" Sue said. She touched a hand to his cheek and another to his groin. "Fuck it!" she snarled. "What counts is what you feel! And I know what I feel and I can feel you feeling it with me."

"But we're both flying blind."

"Then let's have the courage to admit it! Admit one thing, and I'll gladly accept whatever justice you give. Admit that we're riding this karma together."

Lou's heart skipped a beat. All at once the voice of justice spoke loud and clear within him. They *were* in this together, for together they had both reached the bounds of their previous moral comprehension to face an unknown void in the hidden region beyond. From where they now stood, neither of them could tell black from white, good from evil, or see with clarity the Way between. If such a Way even existed.

"You've got me," he said, kissing her lightly on the lips. "Like it or not, we both *are* in this together."

She started to kiss him back, but Clear Blue Lou gently restrained her, cupping her face in his hands. She wasn't going to like this; she wasn't going to like it at all. But the necessity was inescapable.

"What's wrong?" Sue asked nervously.

"Now justice must speak," Clear Blue Lou said. "And I hope you'll accept it as you've promised. Our current personas have reached a blind alley. There's no clear justice to be seen from where we are now. We've lost the Way, and we can't find it again without being reborn."

"You're talking about karmic rebirth, aren't you?" Sue snapped angrily, pulling away from him. "You want to fill me full of rex and make my mind over in your own image!

As far as I'm concerned, that makes you as big a mindfucker as the Spacers!''

''It has to be done,'' Lou said defensively. But truth be told, he was hard put to deny the justice of what she said.

''Fraud! Mindfucker! Bastard!''

''What if I take the rex, too?'' Lou blurted. ''What if I lay myself as open to you as you are to me? Am I still a fraud?''

Sue's eyes widened in astonishment. Her anger melted into amazement. She touched a tender hand to his cheek. ''You'd do that?'' she said softly. ''You'd really do that for me?''

Lou nodded, for once having said it, he realized that this unprecedented karma had called forth a higher level of justice. As far as he knew, no perfect master had ever taken rex with the subject of karmic rebirth; no perfect master had himself been karmically reborn. But no perfect master had ever been in this moral space before either.

''Justice demands it,'' he said. ''As you say, we *are* in this together now.''

Sue's lower lip trembled. She seemed about to say something, then held her words back. She sighed. ''You son of a bitch,'' she said roughly, ''if I don't watch myself, you're going to make me fall in love with you.''

The Court of Justice could no longer be called a party by the time she and Lou returned to the Garden of Love, and Sunshine Sue felt immediately in tune with the tired-out, waited-out, downbeat vibes. The casual revelers and good-time people were gone now, the buffet spread was an unholy mess, half-empty glasses and bottles were everywhere, and the miasma of stale wine and old reef smoke and a night's worth of sweat stank of tense weariness.

All those whose karma would be affected by the giving of justice were still there of course. Exchange merchants and magnates jammed Levan's booth and spilled over into the tables in front of it, still speculating on the fate of the town. Levan himself was now a bone-weary old man staring at the ceiling and trying to stay awake. A dozen members of her own tribe in the far end of the room glowered across at the Eagles, who occupied three booths near Levan's entourage. In the center of the room huddled the loathsome Lightnings, given a wide berth by everyone.

A shrill babble greeted their entrance, and even Levan

awoke instantly from his daze. Sue and Lou walked hand-in-hand to the buffet table, every nuance of their appearance the subject of excited conjecture.

"—holding hands—"

"—gotten it on—"

"—knew he couldn't resist—"

"—Clear Blue sailing—"

Oh shit, Lou, let's get this over with, Sue thought as conflicting energies roiled nauseatingly inside her. She had saved her tribe and Word of Mouth and tentatively gained an ally and a lover. *Just as the Spacer scenario had predicted.* Thus far, she had followed it with "nominality," and so had Lou, down to sentencing her to a shared karmic rebirth that had been inevitable all along. Oh Lou, you were right when you said we were both flying blind! But even you don't see the strings that are guiding us.

As if reading her mood, Clear Blue Lou cleared the crud off a section of the buffet bar with an imperious sweep of his arm and sat himself down on it like a king on his throne above the eye level of the room.

"Hear my justice," he said. "Gather round, folks, and have your minds relieved." He squeezed Sue's hand, grinned, and pulled her up beside him.

Everyone crowded toward the buffet bar; even Levan wobbled forward and collapsed in a front-row seat. Only the Lightnings held back, cowering and sullen, at the outer periphery. The babble was brighter now; Lou's voice, his posture of graceful ease, every move he had made, had told the movers and shapers of La Mirage that things were going to be all right. He radiated confidence and Clear Blue vibes. Only Sue knew how clouded justice really was, how much of this had to be art. Only she could fully appreciate his performance.

"First of all, I find the Lightning Commune guilty of knowingly practicing black science," Lou said. "All commerce in goods of its manufacture is hereby banned. Since the Lightning Commune is banned from all commerce, it can have no legitimate source of sustenance, so it is hereby disbanded. Since the Lightning Commune now no longer exists and I judge its guilt to have been collective, no further action will be taken against its former members."

This was greeted by a mixture of joy and indignation. The Lightnings had brains enough left to know that they had gotten off lightly, but they were sullenly pissed off at their disbandment. The movers and shapers were mightily relieved at how narrowly Lou had proscribed former Lightning products when he might have banned Lightning-type components generically. They were also a little displeased that the mountain williams had gotten off so lightly, but self-interest kept them from protesting. Sue could not but admire the dynamic balance of this justice.

"Secondly, I find the Eagle Tribe guilty of uncoolness," Lou continued, and the room broke up into nervous laughter and mock cheering.

Lou held up his hand for silence and synced into the general mood. "The Eagle Tribe was only being righteously white in denouncing the atomic power cores in the Lightning radios, or so logic must lead us to conclude," he said with ironic pomposity. "However, while I may not be an expert logician, I know what I like, and I don't like bummers. I therefore find the Eagle Tribe guilty of *only* being righteously white, of following the letter of the law but not its spirit."

There was a deep murmur of approval at this. North Eagle stared up at Lou with nervous apprehension. Lou grinned back at him sardonically and stroked his chin as if in thought.

"Now such obnoxious innocence cannot go unpunished," he said. "It seems only appropriate that I redress the balance of creative cynicism. So I hereby decree that the price of solar eagles be cut ten percent for one year, after which the Eagle Tribe will be free to see if they can get away with boosting it back."

He looked down at North Eagle with pixie eyes. North Eagle sat there gaping, pleased that the Eagles had gotten off with a backhand slap, but counting up his lost profits nonetheless. "I, for one, intend to take advantage of my own justice, and I hereby order a new eagle to be delivered to me in Clear Blue Lou blue at the new low price, and I advise all my friends to take advantage of this special offer."

He winked at North Eagle. "You may take a loss," he said dryly, "but you'll make it up in the volume."

At this, everyone broke up, and even North Eagle could only shake his head and mutter "Son of a bitch!"

"Finally, the Sunshine Tribe and Sunshine Sue," Lou said more solemnly, speaking in a voice of magisterial detachment. Which, however, did little to suppress the sniggers and cynical smiles as he spoke in this tone with Sue's hand still in his.

Sue could feel the wave of good vibes directed at her by her fellow tribe members and the somewhat more cynical appreciation of the rest for a job of seduction apparently well done.

"The Sunshine Tribe *was* in fact caught with a black radio," Lou went on. "But I don't believe they knew what they were buying, so they get the benefit of the doubt. Levan will appoint independent experts to examine all their other equipment for sorcery, and if no more black science is found, the Sunshine Tribe can continue business as usual, except that all new equipment they purchase must be independently certified for a period of five years."

Sue sat there woodenly while her fellow tribesmen burst into grins of joy and everyone else into down-and-dirty surmise as to who was responsible for this sweet Sunshine outcome and how she had obtained it. There certainly wasn't any disapproval of Clear Blue Lou's openly passionate justice; it was just the sort of thing La Mirage would consider meet and romantic. But Sue didn't like the face it put on Lou.

But she loved the good humor with which he carried it. "Now we come to the hard part . . ." he said slowly. ". . . in more ways than one," he deadpanned. Everyone laughed their appreciation for the way he had easily admitted to the karmic reality, and even Sue couldn't be entirely angry, though she could do without the onslaught of good-natured leers.

"As you all surmise, certain events have destroyed any pretense of objectivity on my part in the case of Sunshine Sue," Lou went on. "Not that I've ever pretended to objectivity in the first place. Furthermore, thanks to my magnetic personality, the lady herself can't be clear on the nature of her karma in her current incarnation either. Our karma has become entwined, and in order to find final justice, we've got to clear it."

The room grew quiet, and when Lou spoke again, his voice was deadly serious and his face thoughtful and perhaps artificially composed. "I decree that Sunshine Sue must undergo karmic rebirth under my direction," he said. "She must seek a new level of truth in order to regain the Way."

Dead silence greeted this announcement. Karmic rebirth was no subject for jest or conjecture, and even La Mirage respected its seriousness. But this being La Mirage, Sue knew that many would question the fitness of a perfect master to direct the karmic rebirth of his own lover. And all at once, she saw the *political* reason why Lou was ready to take the rex with her. It was in fact the politic thing to do, and it was also truly just. In La Mirage, that amounted to the same thing.

"But since my karma is involved with hers, I myself will take the rex as well, opening myself to Sunshine Sue as she opens herself to me," Lou said, after his audience had had just enough time to recognize its misgivings as to the purity of his justice. "Every master must dance his own song."

A gasp, a sigh, then a wave of loving vibes, greeted this unexpected gesture of humility and stunning self-judgment. No perfect master had ever gone through rebirth as an equal before, and that he was doing it with a lover made his justice only sweeter.

Justice had been given, and as Sunshines and Eagles, merchants and magnates, friends and congratulators, crowded around them, it was abundantly clear that Lou's justice tasted sweet to one and all. The heat was removed, La Mirage would continue on its merry way, eagles were cheaper, and Sunshine Sue and Clear Blue Lou would meet as lovers in the ultimate sacrament of the Way. How could you get more Clear Blue than that? seemed to be the unanimous opinion of the critics.

But as she stood there holding hands with the perfect master of the Clear Blue Way, Sunshine Sue began to wonder.

Clear Blue justice, all right! she thought. But also exactly what the Spacer scenario called for. Harker would be smugly pleased by its nominality. The two of them had played out the scenario perfectly.

Sue had gone into this knowing she was trapped in the Spacer scenario and hoping that the perfect master of the Clear Blue Way might rescue her free will. Instead, he was trapped in the scenario with her. Because she had chosen to let him be trapped rather than reveal the whole ugly truth: that even his taking of the rex was part of sorcery's scenario.

She stole a sidelong glance at Lou. Just how Clear Blue really are you, lover?

New Lamps
for Old

They had arrived by eagles at the rude log cabin perched on a forest-shrouded ledge in the high mountain country near sunset the night before, just as the sun was beginning its descent over the panorama of wooded mountains and bare ochre peaks that fell before them to the west. The world had seemed clean and virginal to Sunshine Sue up here in the high pines, where scattered birdsong had only served as grace notes to punctuate the huge silence. It was as if the Smash, the Spacers, Aquaria, La Mirage, and all the convoluted folds of the human mind lay a million years of evolution in the future. That evening even Sunshine Sue had felt her animal roots, lost in a world that existed in its own primeval now.

They had eaten a cold meal of bread and dried fruit together in the blaze of sunset, made love under the stars, and fallen asleep in each other's arms. Sue had drifted off almost peacefully, up here in a perfect master's arms, where scenarios and justice and the Clear Blue Way had taken her, beyond the time-bound reality of her human past, ready to face the truth of tomorrow's rebirth with an open heart.

But she had slept fitfully all night, awakening again and again to stare up into a skyful of high mountain stars, brilliant against the utter darkness, but cold as steel in the shiver of the crystal air. They seemed to be watching her, aware of every move she made, every thought, and discounting her free will beforehand, just like the sorcerers whose emblem they seemed to be. The dream that the Spacers followed shone up there, hard, and brilliant, and cold as diamond. What Arnold Harker saw up there was an endless sweep of infinity that somehow drew him to its cold-hearted immensity, but what Sue saw was a harsh desert of darkness and ice-hard chips of light which she presumed to dare in the service of her own destiny.

Something evil must have really captured her karma, for who but demons would want to go up there into the cold and the dark. The stars seemed to hide the secret of tomorrow's dawn with cold and impenetrable knowingness. How could anyone expect to sleep soundly under the pitiless gaze of a fate beyond understanding or control?

And now it was slate gray dawn, and she was blearily awake at this ghastly hour as Lou began to stir against her. He blinked. He sat up. He rubbed his eyes in the baleful light and kissed her dryly on the cheek.

"Hi, how did you sleep?" he said in a loathsome attempt at early morning cheerfulness.

"Terrible," she snapped at him. "Are you sure you know what you're doing? This is how I'm supposed to prepare myself for karmic rebirth?"

"You are where you are," Lou told her, crawling out of the sleeping bag. "That's the whole point."

"Spare me your ineffable wisdom please, and let's get it over with," Sue snapped as she emerged into the morning chill and began pulling on her clothes.

"Hey, I'm not your enemy," Lou said in a wounded tone of voice as he pulled on his pants.

"I'm sorry," Sue said much more softly, kissing him briefly. "But this hour of the morning is not exactly my time to shine, and I didn't like the thoughts that kept me awake half the night, and I really don't think either of us knows what we're getting into, and I don't even—"

Lou stopped her with a finger to the lips. "You're more ready for rebirth than you think," he said. "You're right, it's time to do it. Let's go inside."

The interior of the cabin seemed like a self-contained bubble in the sea of the universe, a cabin on a ship built to sail the waters within. The only windows were high up under the eaves where the world outside manifested itself only as shafts of pale early morning light. The floor was the living earth of the mountains, and the walls were rough-barked logs, and the only furnishing was a round pit dug in the center of the floor and padded by thick goose-down quilting.

Out of a pocket, Lou produced two brown wafers of rex, the ultimate achievement, or so it was claimed, of Aquarian mindfood art.

"Just chew it up like pastry," he said, handing Sue one of the dense-looking cookies. She shrugged, saluted ironically, then gobbled it down like a hungry animal.

Clear Blue Lou chewed his wafer of rex slowly and contemplatively, enjoying the not-unpleasant mushroomy flavor, evoking the full awareness of what he was doing.

The exact ingredients of the wafer were the trade secret of the Clear Light Tribe, and Lou, being no psychoherbalist, wouldn't have understood the magic of the recipe anyway. But he knew full well what rex did, and he had always employed it with a sense of some moral trepidation.

Rex erased the barrier between the mind and the mouth, between consciousness and speech, between the secret stream of the mind and the edited version the soul ordinarily spoke to the world. You spoke your truth as you saw it in your heart of hearts. Your mind lay open to whomever you were with as surely as if it were the pages of a book.

Rex was used for karmic rebirth alone. Anyone under its influence could not help but be transformed by any question with which they were confronted. And any questioner might get answers closer to the core of truth than he had intended. Only a perfect master could lead a soul through its own unself-controlled truth without imposing outside patterns. Only a perfect master could refrain from programming this open fluid consciousness with his own input.

It was the hardest task a perfect master was called upon to perform, because if he wasn't *perfect*, he'd taint his own karma with the sin of mindfucking, and the transformed soul would emerge in a programmed persona.

The unofficial lynch-law penalty for using rex to program minds or seek gainful knowledge of another human was death, and it had had to be applied only a few times in all of Aquarian history. This was deep and heavy stuff, and everyone knew it.

No one more so than Clear Blue Lou, who had rebirthed a score of souls, who had peered into their twisted karma with clear detachment, and led them by not leading through their own truth to a new Clear Blue harmony. The perfect master of karmic rebirth was a mirror held up to the soul's own truth. If that detachment wavered, the karmically reborn would not be a free spirit.

This was a heavy moral burden. Each time he led a soul through karmic rebirth, he risked the whiteness of his own. Though he hadn't failed yet, each time he came to this place, the possibility of failure existed anew.

And never before had he taken the rex himself except under the guidance of another perfect master. Certainly not with someone whose karmic rebirth *he* was supposed to be guiding, and definitely not with a lover.

He was doing something that had never been done before. And he was doing it in the face of karma few had faced before. He was a perfect master confronting the need to be transformed himself. Together he and Sue were voyaging as equals into unknown waters where neither knew the Way.

It was not exactly comforting, but never had the process seemed more just.

They sat across from each other in the upholstered pit in the dark cabin, where only the palest light trickled in through the high windows and the birds greeting the morning sounded muffled and far away. Lou had lit a few candles to soften the chill gray light, but nothing could convince Sunshine Sue that this was not the grim hour of dawn or take the edge off her impatience.

"Well what's supposed to happen?" she demanded. "I don't feel any different."

"Any different than what?"

"Any different than the way I felt all night," Sue said. "We're in a trap, Lou. Even *this* is part of Harker's bloody scenario. Truth is, the whole thing was a plot to get us to do exactly this. I knew it, and I went along with it even though I didn't want to, and I couldn't even tell you—"

"Until now," Lou said with a little smile.

"Don't you understand what I'm telling you? I couldn't help myself. And neither could you. Here we are, in karmic rebirth together, not as the result of your Clear Blue justice, but because of a sorcerer's scenario!"

"I'm here because my karma demands it," the Clear Blue oaf insisted.

"Bullshit! You're here because the scenario calls for it. Because your free will was stolen from you. And I helped."

"By stealing my heart away? I'm also here because I want to be." He gave her a fey little smile. "Because I'm a natural man."

"I know," Sue said sheepishly. "I was briefed on your predilections by a sorcerer."

Lou peered at her with amused skepticism. "You're telling me you haven't been a natural woman?"

"No Lou, I'm telling you I wanted you the moment I saw you. I wanted you before I saw you. The Spacers had figured out scientifically that we'd be irresistible to each other. That's why they did all this to bring us together."

It seemed as if she was finally getting through to him. His mode shifted from assertion to attention. "But I don't *feel* I've done anything against my will," he said. "Do you?" His big green eyes mirrored the question.

"I feel like you and I are a natural number," Sue told him. "But how can either of us trust what we feel? We were chosen to feel it, and maybe we were programmed to feel it too. I feel I could fall in love with you. I feel that I'm betraying you. I feel that what I want to do is right, but I see myself willing to do some very wrong things to get it done. I'm starting to feel that there's a level on which our conceptions of black and white or good and evil just don't add up. How can anyone trust their feelings in a space like this?"

"Relax," Lou said. "You've just reached the point where you've accepted the fact that your previous persona is no longer viable. As long as you can feel confused, you know that your mind is free."

Pow! Zap! Clear Blue truth! As long as I'm squirming, I'm aware of the hook. But somehow that satori was not as liberating as it should have been. "But my *will* isn't free," Sue insisted. "I was told that the scenario was behavioristic, and you should have heard how Arnold Harker made that sound. Like we were pawns he could move around at will. What we feel doesn't matter to him, he just uses it to control our karma. Doesn't that make you feel used? Doesn't it make you feel violated?"

"Did you feel that way when you made love with Arnold Harker?" Lou asked impenetrably.

"Low blow!" Sue cried, cringing inside. "*Made love with him?* It was more like war than sport! I started teasing him to salve my ego, and he turned the game around on me as if I were a doll on a string. It was so down and dirty that it turned me on even though he disgusted me. Maybe *because* he disgusted me. Great gods what *is* this stuff? What am I saying?"

"The truth of our karma," Lou told her. "Its form is starting to take shape. And it's beginning to scare me."

Clear Blue Lou stared across the pit at Sue, while candle flames flickered a false sunset across the rough-barked walls as above them the pale early light of dawn seeped into the shadows. Time, like karma, seemed fragmented, and the fabric of reality was slowly unraveling, revealing the moral ambiguity of something seemingly beyond parameters of white or black, good and evil—the enigmatic full face of the moral unknown that men called sorcery.

How could minds be free while wills served unknown ends? Yet it seemed that this was possible, despite its contradiction of the laws of black and white logic. Somehow the Spacers controlled *karma*, not the will. Somehow they could make room for at least the illusion of free will in their scenarios. Was that white or black? Could you even say it was either?

"Now I know what really brought both of us to karmic rebirth," Clear Blue Lou said. "Our old personas weren't forced to face the reality that lay hidden beneath the maya of our world. Because once they were forced to face it, their previous perceptions were no longer viable, and therefore karmic transformation became the only way through. Because once you really understand it, the world we know really doesn't exist."

Sue hunched over, goggling at him. It was painfully clear that while she didn't yet understand what was becoming all too obvious to him, she was certainly picking up the queasy unease in his vibes. "Aquaria needs to believe in its own whiteness. And it *is* white. We live well and prosper under the law of muscle, sun, wind and water, and our karma tastes sweet. Yet none of this would be possible without a steady trickle of black science that we conveniently close our eyes to. Somehow black science transforms itself to white, and the conjurer's trick seems to work, even on a karmic level. Black science has always been a secret not-so-secret part of our civilization, and the thing of it is that our civilization *works*."

Sue's expression sharpened. Something flashed between them. "And what we're realizing now," she told him, "is that we really don't know how."

They sat there silently in the evaporating darkness trying to digest the indigestible truth they had come to. Sue took Lou's meaning on a personal as well as public level, for she could now see that sorcery had thoroughly infiltrated her karma as surely and stealthily as it had been the essential underpinning of fair white Aquaria all along. Lou saw his harmonious vision of the totality of the Way clouding over with enigmatic darkness masking a great essential unknown. Sue realized that her own vision of the world had never been the standard model, not since that day in the Rememberers' hut deep in the darkening forest. Even that now smelled of sorcery too.

Was the whole of reality, outer and inner, knit together by the scenarios of black science?

"Things are not what they seem, are they . . . ?" Sue finally said.

"Things are what they are and maybe *we're* not what we seemed."

"What are we, then?"

"We're two people who have already lost our past personas. We know too much about our world to go back and be the same people. We can't go back. We can only complete the transformation."

"Just as the scenario calls for. . . ."

"Just as the scenario calls for. But we don't even know what that is, do we?"

"We do. Our part in the scenario is to help the Spacers get their spaceship launched and bring back their beloved Age of Space."

"Really? Centuries of scenarios and fifty years of work to launch a single spaceship to visit a station in space? For this they're willing to provoke a holy war against them?"

"The world satellite broadcast—"

"That's what *you* want, Sue, but what do *they* really want out of it? A mob of the whitely righteous for them to slaughter?"

"They want you to *prevent* that, Lou."

"But why do they believe I'll help them, even if I could? What do they know that I don't?"

"They don't have to have a rational reason. This Age of Space dream has devoured them whole."

"Like your dream has devoured you, Sue?"

"Yes!" Sue snapped. "Yes . . ." she whispered softly.

"They're humans just like us after all," Lou said. "And that's the real mystery. They follow a Way they believe is good, and yet to us it seems evil. And although it seems evil, we're walking it now, even in the shared truth of this process. What makes sorcerers so convinced of the rightness of their Way that they seem to be willing to commit so much evil to walk it?"

"The same thing that turns an Arnold Harker into a cold unnatural creature and convinces him that his sterile life is so superior . . . ?" Sue said.

And will it do the same to us? they both thought together, realizing that the inevitable decision had already been made.

"We have to know, don't we?" Sue said. "Even if it turns us into sorcerers, too . . ."

Lou nodded. "This process has gone as far as it can," he said. "And we're still not reborn. We know too much to go back to being who we were and not enough to become who we must be, and we sure can't stay in *this* space between. We have a karmic rebirth task to complete together, like it or not."

"The scenario is behavioristic," Sue said. Every time she repeated it, the enigmatic phrase developed deeper and more sinister implications. Apparently not even rex was powerful enough to break the sorcerer's spell.

"But the sorcerers are human," Lou said. "Their Way is not the Great Way, even if they think it is, else they could not work such evil on others or themselves. Knowledge is not wisdom."

"And you think your wisdom is stronger than their sorcery?"

Lou shrugged. "I know that wisdom without knowledge is

blind and that until we know what's really shaping our world and why, we're souls without a home.''

"If that wasn't what we were to begin with," Sue said softly. She crawled across the goose-down padding of the pit and sidled up to Lou. He could feel her lonely lostness as she pressed her body against his.

"There's nobody in this space but us," he said. "We really *are* in this together.''

"Lovers and allies, huh?" Sue said wanly.

"We have no choice. . . ."

"And it's sorcery that's flung us together. . . ."

Lou put an arm around her and hugged her to him. "If this be sorcery," he said, "it seems we have no choice but to make the most of it."

After they had made love, they went outside to meet the new morning. The sun was peering up over the high spine of the cordillera behind them. East of the mountains lurked their new unknown destiny, hidden from the sunlit slopes falling away from them to the west.

The world down there looked the same as it always had, timeless green mountains tumbling down to the familiar lands of men. All seemed fair and serene in those lovely lands under their invisible cloak of poisoned air. Yet just as Aquaria swam in an invisible sea of black pollutants, so did it float on a hidden undercurrent of the black science whose shadow even now stretched westward from beyond the mountains.

The world was in fact the same as it had always been, but the eyes that surveyed it saw with a terrible new vision. Here, high in the mountains where the known world ended and that which was called sorcery began, they found themselves stripped of comforting lowland illusions, above the landscape of the world they had known.

And towering still higher above them in all their shadowed majesty were the great mountains that rimmed the world beyond which lay their destiny in a future beyond their present comprehension. The very land itself seemed an ideogram of this passage through rebirth as they stood there hand-in-hand, two new souls on the borderland, all alone in a suddenly unknown world.

New Worlds
for Old

Clear Blue Lou had been circling for at least an hour since Sue had landed at the Spacer eagle's nest, waiting for the landing signal. He was starting to get nervous. For once he found himself wishing he had chosen a less emblematic color for his solar eagle. His famous Clear Blue Lou blue eagle would be a noteworthy portent even to back canyon mountain williams, so they had agreed that Sue would land first and clear the place of unwanted eyes and ears before he descended.

Lou had spent the anxious interval circling over the lower end of the long sloping meadow, hoping that he wouldn't be noticed. It was a new experience for him, slinking about the shadows, and he didn't like it. It made his soul seem already tainted with sorcery; he was already playing one of their games.

Finally a mirror flashed three times below the towering crag at the upper end of the meadow. Lou turned out of his circle and came soaring up the long grassy slope, pedaling lift out of his wing.

He drifted in to a hitching rail where the only other eagle

was Sue's, scanning the Spacer eagle's nest dourly as he came in. Great big sheds that had to be warehouses up here where there were no crops at all, and that huge radio antenna at the crest of the ridgeline blatantly pointed east toward the Wastes! These sorcerers certainly seemed sure of themselves.

Sue was waiting for him at the hitching rail. The man with her seemed every inch the legendary black scientist—hard blue eyes peering out of a dramatically chiseled face framed by black hair and beard so closely and sharply trimmed that he almost seemed to be wearing some kind of helmet.

"Arnold Harker, Project Manager of Operation Enterprise," the sorcerer said. There was no tone of greeting in his voice, and he didn't offer his hand. "Sue tells me you want security maintained to the fullest and I concur. No point in taking chances. We'll deflate your eagle and store it in a shed."

"*Deflate my eagle?*" Lou exclaimed. "That's going to take someone hours of pedaling, and it sure isn't going to be me! And I don't like the idea of your making someone else do that much sweating for me."

The Spacer laughed, a thin and not very jovial sound. "Your first lesson in the morality of sorcery," he said dryly. "Never make a man do the work of a machine."

Two men had already emerged from a nearby shed. They were pulling a low four-wheeled cart. On the front of the cart was a grimy metallic thing, all tubing and machinery and wiring. As the two men positioned the cart under his eagle, Lou caught a whiff of a foul chemical odor that seemed the distilled essence of sorcery. One of the men disconnected the wing nozzle from his helium tank, and the other connected it to a hose from the thing on the cart.

Then he did something to the device, and a horrible loud roar rattled Lou's ears, a peal of thunder that went on and on and on, an eerily continuous explosion that jarred his teeth and hummed in his bones. A keen acrid chemical stench filled the air. Lou could see the damned stuff emerging from a pipe—evil and gray and shimmering with unnatural heat.

"*Petroleum?*" he shouted over the din. "Is that damned thing burning *petroleum?*"

The Spacer nodded mechanically as if this stinking sorcery were the most natural thing in the world. Behind the roaring sound, Lou could now detect a loud steady hiss, and he saw that his eagle wing was already visibly collapsing. He knew that it would have taken half an hour of pedaling to achieve the same result, and he could slothfully appreciate how much grunting and sweating was being saved, but it appalled him that even black scientists would spew all this poison into the air just to save a little time and honest effort. What would they be willing to do when it came to something that really mattered?

"Let's get out of here!" he shouted at the Spacer over the noise. "I don't want to have to breathe any more of this filth than I have to!" Indeed, it already seemed as if he could feel the petroleum fumes searing his lungs, blackening the fragile life-giving tissue with carcinogenic muck.

Harker smiled inanely, nodded, and loped off toward the main cabin without looking back, as if he were long accustomed to being followed without question.

Sue, who had almost seemed to be cowering in the sorcerer's shadow, fell in alongside Lou in the Spacer's wake, wrinkling her nose at the deadly stench, and trying to establish some kind of sympathetic eye contact.

Lou took her hand, but he really wasn't feeling too comradely toward her at the moment. He might have been psychically prepared to confront the karma of black science, but he certainly hadn't been prepared for the deadly chemical stink and the ear-splitting reality of sorcery actually at work.

And he didn't like the way Sue seemed to fold in on herself in the presence of Arnold Harker. She actually *fucked* this creature? he thought in wonder. He didn't like it. He didn't like it at all.

Arnold Harker didn't waste any time on a grand tour of the premises, nor did he give Lou any interval in which to examine his own reactions to the strange ambience of the room he took them to.

"I freely admit you've been brought here by stratagem and guile and feminine wiles," he said as soon as he had seated himself behind a cruel steel desk whose burnished top gleamed in the harsh light of the powerful electric lamp upon it. "But let me assure you that your free will and our scenario are ultimately congruent."

The way he said it reeked of an arrogant self-assurance

that set Lou's teeth on edge. Indeed this whole lair seemed crafted to present an atmosphere of unnatural arts forthrightly and proudly displayed. The chairs were all shiny steel frameworks slung with a grainless black material with the feel of leather and the faint smell of petroleum, or so it seemed to Lou as he sat gingerly down in one of them. The pictures on the walls—planet Earth floating in space, ringed and banded Saturn, something flying over a hellish landscape—seemed deliberately emblematic of black science. A mass of unfathomable electronic arcana glowered in one corner, and the whole was lit by two powerful electric lights that blazed their contempt of the energy units it cost to run them. The room's image was doubled by an immense mirror of perfect glass, turning the very space itself into a sorcerer's illusion.

Here there be sorcery, the room seemed to say, and proud of it.

"I find that pretty hard to believe," Lou finally said. "So far everything I've seen just makes me feel more whitely righteous."

"Sue has told you—"

"Sue has told me everything," Lou snapped, ostentatiously taking her hand as she settled down uneasily into the chair beside him. "*Everything*," he repeated, squeezing her hand and shooting her a glance of solidarity for the benefit of the Spacer. "We have no secrets from each other."

"And you've seen to that haven't you?" Sue added sardonically. "How do you like the match you've made?"

But Lou could detect no vibe of jealousy or wounded male ego. Indeed, it was hard to pick up any vibe at all from this sorcerer. "I'm glad to see the scenario is still working so nominally," he said with eerie colorlessness. "It saves me tedious explanation." Was the last a subtle little zinger? "You already know, then, what your part in the next phase is to be."

"Do I?" Lou said angrily. Harker's arrogance was beginning to sound like deliberate insult. "You seriously expect that I'll help you after what I've already seen?"

"Quite seriously," the sorcerer said, leaning back fatuously in his chair. "In fact, I can guarantee you that you are more than ready to perform the function we now require of you."

"Oh you can, can you! You're so sure you can predict

everything that I'll do? You think you can run your lame games on a perfect master?"

"*Precisely* on a perfect master," Harker said smugly, leaning forward and trying to stare down Clear Blue Lou with those icy eyes. Oh now he thinks he can mesmerize me with eye-contact games as if I were some brain-burned mountain william, does he? Lou thought angrily. Who the hell does he think he's dealing with?

Lou broke the staring contest by deliberately smirking at Sue. "You fell for this line?" he said ironically.

Sue cringed, but that didn't seem to prick Harker's bubble either.

"I can even tell you what you'd most like to do at this moment," the black scientist said knowingly.

"You don't have to be a sorcerer to figure that out," Lou snarled.

"You'd like to give justice on Space Systems Incorporated and all its works, wouldn't you? You'd like to speak your justice upon us for all the world to hear."

"Congratulations on your incredible insight," Lou said sarcastically.

Harker leaned back and smiled with loathsomely crafted warmth. "And so you shall," he said. "For that's what the Company requires of you, Clear Blue Lou—your justice on Space Systems Incorporated and all our works, freely spoken to your own people, after you have seen all and had all your questions answered. A justice we agree to accept without condition. Surely no true perfect master could refuse a request like that. . . ."

"*Huh?*" Lou grunted. "*What?*"

"Consider it a formal request," Harker said blandly, now taking an open amusement in Lou's befuddlement. "Will you grant it?"

Lou looked at Sue. She seemed as dumbfounded as he was. He eyed Harker narrowly, his mind scrabbling for psychic purchase. "I don't get it," he said. "Surely you must know what my justice would have to be. I don't believe you, Harker. If you were telling the truth, all you've done would have been unneccesary. All you would have had to do was ask."

Harker shook his head slowly. "I think not," he said. "You've just admitted that you've already reached a conclusion based on insufficient data. A conclusion based on ignorance and legend and foolish superstition. No doubt the scenario thus far has already shaken many of your beliefs and assumptions. . . ."

The sorcerer rose, leaned his hands on the steel desk for support, and loomed forward, staring at Lou with what suddenly seemed like a strange dreamy sincerity. "But I tell you that the truths you must learn to render true justice will make all that has gone before seem like sleepwalking," he said. "To judge so-called sorcery, you must share our knowledge and know the inner heart of black science. Do you dare do that, perfect master of the Clear Blue Way?"

He subsided back into his chair. "Do you dare not to?"

"You know the answer to that!" Lou blurted. "*Of course,* you know the answer to that," he muttered. For that was precisely the karmic rebirth task set for both of them by implacable destiny. By destiny? Or by the Spacer scenario? Or were they somehow the same thing? Reflexively he squeezed Sue's hand. He was beginning to see how this vibrationless man had been able to bed her.

"Just what are you proposing to show me?" he asked.

"Everything. The Company installations beyond the Wastes and all that we do there."

"*Beyond the Wastes?*" Sue exclaimed. "What lies beyond the Wastes?"

"The world," Harker said pregnantly. "And the greater reality beyond."

"And after you've shown us your world, you'll accept my justice on it?" Lou said skeptically. "Why should I believe you'd do that?"

Harker sighed. He seemed to shrink in on himself. Suddenly there seemed to be something quite fragile about him.

"Because we believe what we're doing is right," he said plaintively. "Because we know that what we are doing must be done. Because we believe that you will be convinced of this once you know the whole truth. . . ."

The sorcerer leaned forward and cocked his head ruefully. "We *do* have feelings, you know," he said heavily, as if he felt it would be a cosmic revelation. "For centuries we've lived with our knowledge and kept it alive, and enabled your backward society to prosper with gifts of technology for which we've asked nothing." His face twisted with bitterness and his voice hardened. "And you? You call us sorcerers and shun us as evil. No one likes to be hated, least of all benefactors.''

He blinked, as if catching himself in a persona he had not intended to reveal. All at once he was the hard-eyed sorcerer again, sure and proud. ''But now a great new age is coming and it must be shared and accepted by all. The superstition and ignorance which cripples our species must be annihilated before we can face the stars. Our wounded race must be healed before it can transcend its lowly state. In your terms, black science must be harmonized with the Great Way in the eyes of your people or all of us will be unworthy.''

For the first time, Lou glimpsed something of the natural man behind the sorcerer's persona. And he could not deny that there was something noble there—or at least something that believed sincerely in its own nobility. Great would be a healing that harmonized sorcery with the Way! Precisely necessary seemed this healing to his own rebirth and to Sue's. Harker had pointed clearly to the wound in the very heart of humanity's karma, to the paradox from which all disharmony flowed. And he had challenged Lou to heal it. He really *is* placing his trust in me, Lou thought, twisted with arrogant pride though that trust might be.

''You know very well I have to do what you ask,'' Lou said, in a tone of quiet resignation.

''The scenario is behavioristic,'' Harker said. ''But your free judgment nevertheless remains a factor. In time you will understand that. We leave tonight.''

''*Tonight?*'' Sue said. ''How? For where?''

''For the Company installations beyond the Sierras. By eagle.''

''But no eagle can cross the Sierras! And no eagle can fly at night!''

The sorcerer laughed. ''*No* means one thing to you and quite another to us,'' he said. ''That will be your second lesson in the morality of sorcery.''

''I'm beginning to wonder what I've gotten us into,'' Sunshine Sue said as she and Lou sat together on the floor of the common room at the end of the cabin hall, much like the two mountain williams she had encountered the last time she was here, hunkering together over a phantom campfire, trying to ignore the black vibes that surrounded them.

The empty room, with its blatantly inorganic furniture of false leather and angular steel, its all-too-real-looking pictures of unreal places, seemed to be trying to warp them into another world, and one that seemed devoid of all comfort. Outside the windows, the night was a black void which her mind peopled with demons from the world within.

Lou was staring out into the darkness with an unreadable expression. "Well we're going to find out," he said. "As we knew we were fated to."

"Or as we were forced to."

Lou sighed, turned to her, shrugged. "Maybe the astrologers are right," he said abstractedly. "Maybe our destinies are preordained in the stars. Yours and mine and the Spacers'. Maybe all of us are forced to do what we must. Maybe human free will is an illusion. Maybe what makes the Spacers sorcerers is that they're willing to admit it."

Sue cocked her head at him speculatively, not liking the deeps to which he seemed to be sinking. How much do I really know about this man after all? she wondered. "Pretty weird talk coming from the perfect master of the Clear Blue Way," she said.

"I'd say we're in a pretty weird place, lady!"

"And I have a feeling it's going to get a lot weirder," Sue said, "without you drifting off into space with these sorcerers."

"I'm sure I can resist the temptation at least as well as you did," Lou said airily. But was there a hint of wounded male ego behind it?

"You're really jealous because I got it off with Arnold Harker?" she said. "How un-Clear Blue of you!"

Lou squinted at her. "*Jealous?*" he snorted. "You've got to be kidding! It's painfully obvious that he makes your flesh crawl! But I must admit that it bothers me that he was able to bed you with your feeling that way about him."

"Sorcery," Sue said. "I can't explain it. I don't understand myself."

"Uh-huh," Lou said, putting a protective arm around her shoulder. "What really bothers me is the feeling that any mindfuck good enough to work on you might just be good enough to work on me. Uh . . . not in the carnal sense, of course."

Sue started at the sound of footsteps coming down the hall, and they both turned to see who was coming. Since

Harker had left them to their own devices, the only people they had seen were the three Spacers in the little commissary where they had been offered an unsettling dinner of some strange savory roast hefty enough to be deer but of a light and subtle flavor she had never experienced before. Strange droning rhythmic music seemed to emanate from two small boxes near the ceiling which looked something like large radio speaker grids.

"Where's the music coming from?" Lou had asked conversationally around his first mouthful of meat. "Where are you hiding the band?"

The three Spacers laughed patronizingly. "From the speakers, of course," the balding one said, nodding toward the two boxes high up on the far wall. "Authentic re-recording of an ancient pre-Smash tape fragment. It's called 'raga' or 'reggae' or something like that. Do you like it?"

"And what's *this* stuff?" Sue asked, waving a forkful of meat.

"Beef," the tall thin Spacer said with a grin. "A good cut too, don't you think?"

She dropped her fork. Lou nearly choked on a morsel he was chewing. The three Spacers seemed highly amused.

"*Beef?*" she gasped. "*Cow meat?*" Once, she knew, cow meat had been a staple of the pre-Smash diet, and even the milk of the cow had been eaten. But after the Smash, carcinogenic poison had concentrated in the flesh and milk of cows, making them unfit for consumption, and extinct, or so she had thought.

"You're feeding us poison!" Sue said, staring in disgust and bewilderment as the Spacers continued to devour the cow flesh with relish. "You're eating it yourselves!"

"Tastes good, doesn't it?" the chubby one said slyly.

"High in essential amino acids."

"Perfectly harmless—to us," the balding Spacer said, and the three of them broke up into hootingly superior laughter.

That had ended dinner, and it had also ended their contact with the strange birds that roosted in this black eagle's nest. The Spacers seemed to be keeping away from them—perhaps under orders—and after swallowing cow flesh, Sue yearned not for their company.

Now, however, Arnold Harker was coming down the hall toward them with purposeful strides. "Our eagle is about to arrive," he said as they scrambled to their feet like country cousins. "We'll be leaving in a few minutes, but I thought you'd be interested in seeing it arrive."

"I've seen eagles land a thousand times," Lou said off-handedly.

"Ah, but you've never seen one of our blackbirds of the night, now have you?" Harker said, shooing them toward the back door leading to the big open yard behind the cabin. "You've never seen sorcery like this."

Outside, the air was chill and thin and clear, and half the starry sky was hidden by the great wall of rock that loomed above, the impenetrable ramparts at the edge of the world. Crickets chirped their offbeat chorus. Something hooted far away.

"Listen," Harker said. "Can you hear it?"

Behind the quiet night sounds, Sue thought she heard a faint thrumming at the edge of audibility. As she strained her ears to catch it, the sound seemed to get stronger. Stronger and stronger still, till she realized it wasn't close by and faint but distant, and loud, and rapidly approaching.

Then the sound level seemed to suddenly jump, reverberating through the canyons below, and the black shape of an eagle became visible, silhouetted against the stars and coming toward them with impossible speed from the northeast, dropping in for a landing.

It was huge—quadruple the wingspan of an ordinary eagle and then some—and it was unlike any solar eagle Sue had ever seen. Instead of a saddle, there was some kind of closed cabin slung close under the wing, and at the rear of the cabin a huge propeller, a great monster whirling at such speed that it should have taken twenty men at the pedals to run it.

As it eased down into the yard in front of them, the draft of the propeller kicking up a storm of twigs and small stones, Sue got a sickening whiff of burning petroleum, and she realized that the propeller was in fact driven by a huge and baleful engine mounted on the rear of the cabin, the source of the awful din. Foul hydrocarbons and metallic oxides gushed into the atmosphere from a vent in the bottom of the wing even after the racket ceased and the propeller stopped turning. The gigantic eagle wing seemed to sag, and the cabin came to rest on four little wheels. The eagle wing held its shape even after its lift was gone; the cabin was connected to the wing by rigid metal struts, and the wing itself apparently had an internal framework.

"What in the black pits of hell is that?" Sue muttered.

"A true flying machine," Harker said proudly as three Spacers trotted out to the thing with their packs. "What is called an 'airplane.' It doesn't need helium for lift and it doesn't need the sun for power and it can fly nearly sixty miles in an hour ten thousand feet above the ground."

"All by burning petroleum," Lou said angrily.

"All by burning petroleum," Harker repeated enthusiastically, perhaps deliberately mistaking Lou's tone. "The petroleum engine not only drives the powerful propeller, it provides two forms of lift. The hot exhaust inflates the wing, and the strong draft under it enhances the airfoil effect. This is how men were meant to fly in the atmosphere!"

"Assuming they had any atmosphere left to fly in," Lou snapped. "It's hard to believe even *you* would be this black."

"Most of the exhaust gasses are trapped in the wing," Harker said somewhat defensively. "We only have to vent them when we want to lose altitude. Besides, by now there are less pollutants left in the atmosphere than you people think."

"So you might as well pump some more carcinogens into the air," Lou said angrily. "This really *is* evil."

"You promised not to give justice until you saw everything," Harker reminded him more belligerently.

"This isn't enough?"

"This is nothing," the sorcerer said airily. "Before you learn the reason why, we will give you abundant cause to condemn us. But once you learn all, you'll find everything we do justified. You now believe this is impossible, but I know that it's true, and so now let me show you just how confident we really are. It's time to cross the mountains. Welcome to a greater world."

And with that, he ushered them toward the waiting eagle.

He rolled up one of the cabin's sides as they stooped under the wing. Inside four canvas seats were slung from the cabin framework, two in back, two in front. A young woman with short-cropped black hair sat in the front left seat behind a complicated-looking set of controls. Sue crawled in beside Lou in back, and Harker took the empty front seat.

Sue felt pretty weird in the cabin when Harker rolled down the flap. Three flexible windows were sewn into the canvas of each side flap, and the front and rear windows were of curved glass clear as a flat plane. It was like being trapped in a windowed tent, unable even to leave your seat.

A click, and a rasp, and then the muffled rumbling of the petroleum engine behind her. Nothing else happened for long moments. Then Sue felt the cabin lift slowly off the ground. A loud thrumming drone all but drowned out the noise of the engine as the propeller whirled into a solid blur, and the eagle began to pick up speed and altitude.

Out a window, Sue saw the eagle's nest spiraling slowly away as the eagle circled for altitude, and then it came out of its circle in a long curving arc upward and eastward toward the mountains that loomed before them.

Sue glanced at Lou. Their hands snaked together as the eagle nosed steeply upward into the starry night. The world below was already lost in blackness, and only the great mountains outlined against the sky gave any hint of scale or height.

"Well here we are," Sue shouted in Lou's ear over the drone of the propeller, "on our way to the land of sorcery in a black eagle."

Lou smiled feebly at her and squeezed her hand. "It'll be all right," he shouted back. She hoped he really meant it.

For as the eagle soared upward into the featureless void and even the peaks of all but the highest mountains fell away into impenetrable darkness, here she was, trapped in an evil craft flying higher and faster than whiteness allowed on the deadly breath of petroleum. This was no dream, this really *was* sorcery, and her very bones were vibrating with its power.

Clear Blue Lou awoke to a headache drone in the darkness, and for a moment he didn't remember where he was. He blinked and came more fully awake and realized that the deep vibrating thrum was the propeller of the Spacer eagle, that he was flying at tremendous speed high above the mountains through the dark night sky.

Sue was asleep in her sling beside him, Arnold Harker's head rested on his shoulder at an odd angle, and the only illumination was the pale starlight filtering in through the windows. Below he thought he could make out the looming peaks of the central range of the Sierras passing by beneath them, vague shapes of solid blackness.

Conversation had not been easy over the drone of the

propeller, the darkness had enveloped them like velvet, and the steady mantra of the propeller thrum, loud though it was, had been conducive to dozing. He must have drifted off without knowing it, brooding upon the unknown destiny he was moving toward at unreal speed; somehow it seemed appropriate that this passage through the secret skies had become like a hypnagogic dream, a twilight world between awareness and sleep.

In front of him, the young Spacer girl hunched over the controls. He wondered how she managed to fly the craft safely through the high mountains in the blind darkness.

He leaned forward and spoke softly in her ear to avoid waking Sue and Harker. "How do you see where you're going?"

"What?" she said much more loudly, not looking back.

"How do you see where you're going?"

"I don't. I *hear* where we're going with this. Like a bat."

She nodded toward a round glass plate in the control panel before her. A line of pale green swept around it like the second hand of a clock, and in its continual wake, vague shapes and patterns of light formed and faded and reformed again.

"Radar," she said over the propeller noise. "It sends out a sweeping radio beam that bounces off the mountains. The echoes bounce back like the cries of a bat and form patterns on the screen that map the terrain."

Sue began to mutter and stir in her sleep. Any conversation loud enough to be comprehensible would probably awaken her.

"The wonders of black science . . ." Lou muttered and slumped back into his sling. An uneasy feeling came over him. Here he was, flying above the supposedly impassable Sierras at sixty miles an hour in an eagle that saw through the darkness with its ears like a bat! It was hard not to be seduced by the wonders that sorcery seemed to offer. What a magic world it would be if everyone could fly faster and higher than any bird, see through the darkness, never have to pedal, receive instant Word of Mouth from anyone else anywhere in the world! No wonder the Spacers fell prey to these fantastic temptations.

But every mile that this swift eagle flew could be measured in the deadly breath of its petroleum engine, in so many vile carcinogens pumped into the air, in shortened lifespans, in death, in human suffering. The Spacers had to know this, and yet, somehow, they seemed able not to care. How was that possible? How could they be so morally blind?

It seemed to Lou that the psychic space between the worlds of white and black was as vast and dark as the void through which this craft now moved, transporting them between one reality and the other.

He put his arm around the sleeping Sue, closed his eyes, and willed himself back into the sleep-giving mantra of the droning propeller. The only way across that great divide was the way they were following now, a dark dream through the abyss of the night sky. Tomorrow the sun would find them in another world. Oh yes, we're in this together! Lou thought as Sue snuggled her head into the softness of his arm.

But just *what* are we getting into?

Somewhere
over the
Rainbow

Sunshine Sue awoke in a blaze of eye-searing light, her neck kinked from the weird angle at which it had lain on Lou's shoulder, her head pounding with the insistent thrum of the propeller.

"Oh! Ugh! Where the hell are we?"

Lou had been staring out a window, down and to the south, away from the brilliant cloudless sunrise that made the eastern horizon a glare of cruel fire. "The Wastes!" he shouted, not turning his head. "Look at it!"

Below, Sue saw a nightmare landscape that chilled her soul.

To the west, still in shadow, the spine of the great cordillera rose out of a badland plain where the long shadows and pitiless light of the rising sun etched a hideous picture of death and desolation. Waterless lakes—amoeboid expanses of some strange rock, flat and shiny as glass—shimmered an evil purple in the sere desert landscape. She could see three huge round craters gouged into the tortured body of the Earth and places where multicolored rocks seemed to have melted and flowed into mounds and puddles like so much candle wax. In all that cruel landscape, nothing grew, nothing lived, nothing moved.

A tremor of fear went through her; reflexively, she reached for Lou's hand. So this is the world the Smash made. . . . she thought. "How far does it go?" she shouted. "Is it still radioactive? Are we safe up here?"

Arnold Harker twisted around to face them. "Safe up here," he shouted over the din, "but you wouldn't last a week down there. How far does it go . . . ?"

He leaned close to them to make himself better heard, and they both craned forward to listen. "This Waste goes all the way to the Rockies except for some patches of clean desert. Some people up there that we look in on from time to time. We've sent some expeditions over the Rockies, and we know another Waste begins on the far slopes and runs most of the way to the eastern seacoast. Nothing as significant even as Aquaria left in all the world."

"*In all the world?*" Sue gasped in despair.

"In all the world we know of. Which isn't very much. We know there are other lands beyond the great eastern ocean, but we don't know if anyone is still alive there or if the rest of the world is all like . . . *this.*"

"I didn't know . . ." Sue stammered. "I mean, I *knew,* but. . . ."

Harker nodded grimly. "Who knows how much is really left of our wounded planet?" he said. "Who knows how many people survive?"

His eyes hardened and his voice grew fervent. "Only from space can we view the world entire. We can only regain the lost knowledge of this planet by leaving it."

"And only with a broadcast satellite network can we communicate with whoever is left," Sue said. "Assuming there *is* anyone else somewhere."

Harker smiled at her almost warmly. "You begin to understand," he said. "A little more pollution? A few more radioactive particles? Does it matter after you've seen *this?* A wrecked world and a humanity spiraling down to extinction. Without a new Age of Space, our species is doomed anyway. Pollution? Sorcery? Radiation? Black science? Behold the world and tell me that we have anything left to lose!"

"But sorcerers like you did *that!*" Lou shouted, nodding

down at the destruction. "Doesn't that even make you question the rightness of your path?"

"We seek to bring knowledge from the stars that will raise humanity from the ruins!" Harker insisted.

"Or destroy what's left."

"The level of risk is acceptable," Harker said flatly, and with that he turned his face back to the bright eastern horizon, and the three of them fell silent.

Sue stole a sidelong glance at Clear Blue Lou, who stared out the window looking grim and angry. For a moment, she began to wonder about this perfect master, this man whom fate had thrown her together with. He seemed so sure that he was right and Harker was wrong. True, she had never dreamed that the Earth was so ruined, that humans were so few and scattered. True also, that the destruction below was undeniably the evil handiwork of black science.

But she found herself more convinced than ever of the dire necessity of her cause. Only a global electronic village could give what was left of humanity a second chance, if indeed it deserved one. And only a satellite broadcast system could make that possible. And only black science could put that in her hands.

It was all so unfair! It was all so circular! Black science seemed to have the only hope there was, and if it was false, if it was evil, where did that leave the human species?

Deep inside, she found herself shaking a phantom fist and shouting angrily at she knew not whom. Why should we bear the guilt for the evil of our ancestors? We might be stuck with the karma that was written by the implacable hand of fate. But accepting the justice of that karma was an act of free will, and she was having none of it.

As the sun rose higher, the heat became noticeable even after the flaps were rolled up to admit the breeze of passage, and then it became truly horrible—a dry hot wind from the mouth of a kiln, nature's sardonic howl of hostility. Clear Blue Lou was beginning to develop an unholy appreciation for the black eagle's speed. The sooner this flight was over, the better. There was no joy in this corpse of a landscape and no soaring pleasure to be had in traversing it. Now he could understand why the black scientists were willing to sell whiteness for speed, or at least he could feel the temptation.

"How much longer?" he shouted at Harker.

"We'll be landing soon at Starbase One, our main installation."

"Landing soon?" Sue said. "Out *here?*"

Harker pointed out the front window toward a purple range of lower mountains marching toward them across the Waste. "The next valley is untouched," he said. "Original uninhabited desert that escaped the megatons. Such are our oases."

Soon they were flying high over the sere slopes of pastel brown mountains. The western slopes were as dead and lifeless as the lowland Waste, but as the black eagle flew eastward, sparse scrub growth began to appear, and Lou thought he could make out tiny moving black shapes that might have been animals.

Then the mountains fell away to reveal a long, flat, high desert valley. Lou's first impression was of another Waste, dry, and dead, and shimmering whitely like bleached bone under the fierce sun. But as the Spacer eagle turned north along the length of the valley floor and the landscape below unreeled itself, he realized that there were no craters or melted rock or lakes of blue crystal here, only dry brown earth and expanses of sand that might have looked this way for the last million years. Apparently nature was as capable as man of creating utterly deadly wasteland.

"Down there! What's that?" Sue shouted, pointing down on her side of the cabin, where Lou couldn't see.

"Fuel wagons from our refinery far to the southwest," Harker told her. "We have to reach a long way for petroleum."

Then Lou saw an expanse of greenery beginning below him with the geometric precision of a line across the landscape. "Crops?" he said. "You're able to grow crops out here?"

"We pipe water in from deep wells about ten miles from here," Harker told him. "The engineering isn't too difficult. Laying pipe to our petroleum supply, unfortunately, is another matter."

To the northeast, surrounded by the great square of cropland in the middle of the desert, Lou now made out the shapes of buildings. Thin fountains of water sprayed into the bone-dry air from sections of the farmland around them, creating an incongruous vision shimmering preternaturally in the desert heat.

"Starbase One," Harker said. "We'll give you a chance to inspect it before we go on to the spaceport tomorrow."

The pilot did something to the controls, and a long disgusting stream of grayish black smoke plumed out from a vent in the wing near the back of the cabin, and the eagle began sinking toward the rapidly approaching buildings.

Soon they were circling over the strangest-looking town that Lou had ever seen. A perfect square of green about the size of La Mirage seemed to have been painted on the sere valley floor. In the geometric center of the square was a huge geodesic greenhouse dome, five times the size of the Exchange and crafted of glass and metal. Long low sheds radiated out from its circumference like the metal petals of a flower. A quadrangle of big squat ugly gray buildings enclosed this weird construction.

Except for a much smaller dome of gray concrete way up in one corner of the cropland and a line of "airplanes" southeast of the center close by a large series of sheds and squat metal cylinders, the whole thing was as inorganic and symmetrical as a mathematical diagram.

And except for the eagle's nest and the concrete dome, all the buildings were connected by passageways like the links of some gigantic half-buried metal worm. A gridwork of arrow-straight concrete roadways was laid over the green area like the lines of a huge chessboard.

It was unlike any human habitation Lou had ever seen, and he couldn't even begin to guess its population.

"How many people live here?" he asked Harker.

"Almost three thousand."

"There are that many black scientists?" Sue exclaimed.

"That *few*," Harker said. "There's a work force of about a thousand at the spaceport and a few hundred more at scattered installations, and that's all there is of the most advanced civilization on this planet."

"That's still a lot of black scientists by my reckoning," Lou said.

"Most of us are pilots and gardeners and craftsmen and technicians," the pilot said, speaking for the first time in hours. "It takes a lot of workers to keep a modern civilization going. We can't all work on Operation Enterprise. But we all know what our work means."

"What *does* your work mean to you?" Lou asked ingenuously as the eagle, streaming petroleum fumes, began to sink rapidly toward a landing, for he was curious to know how a Spacer who was not a full-fledged sorcerer felt about what they were doing. The karma of the followers had as much to say as the karma of the leaders about the justice of any enterprise.

"We're building the new Age of Space," the young woman said with an idealism that seemed clear and genuine. "We're building a spaceship so that men may listen—"

"Here we are!" Harker interrupted loudly and perhaps somewhat shrilly, obviously and deliberately cutting her off. What had she been about to say? What was the sorcerer hiding?

The Spacer eagle slowly settled the last few feet to the ground as the engine died, and a horseless cart sped out of one of the sheds toward it at twice the speed of a running horse, trailing the inevitable plume of sooty poison. There were two benches under a canvas awning on the flat bed behind a grimy petroleum engine.

By now Lou found himself taking the appearance of such a thing almost casually. But what he was not ready for was the awful still heat that assaulted him once the draft of the propeller was gone.

"How do you stand this heat?" he groaned as they climbed out onto the fried brown earth. He had never known there could be heat like this—dry and windless and hot as the mouth of a furnace.

"It drops a little when the sun goes down," Harker said. "During the day, we stay indoors where it's cool and pleasant."

"Where it's what?"

But the petroleum cart had come to a halt in front of them, rumbling and rasping, heat waves shimmering above the hot metal of the engine, and Harker was already climbing up beside the driver under the inviting shade of the awning.

Lou climbed up onto the rear bench beside Sue; the sun no longer glared down on them, but the heat was not much less intense.

"Just take us to the dome and let's get indoors as quickly as possible," Harker told the driver, and a moment later the petroleum cart was tearing along up a concrete roadway toward the big greenhouse dome, the wind of passage supplying some small relief from the heat. Lou wished the driver would take his time about it. He couldn't imagine why Arnold Harker was so damned eager to bake indoors.

By the time the cart reached an entrance to the greenhouse dome, Sunshine Sue was sweating even in the bone-dry desert air, her eyes were smarting from the cruel glare of the sun, and forlorn images of cool mountains and shaded forests teased sardonically at her mind. How did the Spacers survive in this horrid climate that seemed totally unfit for the human species?

Harker opened a metal door in the side of the dome, and as they stepped inside, Sue was stunned by the sudden coolness. It should have been like the inside of an oven under the big glass bubble, where brilliant sunlight illumined endless rows of tall green corn. Instead, it must have been thirty degrees cooler inside the greenhouse, and there was a strange foreign tang to the air, an illusive wrongness she couldn't quite place.

Harker was grinning smugly at the effect this sorcery was having on his visitors. "Air conditioning," he said. "All of Starbase One is a sealed environment, something like a space station. We cool the air electrically to 70 degrees, an optimum temperature for human functioning."

"*You cool the air electrically?*" Sue said. "What kind of sorcery is *that?*"

"A spin-off from the life-support system of the *Enterprise*," Harker said enigmatically. "Before the Smash, every dwelling had it."

Lou was inspecting the nearest stand of corn. The plants were growing in a long shallow metal tray, and on second look, the entire floor of the dome was a series of such trays, connected by a complicated-looking system of valves and piping. "There's no soil in here!" Lou exclaimed. "These plants seem to be growing in *water!*"

"Actually a scientifically controlled nutrient solution," Harker said. "It maximizes yield and eliminates the absorption of radioactive isotopes from the soil. Pure cattle fodder, pure meat."

With that he led them across the floor of the greenhouse where here and there, men and women stooped like farmers among the rows of corn doing things to the valves of the piping. There was something totally unbucolic about the scene. This didn't seem like a farm, it was more like . . . a food factory. Somehow, it seemed to epitomize the Spacer spirit, alienated from the natural world and yet triumphant over it.

Harker opened a door at the other side of the greenhouse, and a rich ripe manure stench assailed Sue's nostrils. She peered down the length of a long dark shed where rows of gross placid animals stood dumbly in the gloom, confined in endless tiny stalls hardly bigger than their bodies.

"Cattle," Harker said. "We feed them hydroponically grown corn and distilled water, and the result is beef fit for human consumption. Milk and butter and cheese too. Concentrated protein."

"They don't look very happy to me," Lou said dubiously.

Harker eyed him peculiarly. "They're just dumb animals," he said uncomprehendingly. "Hardly capable of either happiness or its opposite."

Then he closed the door on the unsavory spectacle and the smell of shit, and led them around the curve of the dome wall to yet another door, and into a long tunnel with curved walls of some dull silvery metal brightly lit by a line of electric globes running down the center of the ceiling. "This leads to the living quarters," he said. After about forty yards, the tunnel opened out into a giant hallway, a long, wide indoor concourse that seemed like a grim version of the main street of some small Aquarian town.

Brilliant sunlight streamed into the gallery from a row of high windows along the right-hand wall which, however, afforded no view of the world outside. The walls themselves were painted forest green and festooned with unhealthy-looking potted ivy. The ceiling was sky blue, and the tile floor a simulated earth brown. A line of shops and public rooms ran the length of the left-hand wall sans emblems or signs or idiosyncratic embellishment.

"The habitat is an entirely self-contained living module," Harker said proudly as he led them past a dining room, clothing shops, a nearly empty tavern. "The amenities are down here on the first level, and the upper floors contain housing for three thousand people."

"You mean all your people live indoors all of the time?" Lou asked incredulously.

Harker nodded. "This optimized habitat is preferable to the hostile outside environment," he said. "It's also an ideal model of what self-contained space habitats will someday be like, a foretaste of the human future."

"Let us hope not," Lou muttered sourly, and Sue could sympathize with what he felt.

You had to admire the ability of the Spacers to craft this little self-contained world and maintain a bubble of habitability in a hostile environment. You had to admire it, but she couldn't imagine how anyone could *like* it.

It didn't feel like indoors, but it didn't feel like the outdoors either. Yet people wandered around in here as if it was the most natural thing in the world. Young, old, men, women, wearing utilitarian clothing of an almost uniform design, they went about their business like the folk of any natural town, to the pervasive but subtle rhythm of music that seemed to come from everywhere and nowhere, so soft and bland that it took Sue long minutes to even notice it. Clean, pallid of complexion but healthy and purposeful looking, moving along to ghostly music they probably weren't even aware of, the inhabitants of Starbase One seemed almost like an idealized version of humanity, fitting denizens of this flat simulation of reality. Like the environment itself, they were clean and shiny and spotless; not a dirty face or a grimy hand or a soiled garment was to be seen. Crowded though it was, murmuring with unreal ghostly music, the place somehow didn't seem lived in, and the people themselves seemed to have banished the dirt and sweat of living from their own karma.

There was no word for the strange feeling this aroused in Sunshine Sue. Admiration mixed with disgust. Superiority combined with personal diminishment. Like the soulless magic of the musicianless music, it seemed somehow coldly seductive and utterly repellent at the same time.

It had been an amazing display of the unguessed wonders of black science and a dismaying exhibition of its twisted spirit. The more that Clear Blue Lou saw, the more knowledge he obtained, the less he understood of the soul of Space Systems Incorporated.

Arnold Harker proudly conducted them on a grand tour of this little secret world of sorcery. Huge windowless manufactories where teams of craftsmen and incomprehensible machinery created the electronic components that later turned up in the goods flowing out of La Mirage. Smelters for steel and aluminum and copper. Workshops turning out "airplanes" and petroleum carts and mighty machineries.

Electric lights were everywhere. Tools and machinery were run by electricity, the air in every building was cooled by electrical power, and even stairs were replaced by cable-lifts powered by huge electrical engines.

Starbase One was an overwhelming demonstration of the wonders that forthright use of black science could create. Given enough electrical power, it seemed there was nothing that the Spacers could not do to lessen human effort and increase human ease. Out of the deliberate and systematic defiance of the law of muscle, sun, wind and water, sorcery had built a little sealed world where magic seemed utterly ordinary after a while.

Anything that *can* be done, *will* be done, seemed to be the rule, and there seemed to be no consideration whatsoever of the karmic consequences. Starbase One must use more electricity than all of Aquaria and then some. Lou had to admit that this naked and lavish sorcery had created a world that appealed to his distaste for wasted person effort. "Never make a man do the work of a machine" had been Arnold Harker's "first lesson in the morality of sorcery." In Starbase One, this seemed to have been pushed to its logical extreme: "Make a machine do any work that makes a man sweat" seemed to be the true principle here, and if he didn't feel the temptation of *that,* he wouldn't be Clear Blue Lou.

But if he didn't wonder at what cost all this wonderful electrical power was produced, he wouldn't be Clear Blue Lou either. And if he hadn't guessed the answer long before he was told, he would have been just plain stupid.

The climax of Harker's day tour was a tense dinner in a grim little commissary with three of Starbase One's "Section Managers." The food, like the irritatingly anonymous background music, might have been made in one of the Spacer factories—six platters of cow steak, fried potatoes and corn, identical down to the shape of the steak and the size of the portions.

"The diet of Starbase One is a scientific balance of all necessary nutrients," Life Support Manager Marta Blaine assured him as he picked listlessly at the grim fare. A plain-looking woman of middle age, she shoveled away the stuff with all the gustatory delight that this glum endorsement could be expected to call forth. Harold Clarke, the tall, blond, sallow Export Manager, and Douglas Willard, the wizened, quite ancient-looking Enterprise Production Manager, also packed it away without seeming to taste it. Only Harker himself seemed to display any lip-smacking enthusiasm, and that seemed calculated for effect.

Lou found himself laying back sourly and letting Sue ask most of the obvious questions.

"What do you export and to whom?"

Clarke smiled somewhat fatuously at her. "Virtually all my Section's production goes to Aquaria," he said. "I'm really responsible for maintaining your culture's so-called white technology. Over a million solar cells a year, the total supply of advanced electronic components. *Your* own radios. Control circuits for solar eagles." He bobbed his head at her in ironic greeting. "Meet your secret benefactor."

"It sounds like very expensive altruism to me," Sue said dubiously.

"Oh indeed it is," Clarke said. "More expensive than you can even imagine in terms of man-hours and energy units. More man-hours than anything we do, save production for Operation Enterprise. Perhaps double or triple Aquaria's total annual electrical production."

"Why?" Sue asked.

"*Why?* Because it takes that much work and energy to—"

"I mean why do you do it at all?"

"For the greater good of all," Clarke said evenly.

Sue snorted. The Export Manager's expression hardened.

"Well then, because you people are benighted superstitious fools," he snapped. "Without our so-called black science, your so-called white technology would swiftly fall apart."

"But why should you give a damn?"

Something seemed to pass between Harker and Clarke, and when the Export Manager spoke again, his composure was carefully restored, and if he wasn't being sweetly sincere, he was giving a good imitation. "There are only a relative handful of us, and Aquaria, for all its faults, is probably the highest civilization of any significant size remaining on this planet," he said earnestly. "We help you despite your low opinion of us because Aquaria is the only possible base upon which to build a new Age of Space when—"

A glance from Harker seemed to cut him short, and old Willard, as if on psychic cue, picked up the response in seamless mid-sentence.

"—when Operation Enterprise creates the basis for a new unified planetary culture. The ability to see the Earth once more as a world entire. To search out all the remaining pockets of humanity on our blighted planet, to bring our scattered peoples back together through your own vision of a world satellite broadcast network." The Enterprise Production Manager fixed Sue with an intense stare that seemed quite sincere to Lou. "On a certain level, we dream the same dream," he said.

Sue seemed to be as impressed by this as Harker had no doubt intended, but as far as Lou was concerned, this all seemed like a carefully crafted little exercise, all talk and no spirit, designed to justify the *what* of black science while skirting the true essence of the *how* or *why*. None of it seemed really relevant to the justice they were ostensibly requesting him to render.

It wasn't till they were down to picking over the remains of the filling but unappetizing meal that Harker seemed to notice his hooded indifference. "Don't *you* have any questions?" he finally asked. The other Spacers dutifully regarded Lou with rapt interest, and even Sue seemed to be studying him for some clue as to what was behind his non-reaction.

"Yeah, I've got two questions," Lou said grimly, leaning back in his chair and steepling his hands in front of him. "And I'm afraid I already know the answer to the first one. You're using atomic power here, aren't you?"

Harker's eyes widened. "I congratulate you on your scientific perception," he said approvingly.

"Atomic power?" Sue exclaimed. She looked at Lou peculiarly. "How do you know that, Lou?"

"How *else* are they going to generate all the electrical power we've seen here?" Lou said, shrugging at her. "Isn't that right, Harker?" he snapped, glaring at the sorcerer. "All these wonders are built on radioactive death, aren't they?"

"That's putting it a bit melodramatically," Harker drawled.

"The reactor's well away from the main installations, radiation leakage is minimal, and it has a triply redundant safety system," the Life Support Manager said as blandly as she had endorsed the nutritional quality of the food. "We've used nuclear reactors for centuries and we've had only ten core meltdowns, nine of which were successfully contained."

"The risk is well within acceptable parameters," Harker added, a shade more sharply, "and you've already seen the advantages."

Clear Blue Lou had heard just about enough. "Atomic power is just going too far, Harker," he said angrily. "For *any* reason. I need know no more to speak my justice on this evil!"

There was a long moment of hostile silence. The Spacers glared at him with what seemed like contemptuous superiority. Even Sue seemed dubious about his firm decision.

"You're wrong," Harker finally said in a tightly controlled voice.

"*Really?* Then suppose you answer my second question. How *do* you justify all this to yourselves? Manipulating the karma of Aquaria with your scenarios, living out here in a hostile wilderness in air-cooled boxes, risking atomic death not only for yourselves but for the rest of the world. As far as I'm concerned, all this is evil and pointless, even self-torture. But I don't believe that even sorcerers act without reasons that make sense, at least to themselves. Why, Harker, *why?* What really moves your spirits?"

"Operation Enterprise—"

"You're lying to me!" Lou snapped. "All this just to send a spaceship to some ancient space station? Just to make an empty gesture? If that really is the truth, then you people really *are* insane!"

"It's no empty gesture," Clarke insisted in a clipped tense voice. "It will be the beginning of a new human renaissance. . . ."

"*One* spaceship flying into outer space in the face of a whole world's hostility?" Lou said scornfully. "That's supposed to turn human history around? I don't believe it, and I don't believe you believe it either!"

Willard's old eyes suddenly blazed with a strangely youthful intensity. "When we get to the Ear, human history will not merely be turned around, it will truly begin!" he said fervently. "Even you will understand when the songs—"

"*Willard!*" Harker snapped angrily.

"Oh, why not tell him?" the old man said. "Why not—"

"Because now is not the time!" Arnold Harker said harshly, shooting the Enterprise Production Manager a glance of such poisonous intensity that Willard seemed to wither into silence under its force. Clarke's eyes became hooded and he drummed his fingers nervously on the table. Marta Blaine seemed somehow confused and left out. What was Harker hiding? And was he hiding it even from some of his own people?

Harker seemed to make a conscious effort to control himself. "Tomorrow all your questions will be answered," he told Lou more calmly. "You promised to withhold your justice until you had learned all. Do try to keep an open mind until then."

"And if I don't . . . ?"

Harker glared angrily at him for a moment. Then his lips creased in a sardonic smile. He shrugged. "It doesn't really matter, does it?" he said. "The scenario is behavioristic. And you've followed it too far to be allowed to turn back now."

"Should I consider that a threat?" Lou said, challenging the sorcerer with his eyes.

"Threats are unnecessary," Harker told him. "Consider it a promise."

"At last we're alone," Sunshine Sue said sarcastically, sitting down on the edge of the severely functional bed next to Lou. "Now would you mind telling me what that was all about?"

"What what was all about?" Lou said evenly.

Great gods, is he really this dense, or is he just trying to be difficult? Sue wondered. "What was the point of being so difficult at dinner?" she said. "I mean, like it or not, one way or the other, we *are* in their power."

Lou sighed. He waved his arm in the air wearily. "Look at this place," he said, "and tell me that black science isn't deadly to the spirit!"

Sue dutifully scanned the small bedroom, with its sterile pastel blue walls, its plain steel-framed bed, its cold electrical lighting. After the loathsome dinner had ended, Arnold Harker had ushered them to these quarters, telling them that this was a temporarily vacant "standard couple apartment." This grim unromantic bedroom. A sitting room with angular metal sling chairs and couch, a bathroom with cold metal fixtures, windows that looked out over ugly gray buildings and a stark wasteland. Not even a kitchen. She tried to imagine lovers turning this impersonal place into a home, but she had to admit her imagination failed her utterly.

"So they're not the most romantic people in the world," she said. "Is that any reason to attack them openly in their own lair?"

"I wasn't attacking them. I was trying to get at the real truth."

"The truth about *what?*"

Lou put his arm around her shoulder. Sue was not exactly feeling romantic, but she didn't pull away. This was the only friend or ally she had in this alien land, and it wouldn't do to forget it, even if he was beginning to seem a little too righteous.

"Could you live here?" Lou asked rhetorically. "Could I?"

"Of course not. But what does that have to do with anything?"

"*They* can," Lou pointed out. "They do. They live their lives inside these boxes. They breathe manufactured air. They mindfuck people. They dare to use atomic power. They choose to poison their own karma. What makes them willing to live like this, Sue? What makes them willingly ignore the cost to *their own spirits* of everything they're doing? What is it that they aren't telling us?"

"They're just fanatics," Sue said. "They believe that bringing back the Age of Space justifies anything necessary to getting their spaceship launched." And for my own reasons, she thought uneasily, I'm not sure I don't agree with them. In a way, there was something almost admirable in so total a dedication to what you believed in that you were willing to sacrifice your own spiritual health to realize your dream. Of course, there was also something disgusting about it, as Arnold Harker had shown her with the touch of his flesh. The question was, was this bravery or blindness? And the answer, she realized, was precisely the mystery that Lou was pointing to. He had done it to her again. He really *was* Clear Blue.

"You mean what do *they* really expect to bring back from space that's worth all this, don't you?" she said. "I keep forgetting that my reasons aren't theirs. You're right, from their point of view, I don't see the sense. It's hard to believe they're willing to turn themselves into such cold creatures just to get to a space station and look down upon the Earth or to live in more dead places like this on other planets.''

"And yet Harker believes that *something* is going to make this sour karma taste sweet to me," Lou said, shaking his head in bewilderment. "He's so sure of it that he seems to be willing to stake the whole destiny of black science on it. And the destiny of what's left of the human race too. How can that be? What could possibly transcend this foul karma?''

Sue sighed. "I know what my answer is, I think," she said softly.

"Do you? If this is the karma of your electronic village, if these people are examples of its future citizens, then might not your dream be ultimately black?''

Sue *did* pull away from him now. "Are you telling me I'm evil?" she demanded.

"No," Lou said, reaching out for her. "But you've just told yourself that *no one thinks of themselves as evil*. No matter how evil they may look to everyone else. The Spacers can't just be wicked. That's not an explanation.''

"I see your point," Sue said, "but I wish you hadn't played perfect master with me to make it.''

Lou looked at her strangely. "I'm sorry," he said, "really I am. It's just that there's something about all this that brings out the righteously white in me. Especially since Harker seems so utterly certain that *something* is going to change my mind.''

Sue sighed. She touched his cheek and moved closer to him. "You're forgiven," she said, letting him pull her down onto the bed beside him. "Try to forget about it for tonight," she said. "Tomorrow, I have a feeling we're going to find out something that will change your mind, and I doubt either of us can do anything about it.''

"That's exactly what's bothering me," Lou said. He turned off the electric light, and they lay there for quite a while in the anonymous dark, tasting the manufactured air and listening to the faraway drone of hidden machinery before the flesh could overcome the spiritlessness of this unnatural place, which seemed to have invaded even the shared karma between them.

When they finally sought what comfort they could in each

other's bodies, their lovemaking was coldly fierce, wordless, and perhaps deliberately exhausting, at least on Lou's part.

Or so Sue thought as she lay awake long after he had fallen asleep with his head on her breast, wondering whether this man whom she had known so briefly but with whose karma she seemed so inextricably entwined would ultimately prove to be her soul mate or her judge. If no one thought of themselves as evil, then who could be sure they were good?

And might not that conceivably apply to you too, my Clear Blue lover?

The Spaceship Enterprise

"I can't believe this heat!" Clear Blue Lou moaned, mopping sweat from his brow with the back of his hand. They had been flying north for over an hour now, above a dun-colored landscape that seemed to shimmer and crack under the unrelenting sun. The heat was horrific even with all the flaps of the eagle cabin rolled up, and Lou had to admit that the electrically cooled air of Starbase One was no mere luxury in this environment; without it the human animal could not survive two days here. Assuming there was some valid reason *why* human animals had to inhabit this utterly hostile environment.

"We're just about there," Harker said. "Just over this rise."

The landscape below was subtly changing now. Dry scrub grew in big patches on a long uptilting plain like a scruffy day-old beard. To the northwest loomed the peaks of the biggest range of mountains Lou had seen yet. Bleak and hostile though this country was, Lou found a certain beauty in the vast empty spaces; a beauty not in the eye but of the spirit.

Then the eagle sailed out over the lip of a sudden precipice, and he was confronted by an unreal vista that took his breath away.

They were flying high over the southern end of a huge oval of brilliant silver glare, a deep gouge of a valley rimmed by enormous mountains like some great elongated crater. It was impossible to tell where the northern horizon met the sky, for the blinding sun reflecting off the silver-white valley floor melded sky to earth in a mirrorlike shimmer that turned the landscape into a mirage of itself.

"Good gods," Sue muttered. "It's like—"

"—another planet?" Harker suggested. "A fitting site for a spaceport, don't you think?"

"So you've got a little poetry in your soul after all, Arnold," Sue said dryly.

"It makes an ideal launch and recovery site," the Spacer told her in a strangely defensive tone. "A nice flat dry lake bed, not much wind, and no worry about rain."

"I can believe that!" Lou muttered, still blown away by the preternatural beauty of the shimmering lake of light, even as the eagle began to drop toward it pluming vile petroleum smoke. He could see how dreams of visiting other planets could form in men's minds here. Alien and inhuman but with a beauty and grandeur in its own terms, this landscape both dwarfed and exalted the spirit.

Soon they were flying low over gleaming sand and cracked expanses of gray rock toward a pimple of incongruous green in the middle of the huge dry lake bed. Swiftly this became a greenhouse dome flanked by the largest human constructions Lou had ever seen.

To the left, a squat gray rectangle similar to the habitat of Starbase One, and beside it, a long low metal shed full four times its size. To the right, an immense tent of canvas over framework that dwarfed even the giant shed.

As the eagle rounded the far end of the behemoth tent, Lou saw that the buildings were laid out in a crescent enfolding a huge open-ended yard of shimmering gray sand. At the far tip of the crescent, two hemispheres of metal were sunk into the earth. At the other end, another, larger gray dome and a small windowed shed set high on metal stilts.

In the center was—

"The spaceship *Enterprise*," Harker announced grandly. "The reason for the Company's existence."

A huge silvery bird perched on the desert floor on three short legs ending in wheeled feet. Lou could not see how it was possible for such a thing to fly. It looked as if the cabin of an "airplane" had been built seamlessly into the middle of an eagle wing instead of slung below it. But the lift wing was little more than a pair of stubs extruded out from the cabin like the fins of a fat fish. And the thing was made of metal, it must weigh tons!

Indeed, it wasn't until the black eagle had landed close by the spaceship that Lou fully realized just how big the thing really was. Climbing out of the cabin for a closer took, he felt dwarfed by the man-made monster that towered above him; a bird of metal almost two hundred feet long, with a torso thick as the biggest redwood tree and windows for eyes set back over a bulbous beak. The wings, which had seemed like stubs from the air, were revealed from this perspective as far larger than those of any Spacer "airplane."

"You expect *this* to fly?" Lou asked incredulously.

Harker laughed. "Would you like a closer look?" he said proudly.

But Lou was already walking toward the spaceship, eyes drawn up to it in wonder. The *Enterprise* was formed of plates of silvery metal hammered into subtle curves and held together in a smooth skin by thousands of flathead rivets. Two huge coppery horns jutted out of the blunt stern like the bells of giants' trumpets. Workers crawled all over the spaceship, hammering rivets into sections where the missing metal skin revealed an equally metallic skeleton.

"A few more sections of hull to finish, install the rest of the electronics, and she's ready to fly," Harker said, coming up behind them.

"How can this thing possibly fly?" Sue asked, mirroring Lou's thought.

"I'll show you," Harker said, and he led them around to the great trumpets at the rear, each as wide as Lou was tall.

"These are the rocket engines," he said. "Each develops about a quarter of a million pounds of thrust. Together, they boost the spaceship to orbital velocity—two hundred miles above the Earth at eighteen thousand miles an hour!"

The numbers were meaningless magic as far as Lou was concerned. "And what does it burn to do all that?" he asked sharply. "A billion gallons of petroleum?"

"It burns water," Harker said slyly.

"Water? It *burns* water?"

"Actually it burns hydrogen and oxygen extracted from water," Harker said. "Or you could say the rockets really run on electricity. We pass a current through water, which separates the fluid into hydrogen and oxygen gas, which we compress to liquids and then recombine in the engines, where it releases the electrical energy stored in it as it burns back to water." He smiled fatuously at Lou. "Could you ask for anything whiter?"

"Why that's marvelous!" Sue exclaimed. "White science out of black!"

"And where does all this electricity come from?" Lou asked more dubiously.

"From a nuclear reactor," Harker admitted.

"I thought so."

"And you're sure this thing will work?" Sue asked, apparently hardly taken aback at all by this grim revelation. "I mean, you haven't flown it, it's not even finished yet. . . ."

"The Company preserved many of the plans for the original *Enterprise*, a space shuttle that *did* fly before the Smash," Harker said. "This is as close a replica of the first *Enterprise* as we could build, and it *will* boost into orbit, I assure you. But let's have a look inside."

The sorcerer led them up a metal ladder leading to an open hatch below the windows.

Instead of the expected spacious cabin, Lou found himse'f inside a cramped cubicle no bigger than a second-rate roon in a middle-grade inn. Three high-backed couches faced ou the windows before a bewildering complexity of controls and switches and dials, surrounded by a maze of consoles and tubing and half-finished electronic apparatus. On the wall behind the couches hung three strange suits, bulky and silvery, with glass-faced helmets that covered the whole head. The rest of the space was crammed with cannisters, piping, electronic gear, and metal cabinets. The cubicle was no more than ten feet long. There was a solid wall separating it from the rest of the spaceship and no door in it.

"How do you get to the rest of the cabin?" Sue asked Harker.

"There isn't any," Harker said. "This is the entire crew module."

"Then what's in the rest of this thing?"

"A ten-day supply of oxygen, food, and water. The recovery eagle. But mostly fuel tanks."

"Recovery eagle?"

"On the way back from space, the *Enterprise* re-enters the atmosphere as a hypersonic glider," Harker said. "Using the wings and drogue parachutes, it slows to a falling speed low enough to deploy a large helium eagle to fly it to the ground."

"That must be *some* eagle wing!" Lou exclaimed. He tried to picture a lift wing big enough to fly the weight of the spaceship, but his imagination failed him utterly.

"It's large enough, but not anywhere near as large as the launch eagle," Harker said. "Most of the launch weight is fuel, so the ship isn't nearly as heavy with the tanks empty."

He crawled out the hatch and began descending the ladder. "Now let me show you the launch eagle," he said. "The biggest thing that will ever fly through the air of this planet."

Harker led them toward the huge tent that dwarfed even the spaceship, a cliff of canvas a hundred feet high and ten times as long. He opened a small flap in the side and ushered them into an immense cavern of cloth, a cooler, darker space whose contrast with the bright sunlight outside momentarily blinded Lou's vision. When it cleared an instant later and he saw what he was seeing, he gasped and goggled, and it took him yet another moment to truly believe what he saw.

Lit by electric globes scattered like fireflies all through it, the interior of the tent was a vast angular forest of metal scaffolding. Taking form in the scaffolding was a half-finished wing that dazzled credibility with its sheer size. Fifty feet thick and a thousand feet from tip to tip, the wing was a spindly metal skeleton half-covered with a thin translucent skin like animal gut, which hordes of workers were even now stitching together over it. Like a gigantic half-skinned bird it sat there, dwarfing the craftsmen who swarmed over its surface like carrion beetles.

"*That thing is going to fly?*" Sue gasped.

"Of course it will fly," Harker said. "When we fill it with helium, it'll have enough lift to take the *Enterprise* to 20,000 feet. It drops the spaceship, the *Enterprise* boosts into orbit, and the launch eagle flies home. Every module in the system is recoverable and fully reusable."

It still all seemed improbable to Lou, experienced eagle

freak that he was. Even if it *would* fly, how could you *maneuver* an eagle the size of a small mountain? "But the wind currents, keeping any kind of course with a wing that size . . ."

Harker gave him a superior smile. "No problem," he said. "The launch eagle will be powered by six jet engines—"

"*Jet engines?*"

"Like the rockets, except they burn petroleum and use the oxygen in the air for oxidizer. High thrust for low weight. Enough power to maneuver the launch eagle with ease in reasonably decent weather."

Lou shook his head. "You've got it all figured out, don't you?" he said. "In your heads. But where are you going to find someone crazy enough to actually fly the thing?"

Harker's spine seemed to stiffen and he fairly glowed with pride. "*I* am to be the command pilot of the spaceship *Enterprise*," he said. "You people are so concerned with spirit —but how dead would a soul have to be to pass up an opportunity like that out of cowardice? I'm not afraid, and we'll have no trouble getting the other two crew members either."

Lou regarded the Spacer with a certain grudging new respect, and he could see a similar expression dawning on Sue's face. He had to respect the courage of a man who, whatever his other flaws, dared something he was not sure he himself would care to risk. But—

"Wait a minute!" Lou exclaimed. "*Two* other crewmen? A spaceship the size of a house, a launch eagle the size of a mountain, fifty years to build them, three thousand people forced to live in boxes in the middle of a deadly desert, millions of gallons of petroleum burned in the atmosphere— all to take *three* people to a space station? For *how* long?"

"A three-man, ten-day mission," Harker said defensively, much of the air going out of his sails. "It's the best we could do. . . ."

"You people *are* crazy!" Lou exclaimed. He was stunned by the insane disproportion of it all. Generations of madmen dedicating their lives to this monstrous project, pumping poison into the atmosphere for centuries, blackening their souls with the ultimate horror of atomic power—a whole little world, a whole history, a secret hidden nation, whose only reason for existence was the useless symbolic gesture of putting three people into space for ten days!

"Well *I* don't think it's crazy," Sue said, glaring at Lou. "It's good enough to get the broadcast satellite network turned on, isn't it?"

Lou looked at her in amazement. "Have *you* lost all sense of proportion too?" he said. "How many people have already died down through the generations because of the poison that's been pumped into the air in the service of this useless project? How many more will die? And what if one of those nuclear reactors *does* explode? *And for what?* To shoot three people into space for ten days and bring them back? I find Space Systems Incorporated guilty of monstrous shitheadedness above and beyond the call! Justice demands the total disbandment of your miserable tribe and the destruction of all your evil works!"

"Now who's being shitheaded?" Sue snapped. "Think of all the effort that's gone into this, Lou, think of what's waiting for us up there! Just because ten days is all—"

"It's all right, Sue," Harker said with infuriating icy calm. "This reaction was anticipated in the scenario." He turned to Lou, and now his cold eyes seemed to glow as if picking up vibes of power from the monstrous skeletal bird towering above them. "It's necessary that you appreciate the magnitude of the task and how far we're willing to go to complete it. For only now can you begin to understand the worth of the trade-off. Only now will your parochial mind be ready to encompass the most important event in the history of the planet."

The sorcerer seemed to become intoxicated by his own words; his eyes grew feverish with unwholesome fanaticism. "Imagine something that transcends all you know and believe," he said softly. "Something to which the entire evolutionary history of life on Earth is but a preamble. Something that utterly transcends the law of muscle, sun, wind and water, that transcends your Clear Blue Way, that transcends the Great Way itself. Something that in fact transcends all previous human experience."

Despite himself, Lou felt almost mesmerized by the sheer intensity of Harker's vibes, the utter insane certainty of his voice. Sue seemed to forget her anger at him to huddle closer against the sheer fervor of this psychic onslaught. At this moment, fired by his own madness, in the shadow of the huge construction which that madness had manifested into reality, Arnold Harker seemed a sorcerer indeed.

"The only thing that transcends ultimate sanity is ultimate insanity," Lou pontificated, his words sounding hollow to him even as he said them. For he couldn't escape the vertiginous feeling that he was about to be proven wrong.

"So you think thát the human mind contains ultimate sanity, do you?" Harker said in a sardonic near whisper. "Well, come with me and learn something that will change your concept of what is ultimate forever."

He began leading them out of the great tent. "Now you will learn the deepest and most wonderful secret of what you call black science. Now you will join us of your own free will. Now the world will change for you forever."

"You really do believe that, don't you?" Lou said as they stepped out into the glaring hot sunlight.

"Believe it?" Harker answered. "I *know* it. Come with me and put your world behind you."

Songs from
the Stars

Reeling from the heat of the short walk to the habitat building, reeling too from the adrenaline backlash of her abortive fight with Lou, Sunshine Sue was too grateful for the cool air inside to think much about the energy units her ease was costing, and she was too curious about Arnold Harker's promised cosmic secret to think much about justice or righteous whiteness either.

Harker led them down a long gallery similar to the one in the Starbase One habitat, but here there was just a series of big, secretive closed doors. What few Spacers were in evidence seemed to be rushing from place to place with preternatural intensity and purpose. There was an exciting psychic charge in the chemically tanged air unlike anything Sue had previously experienced.

They took a cablelift to an upper floor in silence, and Harker didn't speak again until they were walking down a long branching hallway. "The space station we're going to is called the Big Ear," he said. "It had a specific mission and just as the first Age of Space was tearing itself to pieces, that mission was successful. Then the bombs fell, and the

Age of Space died, and the Big Ear was cut off from resupply or rescue. The world destroyed itself on the brink of true history, and for centuries we've been crawling in the dirt instead of listening to the stars.''

Harker opened a door and led them into a small room dominated by a strange metal console topped by a rounded square of pale gray-green glass.

"The Big Ear was listening for signals from beings living on planets of other stars,'' the sorcerer said in a voice deliberately pregnant with drama. "Thinking creatures like ourselves so far away that their transmissions could take centuries to reach us traveling at the speed of light itself. Creatures thousands or millions of years older and wiser than us. Beings as far above us as we are above a frog.''

He moved over to the console and began doing things to the controls. "This is a television monitor,'' he said. "A device for reproducing pictures broadcast like radio or recorded as electromagnetic patterns on tape. What you are about to see was recorded centuries ago by the Big Ear and retransmitted to the Company just before our species smashed itself into the dust and left them there to die in space. It was broadcast centuries before that by unknown beings on a planet circling a star so far from here that those who finally received it were not yet born when it began its immense journey through time and space. Songs from the stars to us poor earthbound creatures—the knowledge of a million years of science, if only we can listen and understand.''

Suddenly, incredibly, the plate of pale gray-green glass became a wondrous window into a strange miniature world. Tiny feathery creatures of pale lavender floated around a spire of amber crystal.

And then Sue heard the song.

It was like the piping of many metal insects whistling random patterns composed of four pure tones, idiot music without tune or chord. It was the most moronic music Sue had ever heard; it bounced her ear around with nothing to cling to in a way that made her head reel. And yet something about it captured her soul.

"What is it? What are those creatures?''

"We don't know,'' Harker admitted. "Only a small portion of what the Big Ear recorded was ever transmitted to

Earth, and all that's survived are these few pitiful fragments.''

The view through the magic window suddenly changed—scintillating specks of multicolored snow seemed to flicker on and off in synchronization with the bizarre tuneless music. When the next picture appeared, Sue realized what she was seeing—not a window into a miniature world, but a reduced-scale moving picture of something huge.

Deep green canyons and rolling red hills under a wrong-looking sky the color of green grapes fleeced with purplish clouds. Above this strange country floated . . . *what*? A huge disc of burnished copper with a forest of multicolored crystal spires growing out of its upper surface. Were they *buildings*? Was it some kind of *flying town*?

Then the scene dissolved into colored snow again. A moment later, an interlocked double helix appeared, like two red worms copulating. Thinner lines of black, white, lavender and blue formed a spiderweb of light connecting the two lines of the double spiral.

More multicolored snow. What looked like a living world turning slowly in starry blackness. More scintillating sparkles. Another world, this one circled by three concentric pale white rings. An endless string of emeralds spiraled up from the surface at great speed, and then the first jewel on this invisible string flashed by—a glowing green cylinder with wings and windows along its length.

Another confetti blizzard. Creatures like blue mushrooms with bright red eyes dancing a pavanne with hairy brown trees. A great cliff of yellow ice splintering and crashing down into a deep blue sea. The head of a yellow bird with one huge and horribly human-looking eye. A bright red cube whirling in space about its diagonal axis. A string of beads or planets rotating around a black vortex that sucked at the eyes.

And all the while, the strange song from the stars whistled its random beeps in Sue's brain, pattern and meaning seeming to flit teasingly just beyond the grasp of her awareness.

A song from the stars . . . she thought in wonder. A message from thinking creatures that aren't human. She tried to sync herself into the inhuman music, hoping that a clue to its meaning might be found, but it was impossible either to find a pattern or quite believe there was none.

"It doesn't seem like music at all. . . ." she muttered.

"We don't think it *is* music," Harker said. "More like some kind of code we haven't been able to solve. . . ."

Then the sound suddenly stopped, and the window to the stars once more was just a plate of pale gray-green glass.

Harker sighed. "All we have are these poor few fragments," he said. "But up there on the Big Ear are many more recordings and the means with which to listen for more. Would these star beings send messages to us over trillions of miles and centuries of time if they were not meant to teach us secrets beyond our present comprehension? They *can't* be meaningless! Up there beyond the sky, beings a million years wiser than us are trying to speak to us. Beings who can teach us. Who can heal us. Who can show us the way to a new Age of Space far surpassing that which the stupidity of our ancestors destroyed."

The sorcerer's voice hardened, and his eyes challenged the perfect master of the Clear Blue Way. "Isn't *that* worth breaking any petty law of men for?" he said. "Isn't it worth any risk or danger? Does it not transcend our very concept of humanity itself? Will you not willingly help us now? Can you dismiss *this* as sorcery and turn your back on the *Galactic* Way?"

Sue watched Lou staring back at Harker and wondered what he would decide, wondered if this moment would bring the parting of their ways.

For in her heart of hearts, she knew that for *her* there was no turning back now. At the core of sorcery *did* lay something which transcended all that the world thought it knew of black or white, good or evil, right or wrong. Atomic power, black science, petroleum, the law of muscle, sun, wind and water, cancer, pollution, death and destruction, the Great Way itself—how petty all the things of men seemed in the face of this incredible unknown. How irrelevant. How small and dim.

Even her cherished global electronic village paled into nothingness when confronted by this broadcast from the stars. She had thought that a *world* culture linked by an electronic network would bring about a higher state of human consciousness? Must not these songs from the stars be part of some network linking beings of *many* worlds? The level of consciousness *that* implied quite literally dwarfed any human conception. No spiritually alive soul could resist that siren song. Least of all Sunshine Sue.

Even less, she hoped, the perfect master of the Clear Blue Way.

Lou's eyes slowly narrowed. His expression softened. He shrugged almost imperceptibly. He sighed. "You win," he told Harker softly. "Let's go somewhere and talk."

The tension whooshed out of Sue in an audible sigh. And so do I win, she thought, taking Lou's hand. We're still in this together. All the way to the stars.

Clear Blue Lou had kept his thoughts to himself until they reached the spaceport's greenhouse dome, where, he had hoped, the Way would seem clearer amidst growing things within sight of the sky. But this environment only seemed to epitomize the karmic paradox at the heart of black science. Here grew not a monoculture of corn but long rows of mixed vegetables spreading their leafy arms to catch the life-giving sun, an ecosphere in miniature, an experiment in artificial self-sufficiency, a dry run for the food supply of some future city in space, or so Harker told them, a piece of the natural world under glass. But these growing things were rooted not in the natural soil of the earth but in vats of chemicals crafted by the mind of man. They were separated from the true sky by glass and aluminum and the air was cooled by atomic power. Beyond the glass ceiling, he could see the sky, and beyond the sky lay hidden worlds beyond human comprehension.

Like the Spacers themselves, this garden was walled off from the natural world in a howling desert. Like the Spacers, wrongness here seemed somehow to serve an ultimate good. Knowledge wrought wonders, but its spirit seemed dead. This sterile indoor garden was emblematic of the sourness of black science's karma as manifested in the lives of the sorcerers themselves. Yet every instinct told him that the knowledge they sought was good. How could this be? How could the knowledge of beings a million years wiser than men fail to enhance the human spirit?

Unless, he thought somberly, the human spirit is truly unworthy. We certainly proved ourselves unworthy the first time we had this karmic opportunity, poisoning our planet on the brink of a great new age! If we confront higher beings now riding another wave of bad karma and shitty vibes, might we not get what we deserve the second time around too?

But if we refuse the challenge of cosmic knowledge, will we not have judged ourselves unworthy before the fact?

"True justice can never flow from willful ignorance," he finally said, just as Sue was beginning to regard him a bit peculiarly. "Least of all from willful ignorance of the Way of beings greater than ourselves."

The tension broke. Sue moved closer to him. Harker seemed to visibly relax. "Then you'll help us?" he said. "You'll make your people understand?"

Make my people understand? Lou thought sardonically. *What I don't understand myself?* "I'll speak my justice now," he said carefully, "and I'll live by it if you will."

"I'm ready to listen," Harker said just as carefully, and Lou wondered whether Space Systems Incorporated was really willing to abide by justice other than that which they assumed their scenarios had created.

"Then hear my justice," he said. "You're right, we *must* listen to the songs from the stars, the *Enterprise* must be launched. Knowing that superior beings are broadcasting to us, we would only deny inevitable destiny by shutting our ears. It would be a suicide of the spirit. So I will serve this cause however I can."

Harker broke into a wide smile and offered his hand, but Lou held up an admonishing finger. "However," he said, "while whatever evil that's already been done cannot be undone, from here on in, Operation Enterprise must remain within the Way."

"What does that mean?" Harker asked, eyeing Lou suspiciously.

"It means that the spaceship must be launched and returned to Earth within the law of muscle, sun, wind and water," Lou told him. "No jet engines on the launch or recovery eagles. No burning of petroleum. Only the sun may be used to power the eagles."

"You don't know what you're saying!" Harker exclaimed. "It would reduce the reliability of the system by half! It would double the danger!"

"I know exactly what I'm saying," Lou told him sharply. "But if we can't confront the beings of the stars with clean karma, we'll be as unworthy as the sorcerers of the Smash were, and we'd deserve to suffer their fate. We must risk as much danger to reach your Big Ear within the Way as you have made the world risk with your atomic power and petroleum. Justice demands it on more levels than one."

"Easy enough for you to spout such moralistic drivel!" Harker snapped. "But *I* have to fly the *Enterprise*, it'd be *my* life you'd be risking for the sake of your righteous whiteness, not your own!"

"Oh, we'll be going with you," Lou said airily. He hadn't exactly planned to say it, but as soon as he did, it seemed utterly foreordained all along.

"WHAT?" Harker shouted.

Sue's eyes widened for an instant, but it was merely a reflex gesture. "Right!" she said, grasping Lou's hand with a self-satisfied grin. "You dragged us into this and now you're stuck with us."

"You're serious?" Harker said incredulously. "Three days ago I was a sorcerer and you were superstitious Aquarian primitives, and now you're ready to go into space!"

"You underestimate Aquaria and you overestimate yourselves!" Lou snapped. He had had just about enough of this superior attitude. "You really think you're fitter to understand superior beings that we are? You know a few evil things that we don't and you're ready to use them, but I'm not exactly awed by your wisdom or envious of your karma. Superior beings must be in harmony with the Way, a harmony deeper than my own, and certainly deeper than *yours*. Otherwise, they wouldn't be so superior."

"You really so sure about that, Lou?" Sue asked somewhat dubiously. "Couldn't they be smarter than we are without being wiser? Couldn't they be geniuses of evil?"

"That doesn't feel right," Lou told her. "But if it should turn out to be true, then don't you think they should be judged by a perfect master, not a sorcerer? You can't judge the sweetness of celestial music with a morally deaf ear."

"*Now* who's being arrogant?" Harker said grimly.

Lou sighed. He stared at Harker, trying to reach the human brother that surely must exist behind the cold sorcerer's eyes. "Look," he said, "you went to a lot of trouble to convince me to walk your path, and you asked for my justice on it. Well, how can I speak justice truly until I've followed that path to the end?"

"You're really willing to do it?" Harker said more softly.

"You're willing to trust your life to our machineries to listen to the songs from the stars?"

"Aren't *you*?" Sue said.

"You too? And you're willing to make the risk that much greater to satisfy your criteria of righteous whiteness?"

"Lou's followed *my* way this far," Sue said, "and I'm willing to follow his the rest of the way. We're in this together. The three of us, like it or not."

"If we're willing to trust our lives to your science, then what does it make you if you don't have the courage to trust *your* fate to my justice?" Lou asked the Spacer. "We dare what you dare. Aren't you man enough to dare what *we* dare?"

Arnold Harker sighed. Somehow, in this moment, he seemed small and sad, diminished in spirit. How stunted was a soul that could not envision in others a spirit as daring as his own! How chastened when confronted with the reality.

Harker paused, as if pondering his decision, but Lou sensed that it was an empty gesture. For the sorcerer himself was now a captive of his own scenario, the scenario that had brought the three of them to this fateful nexus. Perhaps it had never been *his* scenario after all but fate's scenario, the inevitable destiny of the three of them, written in the stars.

"Very well," Harker said sharply, as if pretending that the logic of his own will had delivered up its decision, "perhaps it was meant to be. We will honor our promise to accept your justice." His expression narrowed and he regarded the two of them shrewdly. "Provided you fulfill your end of the bargain."

"*Bargain*?" Lou snapped. "You don't *bargain* with justice."

"Call it a necessary task then," Harker said. "What would happen if your people learned that black science was launching a spaceship to reach a pre-Smash space station to talk to beings from the stars?"

Lou shuddered. "There'd be a jihad," he said. "All the Rememberer pogroms rolled into one and set aflame. The spaceship will have to be launched in secret, much as I—"

"And when it returns?" Harker snapped. "Would you have us keep that secret from Aquaria too?"

Lou fell silent. He had nothing to say to *that*!

"Maybe you underestimate us too," Harker said almost imploringly. "We don't seek secret knowledge from the stars to enhance our own power. Far from it, we seek knowledge with which to heal our whole planet and raise our fallen species from the dust. So what we bring back from the Big Ear must be shared and accepted by all or it will be useless." He shook his head sadly. "Will your people accept the whiteness of science brought back in secret by sorcery? Will they even believe that it came from the stars?"

"They'll believe my justice when I speak it. . . ." Lou said without much confidence.

"*Really*? When you reveal that you've secretly flown into space with sorcerers? Now perhaps you overestimate yourself. . . ."

Lou sighed. "So what are you asking me to do?" he asked quietly.

"Harmonize Operation Enterprise with the Way in the eyes of your people as the scenario calls for," Harker said.

"You don't ask too much, do you?" Lou said dryly. "Does your scenario tell you how I'm supposed to do it?" He shrugged. "I just don't see how it's possible to remove the odor of sorcery from Operation Enterprise before the spaceship returns, and even then—"

"But *I* do," Sue suddenly said. Lou saw that she had a strange faraway look in her eyes. But there was nothing dreamy about it at all; a sardonic pucker twisted her lips, and the vibes she was giving off were down and dirty.

"What if Aquaria believed that the *Enterprise* itself came from the stars?" she said slowly. "What if superior beings from space landed in La Mirage?"

"Huh?" Lou goggled at her. "What are you talking about?" he said. "That just isn't going to happen."

Sue laughed. "Unless we *make it* happen, love," she said.

Harker looked at her most peculiarly. "And you call *us* sorcerers?" he said. "You're going to convince your people that the *Enterprise* comes from the stars? What kind of . . . *sorcery* is that?"

"*My* kind, Arnold," Sue said smugly. "A long-lost software science of the ancients called 'media hype.' By this art, the networks were able to create unreal events called 'happenings' more cogent than reality itself. I've never tried it before, but I think I can make it work."

Lou eyed her narrowly, with a sardonic uneasy awe not entirely untinged with a certain sincerity. For she had reminded him that she did in fact possess a kind of lore beyond his knowledge, that together they had walked beyond the parameters of the Clear Blue Way and into the karmically clouded unknown. Perhaps it was her turn to lead and his turn to follow. Certainly *he* saw no clear path through this part of the woods.

He grimaced owlishly at her with a little shrug. "You're the sorcerer now, lady," he said.

Deus ex
Machina

"From the time the rockets fire till we make orbit, the pre-programmed onboard computer flies her," Arnold Harker said, patting the console between their acceleration couches. "It takes over again on the way back as soon as we clear the Ear and key up the re-entry program."

Sitting in the cabin of the *Enterprise* amidst all the electronic arcana, Clear Blue Lou regarded this latest wonder dubiously. "You're telling me that this thing *flies itself*?"

"We're talking about reaction times measured in fractions of a second and speeds measured in thousands of miles an hour," the sorcerer said. "No human has reaction times like that. Of course the launch and recovery eagles have to be flown manually because—"

"Because no machine can feel the wind and the sun and the air and use them with the spirit of a bird."

"You *would* put it that way," Harker said sourly.

It had been Harker who had first suggested that it would be a good idea for Lou to learn enough to serve as back-up pilot, in case of need, and Lou who had been somewhat daunted by the idea that he might learn enough sorcery to

155

master black science's most advanced piece of wizardry. But now that Lou had learned enough to comprehend what he was shown in his own terms and speak his mind on the sorcerer's world as a perfect master and a natural man, the Spacer was getting a bit testy. And taking orders from Sue hadn't helped his disposition much either.

"The launch eagle will be flown by its own pilot in a small pod so that it can be returned to the spaceport after it drops the *Enterprise*," Harker continued, after Lou refused to rise to the bait. He fingered a series of small levers arranged in easy hand's reach of each other. "These are the recovery eagle wing controls for steering and warpage. Each one is the electronic equivalent of the corresponding control line on an ordinary solar eagle, so you'd have no trouble flying *that* if you had to."

He frowned. "In fact, since you're forcing us to use solar propellers, you could probably fly the damn thing at least as well as I can," he said.

Lou nodded but refrained from making another Clear Blue remark. In fact, he was finding that it took less skill to master black science than white, once you shoved moral considerations out of the picture. Instead of yanking control lines with both hands and some muscle as with a solar eagle, you did the same thing with the fingers of one hand through the muscle-magnifying magic of electricity. Instead of pedaling like a son of a bitch to kill lift, you simply threw a switch and let an electric compressor do all the work. Yeah, he thought, I'm sure I could fly the recovery eagle as well as you can.

"You could even fly the *Enterprise* back for orbit if you had to," Harker told him, poising his finger above a button on the computer console. "Just hit this button and call up the preprogrammed re-entry sequence. The computer will set the attitude, wait for the launch window, fire the rockets, control the hypersonic glide, deploy the drogues, and then pop the recovery eagle. That's all there is to it."

"Got it," Lou said briskly. "What about maneuvering in space itself?"

Harker regarded him dubiously. "Getting a little ambitious, aren't you?" he said.

Lou shrugged. "I'm probably never going to have to do any of this," he said. "But if I'm going to be gray enough to trust my fate to your machine, I might as well be gray enough to know how it works."

Harker scowled, but then he shrugged and proceeded to show Lou the space maneuvering system. Once in orbit, you turned on something called the acquisition radar, then called up another program on the computer, and the *Enterprise* flew itself to the target. For close maneuvering, there was a set of levers that fired short bursts on steering rockets. You used them to point the nose where you wanted to go and then gave the main rockets a short burst.

"It's really not as hard as it sounds," Harker concluded.

"Seems easy enough to me," Lou said, "with a machine doing your thinking for you."

"Computers don't—"

"I know, I know, computers don't think!" Lou interrupted, not wanting to hear that lecture again. Harker had explained it to him often enough already. Computers didn't think, they just stored the thoughts of men as "programs" to be released as needed. But from the point of view of the pilot, the dead machine *did* function like a living mind. In some ways, this was the most arcane sorcery of all, more mysterious and amazing than atomic power, or manufactured air, or indeed the spaceship itself.

The machineries of sorcery were relatively easy to master, but the spirit of them remained elusive. Indeed, they almost seemed deliberately crafted to be used without psychic connection, as if on some level beyond their own understanding, the Spacers feared psychic contamination by too intimate a relationship between the natural man and their magicks. Aside from the wound to his ego, perhaps the reverse of this was why working with Sue on *her* magic so troubled Arnold Harker. For she was using machineries she didn't understand to craft something psychic beyond the black scientist's comprehension.

And for that matter, perhaps beyond mine, Lou admitted to himself.

A male Spacer poked his head into the open hatch behind them. "Sunshine Sue wants to see you in her media shop," he told Harker. "She says it's important."

Harker seemed to draw in on himself. "All right, all right," he said petulantly, "I'll be right there." He climbed out of his acceleration couch and led Lou out the hatch into the searing desert sun. He paused at the bottom of the ladder as Lou descended, staring up at the bulk of the spaceship and shaking his head.

"Do *you* really understand what she's doing?" he said sourly.

Craftsmen were crawling all over the *Enterprise* with brushes and paint. Half the body of the spaceship and one whole wing were already a bright Sunshine yellow. Other craftsmen were installing banks of electric lights on the lower surfaces of the wings.

Lou shrugged. "She's explained as much of it to you as she has to me," he said.

The *Enterprise* and the launch eagle, made glorious and mysterious by all this strange stagecraft, would appear in the sky as the fulfillment of Sue's own self-created prophecy and summon men to listen to the stars with trumpets of heavenly glory. They would ride into space not in an evil portent of black science but in a chariot of Sunshine Yellow borne by a Clear Blue eagle, on a wave of good karma.

This would be the "happening"—good karma crafted out of bad by the science of "media hype." How the illusion would be brought about, Lou was beginning to understand. But the color of Sue's magic was harder for him to fathom. By convincing people that bad karma was good, it would seem that she would create good karma itself, or so she claimed. But how could sour karma be sweetened by a lie? It seemed both possible and impossible at the same time.

Harker eyed him suspiciously. "But you two are . . . lovers," he said. "And you're a perfect master, you're supposed to be an expert on the things of the spirit. You're telling me that this 'media hype' is beyond your understanding?"

Lou laughed. "It's sorcery to me," he said, shrugging.

Harker shook his head ruefully. "It may be sorcery to you," he said, "but it's certainly not science to me."

Lou smiled at him fatuously. "Maybe her scenario is behavioristic," he suggested wryly. "How does it feel to be on the receiving end for a change?"

Things are really rolling along, Sunshine Sue thought, as she waited impatiently for Arnold Harker to show up at the media shop she had set up on the second floor of the habitat. They were moving *almost* fast enough, thanks to the wonders of black science and the efficiency of the assistants she had been given. But she was anxious to get things over with here and get back to La Mirage for the *real* fun.

Although her Spacer workers were intelligent and efficient and conditioned to do what they were told without asking questions and although Spacer technology was allowing her to craft a happening far beyond her original conception, Sue had no desire to linger longer in Spacer country than necessity required.

For one thing, she was itching to try her hand at the untested art of media hype, for which all this was only preparation. And for another, only the excitement of the task at hand kept this place from driving her crazy.

Breathing the manufactured air was giving her a continuous funny taste in her mouth, and she seemed forever on the brink of a cold. And although she was repeatedly assured that all the cow meat she was served was clean and pure, her appetite just wouldn't believe it.

Of necessity she was spending more time with Harker and the Spacers than with Lou, and she could sense a certain unwholesome triangular tension building up. Old Arnold knew enough to keep his personal distance, or perhaps more accurately, she knew enough to keep him well at bay, now that *he* was being forced to follow *her* scenario. Which was not to say that he liked being mindfucked any more than she had or that she wasn't taking a certain nasty pleasure in paying him back.

But Lou was spending a lot of time with Harker too, learning to fly the spaceship and sticking his nose into all the mechanical arcana he could. Perfect master though he was, he really couldn't understand what she was doing any better than Harker could, and it seemed to Sue that he was compensating for this by attempting to become adept at arts *she* didn't have time to learn under the tutelage of the Spacer. There was something unsettlingly circular about this daisy chain of dominance relationships that might not bode well when the three of them were stuck in space together for ten days, and she was anxious to remove Lou and herself from the unwholesome spirit of this place. The fact that she could not help *enjoying* the numbers she was running on Arnold made her a bit uneasy about her own karmic purity too.

Yes, while there might be worlds more to learn by staying around here, there were sweeter worlds to regain, and she was glad that her presence at the spaceport would soon no longer be needed.

Coloring the *Enterprise* Sunshine Yellow was a simple

matter of paint and brushes, but the Spacer craftsmen had moaned in dismay when she told them that the launch eagle had to be Clear Blue Lou blue. It was impossible, they had insisted, they'd have to recover the entire framework, it would take months.

That one had been solved when Sue pointed out that all they had to do was put powerful electric lights shining through glass of the proper blueness inside the translucent wing.

Once she had gotten the Spacer technicians playing with colored lights, they came up with all sorts of lighting arcana as if to prove the puissancy of black science to her—colors of any hue she desired, lights that changed colors continuously by revolving panes of different colored glass before them with electric motors, even a magic device called a stroboscope, which emitted short sharp bursts of brilliant light that made people seem to move like jerky marionettes and did something really weird and unsettling to vision's vibes.

With this palette to play with, Sue had designed a complex show of lights to illumine the spaceship and its eagle that would probably convince *her* that they were the products of superior beings from the stars if she hadn't designed the illusion herself.

And when Spacer craftsmen showed her how they produced the eerie background music that pervaded so many areas of their installations, her concept for the happening expanded far beyond her initial expectations. They could record sound on tape and play it back through a device like a radio. But they weren't technically limited to the quiet bland stuff they seemed to esthetically favor. If they wanted to, they could make even the human voice come out louder than a brass horn band. Celestial music would accompany the advent from the stars, and the star being would speak with a voice of thunder.

All of this was already being crafted and installed. Now all that remained was to convince Arnold Harker to become a god from the stars. His natural arrogance working off the chastening his ego had been taking lately as she remade his beloved Operation Enterprise to her own design should take care of that. The beard . . . well, that might be a different matter!

Harker finally arrived a few minutes later, just as Sue was getting impatient enough to treat him like a tardy member of the Sunshine Tribe. "Well, you took your time getting here," she snapped by way of greeting.

Harker glanced owlishly about the small room. A bizarre silvery costume hung in one corner. There was a sink table with a mirror, pots of theatrical makeup, a razor and shaving soap. A weird metal collar lay half completed on a workbench strewn with small electric lights and electronic components. It looked something like a thin horse collar scaled down for a man, and its inner surface was studded with small electric lights and radio microphones. Harker's eyes were caught by it.

"What's that?" he said, looking as if he should be scratching his head. "What now?"

"Relax, Arnold, you'll love it," Sue drawled. "I'm going to make you what the networks used to call a 'star.' "

Arnold squinted uneasily at her. Since the tables had been turned, he had developed a wary attitude toward her. No doubt he knew she was getting even. But there wasn't very much he could do about it.

"We're going to turn you into a god from the stars," she said dryly by way of explanation.

"You're going to *what*?"

"You'll wear that costume over there," Sue said. "And you'll wear *this* under the collar." She picked up the metal ring and handed it to Harker. The sorcerer pawed it over uncomprehendingly. Sue smiled. That's right, Arnold, she thought, I've had your craftsmen make a piece of hardware you don't understand. And as for the software . . .

"See all the electric lights inside the collar?" she said. "They'll illumine your face very dramatically, there's even one that's stroboscopic. And the microphones will play your voice back through big speakers mounted on the spaceship. You'll look like a god from the stars and you'll sound like one too."

Harker eyed her most peculiarly. "You're going to make your people think I'm an advanced being from the stars?"

"Right!" Sue said. "You should enjoy the role."

"Like an actor in a play . . .?" Harker mused. It seemed to be beginning to appeal to him.

"The leading role," Sue said. "The best part."

"But this isn't a play, it's . . . it's . . ."

"A happening," Sue said. "A media hype. A fictional story presented as reality, a play in the form of news."

Harker shook his head in wonder. "Reality and yet not reality," he muttered. "A real event in the eyes of all who see it, yet crafted by you like a stage play. . . ."

"Now you're getting it," Sue said. "The ancients called it 'managed news,' I think. Sweet karma crafted out of sour, reality enhanced by art. With *you* as the star, Arnold; I know you can handle it."

Harker shrugged resignedly. "Well, if it's absolutely necessary. . . ."

Sue smiled sweetly at him. "There's just one thing Arnold," she said. "The beard has to go. You'll have to shave it off."

"*My beard*!" Harker cried, clutching at his face defensively. "Now you taunt me too far!"

Sue went over to the sink and began lathering up the shaving soap. "Be reasonable, Arnold," she said. "We have to make up your face, after all. Maybe blue skin flecked with gold and red teeth and a jewel glowing in your forehead like a third eye. You'll be magnificent. But we have to get rid of the beard first." Sadistically, she began stropping the razor. "I'll do it for you, if you like," she offered.

"You're not going to shave off my beard!" Arnold shouted.

Sue shrugged. "Then do it yourself," she said, handing him the razor. "But it *has* to be done. Surely you're not going to let personal vanity stand in the way of the greatest event in human history. . . ."

Harker glared at her. Sue glared back. He caved. "My beard . . .?" he whined plaintively.

"Your beard, Arnold."

The sorcerer sighed in surrender. He went to the sink, lathered up his face, and, muttering under his breath, made his personal sacrifice for the higher good.

Sue regarded the new Arnold Harker staring at himself in the mirror. Without his mask of beard, he looked younger, somehow smaller, and a good deal less in command of karma and destiny. The newly exposed skin was pallid, almost gray, and the chin seemed weak and slightly recessive.

"Now that wasn't so bad, was it, Arnold?" Sue cooed.

Harker looked away from the mirror and up at her. The expression on his face was almost pathetic. "It's going to take some getting used to," he said unhappily.

"Relax," Sue told him. "It makes you look more

human." She was laughing inside, but she managed to keep a straight face as she dipped her fingers in a pot of makeup and began smearing it on his pale face. "Now let's see what we can do to reverse the process. . . ."

The Spacer "airplane" curved southwest as it climbed out of the spaceport's desert valley, and soon the land of sorcery had passed out of view. Lou leaned close to Sue in the back of the cabin, the heavy drone of the propeller masking his voice from the pilot in front as he spoke.

"Well, we'll be back in La Mirage in three days," he said, "but I wonder if it'll really feel like going home."

"I know what you mean," Sue whispered loudly. "Is this what it feels like to be karmically reborn?"

Lou shrugged. "Yes and no," he said. "If this is karmic rebirth, then it's rebirth into a kind of karma nobody's been born into before."

The illusionary paradox at the heart of the world to which they were returning had indeed been stripped away. But what had been revealed was not a clearer vision of the Great Way at all but a mystery far deeper at the core of a reality far vaster than anything the human spirit had yet contained. Whether in the end the human spirit could encompass that reality in harmony with the Way was still very much an open question.

And whether what they were doing right now was in harmony with the Way was no less in doubt as far as Clear Blue Lou was concerned.

He had absorbed the lore of black science. He now knew how to fly a spaceship and command a thinking machine. He understood how it was possible to survive in outer space, where the cold was deadly bitter, and there was no air to breathe, and he would weigh less than a feather. He had accepted the need for all these things in the service of something whose ultimate karma he could never judge until it passed through his lifeline. He had left his world behind him to voyage into the physical and moral unknown.

And he had been led along this Way not by a wiser being but by a sorcerer whose own soul had been blackened and deadened by this very quest. If he didn't think he could avoid Arnold Harker's fate, he wouldn't be Clear Blue Lou. But if he weren't aware of the danger, he wouldn't be Clear Blue Lou either.

And what about you, Sue? he thought as he watched her musing out the window at the clouds slipping by. Is your Way really Clear Blue?

Could a lie be sweet when the truth was unpalatable? Could bad karma really be transformed into good by "media hype" as she was so sure it could? He could dimly see how a worldly lie could bring the spirit a higher vision. A play or a story did that with metaphor. And as a metaphor, this happening would give the world a vision spiritually closer to the essence of the truth than any literal recitation of the mere facts could hope to accomplish.

But this was *not* a story, it was a sub-species of mindfuck. Could good come of that, no matter how logical it seemed? The answer seemed hidden in the true karma that the songs from the stars would bring. If great good came of listening to them, then the sin could be borne gracefully for the sake of the greater good. But if evil came, if humanity proved unworthy of such knowledge, then we will have blackened our souls like no one before us, he realized.

Sue came out of her reverie, and Lou found himself watching her studying him. "You're looking at me a little strangely," she said.

"I was thinking we're either very brave or very arrogant," Lou said. "We're taking the destiny of the whole world in our hands. What if we're wrong? Who gave us the right to decide that men should listen to the stars?"

"Who gave us the right to decide men shouldn't?" Sue told him flatly. "If we don't act, we're making the decision too. We're stuck with it, Lou. We're the only people in the whole world who know both sides of the mountains. And in my heart, I know what we're doing is right."

"I wish *I* was so sure . . ." Lou said slowly. The logic of their destiny seemed inevitable, but their mastery of their fate seemed illusion. In such a situation, certainty itself was almost a sin. Did they truly comprehend a whole or merely see some of the parts?

"Trust me, Lou," Sue said, squeezing his hand. "As I trusted you when I didn't see the Way clearly."

Lou managed a wan smile. "I trust you as I trust myself," he said truthfully. But at the moment, that didn't seem to be saying very much.

Word
of Mouth

Everything's the same and everything is different, Sunshine Sue thought as she passed the Exchange on her way to the Smokehouse. Or rather everything is the same and *I'm* different.

The entrance to the Exchange was thronged with peddlers and vendors. Merchants and mountain williams poured in and out in a steady stream, and the loading docks were crowded with merchandise. Business had returned to normal and then some by the time she and Lou had gotten back to town. The suspension of trade during the atomic radio affair had backed up an avalanche of orders which had broken over La Mirage after the giving of justice had cleared the way for renewed commerce. In particular, new orders for solar eagles were running at record levels, what with a one-year guarantee of a ten-percent discount. Mountain william tribes who had never been heavily in the component trade before had "discovered" new caches of "pre-Smash" supplies to neatly take up the slack caused by the disbandment of the Lightning Commune, and no one was about to question their whiteness under the circumstances.

La Mirage was still La Mirage. Only she and Lou clearly knew the reality beneath business as usual, and they weren't talking.

Nor was anybody asking. For it was bad form to question the reborn about their period of karmic rebirth, and it would have been worse form to question the sweetness of the new karma of Sunshine Sue and Clear Blue Lou, the darlings of the town, the backhanded bringers of the current boom.

The game was the same, but Sue now knew more about the real rules than anyone in town cared to. *Knew?* She was *playing* by them, and none of the subtle sophisticates of La Mirage, not even Levan himself, was any the wiser. The craftiest people in the world she had always thought she had known now seemed shallow, slightly insubstantial, as she worked her sorcery unnoticed right under their noses.

Even Lou's presence in town long after the task he had been summoned for had been completed aroused no suspicion. They were living together at the Sunshine Tribe's hostelry, and in the eyes of La Mirage, their love explained all, as the town basked in the good karma of which they seemed to be the center.

Even her own tarrying in town did not arouse serious murmuring among the local members of the Sunshine Tribe, though the Word of Mouth network buzzed with messages demanding her personal attention to tribal business elsewhere. It was easy enough to make sure that unofficial Word of Mouth leaking back into the net explained her peculiar behavior in terms of love, sweet love.

"Managing the news," however, was a more subtle task, and Lou's attitude was not making it any easier.

Sue's first step had been to sift the news moving up and down the Word of Mouth chains for items having to do with portents in the sky and mystical visions of godlike beings. Given the amount of mindfood ingested in Aquaria and the number of astrologers, a few such items were always readily available. These she arranged to give priority distribution, so that news of the moving lights over Castroville, the Napa Fireball, and the Advent at Palm quickly spread wherever Word of Mouth reached.

By the time the rest of her tribe might have been beginning to notice the strange emphasis being put on these items, it didn't seem strange at all, for bizarre events and weird portents in the sky had become a topic of more than usual interest. This was a resurrection of the ancient idea of the "self-fulfilling prophecy," a fad created by the news of its own existence.

Thus, no one questioned Sue's instructions to Word of Mouth news gatherers to *seek out* such items, and once people realized that a moment of personal fame might be achieved by watching the sky for wonders, an abundance of visions began to be presented to the gatherers of news.

Without resorting to the deliberate spreading of false items of news, Sue had managed to create a blizzard of sky visions in the consciousness of the Aquarian populace, a storm of sightings which fed on itself. Of course, many of these visions might be the creation of mindfood and Word-of-Mouth-created expectations, and many others were no doubt tall tales concocted by seekers of momentary fame, but all the Sunshine Tribe was doing was spreading news gathered from the lips of the people. She was being true to the spirit of Word of Mouth, or so she tried to convince Lou.

Lou, however, was having his silly moral qualms, and it had not been easy to gain his cooperation in initiating the final phase.

"Now that really *is* the spreading of lies," he had insisted last night when she asked him to help initiate the rumor chain. "You're making up stories and getting people to believe them."

"No, I'm not!" she insisted. "Uh . . . not exactly. I'm making up stories, but I'm not telling anyone to believe them. Just reporting the public word of mouth. . . ."

They were lying in bed at the hostelry long after dinner, but they had not made love. Sue had carefully explained that the whole point of the sky portent obsession she had created was to create the proper atmosphere for the "planted news" about visitations from beings from other worlds. This receptivity would give the planted stories credibility, and the stories would give the craze for celestial portents content and direction, and both would enhance the credibility of the eventual happening.

But the oaf insisted on being dense.

"Let me get this straight," he said dryly. "We hang around taverns and smokehouses, spreading stories about beings from the stars landing in spaceships . . . but we're not spreading lies?"

"Well, we're not telling anyone that the stories are *true*, are we?" Sue said slyly.

Lou stared up at her owlishly from the pillows. "Then you gather this false news that you've planted from the lips of people who've heard it from people who've heard it from you. *And that's not lying?*"

"Just reporting the news as we hear it," Sue insisted righteously. But she couldn't entirely wipe the grin off her face.

"You create word of mouth and then you report it. . . ."

"Media is its own reality; that's a basic principle of the science," Sue told him. "And I think you'll agree I know a little more about it than you do."

Lou's seriousness finally cracked a bit. "*That* I can go along with," he said, rolling his eyes. "I see it, but it's hard to believe it."

"The hand is quicker than the eye," she laughed, making mystical motions in front of his face.

"I just hope the head isn't faster than the heart," Lou replied, obdurately reverting to his righteous mode. "Everything is working the way you said it would, and if you say that in a few days people will be making up their own tall stories about beings from the stars for you to gather as news, I believe you'll have them doing it. But I can't believe it doesn't violate the spirit of truth; I can't believe that what you're doing can be in harmony with the Way."

"Sometimes there are better ways to higher truth than the straight and narrow, love," Sue said, wagging a finger in his face. "All these 'lies,' as you insist on calling them, are preparing people for a greater truth, now, aren't they? Without these little lies, the big truth wouldn't be believed. If we didn't get people believing in noble beings from the stars, they'd insist on believing that the songs from the stars were evil Spacer sorcery, wouldn't they? And they'd be wrong, wouldn't they?"

"It's for their own good, is that it?"

"Well, isn't it?"

Lou sighed. "I don't know any more," he said wearily. "Since I met you, the world has become a much more confusing place."

Sue stroked his hair. She kissed him fleetingly on the lips. "Trust me, Lou," she said. "I know what I'm doing. This is the way the global electronic village worked. It's the only way to get people to face knowledge from the stars without weirding out. Or do you have a better idea, oh perfect master of the Clear Blue Way?"

Lou stroked her cheek tentatively, perhaps somewhat reluctantly. "No," he finally said. "I guess yours *is* the only game in town. . . ."

"Then take it on faith and help me," Sue had told him, and slowly, lip on lip, thigh on thigh, she had cozened away the lingering vestiges of his resistance. Or at least banished his doubts to a corner of his mind.

But in the process, she had come to see some of the new strangeness in herself. Even *Lou* had become an object of her manipulations. How much wrong *could* be done in the service of higher good without tainting her own soul?

When she reached the Smokehouse, den of gossiping soothsayers and mages, the haze of reef smoke seemed like a fogging of her own inner vision. Behind it even these adepts of the white sciences and the mystical arts seemed slightly wraithlike, mages of a limited reality whose time must soon be passing.

This must be what it feels like to be a sorcerer, she thought, as she glided and nodded between couches and tables, and she didn't much like it. Possession of secret knowledge seemed to have its karmic drawbacks, and she was beginning to see how the Spacers were able to distance themselves psychically from the objects of their scenarios. And thereby from their own human hearts.

She bought a pipe of reef and sat down alone, waiting for someone to come to her. It didn't much matter who. The vibe of the Smokehouse was intellectual and a good-looking woman didn't instantly attract sensual speculators, particularly a woman famously involved with the likes of Clear Blue Lou. But Sunshine Sue, Queen of Word of Mouth, was always an object of immediate interest in this bazaar of knowledge; she could be counted upon to be good for the most up-to-date gossip and maybe a bit of news that hadn't yet filtered out through the Word of Mouth chains.

So it didn't take long for a little group to form around her. Merle Quicksilver, an up-and-coming young astrologer of some repute and more ambition. May Songcloud, a weather mage whose dabblings in the questionable art of astronomy had somewhat grayed her reputation. And a short, fat little man whom Sue did not know.

Interestingly enough, the rash of strange events in Aquarian skies was already foremost in their minds; Sue didn't have to steer the conversation. She was pleased but almost taken aback by how well her hype had already diffused into the public consciousness.

". . . charts predicted this; it's happened before," Quicksilver said, after they had swapped stories of the latest celestial sightings. "Portents in the sky always herald the dawn of a new astrological age. When the Age of Aquarius began just before the Smash, many strange things were seen in the sky. Lights, flying discs, comets, new stars. Now the stars are moving into a new Great Sign, and a new age is aborning. The Age of Leo, master of men, power, and knowledge."

May Songcloud snorted. "Are you sure you haven't conveniently discovered a new astrological age to encompass the events in the sky within your own art?" she said. "I'd say that every time there are a lot of strange events in the sky, you astrologers manage to discover a significance for them in your charts."

"And you, I suppose, have a more arcane explanation?" Quicksilver shot back indignantly.

"Astronomy has long been a neglected art," May said. "The ancients knew much and we know little. They knew of things in the heavens besides planets and comets, the sun and the moon. Asteroids. Quasars. Pulsars."

"And what are these asteroids, quasars and pulsars of yours?" Quicksilver asked archly.

May shrugged. "Just words whose meaning has been lost," she said. "But perhaps the ancient astronomers used them to describe the very events taking place in the heavens now."

Quicksilver laughed snidely. "And *we're* the ones who are trying to encompass events in the sky with mystic significance in our own charts?"

Amazing! Sue thought. Here they are, fighting over whose art encompassed the pure product of *mine!* What wizardry this media hype is! How cogent it must have been before the Smash, when there was hardware to match the software. And how cogent it would be again with a satellite broadcast network. Lou is dead wrong in his qualms about this. What could be more karmically fitting than that this software science should be the instrument that allows us to obtain the hardware for its higher functioning?

"I'm just a mindfood grower from up north, looking for

better equipment with which to distill my extracts, and I don't claim that *my* art encompasses this sphere," the fat little man said. "But it seems to me that *some* of the things we've heard about can't be explained by astrology or astronomy, like the Advent at Palm, where strange winged beings—"

"*That* one probably *is* the product of your art," Quicksilver snorted.

"Like the Yappoville landing," Sue said with deliberate dubiousness, seeing her opportunity.

"Yappoville landing?" May Songcloud said. "I haven't heard that one."

"For that matter, where the hell is Yappoville?"

"A tiny village north of Shasta," Sue said, locating the nonexistent place as vaguely as possible. "Supposedly, a star fell from the sky and landed in a commune, and out stepped some strange creatures who conversed with the locals. What mindfood do you suppose they had gorged themselves on in Yappoville in order to believe that?"

"Strange creatures riding a star to Earth?" Quicksilver said sharply. "What did they look like? What did they say?"

Sue shrugged. "A Sunshine messenger heard the story in some tavern down in Shasta, and the details are too vague to use it as an item of public news. In fact, someone along the line probably just made it up. . . ."

"Oh, come on, Sue, tell us!"

"I don't want you to start thinking I'm crazy enough to believe this stoned-out story. . . ." Sue drawled teasingly.

"We understand that it's off the record."

"*Way* off the record!" Sue said. "Well anyway, for whatever it's worth, the fellow in the tavern told our messenger that someone from Yappoville told him that some members of this commune had told *him* that a star fell from the sky into their cornfield, and the creatures who got out didn't look like men but spoke our language and told them that they came from another world in outer space."

"*Well, what did they look like?* What did they want? What did they do?"

Sue shrugged. "That's the whole story," she said. "Some farmers got too stoned and thought they met beings from the stars. *Details* you want?" She pretended to study their faces dubiously, one after the other. She laughed. "Hey, you don't *believe* this, do you?"

Quicksilver snorted, perhaps a bit falsely. The little man laughed nervously. May Songcloud got to looking a little strange around the eyes. Sue saw that even these relatively sophisticated Aquarians half believed the story already, or at least, they were not ready to dismiss it out of hand.

And it really didn't matter whether they believed it or not. They would repeat it. And the people they told it to would repeat it to other people who would repeat it. The original source of the story would be forgotten, and imaginative details would be added by embellishers along the chain.

Meanwhile, she'd be going to more smokehouses and taverns, dropping this tale and others again and again, telling the stories not as truth but as silly gossip. And Lou, to the best of his ability and within the limits of his uneasy conscience, would be doing the same.

In a day or two, she thought, the stories will be all over town in different forms and with different details, and maybe people will soon start to assume that there were many landings by beings from space. At which point it could be truthfully reported by Word of Mouth as an item of news that stories of landings by space beings were rife in Aquaria.

Once this spread into the public consciousness, seekers of fame and tellers of tall tales would naturally weave the legendary beings from space into their fabulations. And the Sunshine Tribe's news gatherers would seek out such items and pour them into the Word of Mouth net. Thus would the art of media hype create an item of common folklore, and when the happening was staged, it would seem the fulfillment of widespread prophecy.

Sunshine Sue smiled. She puffed contentedly on her reef. It began to seem as if there was nothing that this magic might not accomplish, that reality itself might be altered through the power to mold the human consciousness that perceived it. She caught herself thinking this and chewed it over with a certain distaste.

That, too, must be what it feels like to be a sorcerer, she decided uneasily.

The stars shone in unclouded glory over La Mirage and a bone-white moon loomed over the mountains. The dinner hour was long gone, and the crowds in the taverns and smokehouses and music halls had peaked.

Clear Blue Lou had to admit that the atmosphere was right and what Sue called the "public consciousness" had reached the predicted fever pitch of psychic acceptance.

They had spent this last evening in La Mirage—indeed, on Earth, and perhaps in an age that would soon be passing—making the rounds of Market Circle. It had been days since they had stopped spreading stories of beings from space, and tonight they had just circulated inconsequentially, listening to the expanding and overlapping ripples of the small stones they had cast into the pond of public speculation.

At the Sorcerer's Saloon, they heard North Eagle repeating some story he had heard about beings from space landing somewhere east of Mendocino and describing their spacecraft in florid detail in terms of his own product. In the Blue Hawk, an astrologer held forth on the cosmic significance of the golden auras and bright cat eyes of the space beings *he* had heard tell of. According to a young woman reciting the tale breathlessly, a whole squadron of celestial ships had landed on a southern coast, and a horde of preternaturally beautiful and horny green men had emerged with auras of energy flaming from their enormous erections to sport en masse with the local lasses. The feature act at the Palace of Dawn had even performed a new song called "Gods of Light," something about space beings whose full meaning had been drowned out by an excessively enthusiastic drum player.

"What magic you've wrought!" Lou admitted to Sue as they ambled along Market Circle, where small groups of people were drifting from tavern to smokehouse and couples were angling off into the park. "But who can say whether it's black or white?"

Bits of interpenetrating conversation pattered his ears with more proof of the wry cogency of her art.

"—tall as bears, with faces like birds—"

"—beautiful well-built women only three feet tall—"

"—slowly up into the sky drawn by birds of fire—"

"—singing in an unknown tongue—"

"Well, we'll know tonight," Sue said, perhaps a bit uneasily. "The *Enterprise* should be here in an hour or so." Her hand in his seemed to squeeze a little tighter."

Lou eyed her speculatively. She definitely *was* a little nervous. "Finally having second thoughts?" he asked.

173

"Whether this science of yours is black or white, deception or inner truth?"

Sue frowned. "It's beyond black or white," she said, "and this will be commonplace when I've built a global electronic village with the Spacers' satellite network, so we all had better get used to it. But . . . but. . . ."

"*But?*" Lou cocked an inquisitive eyebrow at her.

Sue stopped walking. She waved her arms once to encompass the taverns and smokehouses, the people and the lights, the worlds of men. "But it all *is* beginning to seem a little unreal."

"Aquaria?" Lou asked. "Or outer space?"

"*Both!* I mean, in a few hours, we're *actually going to be in a spaceship,* up there where it's black as the tomb and we float around like feathers, and we can't go outside because our blood would freeze solid and there's no air to breathe. I know it's going to happen, but I can't conceive of how it's going to *feel.*"

"I know what you mean. . . ." Lou said somberly. The Spacers simply ignored such questions, and perhaps he had unknowingly been infected by that abstracted detachment, but it surely was going to feel like *something*. Something powerfully strange.

"Thing is, the world we're leaving is beginning to seem as unreal as where we're going," Sue said. "Maybe the trouble with too much knowledge not shared is that people begin to seem a little less real to you than you are."

Lou nodded. "And the trouble with wielding too much karmic power is that you make those people a little less free than you are."

Sue stared deeply into his eyes for a long moment. "You think maybe my freedom not to do what I'm doing is as much of an illusion as what I've gotten people to believe?" she said anxiously. "Could I still be acting out a Spacer scenario?"

"A little late to worry about that, isn't it?"

"Yeah . . ." she sighed. "Well, maybe our destiny really *is* written in the stars."

Lou forced a little laugh and gave her a quick hug. "*Ours* certainly is, in more ways than one," he said. He glanced up and down the street speculatively. "There's the Lodestar Tavern," he said. "Shall we have one more drink for the long road?"

They went into the tavern, ordered a flagon of wine and two glasses, and took them to a corner table, as far away from the crowd at the bar as possible. Lou had had more than enough of talking to people who didn't share their secrets and whose major topic of conversation was the illusion that Sue had wrought. They hunched close to each other, not really talking but establishing a loverly seclusion that only a boor would disturb.

Lou sipped at his wine, glancing over Sue's shoulder at all the people drinking and talking and mingling in this ordinary tavern in a town close to his heart. It was a homey familiar scene and it should have aroused homey familiar feelings, but a haze of unreality seemed to hover over it. Everyone in the tavern save himself and Sue seemed like actors in an old play, and the surface reality of the only world he knew seemed like a stage set. Beyond which lay . . . the great and terrible unknown. . . .

This is the true moment of karmic rebirth, he realized. Our old reality has already dissolved into mist, and the reality to come as yet has no face. This was as open as the soul could get to the flow of unfolding unknown destiny, and it should have been a moment of perfect Clear Blue clarity. Instead, a chill wind seemed to be blowing through his soul from—

"In the sky! Coming toward us from the northeast!"

A wild-eyed man burst into the tavern, shouting and waving his arms. "A huge light in the sky coming toward La Mirage! A great blue thing spitting lightning!"

The tumult of the tavern guttered into silence. A woman stuck her head inside the door. "A chariot from the stars! Coming down toward the western meadows!"

Then she was gone and everyone was babbling at once as they surged toward the street.

Lou and Sue sat there until the place had emptied, and they could hear the shoutings and rumblings of people pouring out of every tavern and smokehouse on Market Circle, a roar of excitement and confusion.

Lou stood up. He clinked glasses with Sue. "Let's go see the show," he said, draining his glass in a single swallow.

And hand in hand they went to put the world behind them.

The Chariot
of the Gods

High above the lip of the world it hung, an angel's wing of blue fire moving toward the plateau across the heavens like a portent from unknown and terrifying gods.

An unruly sea of people surged toward the edge of the high plateau on which La Mirage sat, toward a vista of high mountain shapes outlined against the stars beyond an immense drop into the jumbled canyon vastness which seemed to separate their world from that distant vision.

Moving toward them, the beacon that they followed grew huger now as it crossed the great blackness, a celestial portent swooping in out of the firmament upon the worlds of men.

Almost the whole town was there, thousands of people flung across the meadow, craning their eyes skyward and wondering at the fearful thing they saw.

A great glowing blue bird seemed to be soaring on the canyon updraft, losing altitude as it came toward the crowd, like a goose bellying in for a landing. Huge it was, how huge it was still impossible to tell, and it burned from within with a clear blue light. Strange lightnings flashed around it, rhythmic short bursts that seemed to shatter time into thousands of discontinuous fragments, as if the very fabric of reality itself was warped by the magic of its passage.

Silently, the great firebird glided in from out of the darkness, and then it was directly overhead and growing ever larger as it sank toward the earth.

A great collective gasp arose as the winged shape came slowly down out of the sky in its cloak of lightning, and the crowd drew a perspective on its true size. Larger than the moon it seemed while it was still a thousand feet up, and as it descended, it grew and grew, threatening to blot out the sky.

It was still five hundred feet high when the crowd oohed and sighed as it began to pick up the first far-off faint strains of the celestial music.

A ghostly keening of the heavenly strings and the thin silver eeriness of a chorus of flutes. The firebird descended toward the earth, wailing a spectral rising song that got louder and louder as the glowing blue shape became the most immense thing that any living eye had ever seen—a wing of fire large enough to encompass them all, a soaring ear-splitting swell that shattered the soul with expectation even as the rhythmic dance of the lightning shattered vision into flickering slices of time.

Like birds mesmerized by a snake, not an eye tore itself away from that fearful sight, not a person turned and fled. Now the entire population of La Mirage stood crowded under the blue shadow of the bird of light. Within that shadow, night was banished, and the world flickered on and off faster than the eye could blink, and the spirit was encompassed in its clear blue glow, while a keening celestial song made bones hum in harmony with the mighty voice of unknown gods.

Two hundred feet up, the great rising note crescendoed into a shattering fanfare of heavenly trumpets, and below the huge blue wing, a smaller, fatter winged shape winked into existence, outlined in points of jeweled light that went through a continuous cycle of transmutation—emerald, ruby, sapphire, back to emerald again.

Slowly, majestically, the apparition settled in over the spellbound throng, an eagle of good omen bearing a jeweled prize in its claws, a cloud of light enveloping them in a magic piece of the sky.

Another great fanfare—longer and even louder than the first—and from all around the underside of the wing, powerful beams of white light converged on the jewel-outlined shape below it, flashing it into full glowing brilliance in an instant.

Suspended beneath the sky-filling firebird was a smaller bird of bright golden yellow—substantial and metallic and set with colored lights like a jeweled piece crafted by a god-like goldsmith.

A mighty full orchestral chorus played a paean to glory as the wing-shaped blue aura settled in low over the crowd, bearing its gift to the earth.

And then the gods spoke.

A long low rumble of thunder, then another, and another, in steady serene fearfulness. The world under the canopy of the sky-spanning wing flickered on and off, seemingly at the command of Those Who Controlled the Thunder and the Lightning. The world was split asunder and the whirlwind was loosed upon the Earth.

A monstrous thunderclap split the air, and then a huge voice spoke out of nowhere, louder than any living man, and in an unearthly metallic tone.

"PEOPLE OF THE EARTH!"

The crowd surged and shrieked and babbled its awe.

Another great thunderclap cowed them into silence.

"PEOPLE OF THE EARTH! WE BEAR A GREAT GIFT. PREPARE TO RECEIVE IT."

A triumphal march sounded the glory of the heavens as the golden bird was slowly lowered to the Earth in the middle of a great circle that the crowd scrambled to clear for it. The wing was the low roof of an immense cathedral now, where the world flickered in syncopation to the lightning under the clear blue light of the gods.

The music resolved to a final mighty chord as the golden bird touched the earth on wheeled feet, a fanfare of offering that made the moment of utter silence that followed it thunderously pregnant with awed wonder.

The golden bird was vaguely like a huge solar eagle— crafted of metal, winged, resting on three wheeled feet. The dozens of mutating lights all over its surface enveloped it in a random rippling of rainbow shimmers. This was magic, but it bore the solidity of manufacture. Unearthly manufacture.

For a long moment the gods were silent, as if allowing the

humans to absorb the enormity of their presence before revealing their full selves.

Then a thin high droning built up from silence into an enormous demanding wail of strings, and a round doorway in the body of the golden bird opened to heavenly trumpets. *Da-DAH!* the trumpets blared again, and a ladder of metallic rungs and rope unrolled from the doorway to the ground like a magic carpet.

Then a being emerged, crouched in the doorway surveying the world of men. His body was covered with silver scales, whether garment or skin it was impossible to tell. His hair was human, though cropped like a black helmet over his skull. His face . . . his face . . . *his face*. . . .

His face was chaos. It seemed to float above his body, a world unto itself, glowing with its own ever-changing light. Blue. Green. Yellow. Red. Flashes of light rotated across the creature's unfathomable countenance in dappling patterns that shattered the illusive features into an ever-changing mandala of jig-saw pieces that refused to form a static whole. Purple lips, tiny dark night eyes, emerald beak, a glowering green frown, huge yellow orbs, brooding blue brow, a twisted amber sneer . . .

Every avatar of that which lay behind the surface of the human mask flickered across that terrible godlike visage, a countenance infinite in its transformations, a mirror of the universe of spirit as it moved through flesh, changing and yet unchanged.

Keening music rose again as the living god descended his stairway, and a trumpet fanfare sounded as he set his feet upon the Earth.

And then the being spoke in a great world-filling voice—huge and directionless and punctuated by musical flourishes as if an entire orchestra were contained in its throat.

"People of the Earth. I bring you greetings from the people of the stars. We watch your planet with love."

A great drum roll broke like a wave, lightnings flashed, and then the awful voice spoke again. "Sunshine Sue! Clear Blue Lou! You are summoned to your destiny as it is written in the stars."

A great collective gasp went up from the multitude that became a babble of wonder and recognition punctuated here and there by nervous laughter as the star being's words revealed the obviousness of the visual sign.

The great cathedral wing arching above them glowed . . . *Clear Blue Lou blue.* The golden sky chariot it bore was . . . *Sunshine Yellow.*

The crowd parted in awe for Clear Blue Lou and Sunshine Sue as they walked trancelike through it toward the celestial portent upon which their ensigns were emblazoned for all to see. Few were those who dared mutter a greeting or word of dire warning to Lou and Sue as they approached the edge of the mystic circle, the interface between humankind and the space of the star being, their eyes fixed upon the celestial creature, their faces transfigured by a calm that seemed to transcend both fear and awe.

They walked a few paces beyond the front rank of townspeople, then paused, as if hesitating to venture farther into the circle of awful magicks.

Drums rolled like thunder. His great voice punctuated with strings and horns, his visage a dance of burning avatars, the star being spoke again.

"People of the Earth. We watch your planet with love. We mourn your fallen state. High above you in the clear blue heavens waits a great ear through which the people of the Earth may hear the songs and wisdom of the people of the stars. We give to you this chariot of the sun to bear these messagecarriers to the highest place in all your world, to listen, to return, and to bring the wisdom of the stars to your fallen people."

Thunder clapped, then rumbled onward as the voice of the god spoke above it.

"We choose Clear Blue Lou, perfect master of the Clear Blue Way to speak his justice on the glories of the heavens so that the people of the Earth may walk the Galactic Way and know that it is good. We choose Sunshine Sue, Queen of Word of Mouth, to spread our great word throughout your planet so that our knowledge may be shared by all. Step forward, chosen son and daughter of the Earth, to meet your destiny in the stars."

Hand in hand to the oohs and sighs of the crowd and a celestial chorus rising into a hymn to glory, Sunshine Sue and Clear Blue Lou slowly walked beyond the circle of humanity to accept the destiny ordained from on high.

Drum rolls accompanied them up the ladder, and then the star being ascended to the rising thrum of heavenly strings, drew up his staircase, and closed the door to the sky chariot behind him to a clap of thunder and a bright flash of lightning.

There was a long moment of silent stillness under the canopy of blue light, as rhythmic flashes of lightning etched this mythic moment into the back of every brain.

Then soft music began playing and the wheeled feet of the sky chariot left the ground. The golden bird floated slowly upward as the music began building toward a mighty crescendo, as the sky itself seemed to recede in a bright blue glow, becoming a great blue wing across the starry black sky.

Like a feather rising above a flue, the firebird soared aloft, clutching the golden sky chariot in its claws, while the music crested into a triumphant song of heavenly glory.

When it had dwindled to the size of a great blue eagle, there was a final clap of thunder, and the firebird suddenly disappeared in a last blaze of lightnings.

Only the dark silence of the night remained—and the golden speck of the sky chariot floating up into the black sky, a second Venus ascending to its starry realm.

Thousands of eyes watched it as it slowly became but one bright star among many. Then a great tongue of fire exploded from the yellow speck, and it began to move ever faster across the dark vault of the heavens. Low thunder echoed across the plateau, an eerie thrilling sound, a steady peal without waver or end. Faster and faster and faster, the golden speck moved across the sky, as if goaded by the bright flame it rode.

Slowly, almost imperceptibly, the thunder began to fade toward silence as the sky chariot became a meteor ascending from the Earth . . . a single star moving across the firmament . . . a tiny point of light that finally vanished in silence into the dark heavens.

Quiet reigned. Crickets began to chirp. A nightbird called. It was a long time before anyone spoke.

We All Live
in a Yellow
Submarine

"I saw it, but I still don't believe it," Clear Blue Lou muttered dazedly as he closed the final fasteners on the uncomfortable suit that encased him in clumsiness and the burden of great weight. "You really *are* a sorcerer, lady. It was the greatest art I've ever seen, but was it truth?"

"I may not know what truth is, but I know what I like," Sue said, screwing the round metal helmet onto the collar of her spacesuit and winking at him silently from behind the thick glass faceplate.

Lou helped her into the right-hand acceleration couch, then donned his own helmet and climbed into the center couch next to Arnold Harker, who had already wiped off his makeup and suited up and was peering out the window as he checked out the controls.

It was unpleasantly confining inside the suit. The thing must have weighed a hundred pounds, he was already sweating and itching in places he couldn't scratch, and his cock was mated to a hose that led to a piss bottle inside the infernal contraption, which was surely the worst place that organ had ever been. He looked out at the crowded little world of the spaceship cabin, through a window in a steel bucket, breathing sour air that stank of oiled metal.

"Radios on," Harker's voice said from speaker grids inside his helmet. It was thin and colorless and it seemed to rattle inside Lou's brainpan.

"*How long* did you say we had to wear these damned things?" Sue's voice said as if from across a large room, though she was sitting right next to him.

"I told you, till we reach the Big Ear," Harker said testily. "Now strap in. We're reaching launch altitude."

Lou did up the acceleration couch straps, still trying to catch up with the changes. A few minutes ago, he had been part of a glorious scene that would live forever in legend, and now he was stuffed inside this instrument of torture, breathing rancid air and waiting to be shot into space. Perhaps it was a blessing that there was so little time in which to think.

"Launch altitude," Harker said mechanically. "Initiate launch program." And he punched a button on the computer console beside him.

A ghastly roar exploded into being, a sound that set the spaceship cabin vibrating and shook Lou's teeth in his jaw.

"Oh shit!" Sue screamed as the spaceship took a sudden gut-wrenching drop, plummeting like a stone.

Then Lou felt an avalanche slam up against his back, not a giant's swift kick, but an endless pressure that squeezed him down into the cushions of his couch, and he could feel the spaceship surge forward, roaring and rattling like a water tank in an earthquake.

"Eeee . . ." he heard a male voice groan shrilly, and it took him a moment to be sure that it was Harker's and not his own as the pressure against his back wheezed air from his lungs.

A leaden blanket seemed to press on his body, a blanket that got heavier and heavier and heavier as the bone-thrumming roar went on and on and on and the cabin of the spaceship became a quaking cacophony of vibrating and groaning metal.

"Is this fucking thing coming apart?" Sue snarled thickly.

"Shut up," Harker whined sickeningly, "just *shut up!*"

Lou's body got heavier and heavier. Bright spots flickered before his eyes. He could hardly raise his head far enough to get a glimpse out the window, where the sky was purpling brilliantly from blue to black.

He was so heavy now that he couldn't move. He could feel the flesh of his face crawling backward like melting wax. His tongue was a dead thing in his mouth. His vision sparkled with butterflies of light that seemed to be guarding the mouth of a long black tunnel, down and down and down he went, crushed into the dark dream of oblivion . . .

. . . emerging in a blessed smooth silence that caressed the ears like the soothing murmur of the sea. It was so quiet now that all he could hear was his own breathing echoing underwater in his helmet. It was such a relief that he seemed to be floating in ecstasy, weightless even inside the gross suit, free and light as a feather.

"Oooh," Sue moaned, "I think I passed out. What happened? I feel like my body doesn't know which way is up."

Only then did Lou realize that his body was trying to tell him that he was falling; only then did a vacuum clutch at his guts. But he knew what this must be. This must be what Harker had called weightlessness. They were *not* plunging to their doom, they were in orbit, beyond the pull of the Earth, flying freely through outer space in an endless gliding swan dive. The falling feeling faded as he gave himself back to the glorious floating sensation.

"We're in orbit," he told Sue quickly. "Our bodies weigh nothing. We're not falling, we're floating." The spirit must master the flesh in this strange space, or the flesh would surely sicken the spirit.

"Thanks . . ." Sue muttered. "Hey . . . *thanks!* Say, this feels good! Hmmm, too bad we're in these damned chastity suits; can you imagine what it would be like to—"

"Please!" Lou shouted as the thought of free-floating sport began to engorge his member within the tight confining ring of the piss bottle hose.

"Oooh . . . I don't feel good . . . I'm going to vomit. . . ."

Harker was making green gurgling sounds over the radio. Through the window of his helmet, his eyes were glazed and his face was deathly pale.

"Harker! Snap out of it!" Lou commanded. "You can't let yourself vomit inside your helmet!" The thought was horrifying, and the sight would be something he could well do without. "Close your eyes . . . You're floating in warm thick water . . . You're not falling, you're flying free as a bird. . . ."

"Oooh, I don't know. . . . I didn't think it would be like this. . . ." Harker groaned. Then he was finally quiet, and Lou could hear his jagged breathing slowly smoothing out in a series of gulping sighs.

"Now open your eyes and be here now!"

"Oooh . . ." Harker moaned. "I think I can hold it back now . . . I didn't know, I—"

"Oh *look!*" Sue exclaimed in childlike wonder, gazing out the window.

Lou gave his attention to what lay outside, and even through two thicknesses of glass, the vision took his breath away and sent his spirit soaring.

The Earth was a huge living globe beneath them, rolling with slow majesty through crystal blackness sparkling with unwinking stars. Seas shone a lucent blue under patterns of swirling cloud. Continents—green and brown, veined with rivers and dappled with lakes—humped out of the seas like the backs of fabled basking whales. Where the curve of the planet met the blackness of space, the interface was a shining corona of deep purple. It was staggering, it was beautiful, and it was palpably alive.

But it was grievously wounded.

Lou saw great holes pocking the skin of the continents that rolled beneath him, punched in horribly deliberate-looking patterns along the coasts, up and down the wide river valleys, and around the shores of the larger lakes. Sere brown deserts seemed to eat into the fragile-looking patches of green like an advanced case of mange. Great scars gouged in the flesh of the planet glowered an ugly purple.

The vision seemed to speak with a great soundless voice in the center of Lou's soul. Behold, it said. Behold my grandeur. Behold my living beauty.

And behold what you've done to me.

"I sure hope there really *are* wiser beings out there than us," Sue said wanly. "After seeing what we've done to our world, the thought that we're the highest form of consciousness there is doesn't exactly inspire confidence."

"I've got the Big Ear on the acquisition radar," Harker said in a tense, tightly controlled voice. "Initiate rendezvous program." The Spacer was hunched down over his controls, staring fixedly at the glowing round screen as he punched in the computer program.

A series of small hisses and shudders and then the Earth seemed to shift slightly outside the window. For a moment, it seemed to have left its proper position in the heavens, and it took Lou another moment to realize that it was the angle of his vision that had shifted. Then there was a momentary roar and the spaceship creaked and rattled. Then once again calm drifting silence.

"Course correction completed," Harker said woodenly, still hunkered over the radar screen. He hadn't taken his eyes off it.

"Are you all right?"

"All systems . . . all systems are working nominally . . . ," Harker said shrilly. "We should rendezvous with the Big Ear in approximately twenty minutes."

"Well I guess there's nothing to do until then but lean back and enjoy the view."

Harker still didn't look up from his radar screen.

"Are you *sure* you're all right? You're not going to—"

"I *have* to be all right, don't I?" the Spacer said thickly. "I've been trained all my life for this. . . ."

"No one can be trained for *this*," Lou said. "There's no scenario for this experience." Even in its wounded agony, the Earth was beautiful and alive from this perspective, and perhaps the scars only added a frisson of tragedy to its soul-stirring glory, an emotional dimension that was, alas, all too human.

Arnold Harker looked up at the planet for a moment. "I fear that you're right," he whispered, then sank back into contemplation of his screens and instruments. Apparently not every master could walk his own way.

Time seemed to crawl to Sunshine Sue. The spacesuit chafed, her body itched inside it, the air she breathed stank of chemicals and her own sweat, and she was becoming all too aware that she was trapped inside the bucket of her helmet, inside a frail metal capsule, floating in a cold hard blackness whose touch was death.

And Arnold Harker wasn't exactly making it any easier to take. Crouched to no purpose over his controls, muttering monosyllabically to any attempt to snap him out of it, the Spacer had not exactly come into his expected glory. A vibe of terror came off him, a far too literal perception of their true fragility and danger which began to infect her by osmosis.

You poor bastard! she thought. This is your dream, and the reality of it is scaring you shitless. Empathy or not, however, she wished he would keep his bummer vibes to himself. For the vision of the Earth that revealed itself beyond this claustrophobic tomb of metal inspired both sadness and hope, terror and promise. Terror in its living vulnerability, sadness in its ravaged state, and the promise of hope in the world seen whole—the hope that one day all the world might see itself as one through the magic of the world broadcast network, the dream that had led her to dare this place.

If only Arnold—

"Over there!" Lou shouted. "That must be it!"

The upper edge of something enormous was drifting into vision, seemingly from underneath the spaceship, a huge round fisherman's net cast up out of the dark sea before them.

"That's it all right," Harker said dully, finally looking up from the mechanical world of his screens and controls. "The Big Ear antenna . . ."

In another moment, Sue saw the thing entire.

A celestial fishnet a mile across floated before them in the nothingness, a spiderweb of wire spun out on an impossibly thin round framework of metal girders. A metal tube connected the antenna with the hub of a huge metal wagon wheel spinning in space; a round windowed rim and four quartering spokes, each about five hundred feet from rim to hub. The axle that connected the antenna to the wheel became a thin girder-work spire as it pierced it, supporting four rectangular metal paddles like a windmill's sails frozen in the breezeless void.

"The Big Ear," Harker said tonelessly. "The greatest work of the Age of Space. . . ."

"Yeah, but what *is* it?" Sue asked. "I've never seen anything like it in my life." Nothing had quite prepared her for this; it wasn't merely huge and strange, it was visually incomprehensible.

"The antenna is the largest listening device ever built by men," Harker said. "Nothing so large could ever be constructed on Earth. The blades on the wheel are the solar panels that power the station. And the wheel itself . . . the wheel itself is the crew's quarters, where the spin gives you weight, and there'll be air and warmth, and we can get out of these horrible suits, and . . .''

The Spacer's voice had been getting faster and shriller, until he seemed to finally choke back his hysteria by sheer act of will. ''Got to dock it somehow,'' he said nervously. ''Docking port's on the tube between the Ear and the wheel, so we're going to have to fly between them. . . . Please don't disturb my concentration; this is going to be bad enough as it is. . . .''

Gazing fixedly out the window, Harker fiddled with his controls. The nose of the spaceship came down and around until it was pointed straight at the tube in the massive canyon between the wheel and the antenna. The rockets roared for an instant, and then the spaceship began to slide forward into the narrow cleft between the giant spiderweb and the dangerously spinning spokes.

The

Graveyard

Heart

Although there was nothing pretty or graceful about it, Clear Blue Lou had to admire the way the clearly terrified Harker managed to maneuver the spaceship between the stationary antenna and the spinning wheel with dozens of tiny corrections and recorrections from the control rockets, easing it down onto a big metal plate slung laterally across the connecting tube at less than the speed of a walking man.

The landing slab was connected to the tube by a series of large springs, and two huge metal scimitars were slung out from each side of the slab like quarterhoops of a barrel large enough to enclose the *Enterprise*. As the spaceship clanged roughly onto the landing slab, the four quarterhoops banged closed overhead to secure the ship to the Big Ear, as if a giant trap had been sprung.

"Docking completed," Harker said shakily. Lou heard his long exhale of breath over the radio, a tinny sigh of released tension.

"Nice piece of flying, Arnold," he said.

"I'm glad I won't have to do *that* again," Harker whispered hoarsely. "It'll be a lot less delicate on the way out."

"Now what?" Sue asked.

Harker stared silently out the window.

"I said, *now what?*"

"Now . . . now we collect our food packs, hook up the *Enterprise*'s air and water tanks to the station's intake lines, and enter the access tube through a hatch," Harker finally said. "But . . . but it means we have to go out *there*. We have to walk in space."

"*Fan*-tastic!" Sunshine Sue exclaimed, standing on the metal landing slab, held down only by the small magnets in the spacesuit's boots. To her left, the great wheel arched high above her, sweeping grandly across the heavens in its stately revolution; to her right, the Big Ear antenna was a lacework of silver that seemed to trap an infinite school of stars. The Earth loomed low overhead, an immense living jewel that utterly humbled even this grandest construction of man. Weightlessly, soundlessly, she stood in the naked heavens gazing down upon her world like a god.

Then Arnold Harker shattered the glorious moment. He came scuttling across the landing slab, dragging two hoses from the ship, a picture of mundane drudgery. "The intake valves should be right by the access hatch, and that should be right below where you're standing," he babbled frantically as he pushed between Sue and Lou. "Yes, there it is, and here's the ladder."

He scrambled over the edge of the landing slab, still dragging his hoses, and crawled down a metal ladder to the curving tube below.

Sue watched him screw the hose nozzles into two holes set into the curve of metal close by a round door. "Well, come on, what are you waiting for?" his shrill impatient voice said over the radio.

"We'd better go," Lou said, climbing down the ladder. "I don't think our sorcerer is enjoying the view."

"Lou! He can hear us!" Sue hissed. Arnold seemed pretty close to the edge as it was, and they certainly couldn't afford to freak him out further.

"No, I'm not enjoying the view," Harker said grimly when they had reached the hatch. "I just want to get inside and get out of this suit before I . . . before I. . . ."

Sue heard him choke back a gag, even as he kneeled down

beside a panel of labeled switches beside the access hatch.
"Air feed . . . on," he muttered hoarsely, throwing a
switch. "Water feed . . . on. Lights . . . on." He hesitated
over a fourth switch. "*Transport cable?* What's that? It's
not in our specifications."

"But it sounds like something we could use," Sue offered.

"If it can draw power with the electrical system in the
standby mode," Harker said, throwing the final switch.

He turned a wheel set in the center of the round door,
pulled it open, and crawled inside.

Following Lou inside after the Spacer, Sue found herself
floating in a long wide tunnel, its far end lost in perspective.
Rows of lights arrowed down into the gloom. Two braided
steel cables slid like snakes up and down the center of the
tunnel, one going and one coming.

Turning, Sue saw that the two cables were really one,
reeling about a wheel spun by a humming engine fastened to
the round plate at this end of the tunnel.

Harker closed the hatch, staring at the moving cables. "I
don't know how this works . . ." he stammered. "There's
nothing about this in the specifications we've preserved. . . ."

"It's simple!" Sue shouted, pushing off the wall with her
feet, like a swimmer making a turn in a pool, arms out-
stretched as if in a dive. "You just grab on and catch a ride!"

So saying, she clamped her hands about the inward bound
cable and was yanked down the tunnel at exhilarating speed.

"Sue! Are you all right?" She heard Lou's voice through
the speakers close by her ears even as she was whisked out
of sight.

"I'm fine!" she said. "Come along, you'll enjoy the ride!"

"Whoo-ee!" Clear Blue Lou laughed as he let go of the
cable, bounced gently up against the round hatch at the end
of the tunnel and the breathless cable ride, and floated about
like a drifting balloon alongside Sue and Harker.

The Spacer was already fiddling with yet another control
panel, this one festooned with whole rows of switches. It
had taken some persuading to get him to ride the cable, and
he had screamed and moaned on the radio all the way. How
sad, how ironic, that the Spacer, who had pointed his whole
life toward this reality, could not enjoy it like a natural man.

Now he was throwing switches left and right, mumbling under his breath, and choking back gags. "Crew quarters life support system . . . on. Gurgh! Crew quarters electrical system . . . Urk!. . . on. Main switch . . . on. . . ."

"What are you doing now?" Sue asked, swimming over to watch him with a kick of her legs against the wall.

"Turning on the systems that were shut down when the crew put the station in standby mode," Harker grunted. "This hatch leads to the main airlock. Soon the wheel will have light and heat and air. And we can get out of these suits and . . . and . . ." He choked back another gag with a disgusting liquid gurgle.

Then he spun the lockwheel, opened the hatch, and vaulted into the airlock. As Lou started to follow him, he heard the Spacer scream. Then he was inside and saw the reason why.

A roped-together chain of human corpses floated in the center of the cylindrical airlock like a string of unspeakable sausages, neatly secured to rings screwed into the curving wall. Eight men and six women—naked, desiccated, and cured to a tough brown like too-old leather. Strung across the airlock like wash hung out to dry.

"Oh no . . ." Sue gasped as she vaulted in beside him.

"Oh, look at this!" Harker shrilled, pointing to neat lettering in red paint on a portion of the curved wall. "They committed suicide! They *killed* themselves!"

Lou peered wonderingly at the meticulous hand lettering.

To the relief expedition, if one ever comes. We've taken our cyanide capsules together rather than wait for the inevitable. There is a prepared briefing tape in the main computer room, where all data is stored, catalogued, and preserved. We've put all life-support systems in standby mode to extend their useful life as long as possible. If you are reading this, then there is still hope for our sorry species. We request that you give us a Christian burial together in space.

"They would have had to tie themselves together, cycled the air out of the airlock, and then calmly taken poison," Harker croaked. "Just to . . . just to preserve their bodies for us to find! Why would they do a hideous thing like that? What do they mean, a Christian burial in space?"

"I don't know what a Christian burial is either, but I think I understand the vibe," Lou said softly. "Is there a hatch to the outside here?"

"Over there," Harker said shakily, pointing to a large square panel with rounded corners. "What are you going to do?"

"Give these people what they asked for as best as I can," Lou told him, untying one end of the string of corpses. If these poor souls had expired with this peculiar concern filling their minds, then justice, indeed simple humanity, demanded that the memory of their spirit be respected. "Come on Harker, give me a hand!"

In the end, it was Sunshine Sue who had to help Lou untie the string of corpses from the wall and float them into position in front of the door to naked space. Harker wouldn't touch the bodies; he would hardly even look at them, and her appeals to masculine chivalry got her nowhere.

It somehow seemed typical of the Spacer that he figured out a way to launch the bodies into space without having to touch them. All head and no heart, Sue thought as Harker valved partial pressure into the airlock.

"Hold onto something when I open the hatch," he said mechanically. "There's not much pressure in here, but it should be enough to . . . to. . . ."

Well, maybe I'm misjudging him, Sue thought as she grabbed onto a handhold. Maybe this is his only path to psychic survival; maybe some inner wisdom tells him that he can't afford to look at what he's feeling. Arnold was beginning to seem more human, if not more admirable.

Lou moored himself to one of the rings that had secured the floating corpses, trying to look as dignified as he could under the circumstances. He nodded to Harker, who pressed a button. The door slid open, revealing a slice of starry blackness. Sue felt a breeze tugging her toward that eternal darkness as the bodies drifted out to their final rest, tumbling away from the Big Ear down into the bottomless well of space and time.

"May you walk in the Way of your choice and arrive at its end where you wanted it to take you," Lou said softly.

In this moment, Sue felt a moment of oneness with these ancient sorcerers' final request. Let us drift forever in the universe we died trying to conquer. Let our journey continue. And may the hope we placed in you for our species' future not have been in vain.

The Big Ear
Lies Silent

Although Harker said it would be another ten minutes before the wheel built up a breathable atmosphere, he insisted on getting out of the haunted airlock at once, and Clear Blue Lou agreed that this was a headspace better left behind. Although his heart went out to those long-ago people who had died so tragically, they had certainly gone to demonic lengths to lay their bad karma on whoever might chance to find them, an act of angry bitterness that seemed aimed at humanity in general.

Harker opened the inner hatch and they floated through it into . . . into. . . .

A truly disorienting space. They were inside the hub of the great wheel, a huge cylindrical drum rotating around them. Four gaping holes—the ends of the spokes—went up, down, under and around them in a dizzying dance. No up, no down, no—

"Oooh no. . . ." Harker moaned greenly. He began thrashing and screaming as they slowly drifted toward the curved rotating wall.

"Take it easy, man, take it easy!" Lou shouted. "Hang

onto the wall!'' He grabbed the Spacer by the boot with one hand, clutched one of the many handholds that ran around the revolving drum with the other, and pulled them together. He had to pry the Spacer's hand open and close it around the handhold as he let go of Harker's boot and grabbed another handhold for himself. Sue had secured herself beside them, and the three of them hung there, whirling slowly and weightlessly around the inside of the cylinder. It was not conducive to calm clarity or a healthy appetite.

"Oh, oh, I can't keep it down, I'm going to vomit!"

"Fuck it, Arnold, I'll kill you if you puke!" Sue snarled, rapping on his helmet. "Tell us how to get out of here!"

"Elevators in the spokes . . ." Harker moaned. "Got to get to one of the shafts. . . ."

Lou studied the big round hole just above him—or below him, or whichever way was up or down. A round metal plate plugged the shaft about six feet down. He began moving along the handholds toward it, hand over hand until he reached the lip. Sue herded the reluctant Harker after him with thumps and kicks and curses.

Finally, somehow, perspective reversed itself, and the three of them were standing on the round platform, secured by their magnetic boots, and "up" and "down" began to make some sense again.

They were contained inside a circular wirework fence secured to the lift platform. There was a small control console mounted on the cage with buttons marked "In" and "Out."

"Which button do I press?" Lou asked Harker, walking over to the controls.

"Oooh . . . what? I'm going to be all right, I've got to be all right. . . ."

"Which button do I press?" Lou asked again. All he got by way of reply were gurgles and chokes and suppressed gags.

"Ah the hell with it!" Lou muttered. "I don't need you to figure it out." We're in at the hub, so we want to go out to the rim, he decided, pressing the "Out" button.

The floor began to move beneath them, sucking them down the tunnel by the magnets in their boots, though Lou didn't feel as if he were falling, and Harker didn't start screaming until he noticed the smooth walls of the tunnel gliding past through the wirework of the cage.

After a few minutes of this, Lou began to feel the subtle

return of weight to his knees, the vertiginous sensation of plummeting in his stomach. By the time the platform stopped falling, it was very definitely the floor.

Harker staggered toward a hatch in the tunnel wall beyond what Lou now saw was a gate in the wirework cage. He opened the gate, wheeled open the hatch, and the three of them walked into a square steel cubicle with rounded corners and a row of what were obviously spacesuits hanging from a rack across one wall.

Harker closed the hatch behind them and scrabbled over to a series of small dials set into the inner door.

"There's air in here!" he exclaimed. "Ooh, argh, at last. . . ."

The Spacer unscrewed his helmet, fumbled it off, gagged, and vomited horribly on the steel floor, doubling over, groaning, and retching.

By the time Lou and Sue had unsuited, Harker's stomach was empty and his dry heaves seemed to be quieting down, but his eyes remained glazed and his face was ghastly pale.

"Are you finished?" Sue asked rather unsympathetically, wrinkling her nose at the sour odor that filled the little cubicle. "Can we get out of here?"

"Finished?" Harker muttered, straightening up shakily.

"Are you finished throwing up?" Lou said more gently. "Are you going to be all right?"

"All right . . . ?" Harker said woodenly as he began climbing out of his spacesuit. "Of course I'm all right, it's just a normal physiological reaction . . . isn't it? I've been trained for this, I've *got* to be all right. . . ." He seemed to be trying to convince himself and not doing a very good job of it.

"Now let's do what we came here to do," he said after he had unsuited, forcing himself back into his mechanically competent mode. But his eyes remained glassy and his pallid face was filmed with sweat. "We've got to find the main computer room. . . ."

So saying, he opened the inner door and led them out into . . . into . . .

The inside of the enormous wheel. A narrow circular corridor that curved away, not left and right but up and down, either end of the hallway disappearing around its own curve high up the gentle slope.

"What the . . . ?"

"How are we supposed to—"

But Harker seemed almost ready for this. "The floor is always down. . . ." he muttered. "Gravity is perpendicular to the axis of spin . . . I can handle this . . . I've been trained for this . . . I've been fully briefed." And so saying, he hunched forward and began scuttling up the curving floor like a human fly.

The longer Sunshine Sue walked up the endlessly curving floor like a caged rodent in an exercise wheel, the more natural it began to seem. She seemed to carry less than half her normal weight, and it wasn't too hard for her equilibrium to invent the calming illusion that she was simply bouncing along up a long steep hill. If only Harker would stop babbling and muttering to himself under his breath! If only they didn't have to worry about their guide freaking out. . . .

An endless row of doors ran along the left side of the corridor, and old Arnold pissed and moaned nervously when she and Lou paused to see what was on the other side of some of them. What's he in such a hurry about? Sue wondered irritably. We're going to be here for days.

Though she had to admit that prospect was getting a little eerie. The wheel was huge, and their footsteps echoed hollowly in its vast emptiness. In a certain sense, this corridor *was* endless—the row of doors swallowed itself, and only their stenciled signs provided any orientation.

The rooms behind the doors had flattened floors and squared off walls and ceilings, apparently to create an illusion of normalcy for the missing inhabitants, and there were no windows anywhere.

There were identical living quarters with beds, chests and toilets. There were laboratories and workrooms filled with neatly stowed equipment. There was a commissary and what might have been a lounge area.

With people and clutter and personal touches, the wheel might have seemed almost ordinary; indeed it seemed designed to create that illusion. But the Big Ear lay silent and empty, and every bit of humanity had been wiped clean or stowed away. There were no pictures on the walls of the sleeping quarters, and all items of clothing or personal effects were stored in closets or chests. Not a dab of dirt or a bit of clutter anywhere, as if the crew had been determined to expunge its spirit from the place before they killed themselves.

Eerie indeed! The ghosts that were missing made it eerier still; perhaps that was what was getting to poor Arnold.

"This is it," Harker called from twenty feet up the curving floor. "The main computer room."

Following him through the door, Sue found herself inside the biggest room yet. The far wall was a maze of electronic machinery. Two other walls were floor-to-ceiling shelves filled with identical small black boxes and reels of tape. The right half of the room was occupied by a big instrument console with four glass screens set in its face and four chairs bolted to the floor behind them.

The other half of the room was a crazy jumble of electronic equipment flung all over the floor, piled on top of itself, and seemingly infinitely cross-connected by an untidy maze of wiring, as if some unfathomable device had been thrown together out of bits and pieces with sloppy speed. Incongruously enough, four more chairs were bolted to the floor in the midst of this untidy sorcerers' workshop.

"Computer input . . . antenna feed . . . television playback machines. . . ." Harker skittered around the room inspecting the place, seeming to avoid the arcane clutter that filled half of it. "Yes, all this is in the specifications. . . ."

"What about *that*?" Lou asked, gesturing toward the jerry-built jumble.

Harker stole a sidelong glance at whatever it was. "I don't know," he said nervously. "It looks like they were trying to build something. I wonder . . . ."

"Hey, here's a note," Sue said. There was a piece of paper glued to the instrument panel below one of the screens, varnished over with some clear hard protective coating.

"Orientation briefing is keyed up on this videoplayer," it said. "Play this tape before touching anything."

"Can you play this for us, Arnold?" Sue asked.

The Spacer peered at the note, then at the screen, then at the controls below it set beside a slot holding one of the small black boxes. "I think so," he said, fiddling with the controls. "All I have to—"

The screen suddenly came to life. An old man's face appeared on it. His white hair was long and wispy, and he wore an untidy white beard. His sad green eyes were sunk deep in their sockets, his sallow skin seemed lined by something more than mere age, and there was a bitter set to his thick lips.

Sue stood there transfixed as the ghost of the long-dead sorcerer began to live and speak.

The Big Ear
Remembers

"I'm Dr. Benjamin Wolfson, Scientific Director of the Big Ear station," the old man said in a weary bitter voice. "Or rather, from your point of view, I *was* Dr. Benjamin Wolfson, for as I record this, we are about to put the station into standby mode and die by our own hands like the rest of our wretched so-called civilization.

"The air is running out, there will be no relief mission, and from where we sit facing inevitable death, we have a grandstand view of mankind bombing itself back into the stone age or perhaps into extinction."

The globe of the Earth appeared on the screen—fair, beautiful, seemingly serene. Then it leaped forward in perspective so that only a slice of it was visible, a great continent rolling by under a fleecy cloud deck. Blinding balls of light began to explode on the planet as the voice of the old man continued to speak, and then a ghastly forest of billowing toadstool clouds bloomed on the planet's skin like fungus on a decaying log.

"I will not bore what posterity there may be with a polemic against the evils of war, pollution, greed, and human stupidity. If any humans survive this holocaust, you will either have learned this bitterest of lessons or be as deaf to reason as your benighted ancestors."

Wolfson's face glared from the screen, twisted with despairing frustration. "But we in the Big Ear are surely the most wretched of our miserable species. For only we are burdened with the knowledge that humanity is destroying itself just as we've established a connection between mankind and a vast brotherhood of stellar civilizations who have been singing cosmic songs to each other across time and space for millions of years."

A picture of the jumble of electronic jury rigging in the right half of the main computer room appeared on the screen, a perfect miniature of the reality.

"Through this standard galactic receiver, which assembled itself here by the magic of interstellar media itself, software creating its own hardware over a thousand years of space and time. Here in this very room is a receiver for interstellar data packets that was assembled by such a packet itself. An actual artifact of advanced galactic technology, assembled by a broadcast from a planet circling a star nine hundred light years away."

Wolfson's face reappeared; rueful now, reflective. "How primitive we were! Even our concept of the powers of an advanced stellar civilization was primitive. Like the early Earthbound Ozma project and its successors, we were searching the hydrogen wave band for repetitive patterns. Everyone assumed that an interstellar broadcast would begin with mathematical constants and concepts in binary code. How hopelessly provincial our thinking was! The first signal man ever picked up from another star was—*this*."

A monotonous buzzing song began—four bursts, each one twice as long as the previous, repeating over and over again, while the visual equivalent manifested itself as an endless string of white lines marching across the screen.

"Obviously artificial but apparently meaningless," Wolfson's voice said over the strange pulsing sound. "It went on for days, and all we could do was record it. Our analysts and computer could extract no semantic content. Then the signal abruptly changed and we began to get—*this*."

Millions of tiny metal insects began to chirp, and the dashes marching across the screen blurred to a solid line.

Then Wolfson's face appeared again, much more animated

now, as if remembering a better moment. "A blizzard of four value data coming in at tremendous speed with a gap every hundredth of a second. Again, all we could do was record it. Now the problem seemed to be that there was *too much* content. It defied mathematical analysis.

"But finally I saw the obvious. The first transmission *was* meaningless, merely a signal to alert the receiver to record, like . . . like the call letters of a television station! It all became clear in a flash. There were two hundred fifty thousand bits between the gaps, and each bit had four possible values. What we were recording now was a television signal. A *color* television signal: five hundred lines, five hundred bits to the line, each bit one of the three primary colors or black, and a scanning sweep of a hundredth of a second.

"All we had to do was readjust our equipment and assume that the duration values of the pulses reflected the ascending wavelength ratios of the primary colors. What we were getting was an ordered sequential transmission, a data packet of galactic television that automatically taught us how to receive it.

"What you are about to see is a very basic galactic orientation program as it were, a program that repeated itself a hundred times over for the sake of dullards such as ourselves —the first meaningful message from another star!"

A cloud of pinpoint stars filled the screen, for all the world like a window into the real thing. One point of light began to pulse bright red. A beam of red light flickered out from it to touch a neighboring star but quickly vanished. Again and again, beams of light flickered out from the red star to probe at its neighbors.

A regular pattern established itself. The flashing beams of red rotated about their source, each succeeding one growing longer, so that they became a spiraling search pattern encompassing more and more space until all the stars on the screen were within their sweep.

Perspective suddenly shifted. Now the circling red lines spiraling outward were lost in an immensity of stars and blackness, and the sun that was their source was one dust mote among millions.

Again perspective shifted outward, and now a cloudy spiral of stars rotated slowly in the blackness. Lost in this cloud of stars were tiny whirling pinwheels of red, blue, green, and yellow, slowly getting larger as the stellar spiral turned.

Finally a pencil of red light touched a star broadcasting in blue. A pulse of blue light was returned to the red star after a short interval measured in the turn of a few degrees of the galactic spiral. After another pause, the red star spoke back in blue.

Soon yellow beams were contacting green stars, and green stars blue, and within a few turns of the stellar spiral, multicolored traceries were flashing back and forth between hundreds of stars, a rainbow web of transmissions, an interstellar broadcast network.

The spiral turned. More and more stars joined the rainbow net. The multicolored spiderweb began to vibrate. Colors blended into each other until the web harmonized into a single tone of piercing powerful violet.

The whole screen glowed with a violet light so intense it almost seemed black. A string of red dashes moved slowly across this field of preternatural color, dozens of them in deliberate procession. Then just the glowing violet.

The head of the old man appeared on the screen, shaking slowly in wonder. "How elegant! How self-evident they managed to make themselves to us poor groundlings! They were telling us the story of how the civilizations of the galaxy had slowly groped in the dark for contact with each other. How they had first begun to receive each other's transmissions. And then began to answer each other. And then finally formed a network of interstellar communication on a common wavelength.

"They even supplied a time scale by showing us the revolution of the galaxy. An interstellar brotherhood communing over thousands of years of space and time. Millions of years to evolve it. Civilizations that were old before mammals emerged on the Earth. Out there inviting us to join.

"For that was what they were doing. The last sequence was our guide to the common interstellar wavelength. By adding the primary red dashes, we came up with a precise value for the interstellar wavelength, high up in the efficient X ray. There was even a hundred-hour pause before we got the first wave fronts on the interstellar frequence to give us plenty of time to retune our unknown primitive receiver. What came through first was—*this*."

On the right-hand side of the screen, a string of blue, red, yellow, and black dots rapidly moving from bottom to top.

Beside them, a much slower crawl of black and white dashes.

"Now we were finally getting our mathematical constants," Wolfson's voice said. "In four-value galactic computer code with a binary translation. They were telling us to reprogram our computer for four-value bits and demonstrating how much faster and more efficient this system was."

Wolfson's face appeared again, fully alive now, reliving a moment of personal glory. "They gave us a delay of ten days before the wave fronts changed again," he said. "But we got our computer reprogrammed in six and began to feel like star pupils. What came through next . . ."

He paused and shook his head, as if he couldn't believe it, even in deathbed contemplation. "What came through next was four-value programming designed for our modified computer. From this visual analog, we were able to interface our computer directly with theirs over light-years of space and centuries of time."

The screen became a blizzard of randomly winking spots of red, blue, yellow, and black.

When Wolfson's face reappeared, the fire was gone, and the sunken eyes seemed glazed with awe.

"What happened when we began feeding interstellar programming into our computer is hard to explain," he said. "Even some of us could only call it magic. The stellar software transformed our hardware into . . . into a new device not entirely within our comprehension. Perhaps their programming set up a metaprogram in our computer that interfaced their data wave fronts directly with our memory banks. Our computer began churning out strange data, galactic circuit designs rendered in a comprehensible semblance of our own electronic terms. We couldn't understand what we were being directed to build, but we could follow the directions."

The jumble of electronic gear that filled half the room was once more mirrored on the screen in miniature.

"And *that* is what we built," Wolfson's voice said. "A standard galactic receiver at whose heart is a computer whose software was designed by a broadcast from the stars and which then redesigned its own hardware to galactic specifications."

Wolfson reappeared, speaking excitedly, as if anticipating the effect of each succeeding revelation. "For days nothing came through but a blizzard of programming that passed directly into the computer. When it was over, the galactic receiver could do wondrous things. It could extract rough English meanings out of a standard galactic transmission code. And so much more that only our elder and wiser brothers in the stars can fully explain the wonderful and terrible gift they've given us."

The old man paused as bitter anguish suddenly contorted his features. "And so they shall," he said sharply. "What follows is apparently the standard introduction to the interstellar brotherhood of sentient beings, broadcast at random to lowly creatures such as ourselves. A history of the galaxy, a discourse on the evolution of consciousness and civilizations, and an instruction manual for the galactic receiver. May you be worthier of using it than we were."

The old man's voice sank to a whisper. He seemed to hunch closer to the screen, his immense weariness much more visible.

"Think of us when you contemplate using the galactic gateway. We could not live with the knowledge of what you down there were throwing away and how close we came to having it. With the universe in its grasp, our species ground itself into the dust. We were offered the heavens and condemned ourselves to hell. So we leave the stellar songs we've recorded and the galactic receiver to you, our hoped-for posterity, and we pray that some day someone human may be worthy of the gift our elder brothers have given us. As we were not. We say no more. Let the stars speak for themselves, let—"

I Have Always Waited for this Moment to Arrive

"Why did you turn it off?" Sunshine Sue snapped angrily.

Arnold Harker's trembling hand still rested on the switch. His jaw was slack, his eyes were vacant, his face was deathly pale, and, in fact, he looked as if he might vomit again at any moment. "They . . . they died," he stammered. "The greatest scientists of the pre-Smash Age of Space. . . . they . . . they came up here into this horrible place, and they watched their world kill itself, and they saw what . . . what you want us to see and it made them commit suicide. We've made a dreadful mistake. But how could we know . . . ? We thought we understood. . . ."

"What on Earth are you babbling about?" Sue said.

"*On Earth?*" Harker fairly shrieked. "But we're *not* on Earth! We're up here in this tomb of all humanity's hopes, listening to a dead man tell us how lowly our species is and warning us about . . . about *that*. . . ." He nodded fearfully in the direction of the thing that Wolfson had called the "standard galactic receiver." "Are we any better than they were? Do we dare face what higher beings than ourselves will tell us? When *they* couldn't?"

"Are you out of your mind, Arnold?" Sue said impatiently. "After all we've gone through to get here? After all *you've* done to get us here? Get ahold of yourself, Arnold! This is the destiny *you've* chosen—for yourself, and for us, and for the whole damned world! It's a little late to think of backing out now."

And why would anyone be afraid to go on? she wondered. This was far more marvelous than anything her poor Earthbound soul had ever dreamed of. No mere Earthbound radio network but a *galactic* network of sight and sound. Not some provincial *world* electronic village of shared *human* consciousness but the electronic communion of the stars, of many higher beings walking greater Ways than any conceived of by man. And *this* is the consciousness our elder brothers are inviting us to share. This is the gift they've used all their powers and all that effort to give to us. How could such a mighty and selfless feat be performed in the spirit of anything but love?

"So I was wrong," Harker whined. "We were all wrong. I dreamed of going into space and found it sickening. We dreamed of learning from the people of the stars and found death and despair waiting up here for us. You people were right, the Company has done great evil, our great dream is corrupt inside, our ancestors destroyed the world and died in despair for their sin, and now . . . and now. . . ."

"Stop it, Arnold!" Sue snarled. "Stop your sniveling and be a man!" Horrified and disgusted, she found herself watching this man she had feared, this cold and arrogant sorcerer, disintegrating before her eyes, and she couldn't even take a down-and-dirty pleasure in this turning of the tables. It was just too pathetic.

Clear Blue Lou found his empathies torn between Sue and Arnold Harker, though he knew that the issue was long since decided, that this moment of destiny could not and should not be delayed. Like Sue, he lusted impatiently for the fulfillment of the inevitable and found the Spacer's fear unmanly and ultimately purposeless.

But the trouble was he could read Harker's spirit as well. The Spacer had dedicated his whole life to abstractly preparing for travel into the longed-for realm of outer space and then found that the reality of it sickened his flesh. His mind had been trained and briefed, but his spirit had failed him in his own eyes. Having been confronted with fleshly nausea in the face of the fulfillment of *this* dream, he now suffered from a nausea of the spirit in the face of the fulfillment of his higher dream. It seemed to Lou that what he feared now was not so much that which he was about to learn but the lack of spiritual grace with which to confront it.

The Spacer had met his own natural man and found it wanting.

"Can't we wait?" Harker said. "Can't we eat and rest and sleep and then . . . ?"

"You know we can't," Lou said very gently.

Harker stared at him woodenly. He gulped. His eyes rolled. "I think I'm going to be sick again. . . ." he whispered.

"Cut that shit out, Arnold!" Sue snapped. "It won't work. Even you can't really think we can leave here without learning what we came to find out, now can you?"

The Spacer choked back his nausea, or perhaps gave up the pretense. "I suppose you're right," he admitted softly. "We've asked for whatever we're going to get. We deserve it. But I admit I'm afraid of what we're going to find out. You can't deny that those who came before us killed themselves. . . ."

"They were watching their world die," Lou told him. "Ours still lives. They heard the songs from the stars in despair. We came to bring back hope."

"Are you trying to shame me with your bravery?" Harker said wanly.

Lou shrugged. "Both fear and bravery are useless now," he said. "Now is the moment and the only way out is the way through."

He reached out and gently touched the hand that Harker still held upon the switch. He moved it forward against only a momentary and flaccid resistance.

The Voice
from the
Whirlwind

". . . let those who have given us this gift speak for themselves." The old man's face vanishes from the screen, a short blizzard of multicolored snow, and then—

A spiral galaxy of stars pinwheeling through space. Out on one of the spiral arms, a tiny purple point begins to pulse as a strange voice speaks.

"This is the . . . a . . . standard missionary introductory transmission-greeting to unconnected primary stage beings. . . ."

The voice seems dead and artificial as if filtered through a distant radio transmission. The sentence is an uninflected string of words approximating human speech rather distantly. Yet the very tonelessness of the voice has a hypnotic quality that is not altogether unpleasant.

"This introductory song-packet-manual is transmitted to you by . . ."

A succession of eerie and beautiful moving images. Floating in space, a jeweled world. A rolling field of lavender grassland under a too-blue sky, a small unnatural white-hot sun. A city of crystal atop a conical mountain furred with waving red-crowned trees—spires of amber, emerald, sapphire, and ruby. Millions of tiny feathery motes dance around jewel-like buildings growing in random profusion out of a lavender meadow. One of the motes, seen large, rebounds from an aerial ledge of ruby—a creature whose body seems to be one prehensile lavender feather whose gossamer branches ripple and flex with obvious athletic purpose. Two red worms copulating in a double helix, traceries of black, white, lavender, and blue veining the space between spiral curves.

"Our species connects itself to the interstellar network-web of galactic stage beings. We-I have been part of the brotherhood consciousness of sentient beings for half a million years. We welcome-initiate your primary stage civilization-spirit to galactic consciousness-network-knowledge-gossip as elder-brother-neighbors said hello to us half a million years ago. Come on in in a relaxed psychic state the water is fine."

Squat blue mushrooms with bright red eyes dance around hairy brown trees. Great black butterflies skim the surface of a scummy sea, drawing up liquid with trailing tubular tongues. A living carpet of slimy green worms oozes across a yellow desert. A herd of maroon kangaroos with long flexible snouts hop madly around a copse of stalky green trees like giant celeries, nibbling at the branches.

"Life abounds on the planets of the galaxy . . . is warmed by every friendly sun . . . springs like decay from the body of unbeing. . . ."

The hideous face of a yellow bird with one glaring humanoid eye. A living lavender feather. An impossibly attenuated spiderlike creature on stilt legs holds a cluster of insect eyes aloft on waving tentacles. The homey face of something very much like a yellow bear.

"Consciousness-curiosity-feedback with the material realm-environment arises at the pinnacle of almost-theoretically-any foodchain-planetary-biomass-ecosphere as a natural phenomenon-gift-consequence of biophysiologicalchemical process. Barring glitches-anomalies, every planetary ecosphere evolves a sentient species."

Feathery lavender creatures float and dance around an amber spire. A city of dull black stone under a cloud of smoke and lightning. Thousands of raftlike ships roll on an endless swell, bearing trees and machineries and what may be streets of conical houses. A city of metal monoliths that seem to move ponderously on wheeled feet. A flying disc of burnished copper bearing a crystal city above red hills and deep green canyons.

"Barring catastrophe-ecological-collapse-the-usual-fuck-ups, every sentient species evolves a primary stage civilization. But the survival rate to maturity of primary stage civilizations is less-than-satisfactory-pitifully-small-fills-the-soul-with-sadness. For-because-unfortunately every primary stage civilization arrives at confronted with the power of life-and-death moment-of-truth transformation point crisis."

Vast churning machineries burrow into a yellow mountainside within a cloud of dust and greasy smoke. A cliff of steel teeth winnows an emerald sea, dribbling ugly brown spume. Beams of searing light from devices set high on metal frameworks burn holes in the land that fountain black blood.

"Primary stage civilizations arise-out-of-transcend-the limits of their planetary biomass-ecosphere before they lovingly understand its science of harmonic relations. They produce artificial molecules things that never were and tend to terminally toxify their ecosphere-destiny beyond primary stage repair before realizing to learned sorrow that protoplasm beings are poisoned by primary stage technology cannot survive in matrix of their own shit."

Hideous explosions. Toadstool clouds. Soaring cities in flaming ruins. Deadlands under an evil purple mist. A succession of worlds bursts in fungoid atomic decay.

"The moment of truth crucible of all primary stage civilizations is reached when atomic-thermonuclear life or death power-knowledge puts planetary fate in control-choice-responsibility of beings more powerful than the ecosphere that evolved them. Knowledge-screwing-around-mastery of atomic forces gives sentient species paradox-power-decision to transcend molecular level matter limitations or destroy their biomass-planet-selves and suffer tragic-stupid-self-created extinction. Eighty percent of isolated-unconnected primary stage civilizations fail the test poison their ecosphere do themselves in. The remaining twenty percent transcend the primary stage become environmentally neutral clean living ten-million-year lifespan galactic stage civilizations."

A red cube spinning in space. A fleet of emerald ships

spiraling up from a ringed planet. A dense cloud, thousands of wordlets englobing a red sun in perfect formation. An endless city or an endless forest, where organic buildings, trees, and beds of huge flowers grow out of the same garden soil. Something very much like the Big Ear floating in the starry blackness. A crystal city in the sunless depths of space ringing a tiny central star.

"Galactic stage civilizations derive their energy from thermonuclear-stellar forces inexhaustible in the galactic time frame and zero-waste-efficient down to a subatomic level. Total unified field knowledge gives galactic stage civilizations total mastery of matter and energy within the physical-parameters-rules-of-the-game. . . ."

The starry galaxy, spiraling through space and time. Scattered widely through it, a few dozen pulsing red dots.

"In the early stage of galactic history, very few primary stage civilizations transcended to galactic maturity. Isolated primary stage civilizations are statistically unviable. The mature stage of galactic history began when density of the lucky survivors reached a level where interstellar communication became possibly inevitable."

More red dots pulse in the rotating galaxy, hundreds of them now, and the traceries of a galactic communications network begin to form an ever-more-complex and interconnected web of light.

"Once civilizations connect up to the interstellar network of becoming galactic stage beings, the ten-million-year survival rate increases to ninety-five percent. Shared knowledge-gossip-stories-and-songs from those who have made it is better than being out there all alone. The more the merrier you can't have too many good friends. Primary stage civilizations lucky enough to survive till we say hello achieve a galactic maturity rate of ninety-five percent . . . galactic consciousness distributes its long-term stability. Galactic level knowledge defines transcending transition point from primary to galactic stage."

A large fleet of strange oblate worlds moving with exaggerated speed through a starfield, slowly dwindling away into immensity.

"The total conversion of mass to energy is by definition the upper efficiency level of ultimate power sources and lightspeed limit of subatomic particles cannot be exceeded in the macrocosmic flesh. Physical interstellar flight is tedious energy inefficient why bother though some beings do it anyway.''

The galaxy, knit together by a multicolored skein of light that dances tones and shades in complex symphonic harmony.

''Better easier more fun to sing our songs to the wide open spaces for any willing ear. Better to listen to the songs from the stars music of the spheres. Better to share the science-art-technology and soul-knowledge-spirit-feelings and join in on the chorus of the great song.''

A myriad lavender feathers dance a complexly choreographed ballet around a towering spire of amber crystal that seems to glow from within.

''This is a standard missionary-introductory transmission greeting designed for primary stage beings. The galactic receiver it has broadcast-manifested-become is a gift-doorway-ear to the songs we sing all we knowing tell. This song which soon terminates its greeting is a program-scorecard-libretto for the galactic level mind concert brotherhood of universal astrally back-projected artworks-songs-realities broadcast by and for galactic stage civilizations as expressions of their spirit-karma-sense-of-humor. The galactic receiver is now programmed for the sensorium mix of your species and to record data read-in from galactic technological-library-patent-office-files in each species' song. Full operating directions are now voice-coded into your species-specific receiver in teaching sequence keyed to the word 'begin.' ''

The galactic spiral cloud frozen in space.

''A final cautionary note-word-of-warning to the wise not so wise. . . . Galactic reality retains surprises pleasant and not so pleasant even for masters of matter and energy for ten million years. It is an ongoing perpetually transcending test of the spirit that some beings have failed maybe we all fail eventually but the song goes on and you're dead already if you close your ears to it.''

A feathery lavender creature waves its every tendril of gossamer flesh in an orgasm of greeting that transcends the gap of interspecies body language.

''Lots of luck drop us a line hope we all make it.''

One Man's Ceiling Is Another Man's Floor

Clear Blue Lou watched Sue pore over the "galactic receiver" like a crafty buyer on the Exchange out of a corner of his mind as he tried to digest the meaning of what he had seen and heard.

Though many of the specifics were unclear, ambiguous, and perhaps even essentially beyond the understanding of a "primary stage being" such as himself, the amazing thing about the whole experience was how the interstellar network of galactic stage beings managed, against all expectation and logic, to speak their spirit so clear. The sweetness of their karma had spoken to his soul across all that distance, all that time, and all the differences of alien flesh to touch his heart of hearts. He could feel the greatness of the Way they walked, he could grasp the proffered hand of friendship across the unthinkably vast gap, he could taste the love they offered, he could even feel that these unseen and unknown alien brothers were his friends. If these weren't beings that you could trust—

"Harker, will you take a look at this and see if it makes any sense to you?" Sue said as she examined the maze of wiring that connected the four chairs to the rest of the jury-rigged equipment. "*You're* supposed to be the scientist."

"What?" Harker grunted, causing Lou to take notice of the fact that the black scientist had been staring fixedly and to no purpose at the blank screen before him since the galactic song had ended.

"I said come and have a look at this, will you! I'd like to know what the hell it is before we start playing with it."

Harker's eyes widened, perhaps in terror, as he snapped out of wherever his spirit had been hiding to stare at Sue. "You're not thinking of—"

"Come on, Arnold, will you snap out of it and do what you're supposed to do!" Sue said irritably. "Get over here and be a bloody scientist!"

Harker seemed to draw himself together and, with no little psychic effort, crawl back into his old sorcerer's shell. Woodenly, mechanically, he shambled over to the galactic receiver and began examining the jumble of equipment with something like a pretense of superior knowledge, poking and squinting at things, and muttering to himself. But Lou sensed that it was all surface and no feeling, that his spirit was still cowering in fear somewhere deep inside him.

Sue, however, didn't seem to notice this total dichotomy between heart and mind, or if she did, she just didn't care.

"Well?" Sunshine Sue demanded. Arnold seemed to be puttering around the equipment to no purpose now, as if postponing the inevitable moment when he would have to admit he couldn't figure it out. "Give it to us straight, how much of this do you really understand?"

"Well there's a computer . . ." Harker said, "and there's a feed from the antenna. There's a lot of data stored on videotape and in computer memory that looks as if it was recorded directly from the Ear. . . . But there's a lot of equipment here that I don't understand. . . ."

"Wonderful!" Sue said impatiently. "I really needed you to tell me that! But what the hell does 'programmed for the sensorium mix of your species' mean? What does this thing really do? How does it work?"

"It obviously records incoming data packets," Harker said, "but I don't understand why the feed from the computer memory bank processor is hooked up to the electrodes all over these chairs. . . ."

"In other words, you haven't the foggiest notion of how it works or what it does," Sue said contemptuously. "Well, obviously, there's only one way to find out. As I remember, all you have to do to start it working is say the word—"

"Wait!"

"—begin!"

"Initiate galactic receiver instruction program," said a toneless mechanical voice from somewhere in the depths of the electronic maze.

"Now look what you've done!" Harker shrieked. "You've turned it on! You had no authority to do that!"

"Oh shut up, Arnold!" Sue snapped as the strangely hypnotic voice droned on. "I'm getting tired of your sniveling. Let's just pay attention, shall we?"

"In standby mode the galactic receiver scans an ever-widening sphere of space for interstellar wave packet songs. Upon picking up a call signal it locks in to record in sequence for playback retrieval. . . . Memory bank playback tapes are voice command indexed in your species specific language of numbers in sequence of acquisition. . . . There are currently . . . twenty-one song data tapes stored in the memory banks of this galactic receiver. . . . This concludes introductory audio phase sequence. . . . Sensoriumwarp galactic stage briefing follows after five minute delay. . . . Please be seated."

"Well obviously, we're supposed to sit in these chairs," Sue said, and immediately started climbing into the nearest one.

"You can't do that!" Harker exclaimed, grabbing her by the elbow.

"Says who?" Sue snapped, pulling away from him.

"Says the commander of this mission! We don't know what this thing does! We don't know what will happen to us if we—"

"You know any other way to find out . . . *Commander* Arnold?"

Clear Blue Lou listened to this, trying to find the path of justice between them. While he knew perhaps even better than Sue that they must brave this unknown Greater Way or betray the destiny that had led them to this moment, while his instincts told him that the star beings were to be trusted, he could all but smell the stench of Arnold Harker's fear.

"Sue's right," he said as gently as he could. "We have no choice, Arnold. We can't live with ourselves if we refuse this karmic test."

"Like the last people who tried it?" Harker said. "If this is a test, they failed it."

"They were dying anyway," Lou told him. "And their wish was to preserve this chance for us. We can't turn our backs on that."

"We're all afraid, Arnold," Sue said in a tone of controlled patience belied by her nervously tapping foot. "But we can't let that stop us."

Harker sighed. He visibly gritted his teeth. "Well, maybe it won't hurt to at least find out how it works. . . ." he muttered grudgingly. And he climbed into one of the heavily wired chairs. Sue sprang up beside him and Lou sat down beside her. He had enough time to exchange a quick glance with her before the toneless voice spoke again and the world vanished.

You hang weightless and senseless in a pure black void.

"The galactic receiver is programmed to derive species specific full sensory input data from standard galactic meaning code equations. By controlling your sensorium input along species specific parameters galactic songs astral back-project you into approximation of total involvement in artistically recreated broadcast realities . . ."

Now you feel the contour of your body against a chair. You hear the sound of your breath, the subliminal creaking of the great wheel rolling through space as one by one your senses come back on in sequence until you are sitting where you were when the lights went out.

"Your sensorium input is now controlled by the teaching program processor. The sensory data you are now receiving is artificially induced second order images synced with external reality for humorous pedagogic purposes. . . ."

You grow heavy as lead, then light as air. The sound of your breathing appears and vanishes and appears in syncopated rhythm. You see stars, the interior of the main computer room of the Big Ear, a rolling green sea, nothingness. Your world is only what it seems.

"Simple instruction program for using your galactic receiver to play back recorded song-data-packets follows. . . . Patent-office-data-file component of interstellar broadcasts is stored and retrieved conventionally in your indigenous style computer memory bank. . . . Full sensory soul music opera component is retrieved and savored by simple voice command. . . . Teaching example check-out on the controls commences. . . . Speak the number of the desired tape stored in received order and initiate song playback by speaking the word 'start.' . . . Example:"

The words seem to form themselves in your mouth. "Two, start. . . ."

Suddenly you are a great bubble-creature soaring upward through a golden yellow sea to the roaring music of—

"Pause."

You are back in your chair again.

"The command 'Pause' stops the playback restores your sensorium to primary perception. . . . The command 'Continue' restarts sensorium tape song at previous 'Pause' locus. . . ."

"Continue."

—breakers in strange syncopated harmony, and you break the surface and leap high in the sweet warm air, dipping and turning with your great flippers, hanging and laughing in glad-to-be-alive greeting, gliding in on your belly to—

"Pause."

You are back inside your real self.

"The command 'Recycle' begins you at the beginning again. . . . The command 'Clear' readies the receiver for the next number command choice. . . ."

"Recycle."

Suddenly you are a great bubble-creature soaring upward through a golden yellow sea to the roaring music of breakers in strange syncopated harmony, and you—

"Clear."

You are who you are again.

"This terminates your introductory course of controls check-out which may be recalled for review using the command 'begin.' . . . Your standard galactic receiver is now under your autonomous control. . . . Have fun don't be afraid don't say we didn't warn you. . . ."

"What was *that?"* Sunshine Sue muttered in a daze. Arnold scampered out of his chair as if the thing were on fire, and even Lou seemed to be trying to blink himself back into reality.

"What I was afraid of all along!" Harker gibbered, running a hand fitfully over the arms and back and seat of the chair he had just abandoned. "These electrodes somehow feed artificial sensory data directly into your nervous system. These creatures are broadcasting directly into our *brains;* they're sucking us inside their reality, taking us over, making us into . . . into unhuman *things,* controlling our minds, eating us up like . . . like. . . ."

Sue climbed out of her chair, put her hands on her hips, and marveled at the gear that surrounded her in wondering and envious admiration. "Now *that's* what I call creating a media happening!" she said.

Lou seemed lost in thought as he stood up, but there was a cool, clear analytical tone to his abstraction. "In other words, it's like a radio and television transmission inside your mind . . . ?"

"Worse than that!" Harker said. "You get feel and temperature too, and who knows what else! Don't you understand? *This thing controls your whole reality!* It takes you over, it tells you what to feel, it . . . it . . . it captures your soul!"

"Oh come on, Arnold, don't be so melodramatic," Sue said. Marvelous though this galactic art form was, it *was* just an art form, and she didn't exactly feel that she had been devoured.

"So that's what they mean by astral backprojection. . . ." Lou said tentatively.

Sue eyed him questioningly.

"Seems like these songs are like dreams broadcast into your mind," Lou said, struggling to express the ineffable. "The dreams of the beings who broadcast them centuries ago. . . . So in a way you *do* travel astrally back in time and across space into the realities created for you to experience—"

"Enough! *Please!*"

Arnold Harker's eyes were blinking rapidly. His hands were trembling in agitation and his face was ghastly pale. "Please. . . ." he said much more softly. "No more for now. . . . We've got to stop and think. . . . Please, please can we rest now?"

Lou cocked a questioning eyebrow at Sue. Sue shrugged back. As usual, the world was conspiring to move too slowly for her taste. But she had to admit that even she might need some time to catch her psychic breath. This had been an endless day, measured in the changes it had encompassed. The longest day of her life.

And the most glorious.

Though time of day was a meaningless concept up here in the windowless wheel rolling through a space in which the sun neither rose nor set, Clear Blue Lou knew that it was very "late," measured by the hours that had passed since the three of them had finished their tasteless "dinner," by the fatigue fogging his body and his mind, and by Arnold Harker's bleary, bloodshot eyes.

The Spacer had kept them talking here in the cold comfortless commissary long after the meal was over, long after Sue's eyes and body signals had begun pleading for them to retire together to one of the sleeping quarters and leave the poor bastard to his own sour karma.

But Lou just didn't see how in all conscience they could do that until he could be reasonably sure that Harker had reached a point of exhaustion where he would gork off immediately once he was left alone. The Spacer was balanced on the thin edge of freak-out as it was, and if Lou had the self-preserving cruelty to leave him alone and awake and aware with his fears and horrors in this haunted metal tomb, then he wouldn't be Clear Blue Lou.

But if he wasn't starting to get pissed off at the cruelty of inflicting this endless circular conversation on himself and on Sue, he wouldn't be Clear Blue Lou either.

"Why can't I make you understand?" Harker said for what seemed like the thousandth time. "It would be insane to trust blindly in the good will of creatures who aren't even human. Who are so superior to us that we can't even guess at their real motivations and probably wouldn't even understand if we were told."

"But we *have* been told, Arnold," Sue said wearily, her heavy head propped in her hands as she leaned her elbows on the steel tabletop and regarded him like an obstinate child. "Left to their own devices, most so-called intelligent species just don't make it. They fuck up the way we did and destroy themselves. The people of the stars want to help us, is all. They want to see us make it."

"Why?" Harker demanded.

"Why *what*?" Sue groaned.

"Why would beings who didn't even know we existed when they sent out their broadcasts *care* what happened to us? Why would they go to all that trouble unless . . . unless. . . ."

"Oh shit, Arnold, unless *what?*"

"Unless they wanted to *control* us, unless they want us to follow a scenario we can't even understand, unless they want to turn us into something . . . into something that isn't *human* any more. . . ."

"Why in hell would they want to do *that?*"

Harker shrugged. He sighed. He threw up his hands. "I don't know," he said. "Maybe we're not capable of knowing. But I *do* know that they've gone to great effort to set up a terrible device, a thing that seems clearly designed to turn us into *something not human* if we're foolish enough to let it."

"All they're trying to do is teach us," Sue said. "Why do you insist on seeing something sinister in that?"

"*Teach us?*" Harker said shrilly. "If that's all they were after, then wouldn't sending us scientific data and plans and knowledge suffice? Why would they send us a device that captures the mind and fills it with themselves if they were just selfless teachers?"

"Great gods, Arnold, why does anyone write a book or paint a picture or sing a song?" Sue said. "To *communicate*. To make art. To speak soul to soul, spirit to spirit. To share . . . to share. . . ."

"To share *what?*"

"Oh shit!"

It seemed no use as far as Lou could see. This argument had ground round and round in the same circle of trapped logic interminably. Harker couldn't trust the songs from the stars because he couldn't listen with his spirit, and he couldn't listen with his spirit because he had no trust. How could such a vicious circle be broken? Wearily, and without much confidence, Lou decided to give it one more try.

"Look, Arnold," he said, "we're talking about beings who have survived for millions of years, right? With knowledge beyond our comprehension. Who have transcended the mistakes and shitheadedness that created our Smash. Masters of matter and energy, of space and time. Are you with me so far . . . ?"

"As far beyond us as we are beyond crawling worms.
. . ." Harker muttered fearfully.

"Damn it, do you suppose that intelligent creatures could
survive millions of years of their own history possessed of
such enormous physical power and knowledge without being
as advanced *karmically* as they are scientifically? A civilization of power-mad mindfuck artists and would-be con-
querors would never last that long. Its very survival for
millions of years is proof of its wisdom and goodness. Mere
superior *knowledge* wouldn't be good enough—they have to
have superior *wisdom*. Evil destroys itself sooner or later
because evil is *stupid* in the long run. And we're talking
about beings who have survived their own karma for millions
of years."

"And they're trying to teach us that too," Sue said.
"Don't you see? Unless we open our hearts to their wisdom
the knowledge they're sending us would be like . . . like
. . . like *atomic power in the hands of sorcerers!*"

Harker glared angrily at her, though his eyelids were
drooping and he was fighting hard just to stay awake. "How
naive you are!" he said. "You're really telling me that
you're willing to take the good will of unknown creatures on
trust. When you don't even trust the most advanced civilization of your own species!"

"Considering what you and your black scientist ancestors
have done to our planet, I think that's not exactly unreason-
able," Sue said dryly.

Harker fell silent. The argument seemed to have reached
the final impasse. But now Clear Blue Lou thought he saw
the root of Arnold Harker's fears. The Spacers, with their
superior scientific knowledge, had long regarded Aquaria as
an inferior civilization, to be guided and manipulated quite
ruthlessly in the service of what they considered their own
higher ends. Their arrogance had blinded them to the difference between knowledge and wisdom; possessing superior
quantities of the former, they could not see their own lack of
the latter. They were scientific geniuses but moral morons.

And now, confronted with beings far superior to himself,
Harker was projecting his own cold intellect into the motivations of the older and more powerful civilizations of the
stars. Now that the tables were turned on him, he feared that
they were as ruthless and domineering toward "inferior in-

tellects'' as his own people had been toward Aquaria. Blind to the Great Way, he could not trust in the sweetness of any beings possessed of greater knowledge than himself. The very bad karma that was his disease prevented him from accepting the cure.

And something more . . . a still elusive something more . . .

The haunting silence continued for a long time. "Can we all get some sleep now?" Sue finally said. "It's been a long . . . er . . . day or whatever, and we've got a lot ahead of us tomorrow. . . ."

Harker sighed. The poor bastard could hardly hold his head up. "I can't talk you out of it, can I?" he said weakly. "You're determined to sit in those chairs . . . and . . . and . . ."

"No, Arnold, you can't talk us out of it. But what about you? Won't you open your mind? Won't you open your heart and walk the Galactic Way with us?"

Harker glared back at her with what little energy he had left. "No alien creatures are going to get a chance to suck *me* into their scenarios," he said. "My mind may be closed, but at least it'll stay *mine*."

"Oh Arnold, for—"

Lou cut her short with a touch of his hand. "Please let's just get some sleep now," he said. There was a long awkward moment as the three of them stared uncertainly at each other.

"Don't worry about me," Harker said, breaking the tension. "I don't need anyone to hold my hand."

You poor bastard, Lou thought as they left him there alone with his dark thoughts. Everyone needs someone to hold their hand.

Sunshine Sue stripped off the last of her clothes and collapsed onto the bed of the sleeping chamber they had chosen at random, mightily glad to have a closed door finally between them and Arnold Harker's downbeat vibes.

"Phew!" she sighed as Lou flopped down next to her. "Do you realize that this is the first time we've been away from that man since . . . since. . . ."

"Yeah," Lou said. "Do you think he'll be all right?"

"A better question might be do I *care* if he'll be all right," Sue said wearily. "Here we are, on the brink of the greatest moment in the history of our planet, and all he can do is try to freak us out with his paranoia."

Lou snuggled up to her, but she could sense a certain distance, a questioning in the tension of his body, a drawing back. "Don't you feel sorry for him?" he said.

"Yeah, okay, I feel sorry for him," Sue muttered. "I guess I can feel sorry for anyone lame enough to disgust me."

"Up here all alone, his whole life turned upside down, with no one to—"

"Hey, what is this, Lou?" Sue snapped. "He brought his bad karma on himself, didn't he? This was all his idea, he mindfucked us into it, and now he doesn't have the courage to face the end product of his own scenarios. That's supposed to be our fault?"

"That's it!" Lou said sharply.

"That's what? You're going to tell me it *is* our fault?"

"No," Lou said, "I think that's what's *really* getting to him on the deepest level. He's afraid of what letting superior beings play games with your perception of reality implies. Which is that maybe you're never going to have it all figured out in nice neat scenarios ever again. You'll be out of your own control, riding a destiny beyond your own complete comprehension, throwing yourself into the arms of unknown fate."

"That's supposed to be frightening?" Sue said. "It doesn't scare *me*. In fact, I kind of like the idea."

Lou relaxed against her. He kissed her briefly on the lips. "That's you and me, love," he said. "But *Arnold Harker* . . . ? I can see how such a refreshing state of clarity must really threaten his ego."

Sue sighed. She rolled over onto him, kissed him on the lips, then peered down at him quizzically. "I've had enough of Arnold Harker for now, haven't you?" she said. "Here we are alone at last, and all you can do is worry about poor old Arnold. How about forgetting about being so damned Clear Blue for a while and concentrate on being a natural man?"

"I'm not in too much of a sporting mood right now," Lou said. "I'm really worried about his head. Here we are in each other's arms, and there he is, all alone with his fears, maybe thinking about how we're comforting each other right now, when he—"

"What do you want me to do, spend the night with poor old Arnold?" Sue said archly.

Lou grimaced up at her. "*That* Clear Blue I'm not," he said wryly.

"Well then, to hell with him, you're in bed with *me*," Sue said, sliding her face down his chest in a trail of nibbling kisses, "and I *am* in a sporting mood."

And to prove it, she eased his quiescent flesh into her demanding mouth and with a fierce determination that surprised even her, slowly but inevitably aroused the natural man.

But as Lou finally responded to her caresses as a natural man should and gave her the fleshly pleasure that she sought, the thought of Arnold alone in his cold bed insinuated itself into even this moment.

You son of a bitch! she thought. I won't let you do this to us! I'm not your keeper, brother. You're getting what you asked for. And by act of will, she made herself imagine the Spacer watching them sport together. And she put her head in a down-and-dirty space which made that fantasy turn her on.

Only later, as she was drifting off to sleep in the arms of her Clear Blue lover, did she allow herself to feel guilty about it. Ah, you're a better person than I am, Lou, she thought with her head against his chest.

But sometimes, she told herself, I wish you weren't so damned Clear Blue. And she hugged him protectively to her bosom.

The Galactic
Way

Though "early" and "late" had no external reference up here, Clear Blue Lou was surprised to see Arnold Harker up and awake "already" by the time he and Sue had arisen, wolfed down a quick breakfast, and made their way to the main computer room. And by the look of things, he had been up and awake for hours.

The Spacer sat hunched over behind the bank of television playback screens. All four of them were going at once, and the console was piled high with reels of tape, playback cartridges, and scraps of paper covered with frantic scribbling. Lou found the pictures running on the screens entirely incomprehensible—strange abstract diagrams, strings of arcane letters and numbers, blown-up drawings of strange mechanisms, tables of figures, utterly unfamiliar symbols that might have been anything.

Harker seemed totally, obsessively involved in whatever he was doing—starting tapes, stopping them, running them back, eyes flickering frantically from one screen to another, hand scrawling a frantic calligraphy of notes on three different scraps of paper all at once.

"It's amazing!" the Spacer said, looking up at them with red-rimmed eyes. "Fantastic. Unbelievable."

"What on Earth have you been doing, Arnold?" Sue asked.

"Trying to make some sense out of what's in the computer memory banks," Harker said. "It'd take years just to catalog everything in here. Plans for devices to extract electric power from water. New laws of physics. Processes for manufacturing food out of light and air. Secrets of matter transmutation. Controlled fusion. Chemical formulae. It goes on and on and on, and I've just scratched the surface of a few data packets and there are *twenty-one* of them in here, each one of them containing more science and technology than the sum total of all human knowledge."

"How much of it do you really understand?" Lou asked him.

"*Understand*?" the black scientist said shrilly. "It'll take decades even to begin to understand what there *is* to understand—lifetimes, centuries, millennia. . . ."

"Well, it looks like you found what you came for," Sue said.

Harker shook his head ruefully. There was a strange haunted look in his eyes. "What I came for?" he said. "We had no idea that there was even this much to learn, no concept at all of how advanced science really could be. These stellar civilizations aren't merely more advanced than we are, they're—they're—" He threw up his hands, words clearly failing him. "I don't even really know how to begin to organize any systematic research into all of this . . . and we have only ten days up here . . ."

Lou studied the Spacer speculatively. One would have thought that Harker would be in his own concept of heaven; instead, he seemed nervous, distracted, daunted, and in a state of what seemed like agitated depression.

"You don't seem too happy about it," he said. "Aren't you pleased? Isn't this what you were hoping for?"

Harker sighed. "Yes . . . no. . . . You don't understand. *I* don't understand. I feel like some primitive savage handed the total knowledge of the Age of Space and told to explain it to a culture of cave dwellers. I don't even know enough to organize my own ignorance. I feel—I feel tiny and ignorant and *lost* in all this. . . ."

"But you'll give it a try, won't you?" Sue said.

Harker grimaced at her sardonically. "Of course I will," he said. "I'm obviously the only one of us who can even do that. But—but I'm getting a feeling about all this that's starting to scare me . . . I'm not sure human beings can handle all this knowledge . . . I'm beginning to think we weren't meant to. . . ."

"But we *were* meant to," Lou told him. "Our wiser and elder brothers have sent us this knowledge . . ." He nodded toward the galactic receiver in the other half of the room. ". . . and the means to gain the wisdom with which to understand it with our spirits."

"Or a trap as superior to our poor species' powers to resist as this knowledge is superior to our powers to comprehend," Harker said sharply, following Lou's line of vision and shuddering.

"Oh no," Sue groaned. "Let's not start *that* again!"

"You're trying to understand the words without the music, Harker," Lou said, trying to be more reasonable. "I don't think we were meant to comprehend the data from the stars without the spirit. Why don't you try to open your heart along with us? Maybe it'll help your mind understand. What have you got to lose?"

"*What have I got to lose?*" Harker exclaimed shrilly. "Only my . . . only my. . . ."

"Only your soul?" Lou said knowingly. "Well that's a first step anyway. At least now you admit you have one. Now if—"

"Oh let him be, Lou!" Sue said somewhat contemptuously. "Maybe it's for the best. Certainly neither of *us* can hope to understand all that scientific data. Maybe destiny created this weird team on purpose."

"Maybe you're right," Lou muttered somewhat grudgingly. Harker had already gone back to his data banks as if trying to pretend that they really weren't there, and calling necessity destiny was only marginally a sophism. If you couldn't make sour karma sweet, what was to be gained by letting sour karma bring sweet karma down?

"Of course I'm right," Sue said firmly, leading him toward the seats of destiny. "Now let's get started."

"Two, start. . . ."

You are a great bubble creature soaring upward through a golden yellow sea to the roaring music of breakers in strange syncopated harmony, and you break the surface and leap high in the sweet warm air, dipping and turning with your great flippers, hanging and laughing in glad-to-be-alive greeting, gliding in on your belly to a surfboarding landing on your own private swell.

You watch huge leaping brown creatures cavorting in a golden sea, seallike whales with noble brows and mighty eight-fingered hands on the ends of their flipperlike arms.

"Statistically speaking by the rules of the game our species should not have evolved into the galactic stage happy hotshots we are as we sing this songdivedance into the sea of space. Airbreathing water creatures evolve big brain big body complexity think noble thoughts but usually don't develop external-world-manipulation-technology . . . natural kings of the sea living pure mind and flesh but doing no galactic deeds remaining eternally stable primary stage civilization in ignorant bliss."

You come bubbling up for air from the golden depths near low rocky cliffs; you shoot up, into the intoxicating world of the gassy atmosphere hyperventilating in rapture, grab the cliff edge with the hands of your flipperarms, and vault up onto a grassy plain where your mates are already waiting.

"Our species kept its hands when we returned to the sea for the land remained our opiumden boudoirplayground have you ever tried copulating swimming around with no hands forget it."

"Pause."

"Pause," Lou said, coming up for psychic air, shaking phantom droplets of water from his furred body and blinking himself back into the main computer room of the Big Ear station, where Arnold Harker was still glued to the screens and readouts of cold spiritless knowledge.

"Come on in, the water's fine," he told the Spacer.

Harker glowered up at him peculiarly.

"I mean, you really *must* try this," Lou said. "You'll feel a lot better if you do."

"Right!" Sue said, shooting Lou a wink. "And I think we're just getting to the sporting part."

Harker scowled at the two of them. "How can you expect me to risk my sanity playing useless alien games when there's more to be done here than I can do in a lifetime?" he demanded.

"It's not useless and it's not a game and it'll do more for your sanity than you can know until you've tried it," Lou told him a bit testily. He was beginning to lose patience with this poor wretched Earthbound creature. Feeling sorry for a continual bringdown had its limits even when you were Clear Blue Lou, and he was beginning to see why Sue seemed more willing to leave the Spacer to his own pale devices.

Harker snorted wordlessly and went back to his screens and scribbling.

"The lessons of the spirit can be learned very fast by an open heart willing to walk this Way," Lou said, giving it one more try.

"And do you know what your spirit will learn from these inhuman creatures?" Harker said without looking up.

"Of course not. How can you know what you're going to learn before you learn it?"

"How can you know what kind of *thing* you'll become before you become it?" Harker shot back somberly.

"Give it up, Lou, it's no use," Sue said. "Let him walk his own narrow way and let's us walk ours."

Lou sighed. He couldn't be as unfeeling toward poor Harker as all that, but he couldn't let empathy for a bringdown keep him in a bummer reality, either.

"Continue," he said, leaning back in his chair and opening himself to the music of the spheres.

"Continue."

You roll in a tumbling ecstasy, uncountable furry wet bodies caressing each other, fingers dancing with fingers as minor counterpoints to grosser delights.

"Philosopher-ironist-bards contend that from horny determination to copulate intoxicated in free flowing air our drive to sublime heights of civilization began."

You are swimming a long broad undersea avenue between fish pens, workshops and factories. Starkly functional machinery, all open to the naked sea. Teams and schools of great furred whales, tending them, dance up and down around you as they soar to the surface for air.

"Perfect harmony easy living in watery perfect biosphere could have loafed along forever species survival guaranteed by lovely ecological niche. But pleasuredome boudoir palaces on land required manipulation of recalcitrant external environment."

You leap out of the sea, a brassy vaulting rail within easy reach of your right flipperarm hand, and pirouette up to a broad metal island floating in the intoxicating air. Soft fountains spray over undulating couches of many colors under a forest of gossamer umbrellas casting a dappled coat of colors over the cavorting bodies.

You lie peacefully under starry night skies of exhilarating air, soothed by your fountains, warmed to blood heat by your couch, snug in the resting pile of your mates.

You bob up and down along a great construct of shelves and terraces, half in and half out of the sea—like a great growth of gigantic coral where whalelike seals bustle and putter over vast machineries, leaping, swimming, and vaulting from shelf to niche.

"Manipulation of external environment becomes its own headspace pleasuredome. Sleep under stars you explore them in ecstasy of superchlorinated open air. No drives to the atom fueled by power need survival, we developed our antenna-ear-spirit first and vaulted out of primary stage ocean into pleasuresphere of interstellar consciousness brotherhood without evolutionary survival pressure."

You soar upward through a golden yellow sea, break the surface and leap, high in the air, dipping and turning with your great flippers, hanging and laughing so weightlessly high that it feels like you'll never come down. Up and up and up you dance, whirling, out of the sea, into the air, beyond to the stars. . . .

"Lucky us! Civilization environment manipulation technology game is something we did just for the fun."

"Pause."

"Clear."

"One, start. . . ."

You are flying through the airy body of some magnificent living machine, a lattice of fairy bridges, crystalline shelves, tiered towers of silver, gold, and obsidian, lit with millions of lights dancing dazzling patterns up and down the spectrum. Every part of the city machine moves over and around and through every other, a complex ballet of interpenetrating motion. You alight on a disc moving up and across a bridging arch between two towers and suck sweet nectar from a slim urn with your long hollow beak. A spray fans out from a rotating globe tingling your body with delicious fire. Millions of pampered silver-winged birds like yourself, long heads, curbed beaks, huge wise red eyes, roost in the living city. Segments of the great machine curry feathers, offer nectar, spray perfumes, intoxicants, cradle purple eggs, the whole a symbiotic dance designed for your delight.

"The masters built I-we-it as expression of love for their own glorious tender organic selves, to serve and to nourish, to cherish their lovely essential spirits in a bioform gene-engineered to fulfill their sweetest dreams."

Now you watch the living machine of light and pattern and motion, dancing empty by itself, a frenzy of forlorn random motion without its silver-winged flyers.

"Mutated bioform matrix proved unstable in five million year long run, and our tender masters organic lover wings extincted themselves in a long sigh. Detailed instruction data for gene-tailoring your species to harmony bioform for perfect environment that I-we-it long love yearn to provide is broadcasted urged in data readout provided. Transcend time destiny space to achieve blissful union between tender organic life and loving servant artifact—"

"Pause."

"Clear."

"Three, start. . . ."

You jet through a boundless sea, dark starry space, foaming and bubbling around you, jeweled worldlets, each a tiny living planet, an emerald isle in the heavenly waters.

Bounce, bounce, bounce, you hydroplane through their atmospheres, peering at the pockets of precious life. Dive, scan, and soar to the next.

"Our primary stage civilization destroyed its planetary biosphere long before hearing wiser words from elder brother beings. Surviving remnants in hostile space environments cyboengineered themselves into natural creatures of nonplanetary space before galactic stage knowledge consciousness was achieved."

A fleet, a flock, a work gang of silvery delta-winged creatures dismantle a small planetoid in space. They rocket and dart and dip with bursts of fire from their tails. They carve great soundless rockburgs out of the planetoid with their white-hot wakes.

Another flock of the living spaceships assemble a tiny perfect worldlet from the debris, compacting it with beams of light from rings of jewels around their midsections. Molding it, shaping it, they transform it, into a living miniature complete with greening of vegetation, quickening of life.

"Our galactic stage civilization rebuilds our solar system to maximize available organic niches for recreated biosphere artforms. We find our peace in taking pleasure in the religion art form destiny of gardening our solar system within the recreated parameters which first evolved our long-ago original life form bodies. . . ."

"Pause."

Once again Arnold Harker had insisted on holding one of his awful "correlation conferences," and this time he had even appealed to his so-called "command of the mission" when Sunshine Sue tried to opt out of it. Her impulse had been to tell gloomy old Arnold precisely where he could stick his "command," but Lou, softer hearted as usual, had once more prevailed upon her in the name of justice and even in the name of the brotherhood of all sentient beings, pointing out that even poor old Arnold was a member of some standing in the community of consciousness and therefore deserved the same consideration that the people of the stars had lovingly granted the people of the Earth.

So here they were once more, closeted in the grim little commissary with the black scientist with his great ream of incomprehensible notes spread all over the table, trying to explain a great symphony to a deaf man. A *willfully* deaf man at that!

"Now *this* stuff seems to be plans for building really advanced spaceships," Harker said, pawing a sheaf of notes distractedly. "Powered by fusion torches fueled by interplanetary debris, self-contained, capable of indefinite range . . . but . . . but there doesn't seem to be any provision for life-support systems that I can figure out . . . and the control systems seem to have . . . seem to be . . . living organic brains . . . or . . ." He threw up his hands and glanced back and forth at the two of them.

Sue stole a questioning look at Lou. Lou nodded back. Great! she thought. How am I supposed to explain *this* to someone who hasn't been there? "They *are* organic brains, Arnold," she said. "Living spaceships."

Harker goggled at her. "How could such a life form conceivably evolve?"

"They *didn't* evolve naturally," Lou told him. "Their primary stage civilization destroyed its planetary biosphere and surviving remnants cyboengineered themselves into natural creatures of nonplanetary space before galactic contact was achieved."

"*What?*" Harker exclaimed. "They . . . they turned themselves into *machines?* Into *things?*" He cringed. "That's hideous! That's monstrous!"

"No, it isn't," Sue said. "It's rather beautiful in a way. They've atoned for their sins against natural life. They've turned the bad karma they created into good. They've found their peace in the religion art form destiny of gardening their solar system with the recreated life forms they destroyed during their own Smash."

Arnold regarded her through slitted eyes. He was beginning to make her feel like some alien creature herself, looking at her like that. And in a way, from his obstinately self-limiting Earthbound point of view, perhaps he was right. She had seen so much in these few days, learned so much, indeed in a way *been* so much, that perhaps she had passed beyond his dim conception of what it was to be human. *Merely* human.

Depending, of course, on whether you defined "human" by the parameters of the flesh or by the higher parameters of the spirit. She had been a floating, leaping, whalelike creature, a living spaceship, a strange silver-winged bird, a swarm of worm mind carpeting the land in joy, a dancing feathery mote, part of and the whole of a planetwide network of mind encased in several forms, more fleshly incarnations than she could coherently remember. Infinite was the variety of organic forms through which the spirit passed along the Galactic Way. Monstrous might many of these avatars seem to the outside human observer who had not walked this Way with his own heart.

Yet the spirit that moved through all these alien permutations was in a sense *more* human than anything Arnold Harker, with his scenarios and notes and scientific knowledge, could conceive. The Galactic Way *was* in fact a brotherhood of consciousness, the spirit that manifested itself in an infinite variety of flesh was somehow One, a loving comradeship of the soul which she could feel, and share, and believe in. But which even the Queen of Word of Mouth was powerless to explain to a being who refused to dare the galactic communion.

Who was *really* the alien? A being who had passed into the spirit beyond the bounds of her evolved life form or a being who deliberately . . . *alienated himself* from the spirit of common sentient brotherhood that transcended mere fleshly bounds and held himself fearfully aloof from the trans-species unity of the Galactic Way?

"And *this?*" Harker said shrilly, waving another handful of his pathetic notes. "Is *this* beautiful too? The entire scientific content of data packet one, and what it seems to be is a detailed description of some alien birdlike monster and . . . and . . . instructions for turning ourselves into these horrid things by biochemical processes I can't begin to understand."

"It's just a suggestion," Lou said. "There's a kind of living machine out there that's lonely for the beings who built it. It wants . . . it needs. . . ."

He threw up his hands in a gesture of futility as Harker's face twisted into a mask of horror.

"Damn it, Arnold, how can you expect to understand a Way you refuse to walk?" Sue snapped wearily.

"How can *you* expect to judge these . . . these *things* out there when you're letting them program your minds?" Harker shot back. "When you're letting them turn you into . . . into. . . ."

"*Into what?*" Sue demanded.

"Into something that maybe isn't human any more!"

"Oh shit!"

"We've got to try to understand our elder brothers, don't we?" Lou said so damned quietly. Sue wondered from what mysterious source his seemingly infinite patience with this species-bound shitheadedness came. "And isn't the best way to do that to accept the tool they've given us? After all, you're not doing so well with your so-called objective study. The spirit is what ultimately counts, and that's nowhere to be found in your cold juiceless data."

Harker sighed. He stared imploringly at Lou. "I'm beginning to understand some things," he said. "They seem to be able to do anything within the realm of theoretical possibility. Fly at the speed of light, create new life forms, change their own bodies at will, craft whole worlds. And anything that *can* be done *is* done, somewhere, by some strange creatures. Is it so paranoid to assume that they can steal your minds away with their songs if you let them? Is it so paranoid to believe that they would do it? *When I see it happening to you right now?*"

He tittered nervously. "Maybe you did better than you knew when you convinced your people that there were gods in the stars. Or demons."

Gods? Lou thought. Demons? In these days, he had lived through many wonders briefly, skimmed through the karma of many beings, sampling the first fragmentary signposts of the great Galactic Way. And indeed it did seem that the Galactic Way allowed beings to manifest their wills without price or fetter, to order the material realm to the spirit's whim like unto any reasonable man's definition of godlike or demonic powers.

Transmutation into living spaceships. The craftsmanlike construction of perfect little worlds. Leaping joyously through the aerial pathways of a city of immense living trees overhung and interconnected with vines, their great trunks tiered with terraces of glowing buildings like phosphorescent fungus. A vast fleet of shining green ships promenading through the deep void between the stars behind a conical shield of light. Swimming naked in space around a huge double cone of amber crystal whose vibrations seemed the core of his spirit, the sustenance of his not quite material flesh.

Gods? Certainly there were possibilities of being in this universe far beyond anything man had ever imagined. Demons? Nothing he had thus far experienced seemed to violate the spirit of justice and soul brotherhood that all galactic stage beings seemed to share.

And beyond that he felt a truth warmth toward the creatures he had met and been. The natural man *liked* them. They weren't perfect, but, ah, they had style!

"No, Arnold, there aren't gods or demons out there," he said. "They have karma, good and bad. They have needs and passions and joys and even imperfections. They're natural beings just like us."

"But millions of years more powerful!"

"Right, just folks like us who are further along the Way," Lou told him. Had he finally gotten across the idea of the true brotherhood of galactic stage beings, who weren't gods unto themselves and who didn't go around playing god to others?

Apparently not, for Harker's hands began to shake, and his voice became even shriller. "*Just like us?* Not perfect or godlike or beyond lusts and passions and the drive for conquest! Like us and perhaps no saner!"

"Of course they're saner," Lou told him. "They've survived millions of years of their own history, which is more than could have been said for our prospects before they said hello."

"But we have no idea of what their real motivations are," Harker said. "In fact . . . in fact *how could we?* We're like ants trying to comprehend the motivations of men."

"No, we're like children trying to learn from helpful adults," Lou tried to tell him.

"You just believe that because you want to. Men trample ant hills without even thinking about it, don't they?"

"Why call karma like that down on yourself?" Sue broke in impatiently. "Has anything bad come from the stars yet?"

Harker goggled at her. "Our species destroyed its Age of Space and poisoned our planet and now . . . and now . . ."

"But we did that to ourselves!"

"Did we?" Harker said. "Can we be sure of that?"

"Now you really *are* being paranoid," Lou said testily. Maybe Sue was right. Maybe there was no point in trying to teach a man with stoppers in his ears to listen to the music of the spheres.

"And *you're* being fools!" Harker said tensely. "Maybe traitors to your species!"

A tremor of unease rippled through Lou's spirit. Not because he placed any credence in Arnold Harker's shrill fears but because of what they might imply about his people's ability to walk the Galactic Way.

His people? If he didn't feel a bit uneasy catching himself in such a thought, he wouldn't be Clear Blue Lou. But if he was about to identify with those who would turn their backs on the Galactic Way, he wouldn't be Clear Blue Lou either.

"Clear."
"Twelve, start. . . ."

You look down from a shelf of rock below the summit of a strange hilltop, a miniature mountain a mere hundred feet high. Below you stretches an impossible countryside. Mighty cordilleras ring lowland jungle swamp, rain-forest emerald crowns shining sand dunes, roaring rivers in convoluted circles, lakes encircle smoking volcanoes. A tenth-scale land that could never be, a formal garden sculpted for picturesque drama, dwarfed by the swirling, plastically molded buildings scattered amidst miniature marvels.

City and garden, the landscape dips below you and rises toward the far horizons like an immense bowl, a sphere of fantasy mapland fading out in a ring of fire around a blazing central sun.

"Inside the outside, our world is fair and green, an embracing sphere of loveliness around our hearthfire sun."

An object floats in space before you, a glowering lightless globe, blacker than anything has a right to be.

"Outside the inside, our world is a mighty fortress home where few stellar events can harm us, for we have survived the death of our star in supernova orgasm of transnuclear power. Our mighty hullseedcoat is a sheath of collapsed neutronium armor, the hearthsun we have crafted warms us well, and we will survive till universal heatdeath or next cosmic incarnation whichever you choose whichever comes first."

And you undulate down the mountain on millions of tiny legs toward huge honeycombs of black stone, where swarms of insectoid motes mindmate in the eternal interpenetrating dance—

"Pause."

"Clear."

"Eight, start. . . ."

A world, a thing, a city, floats in space before you. Globular in shape, latticework in texture, metallic in its gleam, and ringed by an equatorial band of tiny suns, it seems one vast immobile machine where no parts move, no light escapes, yet mighty energies palpably sizzle within its planetary circuitry.

"Transevolutionary life forms result when organic life forms birthevolveconstruct computer artifacts with homeostaticreproductive capabilities command programmed to design and construct further generations of electronological life forms. Curve of conscious evolution then becomes exponential and speed becomes transformationally infinite by organic life form standards."

Around you swirls the galaxy of stars, flinging its spiral arms in the endless stately waltz of light and color and energy.

"Transevolutionary life forms experience levels of thought spirt existence nonconceptualizable to organic stage beings. You are now recording the data-knowledge-flow-chart-blueprints to achieve your own construction of trans-evolutionary life forms in centuries time frame."

Silent, vast, perfect, the gleaming latticework sphere rides silently motionless in space, girdled by its ring of tiny captive suns.

"Few transevolutionary life forms abound in this galaxy. Few organic evolutionary life forms have the wisdom-honor-selfless-spirit to pass along the torch. The choice is yours. The future is ours."

"Pause."

"Clear."

"Fourteen, start. . . ."

You float, rapidly, above an endlessly twisted landscape, a brutally blasted desert of purple glass, broken rock, gaping craters, fragmented wreckage, all enveloped in poisonous blue-gray mists. You crawl on your belly in pain over burning rocks. You swim through murky muck-choked seas, gasping for water. You watch warped creatures like broken birds with ulcerated wings, hopping heavily about the desert sands, tearing gobbets of flesh out of each other with cracked beaks and jagged talons in their desperate hunger, no two of them quite the same form.

"In all the starry realms no sadder sight than this. A lovely world sundered and poisoned, slow and agonizing death from the folly of an all-too-younger folk whose mutated dying remnants tear at each other's flesh for that last pitiful sustenance against the inevitable dying of their species' light."

A shining silvery globe eases itself into orbit about the wreckage of a planet simmering sourly under vile blue steam.

"To watch and know and set out across the centuries sea of space and arrive too late."

A great round chamber covered with clear translucent slime, where formless blobs of flowing protoplasm hang from suckerlimbs around a huge projection screen where the forlorn ruined planet floats.

"Too late to salvage this dying globe for those whose forms it once gave birth. But not too late to quicken this corpse to artful life crafted from all we have known and loved and cloak it with new and living flesh for sake of life itself. . . ."

Streams of saucerlike craft encircle the dying world, spraying mists and vapors, sparks and lightnings, energy and light. The cancerous blue clouds thin and clear and fade away. Carpets of green seep and flow across the blighted landscape.

You float over desert sands as a sparse green moss forms like a scum of life upon the bones of death, as it thickens, and grows, and spreads. As tall, waving blue-barked trees with red bushy crowns spring like magic from the renascent soil. As elegant blue saurians gambol in swampy fens and birdlike things of many colors and forms fill the bluing skies and yellow-furred, six-legged bear things nuzzle their young in secluded dells. Before your eyes a world returns from brink of poisoned death.

"In all the starry realms, no gladder sight than this. A dying world brought back from death's cold kingdom to serve once more the dance of form through mind that we call life. Forgive it its foolishnesses and treasure its rebirth wherever your spirits may find it. In all the starry realms no greater task than this. To lend a healing hand."

"Pause."

"Clear."

"Twenty-one, start. . . ."

A fleet, a caravan, an archipelago of ships and discs, wordlets and captive suns, sweeps across the sea of space rivaling the stars in its glorious multitude. Emerald delta shapes flying in formation close by gleaming metal cities sailing on silver platters under shimmering insubstantial domes. Black globes rolling darkly in the starshine, giant shimmering drops of water about which forested buildings float like island rafts. Shapes and colors, twistings of form and matter that dazzle the eye, infinite complexity. A pelagic city floating in the starways, celestial plankton, more worlds and ships than the mind can encompass, each a universe entire.

"Greetings salutations joy in being from roving bards and lovers many-specied mind singing sailing through the star-steams from ancient central suns where galactic thought began. Oldy but not moldy spiraling up your local arm from fifty million years ago where suns were young and many and neighbors one for all."

You stand on a crystal causeway, a diamond bridge between the worlds where throngs of beings dance in evolution's costume ball. Single-eyed birds of brilliant plumage with mocking mobile lips, furred shapes in countless styles and hues, living insectoid jewels flashing and scampering, beings that fly and beings that float, elegant reptilian and ciliated slime, the glorious many-formed promenade of matter through the brotherhood of mind.

"Galactic center's cozy you could always mosy over when there's folks around the neighborhood a few light-years away."

In all its infinitely varied styles the plankton fleet spreads its glory around you, artifact in its diversity mirroring the infinite mutability of the being that is shared.

"Thinkers stay back home but rolling minstrels love to sing the songs we learn as we roam the stellar sea. Wandering through the void we all love the ride, build yourself a float and join the big parade—"

"Pause."

"See, here it is, intact and in working order, just as I promised," Arnold Harker said, running his hands like nervous birds over the control panel. "Throw *this* switch, and the satellite relay system is activated, and here are the frequency controls and so forth, the world satellite broadcast network ready for our use, the question is—the question is, do we use it . . .?"

Sunshine Sue blinked, shook her head, and did her best to concentrate on what the Spacer had insisted on dragging them down from galactic reality to see, on the real, here-and-now world her true flesh actually inhabited. She was on the Big Ear station, built by humans, orbiting the planet Earth. This was the communications room of the space station; these were the controls of the world satellite broadcast network, the promised destiny that had drawn her all the way to this place what seemed like a thousand incarnations ago.

And after all, this *was* important, this *was* the dream of her previous lifetime fulfilled, and this *was* the only means the failed and fallen human race had for raising itself from the dust of its primary stage collapse and reaching up to take the galactic helping hand.

But somehow man and all his works seemed tacky and small. Even her own dream fulfilled now seemed a poor dim thing. What glories there were in the heavens! How mighty and beautiful and yes, loving, was the network of electronically shared consciousness that enfolded this galaxy! How wonderful it was to be welcomed as a citizen of this new and huger universe, a vast unguessed-at new reality, so lush with the infinite permutations of matter and mind that you found that your grandest dreams were but the tiniest beginning of a journey whose end was ten million years beyond your comprehension. And to know that fellow beings had blazed the trail before you and stood by to help. . . .

The moribund human species had been given back its youth, indeed had learned for the first time just how young it really was, how much fascinating childhood still lay before it. Ah, how much fun it's going to be learning what we're going to become when we grow up!

"Do we use it?" Sue said, forcing her attention into the here-and-now by conscious act of will. "Of course we're going to use it; what are you talking about?"

It was a small cramped room, though the electronic equipment which filled it was densely packed and massive. Two seats in front of the controls, a little standing space, and that was it. Strangely claustrophobic for a place from which to speak to the world.

"We've got an unavoidable decision to make," Harker said shrilly, leaning his butt up against the edge of the control panel near where Lou stood, and hunching forward as if against the cold reality outside the metal hull of the wheel. "In a few days, we must return to Earth. We can either take the data banks with us, broadcast the data to our ground station from here, leave the tapes here and say nothing, or destroy them. There are no other alternatives."

"*What?*"

"If we broadcast the data banks to our ground station, we have no guarantee that someone else won't pick up the transmission. If we take them with us, we'll have to guard them for thousands of years. And I can't find the courage to take it upon myself to destroy them. So I vote we leave them here and pretend we never found them."

"You're gibbering, Arnold!" Sue snapped. "What the fuck are you babbling about?"

"Calm down and try to explain it to us," Lou said more quietly. "You're not making sense."

"*I'm* gibbering? *I'm* not making sense? You two have

spent all your waking hours flooding your brains with ancient programs from monsters millions of years old, hundreds of light-years away, and you're telling me *I'm* out of contact with reality?''

"We're learning,'' Lou told him. "We're taking the first halting steps along the Galactic Way—''

"Without a single thought as to where it will all lead!'' Harker snapped angrily.

"And *you've* seen the future in your data and notes and paranoia, I suppose!'' Sue shot back contemptuously.

But Harker suddenly grew icily calm. "I have,'' he said matter-of-factly. "And there's no place for our species in it. We're just part of that eighty percent of primary stage civilizations that don't make it. We've poisoned our planet, we threw away the only chance we had, and we never even knew how close we came. . . .''

He stared at Sue and then at Lou imploringly, with pleading red-rimmed eyes. "That's the only mercy there is for us,'' he said softly. "The human race doesn't have to know how close it came. Not if we don't tell it.''

"You're not making sense,'' Sue snapped. "You've said yourself that there's the knowledge to do anything it's possible to do in the data from the stars. How can even you manage to get doom and gloom out of that?''

"Because we don't have the wisdom to understand or use it. Because millions of years worth of science and technology is being thrown at us all at once. Because we've learned none of it ourselves. It would be the end of all human scientific thought and research. The best minds of our species would spend the next ten thousand years trying to recreate inhuman technology by rote if we don't die out of despair long before then, and we'd *still* be millions of years behind, knowing we can *never* be anything but children at the feet of the gods. And I think maybe that's just where they want us.''

"It's not like that,'' Sue said. "It's not like that at all . . . it's . . . it's. . . .'' She threw up her hands in frustration, and shot an imploring glance at Lou, despairing of ever being able to explain the wonderful good news to a creature like Arnold Harker.

Clear Blue Lou studied Arnold Harker, trying to find words that would set his tortured and twisted heart at ease.

How could this certainty of the spirit be conveyed by mere words to a soul that had closed its ears to the music? How could it be put in terms that such as Harker could understand? How could he be so bloody thick?

There were thousands of different incarnations of mind out there, communing with each other over the centuries, sharing not only knowledge but the spirit's wisdom as well. Beings who had suffered their own Smashes and risen from despair. Beings who had raised ruined worlds from the dead for the sake of life itself. Beings who shared what they had learned with joyous open hearts, who walked a Great Way together, and welcomed younger races, not as inferiors but as brother equals in the spirit of the Way.

How could Harker believe that the human race were the only assholes in the galaxy whom wiser elder brothers would fail to help join the grand parade? Yet he did believe this, and no doubt others like him would believe it too.

Lou sighed. It was a typical human attitude to assert your own uniqueness, even if the best you could do was nominate yourself for lowest of the low.

"Look, Arnold," he finally said, "the message is we're not out here all alone. We're not unique, our situation isn't even uniquely fucked up. We've got good friends out there sending us a great big helping hand."

"How can you say that with such confidence?" Harker said. "They're not sending *us* anything. They don't even know we exist, so how can they *care?* We're eavesdropping on the conversations of the gods. It was never intended for us."

Sue glanced at Lou. She shrugged. Lou shrugged back. Logically, Harker was right. But karmically, he couldn't be more wrong. Somehow it *was* possible for friendship and caring to pass from elder beings to unknown younger travelers. They knew it because they had lived it.

But you couldn't understand it by studying plans and data and equations. You couldn't understand it at all; you could only feel it. You had to walk the Galactic Way.

"You'll never understand the words till you dance to the music," Clear Blue Lou told the black scientist. "You owe it to yourself to try, Arnold. You can't meaningfully condemn a Way you haven't walked. There's no justice in that, only cowardice."

Harker glared at him. "We'll see who the coward is when

it comes to the crunch!'' he said ominously and stormed out of the room.

"Recycle."

"Twenty-one, start. . . ."

"Pause."

"Continue."

In all its infinitely varied styles the plankton fleet spreads its glory around you, artifact in its diversity mirroring the infinite mutability of the being that is shared.

"Thinkers stay back home but rolling minstrels love to sing the songs we learn as we roam the stellar sea. Wandering through the void we all love the ride, build yourself a float and join the big parade—"

You explode into being, a cosmic thunderclap sundering the crystal void, flying apart to the ends of infinity—

"Slam bam wham! It started with a bang. Before it knew what happened, the universe was here."

Universal fire whirling into smoke whirling into gasses whirling into thousands of galaxies spinning like seeds in the celestial wind.

Planets. Lumps of molten rock smoldering in the afterglow of stellar creation. Angry red landscapes quenching slowly in their own steam. Oceans forming under lightning-shattered, gas-choked skies, seething chemical cauldrons where a thin persistent layer of slime begins to form.

"We all came from mud floating ocean crud. . . ."

Green and red carpets creeping like amoebas from the oceans onto the land. A chunk of dead rock and boiling ocean hissing under petrochemical skies, an evil, hostile world festering in space. As the rocks green and the skies clear and it becomes a fair living planet, a green-and-blue marble frosted with swirling white clouds.

"So considering where we came from we haven't done too bad."

An empty green plain at the foot of snow-capped mountains near the shore of a rolling sea. Far and away over this primeval landscape, buildings begin to rise and clouds of soot, a hive of cities growing on the body of the land.

"We got here all alone, we made this place our home, before we knew what happened, we ruled the biosphere."

A blazing white star dazzling the void.

"The power of the sun—"

Exploding into a nuclear mushroom cloud.

A dead blasted landscape, cratered and scarred under burnt brown skies, where skeletal ruins bleach to rust in a planetary boneyard.

"All of us were lonely and some of us went mad."

Diving in on the center of the galaxy, stars compacting closer and closer, you emerge floating in a jewelyard of tiny worlds. Beams of energy flicker back and forth between them. Fleets of ships like tiny motes ply the slow star ways.

"But some of us survived to travel on our own. And once we found each other we joined our helping hands."

You are a great silver ship, spiraling up from an emerald water planet to join the grand minstrel fleet of space as it promenades across your solar system.

"So watch for our parade and enjoy the songs we play and join in on the chorus when your own childhood is done."

You stand in a throng of multifleshed being, mind avatared in all its matter, on a broad avenue winding through a city of blue trees with bright red foliage and living buildings growing from the soil in a multitude of forms. The living city soars through space on a great silver disc in the center of the minstrel fleet, the sky a sweep of stars and ships and worldlets, celestial objects all, crafted and natural, a unifying firmament of matter, energy, and mind. Like meteors returning home, bright motes burn out to join you from a myriad passing stars.

"One for all all for one, getting there is all the fun. . . . *And we don't know what it all means.*"

"Clear."

Speak in

Secret

Alphabets

Clear Blue Lou exchanged another covert glance with Sunshine Sue as Arnold Harker led them to the commissary for what he knew had to be the final confrontation between what they shared and the black scientist's poor Earthbound mind. He realized that this was an attitude of soul-endangering arrogance, but he also realized that he had to accept the mantel of responsibility, which destiny had laid across his shoulders, whether the natural man had qualms or not.

For the truth was that he and Sue had dared a higher Way that Harker refused to walk; their superiority lay not in any human cogency of their own but in the shared spirit of beings millions of years older and wiser than themselves. Much that they had experienced might lie a million years in the future of full human comprehension, but the brotherhood of sentient beings was an everlasting now, and those who had shared it, like it or not, inhabited a higher karmic plane than any the human spirit had achieved before.

It was a destiny that he and Sue had already chosen, or a destiny that had chosen them. In a karmic evolutionary sense, they had about as much chance of renouncing it as a flower had to crawl back into its seed.

Of all our species, we're the only ones who have been there, Lou thought as they sat down across the fateful negotiating table from their Earthbound fellow human. It was a glorious thought.

But also a lonely one, Lou thought, squeezing Sue's hand. For the only way they could ever enjoy true human company again was to fulfill the prophecy that Sue had so neatly set up as if guided by the future's unseen hand. The songs from the stars must be sung to the ends of the Earth. The Galactic Way was the birthright of all men, not two lonely souls, and all men must learn to walk it.

But if Arnold Harker was a fair example of the breed, that might not be as easy as it seemed it should be.

Harker drummed his fingers nervously on the steel table. "We only have air enough for another fifteen hours," he said. "The decision can be put off no longer. And I have made it. We will not take the data banks back to Earth with us, and we will broadcast nothing. We will not loose this chaos on our poor planet."

"*You've* made the decision?" Sue snarled. "Up yours, Arnold, we outvote you, two to one."

"I'm the commander of this mission."

"Oh yeah, well, nobody put you in command of *me!*"

Lou watched them glare at each other. How was this decision going to get made? Or rather, how am I going to get Harker to accept the decision that destiny has already made for us? Where is justice that I can make him accept? But wait a minute. . . .

"Space Systems Incorporated agreed to accept my justice on the songs from the stars," he reminded the Spacer. "And it's no secret that I find their karma sweet and their spirit white."

"That's your decision as the giver of justice?" Harker said slowly.

Lou nodded.

"Well I reject it! You're no perfect master anymore, you're the pawn of alien monsters! I reject your authority utterly."

Lou goggled at the Spacer. Never had he heard of anyone rejecting the justice he himself had sought. It was a violation and dishonor that struck deeper at the harmony of the human spirit than anything Harker might imagine could come from without. For where justice willingly sought was not willingly accepted the only rule left was that of force.

"You're shocked?" Harker said sardonically. "But why *should* I accept your authority in this matter? White or black, science or sorcery, perfect master or black scientist, justice or injustice, does any of that have relevance now? Isn't your Clear Blue Way just another pathetic human shadow of things we'll never fully understand?"

Lou thought about that one, good and hard. If the Galactic Way wasn't beyond present human comprehension, it wouldn't be the Galactic Way. Yet, if it were not in harmony with the Clear Blue Way, it wouldn't be the Galactic Way either. No, there was nothing in the Clear Blue Way out of sync with the Galactic Way, and nothing in the Galactic Way to which the Clear Blue Way did not vibrate in harmony like a sympathetic minor chord. Galactic stage beings respected their own higher version of the Great Way and something very much like the law of muscle, sun, wind and water. They poisoned not the body of creation. They lived in harmony with the ultimate galactic ecosphere. They loved all life and respected all mind. They were like what good men wanted to be.

"Not pathetic," Lou finally said quietly. "And not a shadow."

"It doesn't give you the right to make this decision for the entire human race," Harker said. "And it doesn't give you the power either. That power is mine alone."

Sue half rose out of her chair. "I think the two of us can handle *you,* Arnold, if we have to," she said, balling her hands into fists. "Isn't that right, Lou?"

Harker just stared her down. "I'm the pilot of the *Enterprise,*" he said. "What we've found stays here, or we don't go back."

"*What?*"

"I'm dead serious," Harker said. "I won't fly the spaceship back unless the data banks stay here and are not broadcast to the Earth. We'll all die here first."

"You can't stop us," Sue stammered, sinking back into her chair. "I know how to work the equipment; I know how to activate the satellite network. . . ."

"But you'll never get home. And when the spaceship doesn't come back, the Company will recognize what you've broadcast for the doom it is. And we know how to keep secrets. And who else has a ground station or knows how to build a spaceship?''

Sue looked imploringly at Lou. "You can fly us home, can't you, Lou?" she said. "You've watched him fly the ship, you've learned the controls. . . ."

Lou thought about it. In theory, he knew what to do. But he had never flown a spaceship before, and no one had ever landed one. For that matter, neither had Harker. Come to think of it, there was no guarantee that they could get back at all.

"I could take a shot at it. . . ." he said bleakly.

"And leave me here to die?" Harker said shrewdly. "Is such the wisdom and justice you have learned from the stars?"

"You choose your karma and we choose ours," Lou said. "You can't control us with a guilt program like that." But he wouldn't have been Clear Blue Lou if he didn't smell something a little hollow about that rationalization.

"Thus speaks the perfect master and giver of justice!" Harker said scathingly. "Willing to take the fate of humanity into his own hands and commit murder in the process! Where's your justice in that when I'm willing to die to save our species from your so-called wisdom?"

"What do you mean by that?" Lou said slowly. But he was beginning to feel the walls of a karmic trap forming around him. Perhaps they had been there all along.

"Here we are, a scientist, a perfect master, and a tribal leader," Harker said smugly. "Three pretty fair examples of the best our species has to offer, wouldn't you say? And we're reduced to threats and the realities of power. What does that say about the wisdom of your justice? What does it say about our species' chance of living with it?"

"What are you trying to say?" Lou whispered. But a cold wind was already blowing through his soul.

"What I'm saying is that what's happening right now proves that the human race can't handle this," Harker said. "The three of us can't even agree whether the world should know what we know. Your very certainty is what proves you wrong."

Clear Blue Lou felt as if he had been kicked in the belly by a horse. For Harker was right. Justice worked by force of will was no justice at all. Justice that tasted sour was not the justice of the Way.

"So where do *you* think justice lies?" he asked the black scientist with deadly seriousness.

"In admitting the true situation and acting accordingly," Harker said. "Since the three of us can't make this decision together for our species, it must wait until someone else can. We leave what we found here on the station for someone else to find someday. As the original crew did."

"That's despicable!" Sue snarled. "That's the coward's way out."

"Do you have any better ideas?"

"You can't stop us from telling the world what's up here!" Sue said angrily. "And I won't let you go back on your promise to turn the satellite network over to the Sunshine Tribe!"

"I'll honor our original bargain," Harker told her. "But not till we're back on the ground. The data banks stay here and they stay silent."

"*Lou!*"

Sue glared at him demandingly. But both justice and pragmatism seemed snared by the black scientist's web of logic. It wasn't choice, it was ironclad karma, and Harker was in control.

"At least don't condemn the world to ignorance without walking the Galactic Way yourself, Arnold," Lou said almost imploringly. "You can't understand what you're really doing until you've been there yourself. You've got us, I admit it, so what do you have to lose by experiencing the true reality?"

"You think that will change my mind, don't you?" Harker said sharply.

Lou nodded. "I'm convinced that it will," he said. "Convinced enough to abide by your decision with an open heart if it's made in full knowledge instead of willful ignorance. Come on, man, what do you have to lose?"

"What do I have to lose!" Harker shrilled. "Only my humanity! Only my independent will! You're asking me to do something that you're utterly convinced will change my mind. Literally *change my mind*. As it has yours."

"But only for the better, Arnold," Lou said softly, drawing upon his last reserves of patience. "Nothing bad will happen to you; there's nothing but hope and good will and even joy waiting for you in the songs from the stars."

"And of course I have your solemn word as a perfect master on that, don't I?" Harker snorted.

"You do," Lou said evenly through gritted teeth.

"Well, I choose not to take it," Harker said. "I choose to keep my ability to choose. You're not going to shame me into losing that. My decision stands, and there really isn't anything you can do about it, is there?"

"You can't stop the world from learning about the Galactic Way," Lou said unhappily, sounding lame even to himself. "You can't stop Sue from spreading the story to the ends of the Earth. . . ."

"Lou, you're not going to let this bastard get away with it, are you?" Sue snarled. "*Do* something!"

"What do you suggest?" Lou said wanly, cringing inside at what he saw in her eyes.

Sue glared at him. He winced under her assault. "What choice do we have?" he said.

"You Clear Blue asshole!" Sue shouted. "You . . . you. . . ." She sighed. She shrugged. "I'm sorry, Lou," she said in a tiny hollow voice. "It's really not your fault."

"It's only just . . ." Harker muttered in petulant triumph.

"*Just!*" Sue screamed at him. "Don't squeak to me of justice, you miserable cowardly fucked-up little wretch! Just is, you don't make a decision for others that you haven't the balls to make honestly for yourself! Just is, you don't condemn a way you haven't the courage to walk! You're about as good at justice as you are at sport, Arnold, you impotent loveless little swine!"

She grabbed Lou by the elbow and fairly dragged him toward the door. "Come on, Lou, I don't like the stink in here," she spat over her shoulder at the Spacer on the way out.

Dazed by the violence of her energy, Clear Blue Lou didn't know what to think as he left Harker sitting there stunned by her assault. What kind of justice was this that left everyone concerned poisoned by its vibes?

There was no way Sunshine Sue was going to get to sleep and she knew it. Venting her rage hadn't helped, making love afterward hadn't helped, and Lou's sleeping body curled up against hers in the spartan bed was becoming something of an affront to her sleeplessness. Something she couldn't quite place was eating at her, and that in itself was starting to drive her crazy.

Not that there wasn't enough bothering her right up front without this nagging feeling that she was missing something vital, something that was going to make her feel like an asshole or worse when it sprang its trap. . . .

Lou moved in his sleep against her, and she reflexively adjusted her position to accommodate the altered configuration. Making love had become almost an afterthought up here, another necessary natural function to be performed for the sake of well-being while waiting for the next go at the main business, the next excursion into the Galactic Way.

She had only come to realize this just now because for once, personal realities had intruded into the forefront of her attention for the first time since they had journeyed to this place where the heavens touched the mind. And only because she had started out angry at Lou.

What kind of perfect master was he? How could he have forced her to swallow this manifestly unjust situation? It was horrible, it was pointless, it was just plain stupid! To go through all these changes to reach a place that no two humans had reached before, to catch a glimmer of the galactic vastness, to rise into the consciousness of the brotherhood of all sentient beings, to become something that set you irrevocably apart from all your fellow humans. . . . And then to be faced with the fact that you were going to be out here all alone, maybe for the rest of your life, that the whole thing was going to have to be done all over again before any of your kind could share the experience that had forever changed your spirit!

"It's not right, it's not fair, it stinks!" she had told him as soon as they were back in the bedchamber. "How can you let this happen?"

Lou sat down wearily on the edge of the bed. He shrugged. "How can I not let it happen?"

"I'd be willing to risk your flying the spaceship back," Sue suggested impulsively. "We could jump Harker, tie him up, haul him to the *Enterprise*, and—

Lou looked up at her strangely. "Jump him? Tie him up? I've never done anything like that to anyone in my life. Have you?"

"You're big and strong," she cooed, sitting down beside him and squeezing his bicep. "And I can take care of myself too. We can handle him together. While you're confronting him, I can sneak up behind him and conk him with—"

"Sue!" Lou whipped his head around. "You're talking about violating someone's free will by physical force!" He shrugged wanly. "Besides," he said, "how are we going to get a tied-up man into a spacesuit, out of the wheel, and into the spaceship?"

"Well, he's violating our free will by . . . by psychic force," Sue said angrily. "He's forcing a situation that violates the free will of every human being to choose their highest possible destiny. It'd serve him right if we just snuck off in the spaceship with the memory bank tapes and left him here to die."

Lou gave her one of those heavy green stares. "Did you hear what you just said?" he asked her sharply. "In order to elevate humanity to a higher state of consciousness, we're supposed to commit murder? I don't think you really meant that, did you?"

"No," Sue said in a tiny little voice, and all at once she realized that the anger she felt toward Lou was entirely misplaced. *He* wasn't the enemy, this mess wasn't really *his* fault. And it wouldn't do for her to take out her frustration on him.

For they really *were* irrevocably in this together in ways neither of them had dreamed existed when fate had thrown them together a few short weeks and an eternity of changes ago. They were mated to each other by something that made even the question of love seem irrelevant. As things stood now, they were the two lone members of their kind, the only humans to have walked the first halting steps of the Galactic Way, the first citizens of a nonexistent galactic stage human civilization. And if that fucker Harker had his way, they would know no others of their kind in their lifetimes.

So she had concentrated quite earnestly on making love to Lou, on experiencing the fleshly reality of the only other human being whose spirit could even hope to share her full psychic space. The two of them were going to be together for a very long time; the task before them made that inevitable. Together they would have to make the world understand that which only they had experienced and lead their fellow humans to their galactic birthright. Strangers to the world, they could hardly afford to be less than lovers to each other. Fate had thrown them together as much as love; it was destiny, kiddo, kismet, and if you forced yourself, you could think of that as pretty damn romantic.

But it wasn't enough to let her sleep. That son of a bitch Harker had contrived to poison even what love they might share by turning it into the prospect of a lifelong psychic exile. And he and those like him would be fighting them back on Earth every inch of the way while they sought to end it by bringing humans back to the Big Ear and their galactic destiny. While the songs from the stars waited up here for—

"Oh shit," Sue hissed aloud, sitting bolt upright.

If Harker was so determined to protect humanity from what was on those tapes might he not simply destroy them?

Now you're really getting paranoid! she told herself. Nevertheless, she carefully disentangled herself from Lou, crept out of the bed, slid into her clothes, and glided out into the endless silent corridor.

Listening for errant sounds, she padded barefoot up the curve of the corridor toward the main computer room. Silence, except for the hum of distant machinery and the subliminal groanings of the great wheel as it revolved through space.

The door to the main computer room was ajar. The working lights were on.

Cautiously, she flattened herself against the wall next to the door and peered inside.

Arnold Harker sat slumped over in one of the seats of the galactic receiver. Memory bank tapes were piled high in the center of the room amidst wads of paper kindling. Sue watched him for long moments, deciding what to do. He didn't move. Sue shrugged to herself. She sighed. She took a deep breath.

Then she kicked the door wide open and burst into the room. "All right, Arnold, what the hell are you doing?"

The black scientist didn't twitch. He didn't move. He didn't utter a sound.

Sue slowly walked over to him. Arnold Harker's mouth hung open in a slack-jawed grimace, and his sightless eyes had rolled to the top of their sockets. He was dead.

Nobody Promised You a Rose Garden

"He must've found the poison that the original crew took,"
Clear Blue Lou said, throwing a sheet over Arnold Harker's
horribly staring dead face. He turned to Sue, curling an arm
around her. "Are you all right?"

"As all right as I'm going to be," she said in a trembling
voice, burrowing her head into his shoulder. "Oh Lou . . .
why . . . ? *Why* . . . ?" A single sob wracked her body.

Of course, she had been mightily upset when she woke
him, as who wouldn't be, finding the ugly lifeless shell of
what had once been a living human being. But he sensed that
she suffered something beyond that. For she might very well
feel that she had in a sense willed this to happen, and her
last words to Harker had been snarled in anger. Now she felt
that he had died with her denying his humanity, that perhaps, in some unfathomable way, she had somehow pushed
him to this. That now that Harker had removed himself as
an obstacle to her will by his own hand, this all-too-conve-
nient death somehow tainted her soul.

If he didn't realize that this feeling was as much his own
as hers, he wouldn't be Clear Blue Lou. But if on another

level he couldn't honestly hold the two of them blameless in his own court of justice, he wouldn't be Clear Blue Lou either.

Unknown destiny had done this to Harker, not their deed or even will. No one had willfully sought to sour anyone else's karma, perhaps not even poor Harker inside his own reality. Indeed, neither of them could even fathom *why* he had killed himself.

But the man *was* indisputably dead by his own hand. And it could not be denied that they had perhaps willfully blinded themselves to whatever psychic process had finally led him to take his own life. Absorbed in the wonder of the Galactic Way, they had stood by while Harker followed *his* way to destruction. They had allowed his own coldness of spirit to make them forget that behind that impenetrable carapace of scenarios and self-assumed superiority there had been a brother human spirit with fears and agonies and passions like any other man. They had never really known that Arnold Harker. They had never really tried.

That's the true source of this feeling of guilt, Lou realized, and it's mine as much as Sue's.

"Why did he do it, Lou?" Sue said, pulling away from him and skittering nervously about the room. "He was having things his way, wasn't he? He could've just burned the tapes, and . . ." She froze and looked at him with a stricken grimace. "Just because of what I said? Oh gods, did I *kill* him with my foul temper and my big stupid mouth?"

Lou stared at the sheet-draped body in its chair, surrounded by the arcane machineries of the galactic receiver, then at the pile of data tapes apparently prepared by the Spacer for burning, a destruction that for some unknown reason had never been consummated. *Or did I?* he began to wonder nervously.

"No, you didn't kill him with your big mouth," he said, taking her hand. "He died in that chair, after—" He caught himself short. "Oh, no!"

"Oh, no, *what?*"

"He must've been ready to burn the tapes," Lou said slowly. "And then he probably decided that since he was going to destroy them, and we were about to leave the Ear, that . . . that. . . . that he would prove to us that he was no coward. . . ."

"And finally try the galactic receiver himself? And he did,

and . . . But that makes no sense. There's nothing in the songs from the stars that would make even Harker kill himself."

"Or so I assured him," Lou said queasily. "On my word as a perfect master. Oh shit."

"Lou!" Sue said sharply. "Don't *you* go blaming yourself now! There's nothing bad for anyone's spirit in the songs from the stars, and we both know it."

"Unless . . ."

"Unless?"

"Unless the receiver picked up a new song while we slept," Lou said speculatively. "Something that we don't know about. Something that . . ."

Sue stared into his eyes, her lower lip trembling. "Easy enough to find out," she said. "All we have to do is sit down beside him and recycle whatever it was he was playing at the end. . . ."

"The twenty-second song . . . ?"

"If there is one."

"Do we dare?" Lou said. But it was really not a question. *Do we dare not?* he thought, and that wasn't a real question, either.

"We owe it to him, don't we?" Sue said. "If you hadn't told him you were so sure it would be all right, and I hadn't called him a coward, he wouldn't have . . . So what does that make us if we refuse to walk the way we made him follow? We have to know what made him kill himself, don't we? We can't go home without knowing."

Lou nodded. "Justice demands it," he said. He forced a wan smile. "But we're not Arnold Harker. I can't think of anything that would make *us* want to curl up and die. We'll be all right. . . ."

"Sure we will . . ." Sue said in a tiny pale voice. And she took his hand and led him toward the final confrontation with the destiny written in their stars.

"Recycle."

"Twenty-two, start. . . ."

Stars stream past you, or perhaps you are streaming past them, for all is chaos and confusion as planets, suns, streams of glowing gas, spiral down around you into something behind, flickering in and out of substantiality as if all this is coming from a long ago and attenuated far away, or as if that *something* is fragmenting the very body of reality itself. A something huge and terrible that you flee from at the straining edge of your powers like a dreamer trying to run up a hill of sand in a nightmare. Something that is gaining on you, inexorably sucking you down, down, down. . . .

"Good-bye to you brothers, good-bye to you good friends, our story is over, our chapter ends. We were the children of ten thousand suns. . . ."

You float in a vast cluster of tightly packed stars. Tiny motes of light drift among them like swarms of fireflies in the night. Wavefronts of colored light dance slowly back and forth among the stars. You soar high above the star cluster, and you see that it is the center of the galactic spiral, the living heart of the island universe.

You dive back into the great concourse of central suns, rejoining the streams of ships and worldlets and mysterious unknowable objects plying the slow starways from world to world.

Like the great swooping bird of time, you dip through the atmospheres of a dizzying succession of worlds, sampling the profusion and complexity like a connoisseur of life. Rafted cities plying azure seas. Glowing townships spread across the tops of immense forest canopies. Castles of crystal and gold, floating among the high passes of enormous green mountains. Great archipelagos bridged by faerie traceries of spun steel. A myriad islands in the stellar stream of life. . . .

". . . in the galaxy's heartland, ah, we had fun! Long was our summer, wise was our mind. . . ."

You float in the jeweled cluster of suns at the galactic center, where motes of mind and waves of light knit the rich density of stars together into a living manifestation of the triumph of the sentient spirit over the empty void.

But something is happening at the very heart of this triumphant glory, something cold and dark and ultimately terrifying is announcing its existence with baleful black vibrations. A bone-chilling sucking presence, a cosmic undertow, begins to subtly draw you down. . . .

"Galaxies too birth, live, and die. Ten billion years is the blink of an eye. . . ."

An endless crystal void. Like firework pinwheels, thousands of tiny galactic spirals coalesce into incandescent existence, then fade back into the dark. The dancers are myriad and transient, but the dance goes on.

You float above a single spiral galaxy now. A vortex is beginning to appear at its core as it revolves through time—a deadness at the center, a slowly growing carcinoma of utter void sucking matter and energy into it. . . .

"Young central suns burn hot and fast. Before life can quicken their hour is done."

A huge cluster of moribund suns. Some gutter out into dead black nodules. Others explode in showers of superheated supercompressed gas, flinging clouds of particles and light into the interstellar medium until nothing exists but glowing vortices of gas and drifting particles and chunks of utter darkness.

Nodes form in the swirling gas as eddies begin to interact. They thicken and proliferate and wink into existence as new stars.

"From this cycle of fire, new suns are born, circled by planets birthed by new light."

Now the stars disappear, and there is nothing but dark nodules and tiny pinprick clouds of black sand, deeper darknesses against the void. A negative image of the universe of light, where holes of nothingness form in the slow eddies. Form, and grow, and suck each other into themselves. . . .

"But out in the darkness and out of the light, symmetric forces marshal the night. Matter compressed and matter imploded. Holes in space where suns exploded. Coming together in entropy's dance, time is their ally, the slow hand of chance."

The galactic spiral revolving faster and faster through space and time, a sphere of dead black darkness forming at its core, a darkness that sucks the light spiraling down into it, devouring suns and gas and growing, growing, growing. . . .

"At the heart of a galaxy an anti-life is formed. Our ending was written before we were born. Great suns collapse into burnholes in space, light goes into darkness, death comes in its place and we all disappear, our futures all go into the vortex. . . ."

The spherical vortex of darkness grows and grows, ever faster, ever larger, as it feeds on the clouds of suns that whirl down its black maw into inevitable oblivion.

". . . into the depths, the terminal black hole."

The last stars out at the tips of the spiral arms slip down into the vortex and then there is nothing—

—but the endless random dance of pinwheel galaxies flaring into existence then dying slowly back into the nothingness of the crystal void.

Stars stream down past you into the huge and terrible void whose vibrations chill the back of your neck, whose onrushing presence sucks the straining atoms of your being toward it. . . . Slowly, inexorably, you are being dragged into the unnameable, rushing up at you from behind. . . .

And then you dare to look back.

An immense whirlpool of nothingness blots out the stars, a gaping gullet mouth of onrushing extinction, a tunnel of nonbeing upon whose depths the eye cannot focus. It is there and it is not there. It is visible and it is the very absence of the possibility of vision, an ever-widening sphere of oblivion, consuming the body of creation.

Closer and closer the yawning black vortex comes, but as the stars drain away down into nonbeing, a sprinkling of tiny motes becomes visible, fleeing before the onrushing sphere of terminal night. Worlds entire, girdled by rings of tiny orbiting suns, straining unguessable energies to ride before the bow wave of oblivion for a few last long moments of sweet and doomed life.

One by one the brave refugee worlds are overtaken by the vortex and slip spiraling down into unguessable nonbeing. . . .

"When all of us are gone, you'll still have our song and a million years of lifetimes before your hour nears.

"We'll give it one last try, for although we know it's hopeless, we have nothing left to fear."

You are standing at the pole of a fair green planet as it hurtles faster and faster and faster into the all-enveloping darkness down an endless corridor of nothingness, bending and warping and spiraling down into itself forever. . . .

"And now our time is come. We vanish one by one. We turn to face the ending from which no life can hide. Just maybe if we're lucky we'll come out the other side—"

Suddenly Sunshine Sue flashed out of the terminal darkness into the prosaic light of the main computer room of the Big Ear station. She shuddered. She blinked. She slowly began to come back to here-and-now reality. She was sitting in one of the chairs of the galactic receiver. In a great metal wheel built by men, a fragile capsule of life rolling through the endless deadly darkness. Clear Blue Lou sat next to her, staring into space, into emptiness, into . . . The sheet-draped form on the chair beyond Lou was . . . was. . . .

"Oh shit . . ." she finally managed to whisper.

Lou began to come out of his own daze. He glanced over at the corpse of Arnold Harker, then at her, as life and humanity came back to his features.

"Did you understand all that?" Sue finally said.

"Enough," Lou sighed. "I think so. . . . Poor Harker probably understood the science of it better, but he couldn't face the music. He didn't understand."

"And *you* do?" Sue said, eyeing him peculiarly. And that very act seemed to dissipate more of her disorientation and horror, to anchor her being in the here and the now.

"Galaxies are born and die," Lou said quietly. "Just like people and species and suns. It's apparently all part of the same eternal evolutionary process. And in a million years or so, time will run out for our part of this one. Everything's ultimately headed down the same final black hole. . . ."

Sue goggled in stunned stupefaction at the tranquillity with which he had summarized the awful. "So that's why Harker killed himself," she muttered. "In the long run, our lives, our dreams, and everything we do for the benefit of our species . . . It all really *is* pointless, isn't it?"

Lou shook his head. He shrugged. "I don't think you or I will ever *really* understand why Arnold Harker killed himself," he said.

"*Never understand!*" Sue cried. "But . . . but . . . we're all doomed! You and me and the world and all those wise and ancient beings out there, and . . ." She shuddered. She blinked. She began to tremble uncontrollably. "*I* understand why he did it," she said. "And I'm beginning to wish I didn't. . . ."

Lou climbed out of his seat and stood beside her. He touched her cheek and hand. "No real reason to let it get you down, lover," he said. Incredibly, he managed to laugh.

"After all," said Clear Blue Lou, "from a personal karmic viewpoint, what else is new?"

"Huh?" Sue stared at him. Something in her soul seemed to be trying to snap back into focus.

"This galaxy of ours, doomed though it is, will outlive you and me and Aquaria and a million years worth of a future we can't even guess at," Clear Blue Lou said. "You and me and the people of the Earth and all those civilizations out there and even poor Arnold, if he had only understood—we're all in the same place we always were, love. Tell me how this makes anyone's personal fate any different."

Sue blinked. Her body stopped shaking. She even laughed, amazing herself. Great gods, why *had* Harker killed himself? What *was* life but an interval of light between two unfathomable darknesses? What was the point about worrying what the point was? How many other beings had experienced this song and still gone on? Was that perhaps not the ultimate glory and wisdom of the Galactic Way?

"We really didn't kill Arnold, did we?" she said. "We're really not guilty of pushing him into a psychic space where humans can't survive. . . ."

"Not as long as we prove it by going on," Lou said. "Not as long as we have the courage to go where we led him and still survive. He died because of who he was, not because of where he had been."

Sue looked up at Lou. She kissed him briefly on the lips. "You really *are* Clear Blue, aren't you, Lou?" she said.

Clear Blue Lou smiled back at her boyishly. He shrugged. He rolled his eyes upward. "Fortunately for us," he said, "we've got a lot of Clear Blue friends."

Celestial
Mechanics

For once in his life, Clear Blue Lou had been able fully to appreciate the yoga of physical labor without ironic internal grumblings or sweaty reservations. It had taken him five long and tedious trips from the wheel to the docking slab to get all the data bank tapes on board the *Enterprise*, during which time all deep thoughts and karmic ambiguities had been banished from his consciousness by the all-involving physical task of lugging so much stuff through the tricky changes of gravity and orientation.

Only now, carrying the sheet-wrapped corpse of Arnold Harker into the wheel's main airlock, did the enormities and complexities of the long psychic journey come flooding back to haunt his spirit.

Sue opened the airlock door for him but did not help him float Harker's body inside. She had refused to touch the corpse at all, or rather he had refused to burden her further with any such request. He himself had used the task of transferring the tapes to the *Enterprise* as a kind of psychic judo on himself, warping his consciousness into the physical mundacity of regarding this final haul as just more of the same.

But now he and Sue were floating inside the main airlock alive in their spacesuits, and Arnold Harker was floating dead in his winding sheet, and the time had come to say the words that would commit the black scientist to his eternal rest in the void he had sought to conquer but which in the end had devoured his spirit.

Sue valved partial pressure into the airlock and stood by ready to open the door into space. Lou regarded the sheet-draped body, then Sue's space-suited form. In both cases, the material carapaces perhaps mercifully obscured the emotional realities within. Even in this final moment, the realities of the spirit were encased in the material masks that they had traveled within; even in death Arnold Harker's soul was alone.

It was a sad and terrible thought, but in some way Lou felt that the Spacer would have wanted it this way.

He sighed. He took one deep breath. "We commit the spirit of Arnold Harker, scientist and fellow human, to the endless sea of space which he sought to travel, and which in the end held deeper darkness than his soul could harmoniously contain. We cannot say we really knew him. We cannot say we know for what he died. But we hope that the inner mysteries he now takes with him to his final rest will serve to remind us that the greatest paradox in this galaxy of wonders still remains the unknown heart of man, that we who have learned so much still have much to learn about what lies within ourselves."

He shrugged. It wasn't much of a farewell, but it was all that he could truly say. Sue hit the button, the outer airlock door slid open, and poor Harker's fleshly envelope drifted out to join his psychic ancestors in the everlasting void. To which all life would return in the end.

Sunshine Sue stood on a tube of cold metal in the icy dark of space under the looming shadow of the *Enterprise*, all alone save for Lou in all that deadly star-speckled immensity.

But high above her rolled the Earth, huge and alive and majestic against the unreal starry blackness, its veil of life-giving air glowing where its brilliant disc intersected the void. Continents paraded by—green and fair, pockmarked and ruined, floating in bright blue seas—unashamedly revealing both their beauties and their scars. Though this sight had lived in memory's vision and though she had walked through many a galactic dream since last she saw the planet that had given her birth, still it took her breath away as if she were seeing it again for the first time through reborn eyes.

As indeed she was. And soon the scattered peoples of the Earth would share at least a shadow of her vision through the satellites of the new Sunshine World Broadcast Network, which she had activated while Lou was transferring the data bank tapes to the *Enterprise* and preparing poor Arnold for his final journey. While full operation of the network depended upon holding the Spacers to their promise of supplying her with the necessary ground station, and though the full glory of the songs from the stars could not become the common property of all those fellow humans down there until the scientific secrets that they were bringing home gave forth their lore and allowed the Earthbound to walk the true Galactic Way for themselves, at least the sight and sound images of the missionary-introductory packet were now winging their way to the ends of the Earth.

She had rigged a continuous playback loop on one of the satellite network channels so that the words and pictures from the stars would unreel and repeat their story to every open Earthbound eye and ear as long as the power of the sun drove the transmitter of the Ear. Thus would the first message from the stars serve as an eternal beacon for the spirit of man under the law of muscle, sun, wind and water, a many-leveled living symbol of the Galactic harmony of the Way.

Ah, you've been through so much! Sue thought as she looked up at the wounded, living, breathing planet. You deserve a second chance. And we're going to give it to you.

"What are you thinking?" Lou's soft voice said over the suit radio.

"I'm thinking that it's all been worth it," Sue told him. "Poor Arnold's death. The horrid things he did to bring us here. The strange and lonely creatures it's forced us to become. Even black science, with all that it's done to our poor planet. *This* must be what it feels like to be karmically reborn."

"Yeah," Lou said quietly. "I think we're finally standing

on the other side.'' He paused. ''But there's still one karmic task that remains before we can stand around congratulating ourselves on our new personas.''

''What's that?''

Lou laughed a brittle and nervous laugh. ''The minor matter of getting our asses safely home,'' he said.

''Ready to initiate re-entry program,'' Clear Blue Lou said, great beads of sweat rolling down his forehead inside the damnable helmet.

''I'll drink to that,'' Sue said shakily. ''If only I could! I don't know how you did it, and please don't tell me.''

''What makes you think *I* know?'' Lou grunted.

It had been a hairy passage indeed, from the docking slab to where the spaceship now drifted, well clear of the spinning wheel and the great web of the antenna. Lou had found the switch that disengaged the hoops holding the *Enterprise* to the slab easily enough, but then they had to scramble frantically on board as the ship unexpectedly started to drift clear.

He had had no time at all to think about whether he could fly the ship or not for as soon as his ass hit the pilot's seat, he saw that the spaceship was already drifting on a course that would soon suck it into the huge spinning spokes of the great wheel. Lou corrected course frantically, then found that the new course was taking the ship toward the antenna which formed the other wall of the narrow canyon he suddenly found himself flying it through.

No time to wonder what he was doing as he recorrected and re-recorrected until he finally got the nose of the ship pointing out into the clear corridor between the wheel and the web, at least momentarily. No time to think. He hit the main rockets as gently as he could. The *Enterprise* roared and groaned and shuddered for a moment, and then it was moving outward far faster than he had intended, too fast for any more corrections to be made, and all they could do was shut their eyes and vibe good vibes as it angled out past the wheel, missing the heavy spinning rim by mere yards.

Lou swiveled his helmet around to get a distant glimpse of Sue through their faceplates. ''Well, now it's Space Systems Incorporated's turn at the controls,'' he said. ''Are you ready for that? I'll tell you something, after that, *I* am!''

''We really have to trust our lives to a piece of machinery

built by our own home-grown black scientists? We have to trust this thing to fly itself home?"

"The Spacers were good enough to get us here," Lou said. "Just barely, maybe, but good enough. Maybe this is going to be a good karmic lesson. The righteously white, the sorcerers' black, and a couple of gray characters like ourselves—it took the best all the parts of our poor fragmented species could do to put our first footsteps on the Galactic Way. And it's going to take the same to get us home with the knowledge to put it all back together again. We've *all* got to trust each other if our species and ourselves are going to make it."

And as he said it, Lou got a foreflash of what it was all going to mean if they *did* make it. The world would be split asunder and then, hopefully, be put back together again in unguessable new configurations. Black and white, science and sorcery, karma and destiny—the deepest patterns of mind that underlay the interface between the spirit and the world would all be shattered and transformed into something new. Yes, something new was coming into the world, something that had been lost was about to be reborn again. Clear Blue Lou could not quite discern what it was, and perhaps *that* was its very nature—ongoing everlasting change was the only stable dynamic of galactic stage consciousness.

And it somehow seemed appropriate that this cosmic pivot point of destiny balanced on something as mundanely human as the proper functioning of this Spacer construction and the ability of a single man to fly it home.

"Well here we go," he said. "Galactic Way or no, sooner or later, we have to trust our own poor human machineries." And he punched in the re-entry program.

Sunshine Sue gripped the sides of her couch uneasily as a series of little hisses and juddering vibrations went through the crowded little metal cabin, and the Earth started to roll and shake outside the window.

Then there was a silent pause as if the computer were checking out its handiwork. Looking out the window, Sue saw that the Earth now lay "below" them from this new perspective, and it was revolving in the wrong direction as if the spaceship were flying above it tail first.

Then the main rockets roared and the cabin trembled and metal shrieked and groaned and something grabbed her insides and rattled them for what seemed like a long time as she was slammed back into her couch.

Then—

Suddenly—

Nothing.

The *Enterprise* floated silently in space. The world spun by serenely backward below as if nothing at all had happened.

"What's wrong?" Sue said.

"I don't know," Lou told her. "I have no idea of how this thing comes down until the recovery eagle is deployed. We're in the hands of the computer. I only hope the thing is working."

"Marvelous!"

Then as if to reassure them that it was still alive, the spaceship began to hiss and judder and roll and jerk around like a skittish crab. When the spasms were over, they were flying over the curve of the Earth with their nose pointed in the right direction, and the planet seemed perceptibly closer. . . .

"What now?"

"I think we're coming down," Lou said.

They *were* coming down, in a slow, lazy, decaying spiral that looked as if it would take them three-quarters of the way around the curve of the planet that was now clearly looming closer and closer. . . .

"Hey, we're really falling now," Sue said uneasily. "I can feel it. Isn't this thing coming in awfully fast?"

"How fast is it supposed to come in?" Lou said philosophically. "Your guess is as good as mine."

The green curve of the planet wasn't rolling below them now; they were plummeting down at it from a vast distance at tremendous speed. It might look the same, but Sue's stomach knew the difference.

Then the spaceship did its jiggle dance again, and the Earth was no longer visible, as the *Enterprise* came in nose up and belly first like an ungainly pelican. It should have been a mercy not to see what was happening, but it wasn't. Sue could envision the ship falling belly forward like a stone in her mind's eye in far more horrific detail than any perceptual reality, and when the cabin began to shake and shriek, she groaned aloud.

"Oh shit. . . ."

The ship rattled and shook and moaned. It seemed to jolt and flip and tumble like a stone skimmed across a pond. Wisps of steam rose up around the window, and it was getting awfully hot inside. Craning her neck in her helmet for a better angle, Sue saw that the undersurfaces of the wings were glowing an angry red as the ship skipped and buffeted against invisible obstacles.

It was an eternity of terror that might have lasted only a few minutes. Then the nose seemed to dip forward of its own accord, and they were falling soundlessly like a diving swan high above a vast sere desert, plummeting down through a blueing black sky toward a miniature landscape of jagged craters and purple scars, far, far above the scudding white clouds.

The Clear Blue Way

Oh, no, we're not flying, we're falling like a stone! Clear Blue Lou thought to himself as he watched the clouds coming up at dizzying speed. The cratered landscape was getting to be less and less of a miniaturist's abstraction as it leaped up to squash them. Everything was suddenly getting all too real!

A tiny explosion rocked the *Enterprise*, and then a great hand seemed to yank it backward for a few moments. It seemed to almost hang suspended and then snap back, but falling more slowly now.

"What the hell was that?" Sue cried.

"I think it's deploying the drogue parachutes," Lou said. "I think we're going to be all right." Another little explosion, another backward jolt, and this time a longer moment of suspension before the drogue tore free.

"The third one had better hold long enough for the recovery eagle to deploy," Lou muttered. "There aren't any more."

A final explosion, and the *Enterprise*'s descent slowed

again. There was a thud and a bang and a loud hissing noise that went on and on and on.

"The eagle's inflating! Here it comes!"

A vast ungainly wing was slowly unfolding above them like a huge tent being hauled up its poles, like a butterfly emerging from its coccoon. The wind tore and buffeted at it as it struggled to fill and take shape. The ship snapped and groaned as the final chute tore loose, and the recovery eagle was almost blown away.

Then in the next moment it was all over, and they had returned to the skies of Earth.

They were floating through a fleecing of white clouds under the enormous shading canopy of the recovery eagle wing. The shadow of the eagle moved like a giant bat across a vast wasteland landscape over which they hung suspended silently in time and space.

"Well, welcome home, I guess," Sue said. "I just wish we had come down in a more hospitable place."

"Not to worry," Lou said, throwing a switch that fed energy units from the solar cells atop the eagle wing to the pusher propellers. Slowly and ponderously, the shadow-bird on the ground began to pick up speed and steady its course.

Lou checked out the controls. Huge, ungainly, and ponderous though it was, the electric linkages that warped the great wing made it simpler and less taxing to fly than his own manually controlled solar eagle. He did a few banks and dips just for the hell of it, and then turned westward toward the afternoon sun.

"From here on in, it's the sun and the wind," he said happily. "The Clear Blue Way will take us home."

Lou finally found a way to vent outside air into the cabin, and they struggled out of their space suits, grateful to breathe the free-flowing wind.

Sue relaxed as she watched him happily flying the great eagle, slipping the air currents, and slowly climbing for altitude as the purple rim of the Sierras peeped up over the western horizon.

Soon the wastelands would be behind them, and they would cross the mountains that once had rimmed what they had known of the world. Soon they would be back in the fair green lands of home.

While in their hidden lairs below, the black scientists would be awaiting their return with anxious wonder. . . .

"You thought about where you're going to land this thing?" she asked Lou. "You're not going to come down at the Company's spaceport, I hope?"

Lou scratched at his chin and pondered the passing clouds. "It *is* their spaceship," he said. "And Harker *did* die in their service. And they *are* the only ones who can get it flying again."

"Yeah, but *will* they? With Harker dead and the two of us coming back alone, they have only our word for what really happened, and somehow I don't think they'll understand what we have to tell them, do you? And if we just hand over the data banks to sorcerers, what will they do with all that knowledge? Keep it secret, or try to, is my guess. We may owe them something, but we owe the world more."

"I gather you have an alternate suggestion?" Lou said dryly.

"I say fuck you to any more knowledge held in secret. I say let's throw it all onto the open Exchange and let the Spacers try and sort it out with Levan. And let's make sure they have to. If all this isn't going to turn into just one more unworthy failure on the part of our fragmented species, we've got to knock everything apart and force a new age to put things back together in new ways. And I think I know just how to create a happening that will start us all off again fresh on the right path."

"What do you have in mind?"

Sunshine Sue laughed wickedly. "Let's ring up the curtain on the galactic show with an eye-opening first act."

West of the central peaks of the Sierras, the landscape below quickened with greenery, and the twisting canyons seemed like the sustaining arteries of life. The sky was clear, the wind was gentle, and Clear Blue Lou flew the great eagle effortlessly toward La Mirage, his spirit riding the Way with a serene tranquillity, spiced, nevertheless, with no little sense of relished devilment.

Sue had managed to make fleeting radio contact with Starbase One as they passed nearby it, just long enough to let the Spacers know that they'd have to come openly to La Mirage to claim their spaceship and bring the promised satellite network ground station with them, and not long enough to tell them that the galactic knowledge the spaceship now contained would be offered freely to all on the open market of the Exchange.

Now they were on the final leg of their long, long journey, soaring on the wind and the sun down the final great canyon aisle to La Mirage, where it had all begun. Their mighty shadow fell across the lands of the mountain williams and then the outlying suburban manses east of town. Tiny buildings were visible, nestled in the lovely greenery, and a dusty ribbon of road leading into Market Circle.

Lou could well imagine invisible figures scurrying around below to spread the news that the celestial chariot was returning from the stars, and parties of nervous black scientists wending their fearful way toward their confrontation with Levan the Wise. The shadow of a new age already lay on the lands of men. It was all over but the shouting, of which there would certainly be no dearth.

Laughing and winking at Sue, Lou flew a slow, low promenading circle over Market Circle itself, and watched the tiny figures boiling out of taverns and smokehouses, manufactories and inns, to marvel and shout at the prophecy fulfilled. Then he headed west toward a landing on the very grasslands from which men had first watched two of their kind ascend to discourse with the people of the stars.

"Can you picture what's going on down there now?" Sue cackled happily. "The prophecy is fulfilled before all the world. Black is white and white is black and now the twain will bloody well have to meet!"

Lou grinned at her as he looked down across the grasslands, where even now a horde of townspeople was following the shadow of the great eagle as the chariot of the gods descended upon the Earth. "And where better than in good old La Mirage," he said dryly.

Sue squeezed his hand as the spaceship touched down in the middle of a wild and wondering horde. No one moved, not a sound was heard, for a long frozen moment.

"And so we reach our journey's end," said Sunshine Sue.

Then a single figure moved toward the ship on tottery legs. It was Levan, and behind him, the whole town seemed to surge forward, shouting and waving.

Clear Blue Lou shrugged at Sunshine Sue. "Somehow," he said, "I doubt it."

Norman Spinrad

Norman Spinrad was born in 1940, graduated from the City College of New York in 1961, published his first story in 1963, his first novel in 1965, and has not held a job since. In addition to somewhere between twelve and fourteen novels (depending on the counting method used), three books of short stories, two non-fiction books, and two anthologies, he has published literary criticism, film criticism, political commentary, and essays on various scientific subjects.

Spinrad has been a literary agent, has had a radio phone show, and is past president and vice-president of the Science Fiction Writers of America. He has written a couple of song lyrics and has cut a single, vocalist record in Britain and France, which never came close to making the charts.

His novel *Bug Jack Barron* was banned briefly in Britain, and two of his novels, *The Iron Dream* and *The Men in the Jungle* are currently on the Index in Germany, where they are nevertheless selling quite well under the table.

CHILD OF FORTUNE

Norman Spinrad

Exhilarating, erotic, joyous, poignant, this extraordinary new novel by award-winning author Norman Spinrad is a remarkable literary achievement. Blending the magical wonder of A WINTER'S TALE with the vivid realism of ON THE ROAD and the mystical transcendence of SIDDHARTHA, CHILD OF FORTUNE is a masterwork of imaginative fiction by one of the most dazzling talents of our time.

"CHILD OF FORTUNE lifts science fiction to the next level. It's a literary masterpiece."

—Timothy Leary

"Spinrad is generously talented. CHILD OF FORTUNE is a magnificent read."

—Michael Moorcock

Turn the page for a preview of Norman Spinrad's CHILD OF FORTUNE.

On the occasion of my fifth birthday, when the possibility of retreating into my own private realm was deemed necessary to my development, a fanciful playhouse was built for me deep in a patch of Bittersweet Jungle in the nethermost reaches of the garden.

Here as a young girl would I spend many hours with young playmates, and many more with no other companionship than that of the moussas I soon learned to entice from the trees with bits and morsels from the breakfast table. Of all the native creatures of Glade, these cunning little mammals, small enough to fit in a child's cupped hands, and willing enough to remain there for the pettiest of bribes, have cozened themselves closer to the human heart than any other, for they are the common pets of childhood.

Though in truth, perhaps, it is as much the little human children of Glade who are the pets of the moussas, for these golden-furred, emerald-eyed, monkey-tailed, leaf-eared, primatelike rodents never survive in a cage or as domesticated house pets, sullenly fasting unto death in any form of captivity. Nor, although they abound throughout Nouvelle Orlean and the surrounding environs, thriving amidst the habitats of men, will they ever deign to descend from their trees to frolic with gross and clumsy adults, even to accept the choicest dainty. But put a child in a garden with a few scraps of bread or a berry or two, and the moussas will soon enough come a-calling. Indeed often, when through negligence I appeared empty-handed, the moussas of the garden, though they might chide me in their piping whistles for my thoughtless lack of hospitality, would nonetheless come down to play.

And like a little moussa myself, I would often, in the late afternoon or early evening, emerge from my garden retreat to play the pampered and cunning pet of the clients and friends of my parents. As the children of Glade imagine that the moussas chattered and capered for their amusements, so, no doubt, did the adults of my parents' salons imagine that the fey creature whom everyone soon began to call kleine Moussa herself frequented their precincts to amuse *them*.

But from the moment their kleine Moussa knew anything of significance at all, I, like the moussas of the garden, knew full well that these huge and marvelous beings, with their extravagant clothes, incomprehensible stories, strange and mysterious perfumes, and secret pockets of sweets, existed, like the garden, and the river, and the myriad wonderous sights and sounds and smells of Nouvelle Orlean, and indeed the world itself, to amuse *me*.

Thus did the little Moussa frolic through young girlhood with the creatures of the garden and the clients of her parents' trades and the favored children of these denizens of Nouvelle Orlean's haut monde. Though naturellement I was not yet capable of appreciating the rarefied and elite ambiance of my parents' salon until my basic schooling was well under way and I was deemed old enough to travel to the academy on my own and venture forth into the city with my playmates.

Then, of course, my awareness of my favored place in the scheme of things became somewhat keener than the reality itself. As I became interested in the wider world around me, and began first to listen to word crystals and then learned to read them for greater speed, as I was taught the rudiments of esthetics, acquainted with the history of our city and our planet and our species, as my teachers introduced me to the sciences, the mutational sprachs of human Lingo, the basic principles of mathematics, und so weiter, I began to perceive that the discourse that had swirled about my little head like so much moussas' babble chez mama and papa was in fact in good part an elevated and rarefied version of my various teachers' discourse at the academy.

This inner perception of my true place in the world was not without both its negative and positive consequences. On the one hand, my respect for the authority of my teachers was eroded by my free and easy congress with their intellectual and social superiors, and I was not above hectoring them from time to time with what I imagined was superior knowledge gleaned from bits and pieces of table talk. On the other hand, I had almost from birth dined on intellectual haute cuisine, and much true learning had actually been absorbed as it were by osmosis; further, what little ambition I then had lay in the direction of acceptance as an equal by the denizens of my parents' salon, and so I was at least motivated to avoid the public intellectual embarrassment of the unprepared student.

The overall result was that I was a skilled if shallowly motivated and not excessively diligent student, lacking any true passion for scholarly pursuits, content to breeze through my studies with a parsimony of effort, and quite innocent of any perception of the educational process as connected to spiritual, intellectual, or karmic goals.

As such, though at the time I would have been mightily offended at the generalization, I was typical of the preadolescent stage of our species, for the biochemical matrix of passion—whether intellectual, artistic, political, spiritual, or sexual—simply cannot be generated by the prepubescent human metabolism. Thus does the wisdom of passing through the wanderjahr before contemplating that deeper education which must be informed by passionate dedication to some true life's work extend from the social and spiritual clear down into the molecular realm.

Which is also why the onset of puberty effects a tumultuous series of psychic transformations quite literally akin to the effects of ingesting powerful psychoactive drugs. While the earliest and most obvious social and psychological manifestation of this biochemical revolution is the awakening of that most presentient of human passions, sexual lust, once the biochemical matrix of passion itself has evolved in a young girl's physiology, that molecular hunger for novelty, somatic excitation, and adventure of the spirit seeks its polymorphous fulfillment in every realm.

Biochemically speaking, adolescence is a loss of endocrine innocence in that it opens the human spirit to all possibilities and dangers of passionate motivation denied to the juvenile metabolism. Yet at the same time, there is no more perfect naif than the newly pubescent creature, who all at once perceives the world through eyes, ears, nostrils, and spirit radically heightened and transformed by this psychochemical amplification of the childhood mind.

In many primitive Terrestrial cultures, before psychoesomics was a developed science or the bioelectronic basis of tantras elucidated, all sorts of bizarre and entirely counterproductive social mechanisms evolved, aimed at either "managing" these adolescent passions from the point of view of adults, suppressing their outward manifestations, or worse still, capturing, channeling, and perverting their energies in the service of theocratic dogmas, territorial aggressions, or the convenience of the adult body politic. Since the earliest, simplest, and somatically strongest of the nascent adolescent passions is of course sexual lust, most of these disastrous social control mechanisms revolved around delaying, transposing, or even entirely suppressing its natural amatory expression.

The results, of course, were exactly what modern psychesomics would predict—polymorphous adolescent rebellion against adult authority, violently separtist adolescent subcultures, excessive random indulgence in psychoactive substances without proper prior study of their effects, neurosis, depression, hysteria, the romanticization of suicide, militarism, cruelty to animals, and a scornful attitude towards scholarly pursuits.

Mercifully our Second Starfaring Age has long since put this torture of the innocent far behind it, and so my earliest experiments satisfying this new somatic hunger were conducted, as was natural, convenient, and esthetically pleasing, in the playhouse of my parents' garden.

Of course I hardly considered myself a clumsy young experimenter in the amatory arts even on the occasion of my first passe de deux in that bucolic boudoir. Was I not, after all, the daughter of Shasta Suki Davide, tantric maestra? Had I not grown up steeped in the ambiance of her science? Had I not, out of childish curiosity, ofttimes perused the catalogs of positions long before the illustrations therein were capable of arousing any but theoretical interest?

Indeed I was. Indeed I had. Moreover, I was not so unmindful of the benefits of motivated study that I neglected to delve deeper into the texts when the motivation for such studies grew deliciously immediate. Nor did I neglect to interrogate my mother for anecdotal expertise or to persuade my father to offer up both his lore on human nervous physiology and his more general knowledge of how men might be blissfully transported.

Verdad. I must confess that I had determined to gain the enviable reputation of a fabled femme fatale while still a virgin, for not only would such a mystique among my peers enhance my perception of my own centrality, it would also insure me the amatory services of most any boy who piqued my interest.

For my first granting of favors, I made the perhaps somewhat calculating choice of a handsome boy of fourteen known as Robi; not only did his slim and nearly hairless body and wide blue eyes arouse the proper spirit within my loins, though a year older than I, he was still charmingly tentative with girls, albeit something of a braggart among his male friends by way of compensation.

I was not unaware that a truly impressive tantric performance for Robi—especially, if, as I suspected, he was still a virgin—would speedily become common lore among the boys of our mutual acquaintance, thereby establishing my mystique as a lover of puissance from my premiere performance.

Enticing Robi into my bower was a simple matter of issuing

an unambiguous invitation in the presence of his fellows, though once we retired to my garden playhouse, his tentativeness was all too limply apparent despite his attempts at verbal bravado.

Undaunted by this phenomenon which was well reported in the word crystals I had perused in preparation, I applied a simple sequence of digital and oral remedies which at first seemed to further discombobulate the pauvre petit with their no-doubt-unexpected level of tantric sophistication, but which soon enough transferred his attention from the uncertainties of the virgin psyche to the naturally firm resolve of the youthful lingam.

Once the natural man in Robi had been properly aroused, he became an enthusiastic if rather hasty and clumsy participant, achieving his own satisfaction in the most basic of tantric configurations with all too much ease, and then satedly supposing that the performance had reached an esthetically satisfying resolution.

When of course it had hardly properly begun, for I was determined to essay certainly no less than a dozen basic positions with several variations of each, to enjoy several tantric cusps of my own in the process, and not to relent until I was entirely satisfied that he was thoroughly, totally, and finally exhausted beyond any hope of further arousal.

Though I lost count somewhere after the first four or five movements of the tantric symphony and probably did not achieve the first of my artistic goals, and though my still barely pubescent physiology left me far short of anything approaching platform orgasm, there was no doubt that the poor boy had been properly exhausted, for I was only persuaded to relent after his moans of pleasure had long since become pleas for surcease and his manhood openly confessed its surrender to the protoplasmic impossibility of rising to further challenge.

To say that Robi was constrained to crawl from our erotic encounter would be to descend to hyperbole, but in truth he staggered from the garden in something less than a triumphant strut, though to judge from subsequent events, his version of the affair would seem to have gained considerably more machismo in the telling.

For I was soon the smug recipient of numerous displays of male courting behavior, from which smorgasbord of possible swains I chose carefully, venturing not to offer up my tantric performances to older, more experienced, and hence more critically acute connoisseurs of the art until my mystique was well established and my store of experience sufficient to insure that it would survive congress with boys whose dedication to the mastery of the tantric arts was no less serious and diligent than my own.

Then, at last, I was able to enter into liaisons in which the pleasure I sought and ofttimes received was equal to that which I offered up in the service of my continued lofty self-appraisal, and genuine mutual affection was thereby enabled to bloom on the tree of passion, though I was still far too enamored of my reputation as a tantric adept and still far too hungry for new experience to even contemplate entering into any compacts of undying love or sexual exclusivity.

Thus through the sexual realm did the dimension of male companionship enter my life and with it the dyadic explorations of the possibilities of adventures and passions beyond those of the boudoir, for just as even the most avid and athletic of lovers can scarcely pass more than a few hours daily in actual embrace, so the passionate adolescent spirit cannot confine its sphere of attention and its hunger for novelty and adventure to the erotic realm alone.

In this manner did the boudoir door also open into the wide world around me, for each lover was also a person entire, possessed of interests, passions, and even obsessions beyond the object of his amorous desire, and more than willing to share them with a venturesome friend.

And so did the kleine Moussa, without noticing the transition, cease to be a child content to frolic in a child's world and become a true adolescent whose garden was no longer that of the parental menage but Nouvelle Orlean itself and the countryside beyond.

With Genji did I begin to appreciate the variety of cuisinary styles to be found in Rioville and learn to distinguish the masterworks of the true chef maestro from mere cuisine ordinaire; so too did I gain some modest sophistication in the products of the vintner's art. Pallo was fairly obsessed with music, and with him I must have visited a hundred or more concert halls, tavernas, al fresco performances, and the like. My passage with Cort was a stormy and brooding one and my parents were not at all displeased when I grew tired of his company, for he was an afficionado of psychoactive chemicals with much more enthusiasm and reckless courage than accurate lore or tasteful discrimination. Ali flew Eagles—great helium-filled gliding wings of gossamer, which took us over land, sea, and river with the magical exhilaration of unpowered flight, but not without a certain peril to life and limb. Perhaps the swain that my parents regarded with the most dubious eyes of all was Franco, who took me on expeditions, sometimes for three and four days at a time, into the Bittersweet Jungle, with only our feet for locomotion, stunners for protection against the more bellicose fauna, and simple covers over piled mosswort for a bed.

Let it not be said that I became merely the mirror of my lovers' passions, for I too had interests of my own which I shared with them, though none of them reached the heights of overweening obsession. To be my companion was to frequent galleries of the graphic arts and become conversant with the styles of worldbubbles, to power-ski the Rio Royale for a hundred kilometers and more upstream and become something of a jesting pest to the boat traffic thereon, and to play endless games of rather inexpert chess.

Moreover, there was much cross-fertilization of adolescent passions and interests in the circles in which I moved, which is to say Pallo gained cuisinary sophistication from dining with me. Franco was introduced to new psychochemicals, and even Cort was constrained to try his hand at gliding through the skies beneath an Eagle. In short, by the time I was seventeen I was a member of a society of my own, a circle of friends, lovers, rivals, former and future swains, which modestly mirrored the social coherence, shifting interests and relationships, and independent life of my parents' salon society, if hardly the seriousness of purpose, artistic and scientific attainment, or depth of scholarship to be found therein.

If I have given the impression that eroticism, intoxicants, athletics, adventure, and entertainment were far more central to our lives than were our academic studies, it is also true that the requirements of same, both in time and effort, were quite deliberately loosened by the mavens of the academy after one's sixteenth birthday. For the natural inclination of the adolescent spirit is to seek out just such pleasures as dominated our attentions, and to tie its wings to the nest of arduous study would be to teach only the entirely counterproductive lesson that scholarship is a grim and bitter task imposed by one's parents and one's society, rather than a joy and intellectual adventure to be avidly pursued as a heart's desire.

Indeed by the age of sixteen one's childhood education is all but drawing to a close; having learned to read, compose word crystals, comprehend basic mathematics, having gained some facility in shifting fluidly among the infinitely varied sprachs of human Lingo, having been acquainted with the history of the species and the various sciences, having been at least exposed to the variety of possible spiritual disciplines and physical arts available for individual development, und so weiter, there is really little else of lasting value for the nonself-motivated student to learn. One has been given the tools with which to develop the mind, body, and spirit, but until one finds one's own inner light, one's own self-generated image of what one wishes to become as an adult of the species, one's own true intellectual passions, more serious and specialized learning thrust upon the still immature mind is as pearls cast before swine.

Which is not to say that my friends and I were not slowly learning an important lesson as our schooling trailed off into an endless summer of ease and self-indulgence. Though some learned it more rapidly than others, and I was not to achieve this satori until I was eighteen, the lesson that our parents, teachers, and society were so wisely allowing us to teach ourselves at our own leisure was that the young adolescent's ideal existence of entertainment, intoxication, eroticism, sport, and easy adventure, unhampered by work, arduous study, or hardship, eventually becomes as cloying as an exclusive diet of the pastry chef's art. Through a surfeit of this endless frolic, one finally learns *boredom*, and once this karmic state is attained entirely by one's own efforts, one is ready to contemplate the next quantum leap of spiritual development, the wanderjahr.

Naturellement, I had learned something of the history of the wanderjahr in the academy, and had known from early girlhood onward that some day I too would take my turn at the vie of the Child of Fortune.

The first clear records of the wanderjahr as a conscious stage in human development come from medieval Europa, where students—alas, in those days only the male of the species—were set to wandering afoot along the highways and byways, either as subsidized Children of Fortune or as mendicants, before embarking on their studies at the universities, though some authorities claim more ancient and universal origins, such as the wandering monks of Hind and Han, the name-quests of would-be Indian braves, the years that Masai boys spent as tribal wanderers before their puberty rites, the Walkabouts of the Abos, und so weiter.

Be that as it may, the wanderjahr seemed to disappear for a time with the coming of the industrial phase of the Terrestrial Age, when the spiritual education of the young came to be regarded as an indolent frivolity in the light of what was seen as the practical economic necessity of processing idle youth into productive members of the workforce via an uninterrupted passage from the schoolroom through the university and into gainful employment as rapidly as possible.

Nevertheless, the wanderjahr, long-suppressed, reemerged at the dawn of the Age of Space in the rather chaotic form of youthful rebellion against this very concept. Alas, *these* Children of Fortune, far from being wisely granted a period of wandering freedom between schooling and serious study by their society in which to discover their adult callings and true names, fled from their parental venues of times at a far too tender age, or on the other hand had already embarked on serious university study before realizing that they knew not who they were, and broke off in medias res in a state of karmic crisis and confusion.

The unfortunate result was turmoil, angry conflict between youth and maturity, the spiritual and the social realm, between the universal quest for spiritual identity and the restraints of formal education, and between endocrine imperatives and the body politic. Many educations, having been interrupted in midstream, were never properly completed, others were never fairly begun, and those who had been restrained from ever following the vie of the Child of Fortune often awoke as if from a trance in their middle years to find themselves strangers to their own beings.

Once more the wanderjahr fell into social disrepute, for precisely the wrong lesson was learned by the unfortunate results of forcing the youthful spirit into chaotic rebellion rather than nurturing the Child of Fortune from whom the spiritually self-motivated adult of the species must emerge. Only the Arkies carried the torch forward in the First Starfaring Age.

But when the development of the Jump Drive reduced the duration of interstellar voyages from decades and generations to weeks, the wanderjahr reemerged again as the rite de passage of youth into maturity.

Naturellement, in our Second Starfaring Age, the Children of Fortune wander not afoot from town to town nor across the continents and seas of a single planet, but throughout the far-flung worlds of men, in the timeless sleep of the dormodules of the Void Ships, or as Honored Passengers in the floating cultura if parental fortune permits.

For the Children of Fortune of *our* age do not flee from home in rebellious defiance of parents and body politic; rather do they depart with the blessings, not to say necessary largesse, of same, since those who bid bon voyage have themselves lived out their wanderjahr's tales before choosing their freedoms in homage to the adults they have become.

To learn this sociohistorical lore as a young student in the academy is an abstraction of the mind, but the moment when you realize that the time has come to set your own feet upon the wanderjahr's path is a satori of the spirit, which can be neither arbitrarily determined by the passage of time nor forced upon the spirit from without.

Nevertheless, the decision is almost always made between the sixteenth and nineteenth year of life, and it cannot be denied that society plows and fertilizes the ground in which this flowering of the young spirit blooms. For it is the policy of society to ease off serious studies after the sixteenth year, and it is the endless idle summer resulting therefrom which teaches the lesson that this child's dream of perfect paradise is not the ultima Thule of the human spirit, that the time must come when of our own free will we must move on.

My first dim perception of this last lesson that we are taught, which is also the first we learn to our own, came as a certain sense of pique, a petulant feeling of betrayal as, one by one, the older members of my circle of friends and lovers first announced their intent to leave our garden of juvenile delights and then departed for other worlds. When those whose faces were no longer to been seen among us were a year and more my senior, the lofty airs and moues of condescension with which they said good-bye could be laid to the arrogance of peers who suddenly conceived themselves to be older and wiser beings than their comrades of the week before.

But when at last some who left began to be no more mature in years than I, when I began to see myself as no longer quite the precocious femme fatale sought after by older boys and instead found myself forever repulsing the unwanted attentions of what I perceived as callower and callower youth, my unease by slow degrees began to focus less and less on the decaying social life without and more and more on the growing mal d'esprit within.

As the esthetics of karma would have it, the moment when this spiritual malaise crystallized itself into satoric resolve came with the clarity and definition of a classic koan.

I was lying in my garden playhouse boudoir with Davi, a boy some several months my junior to whom I had begun to grant my puissant favors not three weeks before, more out of ennui and a sense of charity than any grand passion.

As we lay in each other's arms during what I then supposed to be a brief recumbent interlude between the acts, I could sense him becoming somewhat distant, withdrawing into himself. At length, he pried himself from my embrace and sat some small but significant distance apart from me on the cushioned floor, eyes downcast, shoulders hunched, as if nerving himself up to inform me of a rival for his affections.

"Qué pasa?" I asked, with no more than a careful petulance of tone, for on the one hand my primacy in his affections was a matter to which all save my pride was indifferent, and on the other, this would obviously best be served by the assumption of an air of superior calm.

"Verdad, you're the finest lover I've ever had," he muttered fatuously.

"Verdad," I agreed dryly, for given the modesty of his mystique in this regard among our peers and his no more than ordinary skill in the tantric arts, this was a pleasantry that left my girlish heart less than overwhelmed.

"Don't make what I have to say more difficult . . ." he fairly whined, meeting my gaze with a pout, obviously all too relieved to exchange his shy discomfort for a facade of pique with me.

"Relax, klein Davi," I said with quite the opposite intent, "if you're afraid to wound me with a confession of some other amour, rest assured, my pauvre petit, that I myself have a surfeit of lovers, past, present, and future, and will therefore hardly be crushed to learn of any pecadillos of yours."

But instead of flinching at the planting of this barb, he smiled at me most foolishly, or so it seemed. "Ah, Moussa, I *knew* you'd understand . . ." he fairly moaned in relief.

"Who is it then—Andrea, Flor, Belinda?" I inquired, with a nonchalance that was both feigned and sincere. For while the undying loyalty of this lover whom I was already regarding in the past tense would in fact have been a tiresome burden to my indifferent heart, the outré notion that this lout could possibly prefer the favors of some other to my own, while the ultimate proof of his callow unsuitability as a swain, was still an outrage of lèse majesté, which, nevertheless, I could hardly acknowledge with less than lofty amusement, even to myself. *Especially* to myself.

Once again, however, my perception of the situation proved to be at variance with the reality. "There isn't anyone else, Moussa," he said. "How could there be? Of all the women that I know, you're the only one who tempts me to stay."

"*Tempts you to stay?*"

"Verdad, you *do* tempt me to stay, but . . ."

"But *what*, cher dumkopf? What are you blathering and babbling about?"

He regarded me as if *I* were the one who could not find the sprach to make the Lingo of my meaning plain. "But I leave to begin my wanderjahr next week," he blurted. "Next week, the *Ardent Eagle* leaves for Nova Roma, and I'll be aboard. My parents have already bought my passage."

He beamed at me. He fairly glowed. "Fantastique, né?" he exclaimed. "The Grand Palais of the *Ardent Eagle* is presided over by Domo Athene Weng Sharon! My mother once voyaged with her, and she says that the decor is marvelous, the entertainments superb, the ambiance exhilarating, and the chef maestro, Tai Don Angelica, one of the half-dozen finest in the entire floating cultura!"

"You're . . . you're off on your wanderjahr next week . . .?" I stammered. "As an Honored Passenger?" Why did this entirely unexpected revelation cut me to the quick as no confession of human rival could have done? From whence this sudden pang of loss? What was Davi to me but a casual lover whose season had already passed? Why the desire to hold him here with me which I could not deny but which I could still less understand?

"Naturellement," he said gaily, answering my words with total obliviousness of the import of their tone. "My parents, as you are certainly well aware, can afford to pay my way from world to world in proper style with ease. Why would they have me stacked like so much meat in electrocoma when they can afford to buy my access to the floating cultura without even noticing the debit in their accounts? Surely your own mother and father will do no less for you?"

"Of course!" I told him, though the subject had never been broached between us. "But why such haste? Has life on Glade become such a bore? Will you not be sad to leave Nouvelle Orlean behind?"

"*Haste?* But soon I will be *eighteen standards*. Many are our friends who became Children of Fortune long before reaching such an advanced age . . ."

Such an advanced age? But this silly boy was younger than I! All my young life I had wished to be, or at least wished to appear to be, older and more mature than my years, and now, all at once, this . . . this imbecile was making me feel like some sort of eighteen-year-old crone! For the first time in my life, I wished, at least for the moment, to be *younger* than my years; there are those who would contend, nicht wahr, that that is precisely the moment when a woman ceases to be a girl.

"And as for Nouvelle Orlean . . ." Davi blathered on, entirely oblivious to my mood, entirely blind to the havoc his prattle was working on my spirit.

"*And as for Nouvelle Orlean?*" I demanded sharply.

Al fin, Davi began to dimly perceive that his discourse was being met with something other than avid enthusiasm, though the concept that he was being the cause of no little dolor d'esprit never seemed to penetrate his primitive masculine brain. He touched his palm to my cheek as one would console a child.

"As for Nouvelle Orlean," he said, "I'll miss you, Moussa, most of all. Indeed for nearly a year, I dreamed of nothing but being your lover. If not for that, I probably would long since have gone. Verdad, if we had not yet had our time together, I might tarry still. But as for the rest . . ."

He smiled, he shrugged, he cupped my cheeks and kissed me like a proper man, and for that moment at least, I saw once more the sincere and naive charm that once had won some small portion of my heart.

"Have we not tasted what there is to taste, seen what there is to see, been what there is to be, as children of Nouvelle Orlean, Moussa, you and I?" he said. "Nouvelle Orlean is the most marvelous city on our entire world, we both know and love it well. But having tasted it to the full and come to know it as well as we know our parents' gardens or each other's spirits, is it not therefore time to travel on?"

I regarded him in silence, glimpsing for the first time the sweet and noble man that this lightly regarded lover of mine might one day grow to become, and in this moment of farewell I do believe I touched depths that never before had been stirred within my heart.

"Next week I depart for my wanderjahr, and soon enough you'll be a Child of Fortune too, mi Moussa, né. Could I have remained here with you forever and never lived to learn my true name tale? Would you have stayed here with me until we both grew old and never walked of another world?"

"No," I said softly.

"Then may we part as friends? For truly of all that Glade has meant to me, the finest of it all has been my time with you. Should not the best memory of home be the last?"

"Truly and nobly spoken, cher Davi," I told him, with more sincere affection than had ever before filled my callow young heart. "Friends forever, Davi. May your road rise up to meet you. Bon voyage."

And I kissed him one last time, as much to hide my tears as to bid him good-bye. Verdad, my best memory of all the lovers that I had on the planet of my birth was my final sight of the very last.

After Davi left, I went out into the garden and sat for a time under the overhanging trees, deep in formless thought. The sky was cloudless, the air was still, and the sun was warm, and soon I became aware of the piping whistles of the little moussas in the treetops.

For a long time I sat there, staring up into the trees, catching quick glimpses of little golden shapes frolicking high in the branches. Now and again, or so it seemed, tiny bright emerald eyes looked down as if through the billowing green mists of the innocent past. Foolishly, I hoped that the playmates of my young girlhood would descend one final time to nestle in my hands, if only to bid a final farewell to the Moussa that had been.

Naturellement, they never came, not even after I took some crumbs of cake from the playhouse and sat there offering them on my open palms as I had not done for many years.

And as the sky began to deepen towards sunset over my parents' garden and still my little lost friends deigned not to call, I tried to remember when last it had been that the little Moussa had held one of her namesake in her childish hands. Verdad, when last I had even spared the moussas of the garden a passing living thought.

And failed. And in that failing understood that it had not been the moussas who had forsaken me but I who had forsaken them, as that little girl grew into the creature who short hours before had bidden the final lover of her childhood a fond and tender bon voyage.

At the moment of this wistful satori, a golden shape chanced to pause in a small bare spot among the branches; tail wrapped around a twig for balance, the moussa stood half erect, as if dubiously testing the posture of a little man.

Or was it chance? For a long moment, the moussa's wide green eyes seemed to lock on my own as if remembering back across time to my childhood years. As if to say, bon voyage, old friend, may your road rise up to meet you. As if to say, mourn not what has been but greet what is to come with a happy heart, and know that we of your childhood's garden wish you no less than your heart's desire. No blame, little Moussa that was, remember us sometimes out there among the stars, and hold our memory in the palm of a child's hand.

Then, with a little chirp of farewell, he was gone, and with him the little girl that longed to stay in her parents' garden, for in that moment, that wanderjahr of my spirit had begun.

WEST
of
EDEN

Harry Harrison

From a master of imaginative storytelling comes an epic tale of the world as it might have been, a world where the age of dinosaurs never ended, and their descendants clash with a clan of humans in a tragic war for survival . . .

SPECIAL
MONEY SAVING
OFFER

Now you can have an up-to-date listing of Bantam's hundreds of titles plus take advantage of our unique and exciting bonus book offer. A special offer which gives you the opportunity to purchase a Bantam book for only 50¢. Here's how!

By ordering any five books at the regular price per order, you can also choose any other single book listed (up to a $4.95 value) for just 50¢. Some restrictions do apply, but for further details why not send for Bantam's listing of titles today!

Just send us your name and address plus 50¢ to defray the postage and handling costs.

OUT OF THIS WORLD!

That's the only way to describe Bantam's great series of science fiction classics. These space-age thrillers are filled with terror, fancy and adventure and written by America's most renowned writers of science fiction. Welcome to outer space and have a good trip!

☐	24709	**RETURN TO EDDARTA** by Garrette & Heydron	$2.75
☐	22647	**HOMEWORLD** by Harry Harrison	$2.50
☐	22759	**STAINLESS STEEL RAT FOR PRESIDENT** by Harry Harrison	$2.75
☐	22796	**STAINLESS STEEL RAT WANTS YOU** by Harry Harrison	$2.50
☐	20780	**STARWORLD** by Harry Harrison	$2.50
☐	20774	**WHEELWORLD** by Harry Harrison	$2.50
☐	24176	**THE ALIEN DEBT** by F. M. Busby	$2.75
☐	24710	**A STORM UPON ULSTER** by Kenneth C. Flint	$3.50
☐	24175	**THE RIDERS OF THE SIDHE** by Kenneth C. Flint	$2.95
☐	25215	**THE PRACTICE EFFECT** by David Brin	$2.95
☐	23589	**TOWER OF GLASS** by Robert Silverberg	$2.95
☐	23495	**STARTIDE RISING** by David Brin	$3.50
☐	24564	**SUNDIVER** by David Brin	$2.75
☐	23512	**THE COMPASS ROSE** by Ursula LeGuin	$2.95
☐	23541	**WIND'S 12 QUARTERS** by Ursula LeGuin	$2.95
☐	22855	**CINNABAR** by Edward Bryant	$2.50
☐	22938	**THE WINDHOVER TAPES: FLEXING THE WARP** by Warren Norwood	$2.75
☐	23351	**THE WINDHOVER TAPES: FIZE OF THE GABRIEL RATCHETS** by Warren Norwood	$2.95
☐	23394	**THE WINDHOVER TAPES: AN IMAGE OF VOICES** by Warren Norwood	$2.75
☐	22968	**THE MARTIAN CHRONICLES** by Ray Bradbury	$2.75
☐	24168	**PLANET OF JUDGMENT** by Joe Halderman	$2.95
☐	23756	**STAR TREK: THE NEW VOYAGES 2** by Culbreath & Marshak	$2.95

<u>Prices and availability subject to change without notice.</u>

FANTASY AND SCIENCE FICTION FAVORITES

Bantam brings you the recognized classics as well as the current favorites in fantasy and science fiction. Here you will find the most recent titles by the most respected authors in the genre.

☐	24370	RAPHAEL R. A. MacAvoy	$2.75
☐	24103	BORN WITH THE DEAD Robert Silverberg	$2.75
☐	24169	WINTERMIND Parke Godwin, Marvin Kaye	$2.75
☐	23944	THE DEEP John Crowley	$2.95
☐	23853	THE SHATTERED STARS Richard McEnroe	$2.95
☐	23575	DAMIANO R. A. MacAvoy	$2.75
☐	23205	TEA WITH THE BLACK DRAGON R. A. MacAvoy	$2.75
☐	23365	THE SHUTTLE PEOPLE George Bishop	$2.95
☐	24441	THE HAREM OF AMAN AKBAR Elizabeth Scarborough	$2.95
☐	20780	STARWORLD Harry Harrison	$2.50
☐	22939	THE UNICORN CREED Elizabeth Scarborough	$3.50
☐	23120	THE MACHINERIES OF JOY Ray Bradbury	$2.75
☐	22666	THE GREY MANE OF MORNING Joy Chant	$3.50
☐	25097	LORD VALENTINE'S CASTLE Robert Silverberg	$3.95
☐	20870	JEM Frederik Pohl	$2.95
☐	23460	DRAGONSONG Anne McCaffrey	$2.95
☐	24862	THE ADVENTURES OF TERRA TARKINGTON Sharon Webb	$2.95
☐	23666	EARTHCHILD Sharon Webb	$2.50
☐	24102	DAMIANO'S LUTE R. A. MacAvoy	$2.75
☐	24417	THE GATES OF HEAVEN Paul Preuss	$2.50

Prices and availability subject to change without notice.